For Emily

Anyone who reads and loves this tale should know it was her
fangirl enthusiasm, meticulous feedback, and gentle guidance
that kept my creative flame burning all the way through to the
dramatic finish.

PRAISE FOR THE SYLVAN AND THE SAND

"A vividly dynamic fantasy romance with an explosive collision of opposite worlds."
~*Angelina J. Steffort, bestselling author of Shattered Kingdom*

"The characters in The Sylvan and the Sand grabbed me from page one. They feel genuine and flawed, and I will follow them anywhere."
~*USA Today bestselling author Alisha Klapheke, author of the Dragons Rising series*

"This story was everything I could have asked for and more! A fierce and flawed heroine, a sweet and gorgeous hero and a toe-curling love story makes this a book you won't be able to put down."
~*International and USA Today Best-Selling author Elle Madison*

"Yesenia and Corin are absolute fire! This is the enemies-to-lovers fantasy I've been looking for!"
~*Casey L. Bond, author of House of Eclipses*

INTRODUCTION

There exists a kingdom set upon an isle, surrounded by a sea no one has ever traveled beyond. The Kingdom of the White Sea it is called, or simply the kingdom, for they have no other name for it.

The individual Reaches—Northerlands, Southerlands, Westerlands, and Easterlands—once ruled themselves. Two centuries past, men calling themselves the Rhiagains washed upon their shores, claiming to be gods. From gods, they became kings.

But not all in the kingdom are so entranced by the foreigners who stole the crown.

The Warwicks, lords of the Southerlands, clashed immediately with the Rhiagains, who claimed their mineral-rich peninsula as a rightful prize of their new reign. Generations of strife between Rhiagains and Warwicks followed, resulting in land grabs for the kings and an extensive accounting of losses for the Warwicks and their people.

Farther north in the Easterlands, a much different picture can be painted. The Quinlandens, the lords of the sylvan kingdom high in the mighty trees of Whitechurch, have enjoyed a more advantageous arrangement with the crown. Their proximity to Duncarrow—the rocky isle upon which the Rhiagains reside—has granted them opportunities to remain in the king's esteem and favor…including gifts of the gold mined and stolen from the Southerlands.

"Bootlickers" is the Warwick name for the Quinlandens.

"Treasonous eels" is the Quinlandens' stinging response.

Lords Khoulter Warwick and Chasten Quinlanden trade these barbs from the comfort of their keeps. The two men have never met.

This is about to change.

King Khain Rhiagain summons the lords and ladies from all four Reaches to a grand celebration in Termonglen, the kingdom's neutral ground.

The Quinlandens rejoice over an opportunity to not only win more of their king's favor but for their peers—their competitors—to witness the heights to which they have risen.

The Warwicks know a trap when they see one. To refuse would be an act of treason. Complying is to be beset on all sides by their enemies.

But it is not *only* the lords and ladies invited by the king's command; their children are called out by name, their attendance compulsory.

Yesenia Warwick, the only daughter of Lord Warwick, is among those names. Bold, brave, and defiant, she has never been well acquainted with conformity, and she sees no use for it now, as she and her brothers prepare to enter a den of vipers.

Corin Quinlanden, the meek and oft-forgotten middle child of Lord Quinlanden, is also on this list, to his family's mortification. Denying the king's wish would undo all they've worked for. They have no choice but to bring him.

In celebration of the birth of my heir, the invitation says.

But a celebration of birth is *not* why Khain has summoned the lords, ladies, and their children to Termonglen. He has something else in mind, an event that what will come to be known, for generations, as the Epoch of the Accordant.

By the time the lords and ladies realize the king's deceit, it will already be too late.

For them.

For their children.

And for the kingdom.

SOUTHERLANDS

Lord & Lady:
Lord Khoulter Warwick
Lady Sancha Garrick Warwick (deceased)

Capital:
Warwicktown

Lord's Children:
Khallum, 19
Yesenia, 17
Byrne, 15

Other Warwicks:
Lady Korah, the Widow Holton, sister of Khoulter

Other Southerlanders:
Rylahn Rutland, steward of Whitecliffe
Erran Rutland, son of Steward Rutland
Sessaly Rutland, daughter of Steward Rutland
Samuel Law, son of Steward Law
Hamish Strong, son of Steward Strong
Lem Garrick, son of Steward Garrick
Foss Garrick, son of Steward Garrick
Anatole, personal guard to Yesenia

EASTERLANDS

Lord & Lady:
Lord Chasten Quinlanden
Lady Mariana Skylark Quinlanden

Capital:
Whitechurch

Lord's Children:
Aiden, 20
Gretchen, 18
Corin, 17
Saoirse, 13

Slattery Row:
Mara
Lorne
Riona
Callan
Claire and Tristan

Other Easterlanders:
Mads Waters, son of Steward Waters
Antioch of Streamstowne
Drystan Sylvaine the Elder

Others at the Epoch of the Accordant

Crown:
King Khain Rhiagain
Queen Florian Rhiagain (not present)
Princess Assyria Rhiagain, 18
Princess Correen Rhiagain, 17
Twins Darrick & Eoghan Rhiagain, newborn

Northerlands:
Lord Hadden and Lady Mylannie Dereham
Holden Dereham, 18
Gwyn Dereham, 17
Alric Dereham, 15

Westerlands:
Lord Oster and Lady Cerridwyn Blackwood
Asherley Blackwood, 17
Maeryn Blackwood, 16
Earwyn Blackwood, 14

FOR THOSE THE GUARDIANS FAVOR

ONE
THE COVE

Yesenia rolled her head along the jagged cove wall as Erran's fervent kisses took a delightful turn. She was already reaching for her skirts to tug them higher, fully versed in the next part of their dance. It was why she'd come there with him, like every other day that long springtide. She'd never understood his need for all the play that came before, but he'd never had much in common with the other boys of the Southerlands.

"Enough of this," she moaned into the briny air. "You know what I want."

"I just want you, Sen." Erran eased off his urgency, and she stiffened at the sudden change in him. "I've always only ever wanted you."

Yesenia knew where this was going if she didn't cut it off quick. She bit down on her tongue to keep him from witnessing her frustration. "Well, ye have me now," she purred, thrusting a hand down his still-buckled trousers to bring him back to the moment she'd been longing for all day. He wasn't so far gone into

1

his feelings that she couldn't save this. "But the tide is already lapping at our ankles, ye ken?"

"I donnae just want ye now, Yesenia." Erran sighed as he fumbled back off of her. "I want ye always. Not like *this*, hiding away before the tide comes in. Wouldnae it be nice to wake in each other's arms? To fall asleep after we've…" His throat ebbed. "Without having to sneak about and worry about yer father or the Widow Holton."

Yesenia tensed her jaw as she let down her skirts. She was mad about *the skirts* now too. How she loathed dressing like her mother, who wasn't even around anymore to appreciate the sacrifice. Erran knew good and well she only wore them if they were making a trip to the cove, and she'd only started doing it because he still hadn't figured out how to smoothly get her out of trousers. And he was going to squander their precious time to talk about his *feelings*?

She pressed her legs together, to quell the throbbing ache, and forced a smile. "Ye know it isnae up to either of us, Erran." She stretched a hand toward his face and cupped his cheek with her palm. "So why not make use of the time that's ours?"

Erran backed up in the sand. Her hand fell away, and her smile followed suit.

"It's just…I *love* you, too much to want this for you."

Yesenia cocked her head, loading a sound scolding, but she succeeded in controlling her temper a moment longer. "Ye cannae say that word to me, Erran Rutland. 'Tis *not* fair."

"And why *not*, Sen? I do love ye. Can ye tell me ye'd rather it be Sam, or Lem—"

Yesenia snorted. "It would never be Lem."

"But you're all right with Sam, I ken?"

She thrust her hands down and to her sides. "Why must we talk about this now, aye? Ye have but a few days left in Warwicktown. Could be months before ye come back again." The urge to pull him back to the wall and persuade him to forget these useless thoughts was strong, but her frustration was quickly growing stronger. "Is this how ye wanna spend them, jawing about pointless things?"

"Pointless things?" Erran's whole face changed, melting his vulnerable expression into sorrow. "Ye cannae mean it. All this, all these months…" He shook his head. "Years. I've loved ye for *years*, Sen. Since we were practically bairns."

"Aye, and ye have me now, so what are we even talking about?"

"You're nay listening to me. I've decided I'll go to your father. I'll tell him—"

"Ye *what*?" Yesenia's boots sloshed in the wet sand when she stepped toward him. "No, Erran, ye willnae go to my father about us. Not unless ye fancy yer head on a pike for rutting with the unwed daughter of your lord."

"That's just it. You *should* be married. It has to happen anyway, so why not to a man who already loves ye?"

Yesenia's mouth flapped open and closed in her incredulity. That he was right didn't still her anger but whetted it, flaming it higher. He knew the matter of her marriageability was a rough affair in the Warwick household, and he had to go dredging it up with his talk of love and feelings? He couldn't have just *shown* her, as he was so very good at, so they could enjoy what remained of their stolen moments, before the sand slipped away and everything changed?

"Sen, he'd only ever wed ye to a Rutland or a Law. Which means me or Sam. If ye think I can sit back and watch one of my best mates say the Sacred Promises with the lass I love—"

"Shh." Yesenia held a palm out at him, turning her head. She raised an eyebrow and Erran caught quickly on, nodding. He'd heard it too.

He slowly knelt to retrieve his sword belt, propped against a rock. He fastened it while she stepped around the bend of the cove toward the sea. As she rounded out into the open air, she withdrew both daggers from her boots without breaking her stride.

Foss Garrick held a book above his head, waving it around. His brother, Lem, knelt in the sand next to another figure who was curled into a ball, his identity blocked by Lem's broad shadow.

Yesenia didn't need to see the bullied boy to know who it was.

"Been rutting with the pigs again, Bird?" Lem crowed. "Dinnae ye ken tha' paper is scarce? Tha' book there could feed a family fer a month."

"Aye, a waste, this." Foss cocked his arm and chucked the book into the sea. Byrne yelled in horror but didn't budge from his huddled spot. "I ken Lem is calling it straight. Only a pig-whacker would think vellum was anything but fer important messages. Dinnae ye ken we're at war?"

"Know a lot about pulling your prick out for the pigs, do ye?" Yesenia cried out as she marched down the beach. "Care to give a demonstration?"

The Garrick brothers turned toward her call, each running their mind through their excuses. She saw it in their stupid, empty eyes, their sputtering lips.

Lem stepped forward, quavering through his weak attempt at bravado. "Come to take yer little bird home?"

Yesenia didn't slow when she reached him, forcing him back several steps. She buried the tip of one of her daggers against his vest, feigning a light push. He winced at the phantom stab, sagging.

"It's you who'll be going home. *After* ye apologize."

Foss backed up the beach but nearly ran into the end of Erran's sword. "Where do ye ken you're going? Lady Warwick is speaking. Show some respect."

Yesenia turned back toward Lem. His eyes were fixed on her dagger pressed tight to his belly. "You can either apologize, or ye can leave your innards here on the beach for the gulls to feast upon."

"We're kin, Yesenia," Lem spat.

"Our mothers were sisters. My mother is dead, and I ken ye donnae even know which alehouse yours is in these days. We're nay shite anymore, Lem, and we'll be even less if ye come near my brother again. Now *say it.*"

Lem sucked in air through his teeth. He turned his head over his shoulder, careful not to move, lest she gut him. "Aye, well I ken I'm *sorry* yer such a craven—"

Yesenia pushed the dagger in an inch. Lem howled.

"Are ye feckin' mad? You nearly—"

"One more time. That's all ye get. It's more than ye deserve." Yesenia gave her dagger a small shake.

Lem whimpered. "I'm sorry, Byrne. Aye? I'll get ye another book."

"I donnae want another book. Not from you." Byrne spoke his first words as he stumbled to his feet, backing away from the scene. "It's all right, Yesenia. You donnae have to sully your blade today on my account."

"Too late," she answered, grinning.

"That all then?" Lem backed away. When the dagger pulled out, he bowled forward as if he'd been felled in battle.

"Willnae even need to stitch it, ye bairn," Yesenia chided. "Next time you come for my brother, you'll be coming a lot further down the end of my dagger."

They waited until the Garrick brothers disappeared into the horizon of the setting sun before putting their weapons away. Yesenia rinsed her dagger in the sea while Erran helped Byrne clear the sand from his trousers. She flashed him a look of gratitude but hoped he could also see in her eyes that she wanted him to leave.

Erran started to lean in, as if to kiss her, but then remembered himself. "Think on it. What I said."

Yesenia nodded and watched him leave. "Did they hurt ye?"

Byrne shook his head. He sucked in his split lip. "They're always on me about something."

"You know why, aye?"

"Because I'm not like you? Like Khallum?"

Yesenia clapped both of her hands on her little brother's shoulders. He was only two years her junior, but he might as well have been ten. "Because you *let* them. Boys like that become men like that. This willnae go away."

Byrne pulled the corner of his mouth into a shaky smile. "I ken my older sister will just make them go away."

"I cannae always be here, Byrne. Ye know this."

"I'll never be as strong as them. I've tried, and it's…just not who I am."

Yesenia shook her head with a hard sigh. "They donnae come after ye because you're weak. You have a love for something they'll never understand, because they've never loved anything so much. They'd take it from ye, Byrne, if you let them."

He crossed his arms and gazed out to the sea. "Why aren't you afraid of them?"

Yesenia passed a curt nod downward, between her legs. "Because they're not afraid of me. I donnae have the right parts."

That got her the grin she'd been after. Byrne shook his head at her and laughed. "They're *plenty* afraid of you. I think Lem may have shit himself."

"Tide's coming. The Widow will give us a right tongue lashing if we're late for supper again." Yesenia threw an arm around his shoulder and steered him toward town. "Why do they call ye Bird, anyway?"

"Because of the thing with the birds."

Yesenia exhaled through her nose, wrapping her arm tighter around her brother. Her anger returned. "Oh."

Yesenia and her brothers waited with barely disguised impatience for the Widow to run through her interminable nightly beseeching of the Guardians. It wasn't enough for her to have one ask of each of their five deities. She had an entire list prepared. An impressive feat, Yesenia thought, seeing as she'd had an equally long list the day before.

"And to the Guardian of the Unpromised Future. Oh, we have but one ask of you, that you divert thine eyes from the Warwick table yet another day. For the greatness of our young ones is just beginning!"

Yesenia caught Khallum's eyes across the table. He rolled them with a tease of a smirk and then closed them again before he was caught defying their aunt. Yesenia squeezed hers shut just in time for the Widow to pass her cool smile around the table.

"You may eat," she asserted.

Khoulter, Yesenia's father, already had his face buried in his stew before she'd released her last syllable. He had no choice but to indulge his sister, as she was here on his humble ask, but he was no more fond of her fastidiousness than his children were.

The Widow was what Yesenia and Khallum called her. They were supposed to refer to her as Aunt Korah. Byrne liked to remind them they'd slip up one day and call her the wrong thing to her face, and then they'd really be in trouble.

The late Steward Holton had been gone five years, leaving Korah an empty hearth, her children having started their own families. Khoulter brought his sister back to Warwicktown to fill the hole his wife had created when she had fallen to consumption, leaving him to raise three children alone. In exchange for helping rear the trio, he grudgingly tolerated Korah's peculiarities.

"Khallum," the Widow said, in a tone they were all regrettably acquainted with. "I know you didnae earn that flush in your cheeks meeting with tenants about quarterly taxes."

Khallum instinctively straightened in his chair at her sharp address. He flashed a quick glance at Yesenia before turning a tight smile on their aunt. "Aye. I've just returned from Blackpool."

"Blackpool?" she asked.

"On my order," Khoulter murmured into his spoonful of dark broth.

"Well, whatever for?"

"The floods," Khoulter barked and returned to his meal.

Exasperated, Korah turned back toward Khallum. "What floods?"

"The dam cracked again. Hamish and I, we went to see what the damage was. Ken if it's better to repair it or tear it down and start anew."

"If you were in Blackpool, then who, by the Guardians, was here to meet with the tenants?"

"I was." Khoulter dropped his spoon and looked up. "Hamish? I thought I told ye to take Sam."

"Sam was busy."

Yesenia heard the lie. She wondered if her father did too.

"Erran then?"

Khallum grinned sideways at Yesenia, quick enough for her to catch up. "*Very* busy."

Khoulter's hands landed on the table, on either side of his bowl. "I ken ye like Hamish a good deal, lad. He's a good boy, even if he is a Strong."

Korah snorted.

"But if I wouldnae marry my daughter to a Strong, I wouldnae find him fit to be the best mate of my heir either." Khoulter tipped his head at Yesenia. "And Sam may well be yer brother soon."

Yesenia slowed her eating, pretending not to listen.

"You'd punish your own daughter like that, marrying her to a gold fist?" Khallum asked. "I love Sam, but I wouldnae wish him upon any woman."

"The Laws are prudent, not misers," Korah corrected. "A virtuous quality, one we could all learn from."

Byrne spoke up. "Why not Erran Rutland?"

Yesenia flinched at his guileless delivery; there was more to the question, and one of the two adults would easily pick it up.

"Ye think a sensitive boy like Erran could handle yer sister?" Khoulter guffawed. "Guardians help him!"

"I would like to think I have at least *some* choice in the matter," Yesenia muttered.

"Not this again." Korah sighed.

"Who put such an idea into your head?" her father retorted. "Not that sister of his, Sessaly, was it? I swear, the lass will never marry, a silver tongue like hers. No wonder Steward Rutland cannae find a groom willing."

"What if I…" Yesenia hesitated when she realized all eyes at the table had fallen on her. "What if I just didnae marry at all?"

Khoulter and Korah both gaped at her. Khallum sucked in his lips, bracing for impact.

Her father and aunt burst with laughter.

Yesenia sagged against the back of her chair. "How is that funny, aye? I can helm a ship even better than Khallum. It's me you pick to supervise the Golden Mine when ye need official eyes on the operation. I'm good enough when ye need me to be."

"She's also quite adept with daggers," Byrne offered. Yesenia closed her eyes, waiting for her father's inevitable next question.

"Ye been pulling your knives out again, lass? Who was it, this time?"

"No one."

"When have we begun allowing lies to sit at this table?" Korah mused aloud, her head cocked to the side.

"I'm only suggesting," Yesenia said carefully, "perhaps I have more to offer the Southerlands than making a good marriage."

"What other reason is there for a man to have a daughter?" Khoulter asked. At the horror in her face, he softened. "Yesenia. You can still do, *mostly*, as ye please when you marry. No man with all his wits would challenge a Warwick daughter more than he had to."

"That isnae the point, Father."

Khallum interjected. "Aye, well it's down to Erran and Sam, innit? At least let her choose between the two of them."

"A woman who chooses her husband owns the unhappiness that follows," Korah said. "'Tis a gift, Yesenia, to be removed from this choice, so you may approach your marriage with the open heart of the unwilling."

Yesenia shook her head. "I donnae ken—"

"You donnae have to *ken* anything. All you have to do, lass, is lie back and remember the Southerlands."

Khallum snorted stew through his nose as Yesenia gaped at her aunt in stunned horror.

"Ye want Erran? Prefer him to Sam?" Khoulter threw up his hands. "'Tis the same to me, girl. Just donnae cry to me when ye run circles around the poor lad." He shoved his empty bowl aside. "Aye, well, I ken the talk of marriage will wait a little longer still. We've other business now."

Korah folded her hands neatly atop the table. "We'll all be leaving for Termonglen in a few days," she said, as if her brother had asked her to deliver the news.

Khallum curled his lip with a shrug. "Termonglen? In the Hinterlands? There's nothing there but the forestland."

"Not nothing," Khoulter answered before his sister could. "It's the only neutral ground in the kingdom. Doesnae belong to any Reach except the Hinterlands, and the Medvedev never leave their forests. 'Tis where the ratsbane meets his subjects when he deigns to leave his rock."

"So, never?" Khallum quipped.

"He doesnae want to meet with *us*, surely?" Yesenia asked, stunned. "We're steps away from war with this crown!"

"It isnae war on his mind," Khoulter said. He strained for his words through visible discomfort, his face reddening.

Yesenia's heart sank. She looked at Khallum, but he was waiting for their father to speak.

"Seems all the lords have been invited. The lords and their children both. For a…" He grimaced. "Celebration."

Khallum shot forward in his seat. "Just what could we have to celebrate with this ratsbane—"

"Mind your tongue," Korah chided. She turned toward Khoulter. "Donnae think I missed hearing it from your mouth either."

Khoulter cast his eyes at the ceiling.

Khallum ground his jaw. "With this *king* who is no friend of ours. He cannae be serious, Father."

Byrne tracked the heated exchange in wide-eyed silence.

"Khallum is right," Yesenia said. "We cannae go *celebrate* with the same king who has stolen from our Reach, had our women raped—"

"Is that really supper table conversation, Yesenia?" Korah asked.

"Am I softening my words for the women who were assailed without answer or for you?"

"Sen," Khoulter warned. "I donnae like it any more than all of you. But the Southerlands isnae ready for war. Refusing this invite would bring it upon us, like it or not, prepared or not."

"What is the king celebrating?" Byrne asked.

"The birth of his heir," Khoulter said in disgust and pushed back from the table. "We leave in three nights. Pack light. We'll nay be staying any longer than we have to."

He left the room. Korah, flustered, rushed after him.

Yesenia spun toward Khallum. "He's really serious? He means to go break bread with the Rhiagains? Wants us to pretend the ratsbane usurper isnae the reason half our men starve and the other half steal?"

Khallum's shrug was quick, violent. "Who the feck knows?" With a cautious look Byrne's direction, he added, "But bring your steel, Sen. I donnae trust it."

Yesenia grinned. "Wouldnae dream of leaving them behind."

11

TWO

THE KING'S FAVOR

Remind me again why everyone in this kingdom is our enemy?" Corin asked his older brother. He'd followed Aiden to his chambers, which were a full story higher than Corin's in their sylvan kingdom of Arboriana. A kingdom was what they called it, but the Quinlandens were not kings, no matter how highly Corin's father and brother regarded themselves.

Even in his own apartments, Corin rarely ventured to the perches overlooking the Great Rushwood, despite his love of the forest. He'd always harbored insecurities with height, but only Gretchen, his sister, knew why his fear had worsened. There was no one else he could tell. He already knew what they would say.

The arbor princeling whose commoner love fell from the trees.

Aiden preened at the basin left for his handwashing. He raised his chin, adjusting expressions until he found one he must have liked. "I didn't say they were *enemies*, Corin. I said they were competition." He winked at his reflection. "Though really, they're the same thing, I suppose. Are they not? It's why Father will ensure we're the first to arrive at Termonglen."

"Competing for what, exactly?"

"The king's favor." Aiden wore a disgusted look, suggesting his weariness with Corin's inability to keep up. "What else?"

"We already have that."

"Your problem is you're thinking in finites," Aiden chided. He dipped his fingertips in the water and straightened back some already-smooth golden hairs. "When the favor of a Rhiagain king offers endless bounty."

"Bounty." Corin repeated dryly. "We're already the closest capital to Duncarrow. We're the only lordship who has been invited to dine with the king on his rocky, joyless isle. He offers us shipments of gold, for no reason at all." He twisted his mouth into a frown. "Gold *stolen* from the Southerlands—"

"I suggest you don't finish that thought." Aiden shrugged his shoulders into a heavy sigh. "The Southerlanders are slippery, treasonous eels who would take from the king if he did not take first. We are most fortunate that King Khain is always a move ahead of them."

Corin couldn't comprehend the backward logic his father and brother used to justify their shifty ideals. The Quinlandens held most of the wealth in the kingdom, and much of it had been handed to them by a crown the rest of the kingdom had no love for.

But Corin wasn't built for politics and intrigue, and, as if he didn't already know it, Chasten and Aiden Quinlanden were always at the ready to remind him.

"Where's Gretchen?" Aiden demanded. An unmistakable glint in his eye followed the question.

"I don't know," Corin lied. Their sister was with Ash. She was always with Ash. If Aiden knew, he'd take that from her too.

"She should be packing. We leave in the morning."

"She knows."

Aiden straightened his gold sash. Head high, he faced the double doors and the perch beyond. "A double wedding," he mused to himself. "That's what we'll do."

"What?"

Aiden half turned, looking past him. "Gretchen and I, we'll surprise the guests with a second wedding, when I wed Anestra Edevane. The Sylvaine heir would be a good choice for Gretchen, don't you think?"

Corin's blood took a chill. Perhaps Aiden did know with whom their sister spent most of her time. Was this a test? So many things were with him. "Father—"

"Father will love it!" Aiden exclaimed, assuming, as always, he knew the intent of a question better than the asker. "All of the Easterlands must know by now, how they sneak about. If we make it out like they've been betrothed all along, we might yet save her reputation."

Why would you want our sister to be happy when you've made it your life's purpose to strip away every last wisp of joy she manages to find?

All the things Corin wanted to say to his more conniving, clever relations lived in the back of his mind waiting to be summoned, knowing they never would. He lacked the cleverness for recourse. He lacked so much. The only compliment he could recall ever receiving from his father was that he was the best looking of the Quinlandens. But then he'd added *prettiest,* and what might have been kindness turned to reprisal.

"And…" Aiden went on. "More importantly, ours. Mine."

"And me?" Corin asked. "Why not a triple wedding?"

"You're seventeen."

"What does—"

"A man should wed at nineteen, when he's ready to be a man. Gretchen, on the other hand, is practically an old fishmaid. Eighteen! She should have been betrothed three years ago. It's Mother's influence at work. Father has never been able to say no to that woman."

"It isn't unheard of for a man to be married at seventeen."

"Lesser-borns."

"Father married mother when he was sixteen."

Aiden groaned. "That doesn't mean we should repeat the mistakes of history." He finally looked directly at Corin. "Why are you in such a rush? You have someone you've been sneaking about with too?"

Corin's breath caught. "I...I'm only looking for ways to be of service to our family."

Aiden's smirk called Corin's belief of that into obvious question. "Corin, you could join the *Reliquary* for all we care. Father has an heir already. Gretchen's and Saoirse's bounties will swell our wealth in Whitechurch. Figuring out what to do with you is not high on Father's priorities."

Aiden clapped him on the back with all the affection of a farmer petting a hog. "Pack only your finest, and don't forget to have an attendant bring out your regalia. We'll greet the rest of this kingdom properly—or not at all."

Corin bolted the door linking his apartments with the Golden Stair. He inhaled the fresh air coming off the perch, letting the soft, soothing patter of rain dotting leaves wash over him.

A quick glance around the sitting room revealed one had delivered his trunks. No one had come to help him pack. He wanted neither of those things, but it was nonetheless a reminder of the differences between the Quinlanden children who could bring prestige to the family and the one who brought nothing but burden.

Corin hadn't always seen himself this way.

Once, he'd even been happy.

Venya's death had changed everything. Without her bright light to steady his dark thoughts, he could no longer ignore the derision underscoring his life—the disappointment he'd not been a more malleable champion of their ways. Barbs that had once rolled off him like water on a glass pane now clung to his bones, ran through his veins.

A marriage in a faraway corner of the Easterlands wouldn't fix this, but it might allow him to breathe again.

When they returned from the king's farce, Corin would work up the courage to speak to his father directly.

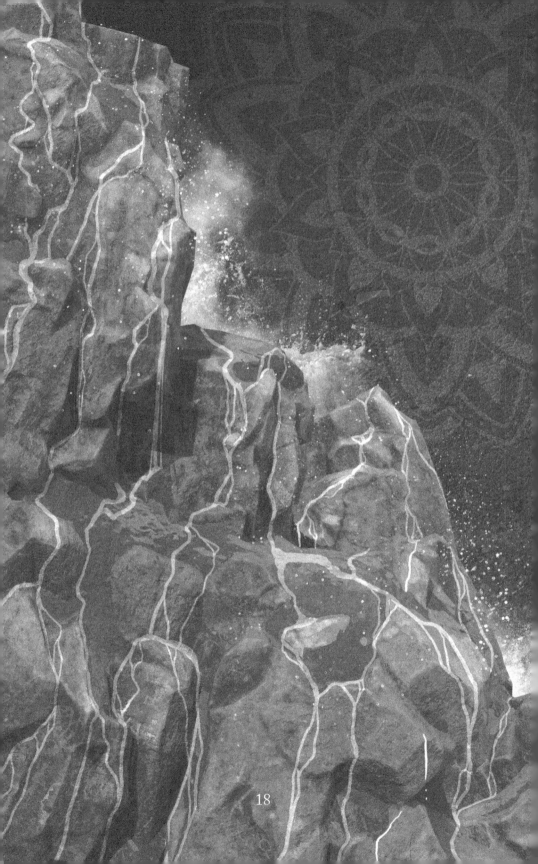

THREE
THERE'S WHAT WE WANT,
AND THERE'S WHAT IS

Yesenia slowed her mare, Kheerai, gradually falling to the back of her father's company. When she was close to the rear, past the eyes of her father's men, she reached inside her leather vest and snuck a swig of whisky from her flask. She sucked air through her teeth with a wince, prompted by both the spirits and the afternoon sun, which was sweltering at this hour, with nothing to shield them except their caps. They were behind schedule, still in the Southerlands. They'd be pulling up to Blackpool when the light disappeared, which meant they'd arrive in Termonglen a half day later than the king expected.

She loved her father for this small rebellion. He may not want to invite war, but he'd take his battles where he could.

Khallum dropped back beside her. "All the men are wondering why you're not riding in the carriage with the other ladies."

"What ladies? It's just the Widow in there."

"Dinnae even know why she came," he muttered. "I'd wager her name wasnae anywhere on the invite."

"She'll be trawling for some fishwife gossip to bring back to Warwicktown, you watch."

"Southerlanders have no time for the chin-wagging of other Reaches."

"Everyone loves a good tale of Quinlanden woe."

Khallum snorted. "Pass me some of that whisky, aye?" He leveled a bemused grin at her when she pretended to not understand.

She handed it over with a resigned groan.

He took a long sip. "And what woe, Sen? Those bootlickers have never been acquainted with the word."

"No? Has to be tiring, craning their necks so far up the ratsbane's arse all the time."

He shook his head. "I donnae ken how I'll stand it, watching them suck each other's pricks for two days."

"Why do ye ken he *really* invited us?"

"Had no choice, if he was inviting the other three Reaches."

"Nah." Yesenia squinted into a frown. "He'd love to slight us if he could. What *I* think is Khain cannae leave Duncarrow unguarded, with his men and Quinlanden's at Termonglen. He knows we'd never overlook such a gift."

"Aye, well he'll have enough gifts to keep us on our toes when we get there."

The glare of midday was blinding. She flicked her leather hat back, letting her scalp breathe, and cupped one hand over her eyes to be sure Byrne was still several waves ahead. "Lem was after him again."

"Byrne?"

Yesenia nodded.

"What for this time?"

"Bullies donnae require a reason," Yesenia answered, casting another cautious glance ahead. "But Byrne said it was about the birds."

Khallum recoiled. "How does Lem know about *that*?"

Yesenia shrugged. She reached for her flask, but it was suspiciously light. With a glare at her brother, she tucked it back in. "Since when do secrets stay secrets?"

"I didnae breathe a word of it. To anyone."

"Nor did I."

"No one else was there but us, Sen."

She sighed. "Does it matter how he knows? He knows. And if Lem knows…"

"Feck all." Khallum hissed through his teeth.

"Aye. We need to do better, looking out for him."

"Sen, he's fifteen. He's gonna have to learn to look out for himself. *That's* what we need to be teachin' him. How to be a man. To hold his own. Not that his sister will come stab anyone who looks at him crossways."

Yesenia eyed him from the side. "There's what we want, Khallum, and then there's what is."

Khallum laughed as he shook his head. "Wisdom *you* should be taking. Father all but said ye could wed Erran, and still ye cannae wipe the despair from your face. You're one of the very few who gets to wed for love, but one would think Father was reciting your dead-given rites."

Yesenia curled the reins tighter around her hands. "You and Erran, with that word."

"Love? The two of ye been slinking about for years now. Lust doesnae last half as long as all that, so if that isnae love—"

"Ye had to bring this up? Cannae even escape it with you now?"

"You'll have to face it soon, like it or no."

Yesenia pushed away recollections of the deeply solemn look Erran had given her in the cave, when he'd changed everything. Khallum was wrong. The only thing she wanted less than marrying at all was to marry for love. That kind of love was a weakness. Erran was her weakness. She hadn't been so certain of this until he'd spilled his heart at her feet, but his words had removed all doubt. Reflected in his eyes was his need for her approval, her returned devotion. She could never tell him that realizing her feelings were not so different from his was exactly why she'd need to end things between them when they returned from Termonglen.

"Always grateful I cannae read your mind, Sen," Khallum said, and they rode the next few hours in silence.

"I have never seen such filth in all my days!" Mariana charged into Termonglen's dining hall, which was coated in years of dust, detritus, and the uncontrolled spread of the invasive flora holding dominion over the modest tower keep. She pressed her sleeve to her mouth in horror, breathing through the thick cloth of her gown. "Two days will not be enough, Chasten. I told you, we should have come sooner."

"We came the day after we received the king's invite, Mariana. How much earlier would you have liked us to arrive?"

"This is *years* of filth. Why does the king not send his own men for this?"

"We brought plenty of workers to get it sorted, and the king will be grateful for it. We'll have an appropriate meal as early as tonight, dearest." Chasten tried to soothe his wife, but she was well past reason. "Why don't you go see that our gifts for the king are properly unloaded and stored?"

"We've been married too long, Chasten. You'll have to be more clever than that to get rid of me."

"Accompany me, Mother." Aiden smoothly slid an arm around his mother's shoulders, grinning an overly charming smile toward her face. "We both know better than to trust workers not to fill their own pockets."

Mariana swept her gaze across the decrepit room once more with a sigh, nodding. "We won't eat a bite if there's even—"

"There won't be," Chasten said to assure her. "Not here, nor the apartments."

Mariana snorted. "For all of our sakes, I won't venture up *there* until they've had a proper go at it."

"Don't worry, Mother," Gretchen said. "Corin and I will have one eye over their shoulders. Won't we, Corin?"

Corin glanced up from the intense scrutiny he'd cast on his feet. He'd been passively listening to the conversation between his parents and siblings, happy to not participate. "We...Yes, of course."

When the others were gone, Chasten turned toward Gretchen and Corin. "None of us much wish to sleep in tents another night, so not a *speck* of dust. Not the *hint* of bird shit. If there's so much as a pillow not replaced with one we brought with us, she'll know it. You understand?"

They both nodded, eager to not disappoint their father, though each for different reasons. Corin had always done whatever it took to stay beyond the reach of his ire, but Gretchen lit up in Chasten's presence, rising higher with every sign of approval and missing, entirely, how the son who tormented her had learned from his father.

"Right. Good. I need to meet with the messengers, get a read on where the others are in their journey. If the king is ahead or behind." He glanced again at them both and left them alone in the dining hall.

Gretchen's smile deflated. She sagged against the slab of wood being used for a dining table, oblivious to the layers of dust that had sent their mother into a pique.

"What is it?"

"Nothing."

"That might work with Aiden, but—"

"Don't say his name!" she hissed, and when she looked up, he saw the purple shadow around the edges of her jaw. "Can't even escape him when he's not here."

Corin's heart sank. He reached for his sister in an attempt at consolation, but his arms fell back at his sides in helpless defeat. "Has he...?"

"No. He likes to bully me. That's all. Even monsters have limits, I expect. But monsters evolve, don't they?"

23

Corin had nothing to say. No power to help her. Aiden *did* have limits, but the boundaries had stretched and bent as he and his siblings aged closer to adulthood. One day, the lines would snap.

"Don't look so surprised. Why would he have ever stopped when there's no one to stop him?"

"If Father knew—"

"Father knows." Gretchen pointed at her face. "What, you think he suspects I just have a problem with stumbling over divans?"

"Then why…" Corin left the question unfinished, joining the many others that lived within him unaddressed. The questions didn't matter because the answers didn't. There was no sense to be made of a nonsensical world. Chasten Quinlanden turned his eyes away from his eldest son laying hands on his eldest daughter because it didn't matter to him what went on behind closed doors, so long as the kingdom saw only the motif of excellence and favor the Quinlandens worked so laboriously to paint.

"Exactly." Gretchen folded her arms. "Let's get this over with. Where are those cursed workers, anyway?"

"Aiden wants to marry you to Ash," he blurted.

Gretchen snorted. "Does he now?"

"I thought that would make you happy. You wouldn't have to sneak around anymore. You'd be free of Aiden."

"I'll never be free of Aiden, Corin. Nor will you. He may not do *this* to you, but does he not tamp you down into the tiniest bits? Even the way you're standing here, looking at me. As if you're nothing. No one. How sad." Gretchen didn't sound sad though. She sounded furious.

"You love Ash though."

"Yes? And?"

"He'll be your husband! You'll never be subject to Aiden's cruelty again. Ash would never allow it."

Gretchen rolled forward off the table. She coughed when a cloud of dust kicked up with her. "You're the smartest of all of us, and yet Aiden has you afraid of your own shadow. Why do you think he's done that?"

Corin had no chance to answer.

"He's not marrying me to my love to satisfy me. He's doing it to remind me that everything I am, everything I have, is because of him. Can be taken by him. He wants me to look at Ash and see *him*." She threw up her hands. "And I will because now that he's put it in my head, I'll never get it out."

"You will. Eventually."

Gretchen squeezed his arm. "You just proved my entire point, brother."

"You get to escape soon, and instead, all you can think about is *him*?"

"Escape? Rushwood is a short jaunt down the road from Whitechurch! It's not even a proper ride. Of course he'd marry me off to a house he could visit as often as he wanted, without missing anything."

"No man would ever allow his wife's brother to lay hands on her."

"Ash may love me," Gretchen replied. "But his love will soon be bought and paid for with Quinlanden gold. More than the Sylvaines will know what to do with."

"What is your point, Gretchen?"

"My point," Gretchen said with a tight smile, "is there is no escape, not for us. We could go anywhere in this kingdom. We could sail to Beyond. He's in us, Corin, and we'll never get the stench of this family out of our hearts."

"I will."

"How? By sneaking down to the Merchant Quarter to be with your peasant friend? Venya, wasn't it?"

Corin lowered his eyes.

"You don't think Aiden knew? That he wasn't aware of every single time you went down to meet her at Slattery Row, where the two of you did…whatever you did. Or that he wasn't entirely

25

aware you brought her to Arboriana, of all places, only to watch her fall to her death?"

"If he knew—"

"Sometimes…terrible things just happen. Sometimes people just *fall*. But sometimes…*sometimes* there's someone there to help them along."

Corin shook his head as the blood plummeted from his face and chest. "Aiden wasn't even at Arboriana when it happened. I only brought her there because he and Father—"

"Came home early that day from Rushwood. Flooding washed out part of the road, and they had to turn back." Gretchen touched his cheek. "Accepting you are not free is a type of freedom itself. Once you do, you can begin crafting the caskets inside of you, in which to bury those parts you could never let him have."

In all the years he and Gretchen had sought comfort in each other from Aiden's cruelty, she'd never spoken so openly. So cynically.

Corin's voice shook. "That's the best we can ever hope for? That what you're saying?"

Gretchen pursed her lips and exhaled. She pulled her red hair back off her face, tying it with the ribbon in her hand. "Ignore me, Corin. I'm tired, and there's too much work to do."

There was more he wanted to say, but Gretchen was done.

"Why do you think the king called all of us here?" He gestured around. "A raven would have been sufficient."

"Not simply to announce he has a son, I know that much," Gretchen murmured. "Let's go find those cursed workers before Mother burns the place to the ground."

FOUR

EPOCH OF THE ACCORDANT

Despite the wave of jittery awe filtering through the Southerland men, drifting back to Yesenia and Khallum, she was not quite prepared for the sight of Termonglen, the towering monolith that belonged to no one. The old stones had become one with the encroaching vines and roots, set in the middle of a valley so dead not even the bootlicking Quinlandens had restored it to life.

Gleaming in the hazy distance was the edge of the Forest of All. Its leaves were the greenest green, and when they shimmered in the breeze, there was a hint of blue and even purple, quick enough to be dismissed as illusion. Trees there were taller than she'd ever seen, taller than the top of the tower.

The Forest of All was off-limits to the kingdom, even to the Rhiagains. It belonged to the Medvedev, the ones who had been there before all men. No one challenged this. The druidic clahnns were the only ones in the kingdom not beholden to the crown and kingdom. This crumbling monument, which sat at the intersection of the four Compass Roads, was their "gift" to the kingdom for leaving them alone. The Rhiagains were the ones who'd named it the kingdom's neutral ground.

Yesenia, seeing it for the first time, thought it wasn't so much a gift as a warning. Just outside all that life, a dearth of it—a reminder of what would happen to the kingdom should they ever forget they were forbidden from the Hinterland forests.

As the Warwick train left the Compass Roads and moved into the brittle grass of the plain, more wonders passed into view, some decidedly more vile. The lords of the other three Reaches were already there, waiting. She noted only a hint of the Northerland banners first, a sign they'd traveled light, intending their visit to be as brief as allowed. The green and silver of the Westerlands formed a larger blanket over the crowd but only just. Both drowned in a thick vat of crimson and gold that wove through everyone and everything in proximity, like an eruption spindling its death outward to swallow all in its path.

"I ken that's the bootlickers being subtle," Khallum murmured, passing a look between them.

Yesenia ground her jaw, letting his words settle over them both. "I loathe everything they stand for. Everything they've allowed this crown to take from us. Do they not think the crown could ever turn on them and do the same?"

"Your loathing cannae be half of Father's or mine, sister. You willnae have to shake their hands and smile at their wives."

"You donnae know the depth of my loathing."

"Aye? I ken that's good, for the both of us. But you'll do the same as Father and me. As Byrne. You'll smile at their jeweled faces and spit at their gilded backs when they can no longer hear you." He looked at her. "Never let them see it. The depth of your loathing. They'll mine it for their own joy."

Yesenia nodded. She flexed her fingers against the leather reins, drawing in one breath after another. Khallum was right. To show them her ire was to give away a part of herself.

Byrne joined them. "Why did they bring so many? Did we not bring enough?"

"Aye, we brought plenty, unless they got the invite wrong and meant to challenge us to a skirmish." Khallum grunted. His jaw slackened. "Are those *feathers* in their caps? It cannae be borne."

"There's more gold in their robes than in our mines these days," Yesenia added.

"They're so pretty. Even their horses are jeweled," Byrne remarked. "Why are they so pretty?"

"Were ye listening to what I told our sister?"

Byrne nodded at Khallum. He started to respond but scrunched his nose instead. "What is that smell?"

"Rot and stew," Yesenia replied. "And myrrh. It's like dropping a rose in hogshit, rather, donnae ye think?"

Byrne closed his eyes as a southerly breeze passed by carrying a foreign but fruity scent in from the forest. "That though, that's nice."

"Aye. Too bad we're not invited in *there*," Yesenia whispered. "Ah, and there's the ratsbane's banners. The crossed swords of Duncarrow. Almost missed them in the sea of Quinlanden blood."

"We're close enough we've gotta start calling him king, Sen," Khallum warned. "I know, I know. I have to remind myself too."

The rest of the company dropped back to allow Khoulter and his children to ride abreast for the rest of their approach. As they fell into formation, presenting themselves before the Reaches, trumpets sounded, followed by a booming proclamation from three young criers forming their high-pitched words in perfect unison.

"We joyously welcome the arrival of Lord Khoulter Warwick of the Southerlands! Lord Warwick is joined by his sister, the Widow Holton, and his three children: Lord Khallum, Lord Byrne, and Lady Yesenia." The criers repeated their announcement twice, allowing Yesenia and her family to draw close enough to the gathering to make out expressions on faces.

Despite her desire to ignore them, her eyes were drawn to the crimson and gold, the darlings of the kingdom and crown. Revered for their beauty, their love of beauty, and their disgust of anything not beautiful, they wouldn't last a day in the Southerlands. A morning.

At the front was Lord Chasten and his family, easy to deduce by the plumage that waved three times as high as anyone else wearing his Reach's colors. His wife cowed at his side, attractive but useless. Stretched to the right and left of the lord and lady were their three invited children: two boys and a girl, like the Warwicks.

Yesenia reprimanded herself for gawking, but her eyes caught those of a boy two down from Lord Chasten. He had light-golden hair and bright-blue eyes, and she thought, for a moment, he was actually *smiling* at her, the fool, but it was only his deep dimples. But then he *did* smile, from the corner of his mouth, with a pink bloom in his cheeks. When his father shot him a hard look, he dropped his gaze to the side.

"Eyes ahead," Khoulter warned.

"What is that, do you suppose?" Yesenia asked, pointing at a large dais ornately decorated with plump flowers that couldn't have come from this barren valley.

"Ye think he was gonna pass the bairn through the crowd?" Khallum quipped.

Yesenia sighed as they angled toward the stables. She didn't share with her brother that something about the way the flowers were arranged unsettled her, like they belonged to another cere- mony than the one they'd been invited to.

She exchanged the thought for another and focused on the eyes following them, courtesy of their late arrival.

Several pages rushed forth to help with the horses. They steered the guard one way and the Warwicks another.

"Everything's ready, Lord Warwick, sir," the boy said, breath- less. "It's *been* ready, ahh, but you know the king. He doesn't like when anyone is late. You have eaten, right, sir? He'll want to start immediately. No more delays, if you understand what I mean. Sir."

"Are we late?" Khoulter bantered, in a voice indicating he knew precisely how late they were.

"It'll be fine, it will. If we can get your horses put up and then I'll see to your bags, sir, which we'll get settled inside—"

"Leave us. Help the others."

The boy nodded, bowed, and happily scurried off.

The Warwicks were alone for the first time on the voyage north. While her brothers and father led their horses into one end of the stalls, Yesenia dismounted outside the double doors, but landed in a large pile of dung.

She groaned, gritting her teeth. Khallum snickered from the other side. After a sharp glare at him, she stepped behind the barn to deal with it.

"Can I help?"

Yesenia stuttered back a step at the intrusion. Steadying herself by digging her already-filthy boots deeper into the mud, she looked up and found herself staring directly into the bright-blue eyes of the Quinlanden son who'd watched her so intently on her ride in. She tried to speak, to say something cutting or witty, but found all she could do was point at her boots.

The boy looked down. "Well, that's quite unfortunate."

"Aye," she muttered.

"Here." The boy turned, offering use of his shoulders. "Use me for balance. So you can wipe them against the wood."

"Use you for balance?" she asked, finding herself again. She tossed her head and laughed. "Ye ken I've never knocked shite off my boots before? I guess ye think I've never wiped my own arse, either?"

The boy turned back, flushing as he had when he'd caught her watching him earlier. "You seem capable of anything to me."

"Do I? Ye say that to everyone ye donnae know?"

He turned all the way back around and offered his hand. "I'm Corin."

"A Quinlanden," Yesenia spat, eyeing his hand like it was ridden with disease.

Corin patted his chest, looking down. "Was it the crimson and gold that gave me away?" He laughed with an upturn of his eyes. "Or the ridiculous feathers?"

She almost laughed with him, but the slip in her resolve, in what she already knew of the boy, only stirred her anger.

"You must be Yesenia."

"And you must be too clever by far to have deduced *that*."

"There are worse things to be," Corin answered. "I really would like to help you, before the others notice and come over to see you standing here with horse dung on your boots." He frowned, turning his head to the side in scrutiny. "Though, not much of a loss then. Those aren't ladies' boots, are they?"

"Do I strike you as a lady?"

"Sen!" Khallum yelled. "Ye crawling about in the mud over there or what?"

Corin lowered his eyes, hiding his grin. "We're supposed to be enemies. But I don't believe that someone I've never met is my enemy, do you?"

Yesenia's grin stretched across her face. She kicked her boot against the barn wall three times and then said, "Aye. I very much do, Corin Quinlanden."

She pivoted on her heels and left him standing there, wishing she could see the stunned look he undoubtedly wore as she sauntered away.

As she was about to turn the corner and re-enter the barn, she heard another voice join him. Her step faltered, and she wasn't quick enough to disappear entirely.

"What are you doing back here, Corin, playing with the help?" A pause, and then he said, "Ahh. You're playing all right, though you've got your eyes on the wrong prize. A Warwick, brother, really? A wild one, but I could tame her in an afternoon. In fact, I might before this is all over. You wanna wager?"

"Don't count on it, Aiden," Corin murmured.

Yesenia regained her step and joined her brothers.

A bloated silence fell over the gathered. No one said what they were waiting for, or why. *Must be the king*, Khallum thought, but he could see nothing except the occasional banner from another Reach catching the wind, rising above the throngs.

It was hogshit was what it was. Yesenia was, as usual, right on the mark, but what kind of lord would he one day be if he couldn't even keep his own sister from starting a revolution?

He pushed forward to where she stood, huddled around Byrne like an overbearing wife. "Aye, and what's so interesting up here?" he gruffed. "Where's Father?"

"All the lords are with the king," Byrne answered. He pointed at a tent across the browned grass. "In there."

"What the feck for?"

"I donnae like it, Khallum." Yesenia whistled through her teeth. "I told ye—"

"That why you were making eyes at a Quinlanden back there, letting him wipe the shit from your boots?"

Yesenia's cheeks darkened. "That lapdog didnae lay a hand on me or my boots. Probably sent by his father to spy. Got nothing from me."

"Except an earful, I'm sure," Byrne said, grinning.

"Well, if you'd have had your sense about ye, you might have thought to do a little spying of your own, Sen."

"Aye? Why not try your hand on the sister, then?"

Khallum's view had improved with his closer proximity to the dais. He could see the front lines of the other Reaches, adorned by those highest born. He swept his gaze over what should be his allies but were not. His appraisal abruptly paused upon a redhead towering as tall as her brothers. She wrapped her arms in her layers as the wind swept upon them, but her copper hair couldn't escape the breeze, whipping across her face. She made no move to address this slight, and something stirred in his trousers as he imagined her applying the same stoic resolve to riding him into oblivion.

"That's Gwyn Dereham you're wetting yourself over," came Yesenia's rude interruption. "Only thing nearly as bad as a Quinlanden is a Dereham."

"And why is that?" Khallum growled, trying to keep his eyes from traveling back toward the alpine beauty wedged between her brothers.

"The Quinlandens at least show us who they are. Traitors. Derehams hide in their icy Reach buried in snow, pretending there's nothing going on south of their borders." Yesenia nodded at the other side. "Now the Blackwood girls? They'd give you a fair ride, I expect."

He followed her gaze to see the three young women of the Westerlands wearing looks so defiant, he had no trouble seeing why his sister respected them.

"Only house who brought three girls too. Wonder why."

"No sons," Khallum muttered. He rammed his shoulder into Byrne's. "Learn to glance, not stare. Otherwise, Lord Blackwood will be insisting you marry his daughter, looking like that."

Byrne shuffled. "I cannae even be curious? You both are."

"Doesnae matter what we think of any of them," Yesenia said, her tone harder than ever. "We listen to the king blather and raise the bairn for us to gaggle over. We go home. We never have to see any of them again."

"Look." Khallum's chest seized at the sight of the tent flaps opening.

The king and his two daughters emerged first, each clutching an infant to their breast.

"It's about t—" He swallowed the rest of whatever he had to say, forgotten and replaced by his attention on the pale looks worn by all four men following the king and his daughters. Gone was their hardened enmity. They had a secret now, something they shared, something they had in common.

"Khallum," Yesenia whispered.

"Aye. Aye, I see it too."

"I donnae like it. I donnae—"

"Hush." He swallowed. "Please. I cannae hear myself think."

A deeper calm settled over the restless crowd. As the small group approached the dais, guards laid down their cloaks at the single stair, bowing as King Khain Rhiagain ascended. He glided upon the stage, a broad bear of a man, with a rigid but satisfied look. Only when his daughters had joined him, one on each side, did he speak.

But Khallum and his siblings were fixed on their father's peaked face and the matching ones of Lords Dereham, Blackwood, and Quinlanden, all waiting to be summoned atop the dais.

"I thank you all for coming, and so swiftly. It has been many years since the leaders of this kingdom have joined together in one place. It is my greatest wish that we do not allow such time to pass before the next event."

"Not ours," Yesenia muttered, but her fire was quenched. In its place sounded like fear.

"We come here today, at Termonglen, to present to the leaders of this kingdom new life. You have all traveled far for this and are no doubt weary and hungry, so I'll not waste words or time. Let us get right to it." Khain nodded first toward the daughter at his left. "In the arms of Princess Assyria, I present to you my heir, Darrick, prince of the Realm, future king of the White Kingdom." He waited for applause.

Khallum weakly slapped his hands together, still staring at his father. Yesenia drew a sharp inhale.

"And in the arms of Princess Correen, a showing from our blessed Guardians that they still, now and *always*, smile upon the Rhiagains. For I was not gifted one son, but two. We have been given twins, and so Prince Eoghan also joins our family, as Prince Darrick's brother, his aide, and his one-day confidante."

The revelation livened the crowd, deepening their applause, and for a moment, Khallum forgot about the bewildered lords standing off to the side.

Both of the king's daughters seemed put out by the task of holding the brothers they'd one day bow to, but Khain's oblivious-ness to this was no doubt an intended slight, as were all his ways of putting those he had no place for in the corner of his choosing.

35

Queen Florian was nowhere to be seen. Had he left her behind in Duncarrow, or was she with the ladies?

"As I say, new life. Promise. Hope for our future. I am nearly an old man now, but it is never too late for those the Guardians favor." He nodded at his heir, Darrick, and then his spare, Eoghan. "As your king, I understand there can be no new life without new beginnings, alliances unburdened by the pettiness of squabbles and jealousy."

"I willnae share a table with a Quinlanden," Yesenia whispered. "There'll be no peace until there's peace for us."

Khallum's response sank to his feet. He again had his eyes on his father, who seemed to be struggling with his breaths. Lord Dereham's eyes were closed, his lips moving, wordless. They already knew what was coming. The lords knew what the rest did not.

"Lords and Ladies Dereham, Quinlanden, Blackwood, and Warwick, I have brought you here with your children to right the many wrongs that have mounted over the years, beginning long before I wore this heavy crown. The fighting, the trade wars, the grudges older than any present here? They end today."

"Is he gonna give us the Wastelands back then?" Yesenia quipped quietly.

"Today..." Khain went on, ignorant of the wind that nearly knocked his daughters and newborn sons sideways. "We come to celebrate the promise of unity. What we do here this afternoon will decide the future of this kingdom, for centuries to come."

Khallum ground his heels into the dirt and ignored the hole-boring gazes both of his siblings had trained on him.

Corin found her in the sea of armor. The Southerlands had come dressed for war but had worn no colors beyond the muted browns and greys of their leather. Salt and sand, they called themselves, words turned to ridicule by his father and brother. Even the Warwick banner, the crested wave, was devoid of dressing.

But Yesenia—every bit the salt and sand of the men gathered around her—was more. Her dark hair snapped in the wind like the sails of her own ship. He pictured her thus, standing at the helm, one hand on the mast and the other directing the men who would follow her anywhere.

Her effect on him was blinding. The urge to fall to his knees, inexplicable.

When he managed to briefly catch her eyes, she rolled hers, but he'd expected her to. He'd stirred something in her, even if it was a hatred older than either of them.

"I can't decide which one I'll take into the menagerie with me first. The eldest Blackwood girl looks arrogant enough. How long will it take for me to knock the smirk from her face? Five minutes? Ten?" Aiden had been reciting through his quest to bed all the daughters of the realm, as if it were as simple as making the claim. To him, Corin supposed, it was so simple, as everything had always been for the heir to the Easterlands. "I'd really like to put the Warwick trollop in her place though. Show her what a real man looks like."

Corin gagged. When he went to find Yesenia again, she was whispering to her brother. Then both Warwicks cast their eyes to the distance, and everything changed.

"Where's Mother?" Gretchen asked, panic rising in her tone. "Why is she not with Father?"

Khallum again caught the redheaded Northerland daughter in his gaze, and this time, she was looking back at him. In her face was the same alarm he felt. She sensed the danger looming in the king's next words, same as he did. She exhaled a deep breath and returned her eyes to the king.

"There will be six blessed unions of marriage on this day," Khain said.

Yesenia halted her restless shifting at Khallum's side. Her animated breathing stopped with it.

"The arrangements have been made with all four lords of the realm, and I will ask all those taking their vows to put aside your quarrels, your sorrows, and step forward in the best interest of all in the kingdom. Know that the bonds you create today will be the foundation of a united realm for all future generations."

"What? No," Yesenia whispered, the word dragging out into a hiss. "No, Khallum, no. He cannae mean…He doesnae…"

Khallum reached down and laced her hand in his. Squeezed, in the absence of words. Released it.

"Khallum!"

"Khallum?"

His sister. His brother. Demanding response. Explanation. What could he do, for either of them, but listen with the same horror? He couldn't even muster the acknowledgement that Yesenia had been right, that they shouldn't have come at all. Because if there was anything more useless than regret, he hadn't yet met it.

Khallum tried to meet his father's eyes, but Khoulter had his tongue between his teeth and his terse gaze cast toward the barren field.

"*Do* something," Yesenia cried. "Khallum!" She lifted her elbows and made for her daggers. "We cannae let him speak another word of this."

Khallum snaked his hand over and clamped it on her arm. "You draw steel, you'll die here."

Yesenia relented, but the tension radiating from her sent a shock through him. "I willnae marry *any* man here, Khallum. I'll run. I'll take a ship and sail to Beyond before I let any of them touch me."

"Then run away," Khallum said. He at last found something useful to say. "Tomorrow. Today, you'll do what the king asks, or you'll be doing him a great favor when he sends his enemy's daughter to her execution."

"Are we not Warwicks, Khallum?" Yesenia panted, leaning into him. The look she wore tore a hole in his heart. "Do we not fight when it matters?"

"We'll sort it, Sen. Byrne. When we can. I promise." He folded his hands over his torso and stuttered his breath inward. "If we donnae listen now, we'll nay know what shite he's sentenced us to, will we?"

Everything blurred together.

The king's talk of new beginnings released a fresh horror through the crowd, which had been, at best, anxious, and was now plotting revolt. Six marriages? Across the Reaches? Corin couldn't have heard him right. That couldn't be what the king meant.

Gretchen sobbed, open-mouthed, her eyes burning holes in the king.

Aiden had stopped his disgusting rants and was, for once, dumbstruck.

"And now I will name these unions so that we may break the bread of the marriage table and return to our lands, and our new lives, at peace," the king said, as pleasantly as one might discuss the evening menu.

"No," Aiden whispered. "No, he wouldn't do that to us. It will be the others, watch. Not us."

"Six unions," Gretchen snapped. "Twelve children invited. Even you can do that math, Aiden."

Aiden gawped at the dais.

"As I call your names, you will present yourselves to me. I will lay the marriage wreath around both your necks, read the vows, and it will be done. If you wish to conduct your own ceremonies, according to your own customs, you may do so when you return home. My blessing will be binding enough under the laws that hold our realm together."

Corin spotted his father standing just beyond the dais. Chasten was green in the face but mustering all he could to preserve the appearance of authority—of amity, with the king. That was when Corin knew his family hadn't known any of this was coming. Today, at least, they had been equal with the other lords in their confusion.

"Asherley Blackwood, first daughter of the Westerlands, you will be joined with Byrne Warwick, second son of the Southerlands."

Corin whipped his gaze to Yesenia, watching, powerless along with her, as she clawed at her younger brother, Byrne. The other brother, Khallum, visibly frightened, shook his head at her and pushed Byrne along.

The two approached the dais. Asherley reminded Corin of Yesenia, tall and proud. At her side, Byrne seemed small, like a child almost.

But they were all children, weren't they? If the king cared about such things, none of this would be happening.

"I hope the king gives me the Warwick slut," Aiden said, recovered somewhat from the shock that had rendered him dumb. "Or the Dereham giant."

The king's next words were reserved for Asherley and Byrne alone. The crowd waited, shifting, restless in the uncomfortable silence of a conversation that excluded all but the young couple standing before the king.

When he finished speaking, the king placed a large wreath of flowers about both of their necks, causing them to stumble in uncoordinated confusion as the guards guided them off the other side of the stage and away from the crowd.

"That's it then? Just like that, and they're *married*?" Gretchen marveled aloud.

"Where are they going?" Aiden asked, clearly annoyed to not know.

"Khallum Warwick, first son of the Southerlands, you will be joined with Gwyn Dereham, first daughter of the Northerlands."

Gwyn's brothers embraced her before sending her off. Khallum showed no hesitation in meeting her, even offering his arm as they ascended the single stair.

Corin turned his eyes back toward Yesenia, now alone. Her intense glower flickered between rage and horror.

"Well, *she's* out," Aiden muttered. "Warwick girl is still in though. You think Gwyn would still let me fuck her?"

"For once in your life…" Gretchen panted. "Can you just say *nothing*?"

Aiden shot Corin an appalled look, but Corin only caught it from his peripheral. He was fixed on Yesenia's struggle as she stood alone, awaiting her own sentence.

"Aiden Quinlanden, first son of the Easterlands, you will be joined with Maeryn Blackwood, second daughter of the Westerlands."

Aiden's jaw parted in disgust. "The *ugliest* one? He'd give me the ugliest one?" He tossed his head in disbelief. "Father will have something to say about this."

"Father agreed to this. You heard the king." Corin murmured, to disguise the quake in his voice.

Maeryn Blackwood approached the stage, her head bowed, and Corin thought to himself that she was actually quite lovely, but whatever beauty she possessed would be stripped and reduced as the wife of Aiden.

"Go on then," Gretchen said through her tears, gloating. "Go accept your prize."

"For now," Aiden said with splintered confidence.

When he was gone, Corin turned toward his sister. "Is this really happening?"

"Yes, Corin. It's really happening."

He shuffled, digging his feet into the damp grass. "What do we do?"

"You ask me that, as if we have a choice?"

"But you're betrothed to Ash! And Father—"

Gretchen nodded at the dais. "You think this king cares? Just because he sends the Southerland gold to Father? Those bounties have a cost, Corin. *Submission.* Can't have even the Quinlandens reaching too far ahead, now can he?"

41

Aiden and Maeryn exited the dais. It was happening too fast. Corin again searched for Yesenia, but he couldn't find her.

"Holden Dereham, second son of the Northerlands, you will be joined with Gretchen Quinlanden, first daughter of the Easterlands."

Gretchen tugged both of her hands to her face with a retching gasp. Corin clapped a hand to her arm, trying to catch a glimpse of Holden. The young man's face was buried behind all his furs. Not that it mattered what he looked like. He wasn't Ash. Gretchen would take a stranger to her bed, just as they all would. There were no considerations for broken hearts or promises.

"It will be okay…" he called after her, neither believing it nor sounding like he did.

If he could only slow this day down, run it backward.

Corin watched his sister through bleary eyes as she was joined to the future lord of the Northerlands. He tried to tell himself it meant she'd be a proper lady, not only the daughter of one. But the consolation was hollow, like every other word or emotion running through his tempestuous thoughts.

"Alric Dereham, fourth son of the Northerlands, you will be joined with Earwyn Blackwood, third daughter of the Westerlands."

Corin's heart dropped to his feet. That was the fifth union. That meant…

He choked on his breath—watched, thoughts divorced from his body, as two people he didn't know were joined on the dais and then ushered off the other side. He waited for the words he knew were forthcoming.

"Corin Quinlanden, second son of the Easterlands, you will be joined with Yesenia Warwick, first daughter of the Southerlands."

Somehow, he found his feet. It was simpler than staying put. Motion gave him breath, left his thoughts behind so he could act, so he could avoid bringing more shame to his father and mother by being the only son of the realm who could not rise to what had been asked.

He nearly bowled into Yesenia as she pushed through the crowd. He offered his arm, like her brother had done for Gwyn Dereham, but she charged ahead of him and stormed up onto the stage.

When he joined her, she gave him neither a greeting nor a welcome glance. It was then he observed she was shaking. His hand twitched at his side as he thought of hers, but that would be the last thing she wanted.

The king looked so much older in person. His wrinkles turned to jowls. His teeth, yellowed and rotting, betrayed the few years still ahead of him.

Could he have not died before this day? Was it treason, for even thinking it?

Corin hardly heard the words. Some kind of vows, he assumed, though not the ones uttered in handfast in the Easterlands, nor, he supposed, the Southerlands. When the flowers were draped about their shoulders, the king looked at them both and said, "You will leave this stage and be taken to a tent, where the two of you will make your arrangements as a wedded couple. Lady Warwick, you may return to your home long enough to prepare a proper trunk, but then you will join your husband, Lord Quinlanden, in Whitechurch. Do you both understand?"

"Yes, Your Grace." Corin needed to be off this stage. He needed air.

Yesenia hesitated. Her breaths rolled slow, heavily. He felt the rebellion rise in her. But then her head came up. She tightened her face into a polite smile and repeated the same words.

"Yes, Your Grace."

"Then go, so I may address the realm once more."

Two attendants awaited them in the tent: an older woman and a younger man.

"Lady Warwick, let me be the first to congratulate you—"

"Save your words," Yesenia barked at the woman. "They aren't for me. I ken they're not for anyone here."

The woman lowered her head. "I know this day must be a shock to you all, my lady."

"But not to you, aye? You've been waiting here, for us."

"Why are we in here?" Corin asked, putting some distance between himself and his new wife.

Wife.

Was this possible?

"We are here," the man said, "to assist with your accommodations."

"Accommodations?" Yesenia stepped aggressively closer to the man, her head cocked. "*Accommodations?*"

The man cleared his throat, avoiding meeting her eyes. "The king understands if tonight you are both not prepared for consummation—"

"CONSUMMATION?"

Corin forced himself into a calm he didn't feel. "Yesenia—"

She threw up a hand without looking at him. "Donnae say my name again, tree-dweller!"

The man and woman glanced at each other and then downward again.

"You may lodge with your families tonight. Tomorrow you will both return to your homes. Lady Warwick, you will have two days in Warwicktown to settle your affairs and then you will be escorted to your new home: Whitechurch."

Corin was astounded Yesenia had let the woman get so many words in.

"That so?" Yesenia's ire radiated. It flowed outward, spreading across the four of them like a blanket of fire.

The woman bowed. "For now, we'll leave you two to get acquainted." She dropped her voice lower. "I know that may not be agreeable to you, but the king will be cross if you do not spend at least *some* time in here, together, as the other brides and grooms are undoubtedly doing. So, for your own sakes…make it work."

The man and woman left.

Yesenia laid her hands on her daggers. Corin took another step away.

"Ye afraid of me then? Think I'd take these to you?"

"I don't know what you'd do to me," Corin confessed. "But I'm not your enemy."

Yesenia laughed.

"We are both victims of the king's games, Yesenia. I—"

Yesenia snapped her gaze at him. "Call me a victim again, Corin Quinlanden."

Corin's heart flipped in his chest. Even brimming with rage, she was stunning. Yesenia was unlike anyone he'd ever known, and he was utterly terrified of her.

"We can sit here, in silence, if you like," Corin offered. "Let the time run down, until it's acceptable to leave."

"Like?" Yesenia dropped into a chair on one side of the table prepared for them. To get *acquainted*, the attendants had said, as if it were so simple—as if they were not in shock.

Corin tentatively took the other chair. He tried to not look at her, her feet kicked up on the table like a commoner, but it was harder than he'd expected, for she was looking directly at him

Glaring.

"Did you know?" she demanded, her nostrils flaring. Her high cheeks flushed crimson.

"Know? About this?" Corin pointed at the tent flaps and the inexplicable events that had just transpired beyond.

"What else could I mean, tree-dweller?"

He shook his head. "No, I didn't know. I didn't know, and neither did Aiden, and I don't think my father knew either."

She snorted and turned her eyes toward the top of the tent. "Right."

"I'm serious. I saw his face. He looked…ill."

He braced himself for more of her ire, but she looked down at her hands, nodding. "Mine did too."

"What do we do?"

"What do we *do*?" Her menacing grin shifted, turning to sorrow. "Feck if I know."

"I'm sorry."

"If you knew nothing, why are you sorry?"

"I just am."

She crossed her arms, shaking her head. "We'll just do it your way then. Let the time run down, until I can find my brothers and sort this mess."

FIVE
WOLFSBANE IN THE PORRIDGE

For once, I have to say I agree with your daughter, Khoulter," the Widow declared, one hand clutched to her waist. A displeased air accompanied her revelation. She fanned herself despite the chill sweeping across the Termonglen plain.

Khoulter grunted and hurled his snot into a rag before grimacing at the tent flaps.

Yesenia would never understand how Korah and Khoulter had been raised in the same household.

"Your opinion doesnae alter the vow I made to the..." Khoulter's eyes flared in defiance. "King."

"He cannae hear ye, Father," Yesenia bitterly retorted. "You donnae have to call him thus. That is unless he's your mate now?"

"Yesenia," Khallum warned.

Yesenia threw her arms out. "Ah, well I'm glad *someone* here is happy. A little too eager to stick it to that redheaded lass though, aye?"

"I'm not pleased about it either," he grumbled. "A Northerlander...in the Southerlands..."

47

"Still somehow better than a Southerlander in the Easterlands."

"Asherley seems interesting," Byrne said, then ducked from the looks leveled at him by both siblings. "We didnae get to say much, in the tent, but she was kind."

"Until she drops wolfsbane into your porridge," Yesenia countered. "You do know you're wedding a poison mistress, I ken?"

Byrne shook his head into his sigh.

"What did the…king say to the four of you, Father? In the tent?" Khallum asked. "How did he convince you to sell yer own kin?"

"Sell my…" Khoulter knocked his ale from the table. "Is that what ye think, son? That ye were all bought and paid for?"

Yesenia lifted her chin. "We donnae know *what* to think! Before this afternoon, I was happily unwed, sneaking about with Erran Rutland in the cove. And now, you've married me to our sworn enemy?"

"Sneaking about…with Erran?" Khoulter squinted at her. His dubious look dissolved in favor of a more pressing one. "There was nothing exchanged. No offer could have swayed me to sell my own children."

"Yet ye did," the Widow said, with a smile Yesenia wanted to knock from her face, whether she agreed with her or not. "I'd just about concluded negotiations for Khallum's marriage to Sessaly Rutland."

"Are ye out of your mind, woman? Why did I even let you come here?" He dismissed her with his hand, though she only backed up and planted herself in a nearby chair. "There was no offer, only a demand. A test. Are we with him or against him. No more or less."

"Against!" Yesenia cried out, laughing. "Isnae a hard question, Father."

"But are we? Really?" Khoulter leaned against the table, weary. "It's as we talked about, before we left Warwicktown. There isnae a chance of us winning anything but a war on words. We have no allies but our own people, and even they've begun to dull their anger toward the crown that takes so much from them. What's the past to them, when the present has them wondering after their next meal?"

"I knew it. I *knew* this was a trap."

"Aye? Lotta good knowing did us," her father replied. "Even a keen rat still takes the cheese."

"Well, I willnae go to Whitechurch. He can come to the Southerlands."

"You will go." Each of Khoulter's words was heavier than his last. "As will Byrne."

"Byrne? But he's a man! The Blackwood girl will come to *him*, as she should."

"She's the Blackwood *heir.* He will leave when you do."

Yesenia's head shook so fast, her vision blurred. There were tears, but she'd offer them no address. "Why are you..." She struggled for breath. "Giving them everything they asked for? What do you get in return?"

Khoulter looked at his crossed feet. "I ken knowing my children are not the enemies of the king, as I've been, was all I needed in return."

Yesenia glared at her father. "How nice for you, that you had the luxury of deciding for us all." She ran from the tent before her tears could overcome her will.

"I just don't understand. I don't *understand.*" Chasten moved aggressively from one end of their tent to the other, stopping only for sighs. "Not even a warning. A *hint.* Perhaps we missed a raven..."

"We missed nothing," Mariana said, her teeth clenched.

"We must have! There's no other explanation. Khain would have wanted us to know. To be prepared."

"At the very least he could've let us pick our brides," Aiden muttered. He quaffed what remained in the wine carafe and let it fall to the ground. "The middle daughter of Lord Blackwood?

Really? Ignoring the obvious slight, we know how the Blackwoods are. It may have been her father who joined you and the other lords in the tent, but *everyone* knows it's the women who rule the west." He shook his head. "I'll have my work cut out, no doubt."

"Could be worse. Could be a Warwick," Chasten replied. "In our house. There will be a cursed Warwick in *our* house!" He feigned a smile his younger son's way. "It will be fine, Corin. We'll prepare you for it."

Corin found his sister huddled in the corner. None of the others had time for her turmoil, of what it would mean for her to leave her love behind and move to the cold, unforgiving north, with a man she'd spent an hour with.

Despite his family's glances his way through most of their conversation, Corin had said nothing in the rapid exchange. His thoughts had moved on to the trial awaiting him.

He'd never leave Whitechurch. Never get away from the Quinlandens and their grasping, cloying ways.

"Sending Gretchen out of the Easterlands will not do at all." Chasten seemed to be just getting started, collecting energy from around himself. "We *need* the payment for her. The Sylvaines would pay double."

"I'm *sure* the king will pay us a bounty," Aiden said.

"No," Chasten answered, bewildered despite his anger. "No, he claims we have all been offered something of equal value, and thus any gold changing hands is unnecessary. We will receive a bride without so much as a scrap of silver, and we'll send one without receiving any benefit. It's *madness*. It goes against the Accord, the agreement that the king shall not tread upon the customs of his Reaches, so long as our taxes are paid on time and—"

"We go home," Mariana said, her voice heavy with reason, stability. "We go home. We pack Gretchen's trunk. We prepare for the arrival of our foreign brides. That's all there is. Anything more does nothing to help us. We must focus on what needs to be done." She nodded. "That's right. That's what we do."

"I need to speak with the king," Chasten asserted. "Alone."

"You will do no such thing," Mariana countered. Aiden started in, as if to scold her for speaking to him so, but she was ready for him. "You are both beholden to emotion at present."

Aiden scoffed. "And you're not?"

"A woman always does what a woman must," Mariana calmly answered. "Chasten, if you go to him now, he will see you at your weakest. You will say things you must never say. You do understand that?"

Chasten nodded, crossing his arms and facing away from them all.

"The king must never see you as anything but his agreeable ally. His most trusted man. His unflappable champion. You can endure anything he gives you. He knows that, and so must you."

"Father already knows all this," Aiden said.

"Of course he does," she replied, looking at her husband. "Everything we already know requires reminder, on occasion."

Aiden spun away from their strange energy and licked his lips at Corin. "Don't look so pathetic, brother. You got the best of the lot. Warwicks are feral. You know what that means."

Corin swallowed and thought of Venya climbing higher and higher at Arboriana, farther than Corin would follow with his great fear of heights. The Sylvan Prince, she'd called him, her last words before he saw her for the last time, lying upon the grass in a pool of her own blood.

"If nothing else, your nights will be satisfying." Aiden shook his head as if imagining it. "Just don't go falling in love with her."

"What?"

"You fall for anything that looks at you, like the merchant girl."

Corin looked away. "That's not true."

"Did you or did you not stick it to her, before she went sailing from the branches?"

"No, never," Corin said. Why he confirmed his truth to the one person who would use it to hurt him, he didn't know. Maybe that was what he wanted. To be hurt. To know pain as Venya had, because pain was, at the very least, something else to focus on.

"Shame," Aiden said, chuckling. "Still. The Warwicks are our enemies. Never forget it."

"How could I?" Corin grimaced at his brother. "When it's all you and Father can talk about?"

Aiden knelt and picked up the dusty wine carafe. He shoved it at Corin's chest. "You want to mope and brood? Then do it while you fetch us more wine."

Yesenia found the Blackwood girl in the menagerie, an unkempt garden of animals carved from bushes. Someone must have tended it once, for the lions and bears were at least somewhat discernible. Who had bothered to create such an ambitious piece of work in the shadow of the abandoned, forsaken keep was a question for another girl, in another time, in another life.

"Asherley, aye?" Yesenia approached the dark-haired heir to the Blackwoods with barely repressed fury. Asherley was pretty, in the same way Khallum's new wife, Gwyn, was pretty. But when she looked toward the sound of her name, there was an iciness to her gaze, a hardness that promised to reveal more only to anyone who had earned the privilege of closeness.

"What a strange place," Asherley replied after a silent appraisal of Yesenia. "Who would bother, all the way out here?"

"You cannae take him to the Westerlands. I willnae allow it."

Asherley folded her shawl over herself and looked up from where she was seated, at the base of an elk-kind missing an antler. "That isn't for you to decide, Yesenia. Any more than I have any say in seeing both my sisters sent off to foreign houses."

"Byrne is a man," she said, when what she wanted to say was *Byrne is a boy.*

"And we are the Westerlands."

Yesenia snorted. "I've heard of what the women are like there."

Asherley grinned. She clutched her skirt when a wind tore down the plain. "Jealous, are you?"

"I have all I need."

"Pray that the Quinlandens allow you to keep it in the Easterlands. Poor Maeryn." She briefly closed her eyes.

"You'll unnerve him, Asherley. He's hardly had time to learn to be a man, and you'd take what little he possesses."

Asherley pivoted on the topiary bench. "I'm not your enemy, Yesenia."

"You're the second person to say that to me today."

Asherley shrugged. "I can only speak for myself. We all lost something here. Lick your wounds and find your way." She returned to staring off into the forest. "As we all must."

Yesenia, flustered, turned to leave, but Asherley stood instead.

"My family will be expecting me. Enjoy the silence, for all that it lasts."

Asherley returned to the sea of tents as Yesenia stewed in her grudging realization that silence was precisely what she needed most right now.

But she was not alone for long.

Yesenia heard him before she saw him. It started with a grunt and escalated to a scream and then a glass bottle hurled through the air. She watched it sail over the topiary fish and land in the tail of the donkey.

"Oh, I…" Corin flushed. She was starting to take his habit, of doing that every time he saw her, as a personal slight. "I didn't think anyone would be out here."

"I was just leaving." Yesenia started to rise.

"No! I mean, you don't have to. Not on my account."

"It wasnae on your account," she replied. "Nor anyone's but my own."

Corin rushed to speak. "My father *was* blindsided by the king. I was right about that. He was just as taken aback as the other lords."

Yesenia balked. She dropped her elbows onto her knees. "Why would you tell me that?"

Corin shrugged. He took a seat amidst what must have been a family of ducks, once. He squinted into the setting sun. "He thinks you'll spy on us."

Yesenia laughed. "Aye, ye can bet on it."

"He's already preparing Gretchen to spy on the Derehams."

"That bootlicker may be a treasonous weasel, but he's no fool." Yesenia waited for Corin to bristle. He didn't. "You're going to let me talk about your father like that?"

"I'll stop you when you've said something out of order."

Her eyes narrowed. "You're a strange boy."

"You're not quite like any girl I've ever met either."

"I'll take that as a compliment."

"Good." Corin glanced at her with a quick smile. His azure eyes sparkled in the twilight. His skin was so pale and smooth, he looked more like the dolls Korah had tried to buy for her when she was little. She was beginning to understand what they said about Quinlandens when they called them ethereal and otherworldly.

"I worry you won't like Whitechurch."

Yesenia reared back. "Of *all* the things that have happened today, that's what worries ye? That I'll nay take to your little fiefdom in the trees?"

"You're my wife now, aren't you?"

She cackled. "Donnae hang your hopes on that."

"You know a way out of it?"

"I will when I find it."

Yesenia thought he looked almost disappointed. It didn't last. Relief flooded Corin's face fast enough for her to take offense.

"I won't be surprised when you do. You're more clever than I am, Yesenia."

He clapped his hands on his thighs and rose. She noted that he didn't look at her. Even when reveling in the tantalizing idea of a reprieve from marriage to her, he hadn't looked at her. She was used to men being afraid of her, but this wasn't that. She sensed the difference, even if she couldn't define it.

"Over there. Atop the donkey's arse." She pointed past where he was looking. "Is where it landed."

"Thank you," he said, turning toward where she pointed. "And Yes—"

Yesenia heard his words die on his tongue as she left him to return to her family.

SIX
COLD, CALCULATED, CUNNING.

Yesenia ushered both of her brothers behind the rock enclosure. The tide was going out, so they'd have a few hours if their needs were determined by the sea, as had been so often true for most of their lives.

"Is this where?" Khallum widened his eyes with a meaningful nod at Byrne, as if he were a toddler requiring protection from adult things.

"Aye, it's where Erran and I come," she replied.

His eyes traveled in a slow semicircle. "Willnae be sitting down then."

"We'll have privacy. No one else comes here because it's a death trap when the tide comes in."

"Feeling much better about it, Sen."

"Open yer eyes, Khallum. Tide's going out, you mudfish."

Byrne backed himself against a rock when Yesenia did, and Khallum joined them after another overdone show of wariness.

"Maybe it willnae be so bad," Byrne said. In his hopeful eyes was something that melted Yesenia's heart. Protecting him had

57

given her purpose, and now, now he was just going to be *sent off*? To a girl who didn't even know him? Didn't know what he needed? Wouldn't know how to look after him?

"Aye," she said, her words raging against her intention.

Khallum must have caught the meaning unsaid and lowered his head.

"But Khallum was right. Father was right." She dug the toes of her boots into the wet sand. "I can admit that now, with a more level head, ye ken?"

Her brothers both nodded. Khallum seemed like he might say something but finished his nod instead.

"Because it willnae be forever."

Khallum snapped back to alert. "What are you up to now? Not forever? What is marriage, if not forever?"

"When it's safe, Byrne and I will come home. We'll return to Warwicktown, where we belong. Salt and sand." She pressed her hand to her chest, and her brothers followed her lead, repeating the words with her this time. "Salt and sand."

"How is rebelling later any different?" Khallum's head fell to the side. "I donnae want this either, but it's just marriage, Sen."

"For you, maybe. For Byrne and me it's a *sentence*. We're being sent away, to foreign lands, to live among enemies. But you? Ah, you get to bed a beautiful redhead who will bend her knees with gladness."

Khallum grimaced. "I'll not lie. I'm rather looking forward to her bending her knees, as ye say, but it wasnae my first choice. It was always supposed to be salt and sand. For all of us. But you're salt and sand wherever you go." He passed a look between the two of them. "Wherever you are. Because who ye are is in here." He pounded a fist against his chest. "Not out there."

"I know you worry for me." Byrne's small voice surprised them both. The tentative way he approached his words alerted her that he was preparing to say something difficult. Yesenia saw Khallum had caught this too. "But you said it yourself, Sen. The boys here will just become men, and nothing will change."

"That doesnae mean you have to *leave*. I'd kill them all if that's what it took to make ye feel safe."

Byrne grinned, throwing his eyes wide. "Aye, I know you would." Khallum laughed with him. "We all know ye would. But I donnae want ye to, sister." He reached for her hands, and she reluctantly granted them. "Do ye not ever tire of having to come to my defense?"

Yesenia's eyes burned. She knit her lips together, protecting herself from the feelings threatening to rise at the very adult look Byrne was giving her. "Never."

He released her hands, nodding. "I suppose that's true. But I cannae be your excuse not to find happiness for yourself, either."

"What? Is that what ye think?"

Khallum started to agree with him, but Byrne rested a hand on his brother's knee to stay him.

"It's what I know. And allowing it to go on indefinitely would be to admit I donnae love ye as much as I ken I do." Byrne's accent grew stronger as his emotions heightened. "And I do love ye. You're the only mother I've ever known, Yesenia."

"Stop," she whispered, using her fist to fight another wave of sadness. "Donnae say another word."

Khallum turned his head away from them.

"I want to go," Byrne said. He stood and moved before her. "Sen, I *want* to go. Asherley told me I could live whatever life I like. All she wants from me is to give her heirs, and will that be so hard a task?" His laugh hid his embarrassment. "She's very nice on the eyes."

"She's cold. Calculated. Cunning."

"Who does that sound like?"

Yesenia scowled. "What if she poisons you?"

"What if she doesnae?"

Yesenia slammed her fist onto the stone. An expected rush of pain followed, but it was what she'd been after, far preferable to the feelings Byrne had unearthed with his rare confession.

Sarah M. Cradit

Byrne wrapped her bloodied hand in both of his. "If I think my wife intends to kill me, I'll write to you."

Yesenia laughed through her blubbering tears. They'd made an appearance after all, despite her efforts. "If she tries to keep me from seeing my brother…" She couldn't finish.

"No one has that power." Byrne kissed her injured hand and dropped it again. "I promise you, Sen. I'll be fine. You taught me everything I need."

"Aye, aye, break it up then," Khallum said, sniffling. "We did-nae come here for this, did we?"

"If Byrne wants to go." Yesenia pulled herself together. There was no choice. Byrne had said his piece, and if she loved him as much as she claimed, she couldn't stand in his way when he'd made his desires known. "If Byrne wants to go, we let him go."

"And you?" Khallum asked.

"Only until I can find or fight my home."

Byrne was the first to return to the keep. Khallum hesitated only from worry for his sister but then wondered if she was hanging back in anticipation of one final roll in the cove with Erran.

"Another hour on the tide, at best," he said.

"I'm not waiting for Erran, if that's what ye think."

Khallum hid his relieved exhale. "You leave in the morning. You donnae wish to see him first?"

Yesenia shook her head. She seemed ready to fall over into the wet sand and let it carry her to sea. He'd never seen her so defeated. He preferred her anger.

"At all?"

"Best that way."

"Best that way? You're not even going to tell him then, aye? You'll let him hear about it from the king's ravens?"

Yesenia's eyes swam with tears. She wore her exhaustion bundled so tight, she seemed unaware of the lapse in the shield she diligently wore to keep others out. "Would telling him myself be any better?"

60

"Aye! *Aye*, it would be much better than just leaving it like this!"

"Like what? We were hardly in love."

"I ken a lie when I hear one."

"I donnae care what ye ken, Khallum. It's done. The king decided things. That *is* what we're calling him these days, aye? King? Sire? Your Grace?"

"Father did what he had to do."

"*I know!*" Yesenia's scream echoed in the cave. What she said next was buried by the roar of the sea, but she repeated it. "I may sound to you like a screaming banshee, but I *know* he did what he had to. It doesnae make it easier, does it?"

Khallum had a decision to make. Though he was the eldest, and the heir, it was Yesenia who had always led them...who had always been the strength molding the trio into an inseverable knot.

But what she needed now was *his* strength, and if he couldn't find the right kind to give her, she'd never trust him again.

"If ye really mean to come home, Sen...I'll help ye. When the time comes."

She looked up. "Really?"

Khallum nodded. He pumped his hands, swallowed the briny air, and drew another breath. "Stand up."

Yesenia used her good hand to push herself off the rock face.

Khallum reached for one of her daggers, but she was quicker.

Hand topping his, she cocked her head, narrowing her eyes. "What are you up to?"

"Ye trust me?"

Yesenia warily moved her hand aside. Khallum drew her dagger and, before he could change his mind, dug a line down the center of his palm, deep enough for the blood to bead and spill over before he'd even finished the stroke.

She watched him with a new look, one of growing admiration, grinning as she snatched her dagger and sliced it down her uninjured hand.

"Now you have no good hands," Khallum said. He pressed their palms together, relishing the burn because the burn meant it was real, and binding. He'd have trouble doing anything of use with the hand until it healed, but it would be worth it. Yesenia would have known if he'd gone easy on himself. "Salt and sand."

"Salt and sand," she replied, running her snotty nose along her sleeve. "Thank you, brother."

He removed his vest and tore the necessary strips to bind their wounds. When he was done, he said, "Please donnae leave without telling Erran. He came all the way to Warwicktown, again, for you. Lesser things have broken a man."

Yesenia tightened the binding on her hand as she turned away. "Aye. I'll think on it."

Yesenia watched the sunset through a gap in the rocks. She climbed high enough to endure the high tide and then made her way back down when it receded hours later. She wondered if she could do it all night. It would be preferable to her own bed, where she'd only lie awake, sleepless in her anger.

If Erran knew she was here…but he didn't. He wouldn't. She'd lied to Khallum when she'd said she'd think about telling him. If she had to look into Erran's eyes, to see again what she'd seen the last time they'd met here…

No, she had to be strong. Strength was the *only* thing she needed going into tomorrow and beyond.

"You missed supper."

Yesenia cringed at her father's smoky voice, a sound that had once soothed any ills. She wanted it to be like that again, but how could it? She might accept his helplessness, but it came at the price of her esteem of him.

"I didnae exactly *miss* it," she answered, hoping her tone sounded teasing and not a reflection of her true mood.

"The Widow made your favorite." Her father climbed over the maze of craggy rocks and settled uncomfortably atop one across from her.

"We've even got you calling her that now, aye?"

Khoulter buried his smile in his bowed head. "Ye know, Sen, ye aren't the first one to come here with someone ye fancied."

"Oh, no." Yesenia waved her hands. "I donnae wanna hear about you and Mother."

"It wasnae your mother. It was the one before her, as I suppose Erran will become for you."

"Khallum has greatly overstated—"

"Donnae defend yourself to me, girl. You're a Southerland lass, born of salt and sand. Not a wide-eyed virgin saving herself for a prince. We do things differently here. Love or nay. I would've married ye to him though, had the choice not been taken from us."

"I never wanted to marry Erran," Yesenia said. She curled her knees up to her chest to avoid a lingering rush of tide. "Khallum had it wrong. You know how I feel about marriage, Father, but the only thing worse than marrying at all is marrying for love."

Khoulter shook his head in soft exasperation. "Aye, so you've said, more than once. Perhaps your coming years will be easier on you then."

"Why? Because I could never love a Quinlanden?"

"I sure as feck hope not, girl!" He looked so serious, she couldn't help but laugh, and it surprised her when he joined in. "These men have stolen from us, and from our people. Donnae forget who ye are. Ever."

"How could I, when it's who I am that makes this so hard?"

"Aye." His face was hidden in the shadows. "I know it, lass. Would that I could take some other punishment to keep ye from yours."

"At least ye admit it now. 'Tis a punishment."

"Maybe." Khoulter kept his eyes on the low tide lapping around the stones. "But there isnae another lass alive more capable of enduring it, nay *thriving* under it, than Yesenia Warwick."

Yesenia shrugged and leaned back. "I'll just take lovers, like other powerful women do."

"You might spare me those details in your letters home." He nodded at her hands. "I'm gonna regret asking, aren't I?"

"One was my fault," she said. "The other, Khallum's."

"A blood bond," he said, understanding. "And what did he promise ye?"

She thought of lying, as she had to Khallum about Erran, but untruths had never sat well with her, not when spoken between kin. She'd regret lying to Khallum one day.

"That when I wanted to come home, he would aid me in that."

Khoulter opened his palms. "The blood dry on yours? Am I too late?"

"Ye cannae mean…" She clambered off the rock and went to her father. "No. Leave the scheming to your children, Father. We're better at it anyway."

"Just the same." He curled his hands into fists. "If it ever becomes unsafe for you in Whitechurch…unsafe, ye ken, for *you*, tough as ye are, *hard* as ye are…I willnae let even a king stand between me and my lass."

SEVEN

THE VELLUM AND THE VIAL

Corin struggled to keep up with Gretchen's frenzied packing. He'd come to help, but her attention was all over the place. She'd begin one task only to abandon it for another, only to remember she had set out to do something different entirely.

Her shattered sobs broke up the otherwise uneasy silence between them. Beyond the open perch, redbuds and hawthorns shimmered in a gentle breeze that might have soothed them both in another time.

"It will be all right." Why did he say it? Lying was Aiden's instrument of choice.

"Tell that to Ash." Her eyes were slivered with red vines darting out from her irises, dilated to full. "And what would you know about it, Corin? You get to stay. You aren't being sent away from your home."

He recalled how they'd had this same conversation only days ago, but in reverse.

"You're being set free, which is another way to look at it." Though equally unhelpful, it was true. Chasten might grant

Corin his own land or even a nominal title, but he'd do it *there*, in Whitechurch, where they could keep an eye on his Warwick wife. He'd never leave now, which was almost as terrible as Gretchen saying good-bye to her heartmate.

Unless Yesenia does figure out a way to end this.

"Free." Gretchen paused with a look beyond the room, toward the trees. She followed her gaze and stepped onto her perch, regarding a basket of fresh fruit with the same suspicion as poisoned stew. "Did you know, there are only two true seasons in the Northerlands? Winter and midwinter." She crushed a peach between her front teeth with a bitter laugh. The light juice stained her dress, mingling with her tears. She chucked the fruit into the forest. They were too high up to hear it land. "Will never eat one of those again."

"You'll never have to see Aiden again either."

"You've missed the entire aim of the Epoch of the Accordant, haven't you? Alliances start with marriages. They don't end with them."

"All right." Corin sensed there was nothing he could say about her situation that she would not have an answer for, and he hadn't come here to drive her further into her melancholy. Nor did he feel safe leaving her alone in such a state. He changed course. "Well, I have to find my way with a Warwick wife. I don't even know where to start."

Her glare was for someone else, someone not present in the room. "Father and Aiden will have plenty of advice for you where she's concerned. Not to worry."

"What does that mean?"

Gretchen dropped a silver mirror on her pile of dresses and spun hard at him. "What do you think it means, Corin? Father is behind this whole thing."

"No. No, I don't think so. You saw his face. You heard him in the tent—"

"Would you have spoken true if you knew one of your children would soon take that knowledge beyond the Reach?"

It was her madness speaking, but he didn't say so.

"Think about it." She wiped her reddened nose, her trunk forgotten as she neared him. "Each of his children, married to a highborn of another Reach? Imagine the possibilities." She arced her hands over her head in a semicircle. "He's already asked me to spy for him."

"Father doesn't have that kind of power, not with the king. He only thinks he does." *Which is what makes his relationship with Khain so dangerous.*

"When he asks you to spy on your own bride, you'll know I'm right." Gretchen wagged a finger close to his face. "And you'll do it, won't you?"

"I…no. I don't know."

Gretchen nodded, assessing him. "You will." She reached forward and cupped his chin in her hands with a sad but loving look. "Because it's the only way you'll find the freedom here in Whitechurch that you'd so hoped to find elsewhere."

Yesenia's carriage crossed over the Southerland border and into the Easterlands just after dawn. Good byes served no purpose beyond breaking a man, and she'd said all she needed to say to her brothers and father. She'd even managed a small note of thanks to the Widow, for all she'd tried to do over the years as a replacement mother.

Yesenia had never paid much mind to the geography of the rest of the kingdom, but she supposed they were just south of Riverchapel, where the Resplendent Reliquary of the Guardians held the tenets of religion. The Guardians had always been there, but the Reliquary was a Rhiagain construct. Where once faith had been personal, it became regulated. How that was acceptable to others in the kingdom, Yesenia would never understand.

Gone were the browns and ochers of the Southerlands. The lush forest they'd entered, illuminated by the first dash of morning sun, was as foreign as anything she'd ever seen. She may as well have sailed to Beyond, for all this would never feel like home.

Khallum would be waking soon. Father too. They'd discover her midnight departure and be angry, but they'd understand. Byrne might not, but the others would.

Byrne, though, was no longer her charge. Not unless he called upon her. *This* was the bitter draught she was still trying to learn how to swallow.

Against her desires, she'd ridden inside a carriage instead of atop her own horse. They couldn't hide the size of her escort, but she didn't have to make herself an easy target either. Her guards were mindful of rogue arrows that might sail out from the woods. She had half a mind to tell them they were being daft, but the problem was she didn't know. She'd have to keep her eyes open for assassins in Whitechurch, of course, but who knew if the Quinlandens were bold enough to dispatch their new daughter-in-law before she even arrived?

Yesenia flexed her wounded hands with a wince as she watched the forest pass by beyond the window. Both lacerations had already bled through the bindings, and she'd need to re-dress them when she arrived in Whitechurch, which meant asking for aid from the last people she wanted anything from. She wished she'd had the foresight to stop by the Widow's apartments to grab some more bandages and retrieve some of her miracle salve.

A pointless regret now, in the midst of so many.

The carriage came to an abrupt stop. Yesenia braced herself until it stopped rocking and then pulled back the curtain. Her personal guard, Anatole, was already standing outside, ready to offer explanation.

She liked Anatole, though to call him a guard was an embellishment. She'd saved *his* life a couple of times, and he'd not yet had occasion to return the favor. But where he lacked in physical prowess, he more than made up for in his keen work with whispers and shadows. It was why she'd chosen him, and only him, to stay with her in Whitechurch when the rest of her father's guard returned to Warwicktown.

"Only watering the horses," he explained, not adding the requisite *my lady*. That was her fault. She'd chastised him for using it once, only to regret it later, something she couldn't admit. The Quinlandens would enjoy that familiarity, no doubt. "We're not far from the Reliquary, if you'd like to make an offering before we make our push east, to the Gap of Ever?"

"I'd not insult the Guardians by making one there," she muttered. She detected a light smile from Anatole, hinting his understanding that she'd been after agreement but not conversation.

"Just the same. Some of the men wish to."

"They can do it on the return."

"Aye, I expected you'd say as much, and I've relayed that suspicion."

"So, we agree." Yesenia cocked her head. "And if we agree, why, then, are you here?"

Anatole stepped closer to the carriage, angling himself so that his back was to most of the waiting guard. He held out both of his fists. "Choose one."

"I have no mind for games, Anatole."

"Go on. Choose."

"Why? Can I not have both?"

"You will have both. The order in which you choose them will determine how we speak of what comes next."

Anatole enjoyed these little amusements, and denying him would only draw this out. She considered only briefly and then chose his right hand.

He grinned. "I thought you might."

Yesenia shook her head at him, looking down and seeing a small scroll of vellum.

Before she could withdraw it, he pulled back a touch. "This was sent to Warwicktown, Yesenia. I intercepted it before anyone else had eyes on it. It is only the two of us who will have seen this."

Yesenia grabbed the scroll before he could play more. She unrolled it and read the overly ornate scrawl. *My Dearest Sister.* She looked up at Anatole, but his face was impassive. *We await your arrival with joy and urgency. More specifically, I await your arrival, and what it means for both of us. Yours, Aiden.*

"Head games." Yesenia handed the note back to Anatole, knowing he would dispose of it properly. "Thinks me his concubine, does he? We'll see."

"Aye," Anatole said in agreement. "But you'll be fighting this battle in his territory."

"He touches me and he'll find himself relieved of a limb."

"To which you'll find yourself relieved of life." He pressed his lips together and inhaled. "It is an honor to serve someone of your strength and vigor. But you will need to quell your quickness to anger and replace it with something more subtle."

"I brought *you* for the subtlety."

"Then allow me to teach you." Anatole opened his other hand. In it sat a vial. "Undetectable poison. A few drops in a man's cup renders him incapacitated. A few more will decide things more permanently."

"How…" Poisons were the business of greener realms, where women like the Blackwoods ruled over their men with unspoken threats. It was cowardice, she'd always thought, to kill a man this way. *You should look him in the eye before you take his life, or you've wasted it, and yours.* "This isnae my way, Anatole. You know this."

"Aye, but it needs to be."

"Father put you up to this?"

"Lord Warwick knows nothing."

"What are you suggesting?"

"Certainly not what you *think* I'm suggesting, dear Yesenia. My only desire is to see you thrive in Whitechurch. But should that not be possible…"

Yesenia nodded. She quickly wrapped the vial in the folds of her blouse.

Anatole smiled. His made his voice louder. "As you wish, my lady. We'll make our repast on the return voyage." He winked, bowed, and left her to ponder his gifts.

Khallum faced his oldest friend and broke the news. He managed a stoic delivery, knowing what would come when he finished. He'd waited until Yesenia was hours gone so the poor fool wouldn't chase after her. He might still.

"*Married?*" Erran's face was as pale as milk. "To a *Quinlanden?*"

"It was an ambush, Erran. None of us escaped it. Byrne leaves today for Longwood Rush. My own wife will arrive in a few days. She's…" It wasn't important. He wasn't here to talk about himself. "Sen's miserable for it. We all are."

"She wouldnae do it though. She'd never go." Erran was lost in thoughts Khallum was relieved to not hear. "She'd never do it. *Not* Sen."

"She had no choice," Khallum explained through his own frustration. Why couldn't she have just said a proper good-bye? Why did she have to leave it like this, leave it for him? "To defy Khain would do more than dishonor the crown. It would bring—"

"I know what it would bring!" Erran's words ended on a howl, a trapped cry. "She couldnae tell me this herself? She sent ye to do it then?"

"I…" Khallum grimaced. "You know Yesenia."

"Aye. All too well." Erran's glossy eyes darted around the room, searching. "All too well." He nodded to himself. "Right, well if I leave now—"

"Nay," Khallum said. He reached for his friend, but Erran dodged the touch. "You'll do no such thing."

"You'd try and stop me?"

"Aye." Khallum rested a hand on the hilt of his sword. "I would."

"If the king had only waited a few more months, Yesenia would have been *my wife*."

"Aye, but he didnae. And she's not, Erran. Aye? She's *not* your wife. She's the wife of Corin Quinlanden."

Erran shook his head as his whole expression erupted into agony. "It cannae be, Khallum. That's our Yesenia. And ye just sent her off, to the den of our enemies? How could ye? And yer father, how..." He tore at his hair. "*How?*"

Khallum said nothing. There was nothing *to* say.

Erran sank to his knees. The sobs followed. "Yesenia...no... Please, Guardians. Let this be a nightmare." He brought his hands to his face.

Khallum breathed in deeply and pulled up a chair next to his friend. He knew this would be the last time he ever saw Erran Rutland in such a state, and he paid this knowledge with the honor it deserved, gripping his friend's shoulder with one hand.

With every few steps, Corin checked to be sure he was alone.

He always was. His father and brother's cold disregard for him was what led to Corin's friendship with Venya. He'd met her on his trips to the Merchant Quarter, safe in the knowledge that neither Aiden nor Chasten would waste their time fraternizing with the poor.

Without the poor, there can be no rich was his father's wisdom on the matter, and Corin thought the reverse was even more true.

Without the rich, there'd be no poor.

Venya had scrubbed the floors of a rundown inn at the end of Slattery Row. An orphan with no memory of her life before, adopted by the innkeeper, she'd accepted Corin's gift of gold and handed it straight to her mistress, whom she'd called Mother.

Why? Your mother has some. You have none.

My mother gives what she has so that I have some too.

Corin never should have shown her his life beyond the Row. Venya had been perfectly content at The Misty Merchant.

He passed from the forest into the clearing, relieved to see the chalet was still there, though there was no logical reason why it wouldn't be.

A chalet wasn't even what it was, just what he'd always called it. It was the remains of an old monastery, humble in size but once great in intention. The old timber had held strong through the tumult of the past two hundred years. When the Rhiagains had washed upon their shores, the old monasteries had been cast aside for a more grand show of the crown-sponsored religion. Relics like these could be found all over the kingdom, his mother had once said, but most people kept their distance, fearful of running afoul with ghosts of the old ways.

How grand this is! Venya had exclaimed as she took in the sparse, single room of Corin's sacred hideaway. *Fit for a king!*

Why could he have not left her wonder there, in the safety of the chalet, and enjoyed it with her? Where had the pride come from that bade him lead her up the spiraling steps of Arboriana, to reveal to her a place truly fit for a king? A place he himself loathed?

With one final check, Corin closed the door and wandered to the cot at the other end of the room. He sank down on it, eyes closed, and pitched forward over his knees, inhaling the old musk like a drug.

The chalet had been his reprieve most of his life. It still had purpose to serve.

It was Corin who needed to find his own now.

He mused on his thoughts as he waited for his bride to arrive.

CRIMSON AND GOLD

EIGHT
CLOTH OF GOLD

There's enough cloth of gold woven into their gowns and cloaks to feed a Southerland village for the next fifty years was Yesenia's first lucid thought when her carriage passed beyond the teeming ivory gates leading from the main road of Whitechurch into Arboriana, the castle stronghold of the Quinlandens.

Her second thought, with a startled glance upward, was *They really do live in the trees. Guardians preserve me.*

Her third: *Only the apple-polishing Quinlandens would use the word castle.*

Silver petals rained from the sky like fat drops of glistening snow, soon joined by pink and purple ones, creating a waterfall of bruised pigment under which her carriage passed. She couldn't make heads or tails of the cloying profusion of scents, all foreign to her nose, clamoring for her attention. A trilling, melodic song played somewhere, created from a symphony of strings and drums and other noises unknown to her Southerland ears.

It seemed everyone in the capital of Whitechurch had come to Arboriana to welcome her. They filled out the right and left of the stone path, some climbing upon the gates and others hanging from them. More awaited at the end, at what the Quinlandens modestly referred to as their castle. Looking up once more, she even saw some waving from the balconies—*perches*, Anatole advised her. The twirling spires of crimson and gold jutting from atop each section of the citadel in the trees resembled spears at their tips. She couldn't see the top from so close, only hints of the same design peeking through thick branches. It was then she saw the open winding staircase that wove through the center of it all.

Yesenia shifted focus to her breathing. She couldn't look as overwhelmed as they so obviously wanted her to feel. She must rise above it, unaffected by the wantonness of their ambitious showing.

I have reached into the sand, and the sand has offered me strength.

I have submerged myself in the salt of the sea, and the salt has offered me courage.

Her carriage stopped. She went to climb out on her own, but two Quinlanden guards, donning the same wasteful gold as their masters—*Southerland gold*, she thought to herself, and had to resist the urge to lay hands upon her daggers—made a formal show of escorting her down the small steps. The ground was unexpectedly solid—rare stone, imported, she thought, from the Seven Sisters of the West. Only the most ruthless explorers could bring back enough marble to pave an entire road.

"Gratitude," she murmured, shrugging them both off once she had her footing. Another look around proved more daunting, as all her earlier observations blended into a chaotic tableau. A chorus of falsettos and sopranos sang along to the music, buried within the blurred horde of colors.

She tried to spot Anatole, but he was lost somewhere in the melee ahead.

Yesenia turned toward the sound of a harpist. The girl plucked a cool song on her instrument as a little boy held it aloft for her, only his feet visible. Yesenia had just enough time to absorb what she saw before the harpist broke off to the side and left her standing face-to-face with Chasten Quinlanden.

She recognized him immediately from Termonglen, but from only several feet away, the familiarity turned to horror. His crisply defined features—a sharp jaw, aquiline nose, and eyes so chillingly blue they looked preternatural—were emphasized in startling relief, as if painted by one who had never actually seen a man with their own eyes.

"Daughter." His glacial smile came too late. He reached for her hands but ended up cupping her wrists. His palms were as icy as his intentions, and she couldn't retrieve her arms quick enough.

She was still too numb to react in any way but compliance.

"You have come to us just on time."

"I'm Mariana. Lady Quinlanden. I regret that we all departed so swiftly from Termonglen, as I'd have liked to have met you then." The woman at his side joined in with eager but practiced enthusiasm. She pressed her lips together and made a soft sigh. "You really are a lovely girl, Yesenia. I believe life at Arboriana will only make you even lovelier. Please, call me Mother, and think of me thus."

The difference between Chasten and Mariana was not the degree of warmth each possessed, Yesenia thought, but the desire and ability to act in possession of it.

Next a young girl stepped forward. She looked like the older one, Gretchen, who was missing from the bizarre display. Yesenia remembered Gretchen would be enduring a similar trial in Wulfsgate, perhaps at this very moment.

"My name is Saoirse. I hope you'll find Arboriana as splendid as we do, and much to your liking."

Yesenia nodded at the civil but kind words, searching for a smile to give the young girl. It died on her face when, just beyond, she saw Aiden, the eldest, leering at her.

I await your arrival, and what it means for both of us.

Yesenia tightened her jaw.

At Aiden's side was the wife the king had sold him, Maeryn Blackwood. Yesenia wasn't buying the cool, dispassionate look Maeryn wore in the face of this garish display, but she *was* curious by it. As Anatole had said, she'd need to learn the smoothness of subtlety.

"I believe that will be my task." Corin gave his sister's shoulders a quick, loving squeeze and then, pivoting to the side, broke through. As in Termonglen, he wore his full ceremonial regalia, but he seemed less comfortable in it here, in his own realm. It clung to his skin like a sticky sweetness he could not wait to be rid of. "Yesenia." He inhaled into a nervous smile. "I hope the journey was all right?"

"Pleasing enough," she managed to say and then she was taking his arm, and everything moved synchronously. The music shifted with them, the petals, still raining, covered the ground before them as they moved up the path. She thought again of her daggers strapped at her ankles inside her boots, not because she had intention to pull them but because they grounded her, reminded her of home in the midst of such madness.

"It's too much," he whispered. Any quieter and his words would have faded into the melee. "I know what you're thinking. I understand."

"You cannae know," she whispered back. Still, there was none she felt safer with than Corin in this new, strange world, where she would never be safe again. He was the lesser of her enemies yet still as dangerous. What if his bumbling sweetness was an act? What if he was even worse than his revolting brother, Aiden?

"Your hand." Corin nodded downward with a hitch in his breath. Her eyes followed to see her crude bandage had bled through again on the one she'd used in her blood oath.

"'Tis nothing," she insisted, hiding it. She nestled the other under their conjoined arms before he could comment on that too.

"That's not nothing. When we get settled, I'll fetch a healer—"

"I *said*, 'tis nothing."

"Right." Corin exhaled, nodding, his eyes back on the path. "Ah, well, we just did this yesterday when Lady Maeryn arrived, so I know what to expect. Our part will be quick, over before we know it. We climb to the first perch and present ourselves to the people. They scream. We smile. They scream some more. We smile some more. Then we go in. The celebrations will continue, well into the night, without us." He bit the corner of his lip. "For our, ah, first night together."

Yesenia wrinkled her nose in disgust. "Tell me that again?"

"It's doesn't mean anything," he replied. "It doesn't *have* to mean anything. It's just tradition."

Yesenia felt the impression of eyes on her. She glanced to the side and caught Maeryn staring. It was not Yesenia she watched though, but Corin. Yesenia knew that look. If Aiden saw Maeryn wearing it, he'd be none too pleased.

They reached the base of the largest tree she'd ever seen. But it was not one tree, she realized as they took the first steps into the courtyard, but a half dozen, all interconnected. Even their roots had become one, trunks bowing and winding, branches swirling around branches, leaves of one tree making life upon another.

Corin escorted her up the next set of stairs, which elevated them above the throngs. When they reached the steps that would take them into the trees, Yesenia hesitated. She was ashamed of it.

"The Golden Stair," Corin explained. "It's not as imposing as it looks. Match my steps."

All she could do was nod. The rest of her effort shifted to not falling through the slats of stairs covered in woven bark. She lost her footing on one and heard Aiden's timely snicker behind her.

When it felt like they'd climbed higher than she'd ever been in her life, Corin guided her onto a platform to the left. A balcony, she would have called it, with columns wound with gold and red metals, but she understood why they called it a perch. She was a bird, on display, in a cage. Powerless.

She held her breath to fight the swoon of disorientation that seized her.

"Great people of Whitechurch! Of the Easterlands! Of the kingdom's most blessed Reach! Please join me in welcome of our newest union as I present my second son, Lord Corin Quinlanden, and his wife, Lady Yesenia Quinlanden." He nodded through the applause, pleased with himself, as if he'd been responsible for it and not taken off guard like the other lords. "Eat, drink, and be as merry as you like! This fete is a gift from us!"

Corin spurred her back into motion as the family unit shifted, leaving the perch. Was that really all Chasten was going to say?

They climbed higher, Yesenia becoming dizzier with every step. They exited into a room whose existence did not seem possible: a banquet hall, as large as any she'd seen. And in the *trees*. It was a splendor she couldn't appreciate in her present state, but rather, she settled her fears deeper, drawing her further from who she was.

"Right." Chasten spun toward the family. "Aiden and I have business, and Saoirse needs to pack for Oldcastle. Is not that so, sapling?"

Saoirse nodded unhappily.

"It's only a year, dear. All your siblings went to university at your age," Mariana said sweetly. "They've reserved my old apartments in Crimsoncastle, just for you."

"Lady Maeryn and Lady Mariana will aid her in this, while you two…" Chasten twirled his wrist, taking Yesenia in. "Become better acquainted."

Chasten left without another word. Yesenia turned toward Corin, to find *something* to say that might restore her some vestige of control, when a hot breath burned at her ear.

"I'll have a more proper welcome for you later. Sister."

"Leave her alone, Aiden," Corin warned.

"Or?"

"Don't you have business with Father?"

Yesenia didn't unclench until she heard Aiden's steps ascending the Golden Stair. "I'll gut him like a fish, he comes near me."

Corin grinned. "What I wouldn't give to see that."

"I'm serious. I'd kill him."

"I know you are." He glanced around the empty banquet hall. "Would you like a tour?"

"No." Yesenia closed her eyes to steady the fresh sway replacing the last one. "I wouldnae."

"Is it the height?"

She didn't answer him.

"I don't like heights myself. Curious, I know, living here all my life, but they terrify me. I rarely ever spend time on the perches."

Yesenia met his eyes. "Never tell me things like that."

"Sorry?"

"Your weaknesses. Never let an enemy know them." She straightened, feeling more balanced. "Make them work for them. Make *me* work for them."

Corin shot her a weary look. "I don't think of you that way, but you're more than welcome to think of me as you please."

"Donnae ken I need your permission for how I think."

"I wasn't suggesting—"

"That's another weakness. You're too agreeable."

Corin was taken aback. "You'd prefer me sparring with you? Is that how men do it in the Southerlands?"

Yesenia shrugged. "I have no preference where you're concerned."

"Yet you seem to have plenty of opinions."

"*Beliefs*. Opinions can be changed."

Corin tensed with a brief shutter of his eyes. "Why don't I take you to our apartments, so you can relax after your long journey."

"Warwicks don't *relax*." Yesenia listened to the singing, the chanting, the joy of the crowd outside. "But, aye, get me out of here."

"Only one bed?"

Corin had braced himself for that question. All her words, questions or otherwise, felt like accusations, and he, the one guilty of her perceived aspersions. If only he could find a way to tell her they were in this together, that they had both lost out in this bargain and, as friends, could at least discover a way to endure it.

"Yeah. Sorry." He saw her trunks had already been delivered. "I tried to have another brought in quietly. I knew it's what you'd want. But…" He eyed the arched door to the sitting room. "I can sleep on the settee, if you like."

"Too agreeable," she reminded him. She perched at the end of the bed, like someone waiting for an assassin to leap out from behind a curtain. Eyes wide. Hands ticking off her thoughts against the quilt with nervous abandon.

"Is that what you really want? For me to be cruel, like my brother?"

"Why do ye ken your brother sees you as such an easy target?"

"Do you care that he hurts me?"

Yesenia's mouth paused in search of words. She closed it without answering. "Is there anywhere I can be alone here, or is this just a more pleasing prison?"

Corin tossed a nod toward the perch. The curtains were drawn wide, and the wind whistling through the trees was peaceful. The view likely was too, but he'd have to be content with his imagination. "Out there. In the forest. Do you have those in the Southerlands?"

Yesenia's lip curled up at the corner as she stared at him. "'Tis a real question, that?"

No topic was safe apparently. "I've never been there. All I know about your homeland is what's told to me by people who loathe you."

Yesenia rolled her eyes. She fell back on her hands, looking away from him, beyond the curtains. "We have some farther north. Near the Easterlands. We'd have more if your family would stop pushing the border, stealing land from us. I heard you want to annex Blackpool next, aye? Well, go on then. You'd be doing us a favor. 'Tis a pit and a curse."

"I don't know anything about any of that," Corin insisted. "No one involves me in their scheming."

She laughed. "Do ye ken I'd be included in anything if I hadnae insisted I be? My father forgets he has a daughter sometimes, and not three sons. That's *my* doing. I wasnae born with the privilege."

"But I don't want that," Corin answered, shaking his head. "That's where you and I are different. I don't want to know. I don't want to know the terrible things they're planning. It's hard enough watching them play out."

Her laugh deepened. She dropped her head back and her dark waves tickled the quilt. "Ah, Corin, is that all there is to our differences?"

"I don't want to be involved in their machinations. I don't even want the name I was given."

"Then what do ye want if not to serve your kin? Evil or nay, it's what you were born into. What you were given. I have cause to loathe the Quinlandens, but your cause is to serve them. That's the way of things."

"I wanted my father to find me a bride as far from home as he could. I didn't even care who, just as long as it took me away from Whitechurch." He lowered his voice. "I'm sure Lord Warwick is a good man. I cannot say the same for my own father."

Her sigh ended in a head shake bordering on disappointment. "You keep feeding me your weak spots. Ye donnae know me. Ye donnae know what I could do with them if I wanted to."

Corin swallowed. How had the king decided these matches? There was no repairing these wounds. They'd only deepen. "You'll do what you must, I suppose."

"Hmm. Agreeable or sly? Do ye only want me to *ken* that you're a good, honest man who's nothing like his shit-grasping relations, or are you really so castrated?"

"I am who I am." He threw out his hands. "And whether we like it or not, we're married. That doesn't have to mean what it does for others, but we're stuck with each other, until one of us spends our promise."

"And another thing!" Yesenia cried, pitching forward again on the bed. "Your father called me Yesenia Quinlanden. Aye, that willnae do. I'll be a Warwick until my last breath."

Corin looked down and sighed.

"Want me to tell him?" she asked.

"No. Better he take it out on me. He holds me in only slightly higher esteem than your family."

Yesenia nodded to herself. "Aye, I'll tell him. Let *me* be the villain. May as well play our assigned roles here." She gave Corin a quick appraisal. "Nor do I wish to see you sulk about all night when he's done with ye."

A knock sounded, followed by a five-second pause. A serving girl wearing a frilly apron took one step into the room.

"Lord and Lady Quinlanden, you are both summoned for evening meal."

"Lady Warwick," Yesenia said to correct her.

The girl cast her eyes away, bowed, and backed out of the room.

"I'm not hungry," Yesenia said when she was gone. "Go on without me. I'll stay here."

"You will not," Corin said, his fear causing the words to fall more forcefully than intended. He was rewarded with an approving eyebrow raise. "If you want life to be livable, you'll learn to be agreeable yourself, when to do otherwise will only invite agony. You want your privacy, Yesenia? You earn it, by serving when it matters. No one refuses a supper invite from my father."

"You've only made me more determined to refuse it," she answered with a mischievous twinkle in her eye. "But I can see he has ye quaking in your little gold heels about it, and I'll not have ye whipped for my defiance." She stood, and he was again taken with how tall she was, as tall as him. "Well? Are we supping or are ye more keen to gape at me like you've just seen a Guardian in the flesh?"

Corin recovered himself and led the way.

Yesenia remembered the way to the banquet hall, for it was the only other place she'd been at Arboriana. She secreted glances to the right and left as they descended the Golden Stair, attempting to discern the rest of the strange arbor castle, while being careful not to appear too interested. At best, they'd think her moonstruck. At worst, spying.

Aye, well I'll do a bit of that too, but they'll not see it so easily. Anatole might think himself the superior at shadows, but a woman uniquely learns, before all else, how to make herself known and how to make herself unknown.

Until her mother died, that was all she'd done, slip about in the shadows, yearning for scraps of intrigue. Yesenia was sensitive to the low heartbeat that thrummed through the center of her household, always had been, and the *not* knowing had been maddening. Khoulter stopped tempering her curiosity when Lady Sancha died. His fight in the matter had died with his wife.

The cavernous room glimmered against the twilight. All the details Yesenia had missed in her initial shock of passing through the strange gallery came into stunning—sickening—relief. The chanting of the villagers celebrating outside had turned sinister. The click of Lady Quinlanden's heels against marble were swords stabbing into ice.

Yesenia couldn't help but wonder at the sheer excess of it all. Curtains spun of even more cloth of gold. Decorated servants in every corner, awaiting a moment of need from their lords and ladies. And the real gold, the *true* gold, everywhere, from the surface of the great table that went on and on to the columns, to the serving benches, and more. Was it a show for her, or was it normal for the ostentatious traitors?

"Here." Corin subtly guided her into the seat already prepared for her. The others needed no such assistance, except Maeryn, who eyed two chairs equally as her memory seemed to evade her. Aiden shook his head, pointing exuberantly with his whole extended hand, as if dealing with a petulant child.

The chair, too, was gold, and the cold charge it sent through Yesenia's back and limbs superseded her control in keeping others from seeing her shudder. Chasten watched her from the head of the table while a servant poured a deep-garnet liquid into his silver goblet. As he took the first sip—a tense moment, everyone hanging upon his reaction, none so more than the poor servant—he kept his eyes on her, and then still as he lowered the chalice with a reverberant but light thud atop the gold.

"That will suit us," he said, bland and disinterested.

A cool relief settled over the gathered. Color returned to the servant's face as he backed away and signaled to the other servants to bring more. Even Aiden appeared to shake off the effect of the prior moment, stretching his neck to the right and then the left.

Yesenia caught Corin from the side calming his breathing. He couldn't know she was doing the same, because she would never let anyone see her the way he was letting his entire family see him now.

The food was brought out in quick but careful choreography, spirited servants dancing in and out of the room without especial notice. They operated strung high off fear, but there was pride in it. There was a hierarchy, Yesenia sensed, and these, the house attendants, were perched at the very top.

"Your feast, Lady Yesenia," Chasten said. "You'll adjust." He waited for the servant to prepare his plate and then dove in without further ceremony.

His words made a sudden sense when she made a closer inspection of her meal. Everything on the table was of bright greens and ochers and yellows, things that had once possessed roots and stems. Fruits she'd never before seen but knew them for their even bolder array of colors. She noted the absence of the rich gaminess that accompanied meat.

"What is this?" she hissed, low enough for Corin but no one else.

"That is a salad," Corin explained. "And that, stew of tubers. In your bowl is an assortment of fruits, all sweet except the bright-red one. Don't let that startle you. It's more of a cleanse between bites, to help you enjoy the next."

"Where's the elk? The rabbit? The deer?"

Corin's face curled in horror. "Do you eat beasts in the Southerlands?"

"Anything we can catch, we can cook."

Aiden's voice carried. "And men?"

Yesenia didn't meet Aiden's challenge. She kept her eyes on Corin when she answered. "What of them?"

"Are men of the Southerlands not beasts? How many of them find their hides upon your tables?"

"The answer to that is a family secret, I'm afraid." Her grin was quick, cutting. She looked at him. The briefest skip in his act told her she was a surprise to him. But a surprise, to men like him, was something to tame, not indulge.

"She's not serious, of course," Mariana said, glancing at her youngest, Saoirse, in a flick of panic. "Though the rumors are colorful enough."

Yesenia ground her jaw. She began to grasp the depth of the smear the Quinlandens had fed their people where the Southerlands was concerned. There'd never be a place for her here. She shouldn't need reminders, but she'd get them all the same.

"Most rumors are born in a version of the truth."

Yesenia felt Corin tense as she spoke.

"Perhaps the origin lies in the land the king stole from the Warwicks. Making the Wastelands his prison came with its share of terrors. Cannibalism becomes necessary when men are forced to starve."

"Oh dear," Mariana whispered.

"Hardly men. Criminals," Aiden said.

"Criminals of political convenience."

"Are we wasting no time then?" Chasten sipped from his goblet. "Yesenia, accepting that you are new here and cannot yet know

89

our customs, I will still ask you to refrain from speaking as a man would at my table."

"Do none of your women have opinions?" Yesenia asked.

Corin sank deeper into his gold chair, presumably attempting to burrow and fall through the floor.

"Who can say? If they do, they have the good sense to keep them to themselves."

"Well." Mariana set aside her fork and pursed her lips. "And your journey here, Yesenia. I take it, it was pleasant enough? Even if you did pass through Blackpool."

Yesenia turned toward Lady Quinlanden and caught Maeryn again giving Corin a dreamy look, as though she were at another table with just him.

"Aye, it was fine. I ken that means you've cooled your attentions on Blackpool?"

"Rumors," Chasten replied. "And *not* the kind based in truth."

"You'll forgive me if history points to a different intention."

Yesenia nearly jumped at the landing of Corin's hand upon her leg. A furtive glance his way revealed a fear that surprised her. His touch wasn't tender. It was a warning.

Mariana tilted her head to the side, wearing a pained look. "Yesenia, dear, I do hope you've packed sensibly." She nodded at her with a light curl in her lip. "And that most of your trunks are not…more of that."

Yesenia looked down at her leather jerkin and pants. "Cannae say I packed a single gown, my lady. I find them vile and ill-suited to my constitution." She couldn't resist adding "then, we donnae lace ours with stolen gold either, so perhaps I've misjudged the experience."

"Salt and sand," Aiden murmured, sharing a private, disdainful gaze with his father.

Mariana pulled her breath through her teeth. "I see. Well, while practical for riding, perhaps, trousers are not suitable for a woman in her daily life." She straightened, smiling. "Not to worry."

"You'll tend to the matter?" Chasten asked as he delicately passed a forkful of greens into his barely parted mouth.

"Of course, darling. I thought it was implied in my response to her."

"I assume nothing," Chasten answered. "Not even when the implication reads as I wish it to."

Corin's hand fell away. Yesenia felt his apology in the way his fingers trailed, passing back to his own lap. Even sharing barbs with his family across the gold table, she'd seen how they disregarded him, as if he were a specter and not a son of the lord.

But she had no sympathy for it. He allowed it. He seemed to shrink and withdraw in their presence and thus permitted these slights. Invited them, even.

No son of the Southerlands would ever allow anyone to treat him that way.

What did surprise her was how nothing she'd said had rankled either the lord or his heir. They hadn't silenced her. Perhaps they were encouraging her. Perhaps their encouragement was the path to the end, for her. And she strode down it willingly, even defiantly.

Channel Anatole. Subtlety.

"Saoirse, I understand you're going to university?" She cooled her blood, found another path. As she waited for Saoirse's reply, she noted Maeryn still wearing the same moony look from earlier, and Yesenia bristled. Her annoyance about it was incomprehensible, but she buried it alongside the rest of her anger.

Saoirse was clearly miserable. "Yes. All Quinlandens attend a full year, before maturity."

"Only a year? I thought the curriculum lasted—"

"As long as it needs to." Chasten cut in. "The Universities of Oldcastle are an Easterland institution. We are a guiding hand in their perpetuity. They have programs specially designed for Quinlandens. Your own children will attend them, in time."

Yesenia's toes involuntarily curled at the implication. Children. Chasten's continued look sealed the point, and his next words removed all doubt of his meaning.

"Aiden wasted no time with his bride. I expect my second son will do no less."

Maeryn at last looked away from Corin, burying her eyes in her lap.

"Corin knows only his hand." Aiden laughed, with a mouthful of tuber stew.

A rise of defensiveness rushed within Yesenia. "A man who knows his own hand knows what he likes."

"Oh!" Mariana exclaimed. "Dear, what had we agreed upon for dessert?"

"No dessert," Chasten muttered. "Just like the night before. Bad for the marriage bed."

Aiden was immune to his mother's attempt to still the tension. "I said *only* his hand, saltlicker."

"Aiden!" his mother exclaimed.

Chasten was silent on the matter.

"Aye? He'll know a whole lot more after tonight, I ken." Now she'd done it. They'd forced her into a corner, and again, she'd walked right into it.

Corin guided his breath through a small gap in his mouth, cheeks puffing as he did. He hadn't touched his food in a while.

Aiden leaned over the table. "And when *you're* ready to know a 'whole lot more,' you come to *my* chambers. *Aye?*" He mocked her.

She fantasized about freezing that look upon his face as she garroted him.

"That's enough," Chasten said. "These unions are decided, and we now decide to make the best of them." He glanced beyond the table, to the purplish haze darkening outside. "We'll adjourn here."

Yesenia cast a forlorn glance at the plate she'd hardly touched. Corin's wasn't much better. He was angry with her, for failing her first test, though he'd never say it. She wished he would. She might respect him more.

Chasten rose. The others rose immediately after, and Yesenia shakily followed Corin's lead.

He offered no further commentary, pivoting with a crisp march out of the banquet hall. Mariana followed in an almost perfect observance of the apparent two steps behind her husband, as prescribed to her as a woman. Did Mariana have opinions? If so, like Chasten had said, she must keep them to herself.

Saoirse, quiet as a mouse, had slipped out in the smooth transition from supper. Aiden guided Maeryn with a clenched hand pinched upon her shoulder.

Yesenia pressed her hand to her belly and breathed in.

"We can't stay here," Corin said, with a touch of panic. "They'll be expecting us to leave the hall so it can be turned over for midnight tea."

"Midnight tea?"

"Exactly what it sounds like. Attendees are those invited by my father, and only them."

"We willnae be…?"

"No." Corin outstretched his hand, pointing at the curved door leading back to the Golden Stair. "There are other responsibilities expected of us tonight."

Mariana caught Yesenia and Corin halfway to the apartments. She stepped out from a room on the right. "May I have just a moment with your bride? I'll not keep her long."

Corin's eyes narrowed in suspicion. He waited for Yesenia's nonverbal confirmation this was all right, then nodded. "You know your way back?"

"Aye," she said.

And then he was gone, and she nearly regretted his absence.

"Your hands, dear!" Mariana exclaimed. Her fingers flitted downward to grab hold of the wounded appendages but only grazed them. "What happened?"

Yesenia shook her head. "I'm fine."

"They look dreadful. I'll send a healer straightaway—"

"No, thank you. I'm fine." She wasn't fine. The wounds burned, one even throbbed with the start of infection, but they were her reminder to stay strong and vigilant. She couldn't abide weakness here.

Mariana placed both of her hands on Yesenia's face, startling her into taking a step back. "My dear. I know this all must be such a shock to you, and the life you come from."

"I see few similarities," Yesenia replied. Wariness spread through her. This woman was showing her kindness, but she was not Yesenia's friend. "But Warwicks are nothing if not adaptable."

Mariana's nod carried on. She wasn't listening; she was judging. "Well, you are not your father, and if your choice is to join this family with an open heart, then I will chip away at my husband so that he does not treat the daughter according to the sins of the father."

Was Mariana showing sincerity or cunning? There was no way to know. The Quinlandens had played a long, commendable game and had won at every step. That had not happened through transparency of intention. "I appreciate that."

"Good. I hoped you might." Mariana crossed her filigree shawl over her bosom. "Your hips are ample enough. Brood mares, we call them here. No trouble bringing the children along, and most survive their first years if they have an easier entrance. Four will be enough, I should think, before you can take your rest and enjoy the years ahead."

Yesenia tried not to sick up what little she'd eaten.

"You might yet be just what Corin needs. He is not what his father hoped."

"That much is evident." And what of his mother? What was Corin to her?

"No," Mariana whispered, a continuance of the prior thought. "Perhaps through you, he might yet find a way to show his value. If you were to, say, allow Corin a certain access that goes against what I see you guarding so closely in your heart, he might find the path to prove himself worthy of his father's love."

"I donnae ken." Ah, but she kenned. She kenned perfectly. A woman apparently divorced of her opinions was speaking to one possessed of nothing but—a young woman who had a *certain access* to her father's doings and might be compelled to see through to sharing some as part of her new wifely duties.

Lie back and remember the Southerlands. Is this what ye had in mind, Aunt Korah?

Mariana's smile blended with the shadow of the coming night. "Think on it, dear. Good night."

NINE
OTHER RESPONSIBILITIES

Yesenia walked into her new apartments for the second time that day and found them changed. Her trunks were open and a mess, a thought she saved for later because more pressing was the obscene quantity of floral dressing draped across absolutely everything in the sitting room. Chairs, tables…anything that could be covered, was. The offensive odor of the dead blooms obscured the fresh pine of the forest. She caught only a hint of it upon the breeze passing through the open doors to the perch.

Gifting Corin an accusing glare, she angled through the arched doorway to the bedchamber. As suspected, the crime was even fouler there. Roses, both whole and de-petaled, were heaped by the thousands across the bed, the sea of crimson madness broken only by the appearance of a lacy nightgown that had *not* come from her trunks.

"It's not personal," Corin said. His wince following was almost expected. "I mean to say the Quinlandens do this for all newly wedded."

"Aye, well it certainly *is* personal." Yesenia whipped her gaze across the mass casualties. It was the Easterlands, so of course, roses probably grew aplenty, but to waste them?

To waste *anything* was a privilege.

"What did Mother say to you?"

"Nothing that should surprise you." Yesenia clawed through a handful of blood-red petals. Their silken texture was startling but more so was knowing that tomorrow they'd be wilted, ugly. Even deader than they were now. Beauty wasted.

"I don't want you to—"

They both turned toward a scream. A bloated silence followed, and Yesenia wondered if Corin had only reacted to her shift in attention, but there it was again, louder. Corin leaned against the wall with a sigh.

"Lady Maeryn will not have a good life here," he said.

Yesenia was horrified. "Does your father know how his son treats his wife?"

"Father has never tempered Aiden's cruelty. My father… He's…" He shook his head. "He has more humanity than Aiden. I suspect he harbors some jealousy over his son's easy abandonment of his conscience."

She watched him over her shoulder as she unlaced her boots. "Why live in the trees?"

"Go to the perch, on the far end of the sitting room."

Yesenia didn't move.

"From here, the people of Whitechurch, of the Easterlands, they look small, like little mice skittering to and fro. They can only look up and guess what it must be like for lions."

"That's the most disgusting thing I've ever heard," Yesenia replied.

"Thankfully, you won't see it much beyond Whitechurch. The wealthy here compete for status this way, but the rest of the Reach has little time for it."

She spun around. "Are you really afraid of heights?"

He nodded. His eyes met hers but then dropped.

"All the more reason for us to live in the Southerlands. Donnae need to climb any higher than a cliff's edge."

"He'd never allow it. My father."

"My father wouldnae ever brook a Quinlanden to sit at his table either."

"So we agree. On something."

Yesenia curled her lip with a half laugh. "Why is that so important to you?"

"Is it not obvious?" He peeled himself off the wall and approached her. With the passage of twilight to evening, the waning light cast an ethereal glow upon his pale skin, causing the flecks of blue in his eyes to dance. "If we are nothing else, Yesenia, I hope we can be friends."

"Friends?" Yesenia twisted her tongue in her mouth, running it through her teeth. If Erran were here, he'd easily read this shift in her, know what it meant: that hard press forward was coming, pushing them into a much different moment.

Corin lost a step as she marched toward him. She bunched his collar in her fists when she became close enough to smell his breath and the weird leaves he'd eaten in the banquet hall.

"Friendship isnae what the king intended for us."

His throat bobbed. His soft mouth opened...closed. Fear lived in his sparkling eyes, but as she let her hands run down his golden dress, Corin's expression became something else.

Did he know what was coming? What would it mean to him? Could he, like her, separate himself from it, become what the moment demanded?

Yesenia's hand cupped between his legs.

He *did* know, or at least suspected.

Unlike Erran, she had no use for needless foreplay.

"We don't have to do this," he whispered. "I would never want to force you—"

"You donnae hold the power capable of forcing me." Yesenia took his bottom lip and scraped it lightly through her teeth. Until the moment was upon her, she hadn't been certain she could summon this part of herself, to do what she must with someone she'd been bred to hate. "Unless you donnae want this?"

"I do...want it. But I need to tell you something first," he said quickly, fighting to get the words out between her commanding strokes. "I've never done this before."

Yesenia released his lip. She licked at her bottom one. "You're a lord's son, who could have anyone he pleased, and you've never done this?"

"Have you?" He rattled a startled laugh. "I guess you have, by the way you...of course. I mean no offense, Yesenia, and—"

Yesenia cut him off by burying her tongue in his mouth. That shut him up, finally. The tension in his back and limbs melted into action as he moved his hands toward her hips and planted them, seeming uncertain but firm.

Yesenia took a step back. A twinge of guilt struck her that she would be his first. She bit down on it, swallowing it whole, for a Quinlanden would have no such remorse if the roles were reversed.

She planted her hands on his chest and shoved. Corin, startled, fell back upon the bed covered in dying flowers. As he struggled to sit, she tugged at the satin pants he wore under his formal dress. He seemed too stunned to do more than gape at her as she deftly slid out of her leather trousers. She enjoyed his flinch at the heaviness with which they fell to the ground, courtesy of her daggers.

"You can stop me at any time, you know," she said.

Corin shook his head, failing to speak.

She left her blouse and vest on, then ripped at his dress until she heard the buttons pop off and land on the floor in little pings.

"Oh." Yesenia buried her awe at the impressive organ he'd been hiding under all the gold and satin. Corin saw her noticing. He looked down, likely trying to decide whether he should feel shame or pride.

She climbed over him. Her hair fell down both sides of her face, running over his.

Lie back and remember the Southerlands?
I prefer he be the one to do that.

Her cry of shock at the size of him was buried in the groan he launched as she slid down over him. Such a prize was wasted on a Quinlanden, but her disgust had no power over her as the unexpected surge of desire washed through her. She moved faster, reaching between her legs to double her pleasure and enjoying Corin's wide-eyed hunger at the way she knew her own body.

His smooth hands caressed her ass, fingers pressed into her flesh to urge her on. The tingle began in her arms as the start of her summit made itself known. Her thighs instinctively tightened around him as the wave surged, and Corin's grunts only fired her up more.

But this was duty, and she couldn't let him think for a moment that it could ever be more.

Yesenia threw her head back and screamed when the orgasm overtook her. Her muscles tightened over Corin, destroying what remained of his resolve. He pitched forward and pressed his lips to her chest as his own pleasure thrummed through him, until it faded to soft, erratic jerks.

She rolled off him, still panting. She'd need to clean herself, to be sure there was no surprise in nine months, but right now she was so *tired*.

With the last of her energy, she turned her head toward him, taking in his flushed face, mussed hair. He was still hard for her.

"'Tis the one and only time that'll happen."

Corin's labored breaths were his only response, until his mind caught up. "I told you, Yesenia, we didn't have to—"

"Aye, but we did. Your father will ask ye tomorrow if your wedding night was productive. You're a terrible liar, but now you willnae have to lie."

Corin rolled to his side, eyes and mouth knit in concern. He hadn't covered himself and seemed unaware of the oversight. "I can handle my father. I don't need your pity."

"Ye think I have pity for you?" She vaulted off the bed and went to recover her trousers. She felt his eyes follow her ass as she moved across the floor. "If I do, it's that ye didnae grasp the expediency of what we just did."

As she removed her dagger holsters and let her pants fall back to the floor, she watched him. Her pretty husband. Erran was a pretty man too, but he had substance. Strength. Mettle. He was not so easily broken nor bought.

"Politics isnae just about reading people, Corin," she said finally. "If ye cannae learn to read a *situation*, you'll always be the one lapping at the heels of those who can." She grabbed a fistful of petals as she shook her head. "A wedding night failure helps neither of us." She dropped the bunched petals to the floor. "I'll sleep on the settee."

"No," Corin said quickly. He recovered his senses, clambering for his discarded clothes. "You take the bed." He made for the door to the sitting room. The look in his eyes told Yesenia this was a battle he intended to win.

She decided to let him. He'd be easier to control if she allowed him his meaningless victories. "Fine."

His nod in return was more gratitude than relief, which was good because it meant he knew she'd allowed it.

He was right, after all, that they were stuck together.

"For now," she whispered to the mess waiting for her atop the bed. She swiped her hands across enough of the carnage to peel back the cover and then dropped in, still in her traveling clothes, and submitted to her exhaustion.

TEN
WIVES FOLLOW HUSBANDS

W here are they?!"

Corin's senses blurred together at the intrusion of Yesenia's panicked demand. He tried first to open his eyes, but the bright-yellow hues of the morning sun blinded him. His head throbbed as if he'd imbibed spirits the night before. The chaos of his wife's stomping and throwing things seemed faraway, breaking through the haze of his unfocused mind every few moments like a shrill whistle.

"Corin, *where are they*? What did they do with them?"

His body didn't respond to the command to rise. The aches in his back lingered in protest, reminding him he'd slept on the cramped settee in order to please a foreigner. An enemy.

Careful. Those are your father's words. Aiden's.

"Where are what?" Corin squinted against the back of his arm, leaning into a half sit against the curl in the couch.

"My trunks!" Yesenia's scream had probably awakened the forest and all of Whitechurch. Her anger had turned away from the

103

mess of the room and was now directed at him, for the audacity of requesting clarity on her panic.

"I assumed they'd just been moved out of the way," Corin mumbled. He used both hands to push himself to his feet. Only upon seeing the disgust in Yesenia's eyes did he realize he was still naked. He fumbled around for something to cover himself. "When we went to bed."

"Are ye so used to folks prancing around your room while ye sleep that ye no longer notice their presence?" Her arms crossed, she passed her rattled eyes around the room she'd torn apart in her search. "I *heard* them come in. I thought it was you milling about but clearly not."

"I'm sure it's only a misunderstanding, Yesenia. The chambermaids probably took them to wash and forgot to bring them back before you awakened."

"Aye, because I'm a filthy Southerlander. That it?"

He sighed. "It's only a guess. I'm not the one who took them."

"No, just your kin, who cannae keep their hands off *anything* that isnae theirs, can they?"

"I just woke up, Sen, I—"

"Donnae ye *ever* call me that."

"Sen?"

"That's for blood. For salt and sand. Never you."

Wind billowed the curtains inward, carrying the welcome scent of freshly baked loaves. Not so welcome was how the reminder had brought forth another: they were overdue in the banquet hall.

Such a slight would not go unnoticed.

"And my hands!" She thrust her palms into the air, waggling them. "You sent for a healer after all, against my wishes?"

"No, I…"

Her hands *were* healed though. Her palms were unmarred, not whatever mangled mess had been hiding under her bandages.

"It wasn't me. I don't know who ordered it."

"I'll get Anatole on the trunks," Yesenia said to herself. To Corin, she asked, "Where *is* Anatole? In the…tree, or somewhere else? I'd like him to stay with me at all times."

Aiden gaped at her. "You want your servant to stay here? In our apartments?"

"Aye," she answered, nodding.

"Eh, well, that might be a problem," Corin answered. "For my father," he added quickly. "Our servants reside at ground level, and first tier. They're only allowed in the royal apartments when in active service."

"Royal…" She shook her head in revulsion. "Anatole is in active service at all hours."

"You know what I meant."

"I need to send for him. Where's your page?"

"I don't have one. Not personally," Corin said, flushing with shame. "But we can ask about Anatole and the trunks at breakfast."

"Breakfast?" Yesenia laughed. "With your family again? Nay."

"We have to go. It's not about what we want."

"Ye said that last night and walked me straight into a trap."

Corin pulled on the fresh shirt someone had folded and left for him. His dressing gown, which Yesenia had freed of its buttons the night before, was now mended, hanging. There *had* been others in the apartment overnight. The first tendrils of dread spread through him at the nocturnal intrusion, which had never happened before Yesenia's arrival. Telling her that would help nothing.

Dressed, he turned back toward her. "I'm sorry. It's like that for me too. But duty is duty." He disliked himself for his next words, but they were the right ones to appeal to her. "I may not know much about the Southerlands, but I know they place duty above all else."

Yesenia's smooth, motionless expression chilled him. The slow smile that followed was evidence of his overconfidence. "Ye think I'm just a harp you can play by calling to my sense of honor?" She shook her head at him, like she might if dealing with an unruly

105

child. "Aye, I'll go to breakfast, Corin. Not because of *duty,* but because I'll be asking your father and brother where to find my clothes and footman."

"Wearing that?" Corin asked as she reached for the door.

Yesenia looked down, unbothered by the realization she still wore the same clothes she'd traveled in. "Aye. What else am I to wear when they've taken my trunks?"

Corin realized she hadn't seen the rack of gowns near the entrance to the perch. He should tell her. She'd be expected to wear them, and when she didn't, his father and brother would punish her.

Yet despite the blood burning in her cheeks and the mad energy swirling around her flesh, he saw in her eyes the same fear known to a trapped animal.

He pretended to not see it, just as he'd pretend to not know about the gowns.

"I sent him home." Aiden directed his words at the jam he spread over the top of his steaming bread loaf. "Mother, will we have cow's milk any time soon, or are we expected to imbibe this watery swill from the Slattery goats?"

"The enchanters have cured the bovine disease, dear, but we still must wait for the food and drink testers, to be certain it's safe for your consumption. You know the rules. If a hundred citizens can drink it without incident, then we will again find it upon our own tables." She nodded at a bowl in the center of the long table. "Sop your bread in the pureed apple, darling. It used to be your favorite."

Yesenia waited impatiently for Mariana to stop pandering to her son. "Sent him home? You sent my footman home? Anatole?"

"Yes, I did." Aiden reached for the carafe of viscous cranberry-hued juice that looked like blood but with seeds. Bile formed in the back of her throat. "Or do I need to say *aye* for you to understand?"

106

"That wasnae your decision to make." She ground her tension into the chair. "He wasnae your man to command."

"All men here are mine to command," Aiden said to correct her. "And women."

Maeryn flashed her a look of warning. Yesenia pressed her tongue to the roof of her mouth. It was her anger they wanted. To offer it would be a gift to them and a loss for her. "And my trunks?"

"Oh!" Mariana dabbed at her mouth. She set her napkin neatly to the side. "Dearest Yesenia, I can explain that one. I had my women go through them, and really, I don't have to tell you how atrocious your options for fashion are in the Southerlands. I've had them thrown out and replaced—"

"Thrown out? You've had my clothing *thrown out?*" Yesenia should not be this shocked. She should not be this exposed.

"Of course," Mariana said, wearing a pleasant smile. "But, darling, the gowns I've left for you have been designed to favor your dark hair and eyes…your generous curves, which are wasted in all that leather." She pointed at Yesenia as if preparing to pluck something from her face. "The dark glow in your cheeks will, over time, lighten, and you'll be a vision."

"You mean her masculine ruddiness, Mother," Aiden replied. He shared a conspiratorial look with Maeryn, who shrank lower when his eyes passed away from her. "Common in women who fancy themselves as competent as men."

Yesenia didn't rise to his bait. She ignored him, focused on Mariana. "I would like my trunks returned to me, Lady Quinlanden."

"Call me Mother. Please!" Mariana shook her head. "And I'm afraid that will not be possible, darling."

"Not possible?" She at last realized the absence of Lord Quinlanden.

"Not possible," Mariana said again, her smile faded. "Did you not see the gowns left for you? The best hands in the Easterlands worked to make them just perfect for you."

"Mother, perhaps Yesenia could have both?" Corin asked. "If she agrees to wear the gowns, should we not let her keep her own things?"

"I donnae need your help," Yesenia said from the side of her mouth.

"Corin, dear, you know we do not linger overlong on unpleasant subjects. If your father were here, this conversation would already be well ended," Mariana said. "And your wedding night? Was it as pleasing as you both hoped?"

"Our wedding night," Yesenia repeated. "Ahh, aye. That."

"Yesenia," Corin warned. He could already read her, sense where she was going.

She hated him for it. Hated his simpering mother and pathetic but dangerous brother.

He could choke on his caution.

They could choke on their inedible food.

On their sly, witty barbs.

On their loathing for her, which was not half of what she bore for them.

Yesenia thrust back from the table and stormed out of the banquet hall. On her way out, she ran into Lord Quinlanden, whose greeting died on his lips as she ran down, down the dizzying steps until she reached the base—and freedom.

"And where are you going?" Chasten demanded. He blocked the way, forcing Corin back a step.

Corin tried again, but his father was immovable.

"Not after her, I hope?"

"She's my wife," Corin replied, set to the tune of Aiden's neighing.

"Wives follow husbands. Not the inverse." Chasten looked past his son, toward the others. "Mariana. Maeryn." He didn't move, waiting for his wife to pick up on his request and follow it.

She at last tucked her napkin into the side of her plate, rose, and departed the room. Maeryn was several steps behind her, training her confused eyes on Corin as she exited the banquet hall.

"Aiden," Chasten said when the women were gone.

"Me? You want me to leave?"

"You frighten your brother. I need him to hear what I have to say."

Aiden balled and tossed his napkin across the table. He shoved back and, on his way out, made a point of shoving Corin to the side while he grinned through red-stained teeth.

"Now then. Sit." Chasten stayed planted in the doorway until Corin obliged.

Corin fell into Aiden's seat. It felt wrong, but if he moved, the reason would be obvious. He rolled his hands over the arms of the chair, waiting.

Chasten kept a methodical pace as he entered the room and settled into his own chair. As always, he looked well-rested, at his absolute best. Not a hair was askance, nor a wrinkle in his garments. His light-blue eyes never left Corin as he inched his chair closer to the table.

Half of Corin's thoughts were rooted in fear of what his father would ask him; the other ran alongside Yesenia, guiding her to a place where she could be free, even for a short time.

"Your wedding night," Chasten stated. "Tell me about it. Was it productive?"

Corin swallowed. He nodded. "It was."

"She put up a fight?"

Corin shook his head, flushing and recalling the way she had shoved him back onto the bed; how formidable and exquisite she had looked climbing over him; how menacing she was in what had followed; and how, even in her dark command, there had been pleasure burning in her eyes, pleasure she took for herself but also gave, whether she'd intended to or not.

He could hardly wrap his mind around what had happened in those short but potent minutes, but each time he replayed the night's events, he saw them differently.

Chasten's brows rose as if watching Corin's thoughts.

"Her move then," Chasten replied, nodding. "She's cunning, that one. She knew I'd ask you this. Knew you'd lack the wits to lie. Did you at least finish?"

"Yes." Corin didn't recognize his own voice, strained and distant.

"Inside of her?"

Corin lowered his eyes and nodded.

"Did she tell you never to come to her bed again?"

How did his father know all this? He surely had spies planted outside their apartments, but that wasn't the impression Corin took from his father's choice of words. Chasten seemed proud in the way he had pieced together, on his own, the prior night, as if it were a game to play and win.

"No," Corin lied. He lifted his chin.

"Is that why you slept on the settee, while she sprawled herself out in your bed, alone?"

"Does it matter where we sleep, as long as our duty is fulfilled?"

"You are not twenty years married, Corin, embittered with each other. She had a choice to sleep next to her new husband or on her own. Her choice is telling."

"She's not used to sleeping with someone else. Nor am I." Corin spilled his words in careless order, flustered. It didn't matter what he said or how he said it. His father never asked questions when he wasn't already confident in the answer.

"I didn't sit you here to listen to you recollect your wedding night with half-truths. I don't care if she enjoyed it or if you did. If she's not carrying your heir within her first few months at Arboriana, then the king will look to me as the source of failure. I don't care if you have to chain her to the bed each night, nor if you have to conjure up the image of some poor alley girl from Slattery Row to make your cock hard. None of this is important. Only what must result."

Corin nodded through his aching discomfort, ignoring the crude mention of Venya intended to wound him. He thought of Yesenia, running through the forest angry and defeated, and wondered why he thought of her so much when she never thought of him at all.

"Are you listening to me?"

"Yes, of course."

"Then hear me when I say this. If you cannot bring your wife to heel in the bedroom, then Aiden will. It's no matter to me whether she's carrying yours or your brother's child, so long as the child is a Quinlanden. I'd do it myself if I had the time." He cleared his throat. "I need to know I can count on you. That while I'm easing an uprising in Rushwood over the broken betrothal between Gretchen and the Sylvaine boy, you're attentive to your own duty. Your *only* duty, Corin. You understand? I have never asked anything of you because I have no faith in your competence, but any man can spill his seed. Any man can father a child." He fingered his lord's ring, spinning it. "Aiden is practically gnashing his teeth to get at her."

Corin squeezed the seat of his chair to bury his horror. Those were no idle threats. He should tell Yesenia, warn her, but would she believe him? Or would she think he told her this to convince her to return to his bed?

No, he couldn't put that on her. He was the one who had to take control of the situation. "That won't be necessary, Father. Yesenia and I are…compatible in this regard."

"Compatibility is not my concern," Chasten said. "What *is* my concern is that she's not been here even a full day and she's already speaking out of turn, running off without being dismissed. This is a lesson for you to learn early and hopefully not often. You cannot allow your wife to do as she pleases." He leaned his head to the side with a searing look. "I will say the words once more, so you receive them in the manner intended. Control your wife, Corin, lest it become the job of other Quinlanden men. Do you understand?"

"Yes, Father."

"You say 'yes, Father,' and yet you allowed it."

Corin sighed. "This world is new to her. I'm trying to be understanding of this, to—"

"What I hear you saying is you are allowing your wife to determine the course of action," Chasten stated. "Which concerns me, Corin. It concerns me a great deal."

"There's no reason for you to be concerned. I'll talk to her. She's not used to the way of things here yet, but I'll help her get there." What little Corin had eaten turned to a rock in his belly. He couldn't help but wonder, amidst these interspersed threats and promises, if Aiden had exploited the opportunity to go after Yesenia...if Aiden was already carrying out these plans to subdue her. "She might have responded better had we not taken her clothing and her footman."

"Are you questioning my choice?"

"Only...trying to understand it."

"I don't require your understanding," Chasten said. "Only your loyalty." Chasten reached to his wife's abandoned setting and picked a handful of berries from her plate. He smashed them into his mouth, and they formed a dark stain on his lips and the corners of his mouth. "I want to know everything she knows about what Lord Warwick is doing in the Southerlands."

Corin caught his gasp midway. "What?"

"They treat their women differently there. It's unnatural, but it works to our advantage. She knows things, Corin. I want to know all of it. No matter how inconsequential."

"So you can tell the king?"

"What did you say?"

Corin's pulse quickened. His father was asking him to train his wife to be more agreeable and, in the same breath, spy on her. Yesenia was far too clever for that, even if Corin were inclined to do it, but Chasten knew that too. It was a test, and he was failing.

"You don't think she's spying on you, boy? That she's not reading you at every chance, making note of everything you say or don't?"

"Even if she was, you'd never let her get a message out, would you?"

"I should hope you wouldn't either. This is your Reach too. Or have you forgotten?"

"She has no power here. She knows that better than anyone."

"Does she?"

Corin pushed back in his chair, unable to hide his escalating irritation. "When have the Southerlands ever posed a threat to us, Father? They've suffered more than any others in this kingdom while we've thrived, at their expense. Isn't that enough?"

"Beware your words, son. Some things cannot be unsaid."

Corin shook his head, his mouth parted. "I won't do it. I won't spy on my own wife."

"Remember who gave you this wife." Chasten's eyes narrowed. "And then you might grasp what I'm telling you. Why would the king, our friend, bring a Warwick to spoil our lands unless there was a purpose? An opportunity for an act of service?"

"Even if I were agreeable to this," Corin said, his words coming faster, bolder, "and I'm not, I'm *not* going to do it. But even if I were, she'd never say a word against her own father. She's loyal, perhaps to a fault."

"There is never fault in loyalty."

"So long as that loyalty is to you or our king, right?"

"That's enough!" Chasten slammed his palms onto the table, causing Corin to jump back against his chair. "You never used to speak to me this way. Has she already wound her poison through your heart?"

Corin reeled in his anger, settling in his chair, just as his father expected, as he knew he would. Corin had become an imperfect soldier with nothing to offer, except as a set piece to be moved around at the whims of his father and brother.

This time he restored his calm not for himself, but for Yesenia.

Until now, he'd not grasped the extent of danger awaiting her. The traps had already been laid, set for her to walk through. The calculating minds of his father and brother never rested.

"If she reveals anything of worth to the Easterlands or the crown, I'll be sure to tell you." Corin forced his words through clenched teeth, his eyes cast to the side so he wouldn't crumble under the uncompromising gaze of his father. Chasten knew his youngest son was only saying what he wanted to hear, and he would use it as a weapon later.

"See that you do, yes?" Chasten replied, a light hiss at the end of his final word. He raised a hand.

Corin was dismissed.

Yesenia yanked the tip of her dagger from the tree. She grunted, stumbling a step. She checked the edges for chips and was relieved to find none, though it was a reminder to not be reckless. She'd thrown it a little too hard. Practicing her daggers was how she was keeping from losing herself to her many competing emotions. She was dangerously close to blurring that line. To becoming what her new gaolers already believed her to be.

They're just clothes, she told herself. *And Anatole was a comfort in a place where I'd be wise to have none.*

The Quinlandens wanted her to feel the loss. To be forced into their golden gowns, wearing the air of assimilation but none of the advantages. To be isolated from everyone and everything that reminded her of who she was.

As if she could ever forget.

She was Yesenia Warwick, daughter of Khoulter Warwick and made of equal parts salt and sand. She would never, *could* never, be like any of these monsters.

No matter what clothing she wore. No matter what soil her boots stood upon.

She cocked her arm back, locked her eyes on the specific spot she wanted her steel to land, and eased off.

Her outward breath when she released the dagger, when she heard the sharp passage through the air, and when it decisively stabbed into bark became one of relief.

Yesenia stiffened at the distinct crunch of leaves behind her. She wrapped the worn hilt of her second dagger with her palm, listening, reading the situation. Whoever it was came no closer. The reason for their hesitation was unclear, as was the danger in it.

But then she heard the trespasser turn and leave.

At once, she knew it had been Corin, and she knew why.

He might believe he was only checking on her, worried about her sudden flight from the dining hall, but he was still his father's son, in more ways than he was aware.

Yesenia resisted the urge to turn by drawing her second dagger. This time, she didn't even pause to line her sight. She released it, her precision perfect as she landed it inches from the first.

Once she freed both daggers from the bark, she chanced a brief glance back.

Alone again.

She shook off her unease and began again.

ELEVEN
THE HUNT

On her second morning in Arboriana, Yesenia woke and discovered she was alone. A quick check of the five rooms of their apartments offered no sign of Corin, until she noticed a small note scribbled on vellum sitting upon an ornately carved desk, which seemed more for show than use.

My father insisted on a hunt today. Expect my return by supper. Safest for you is here, in our apartments, until I return.

"As if you could protect me from anything," she muttered, balling the note. She searched for a hearth in which to toss it but recalled Corin explaining that they didn't have them at Arboriana. Lighting fires in their pretty little tree kingdom was too great of a risk.

She mused at the possibilities.

He wanted her to stay cooped here in the apartments where she couldn't cause him trouble, did he?

Yesenia laughed to herself, searching for her trousers and vest. She'd slept in her tunic, the balmy air drafting in from the perches reminding her, despite the infinite differences, of home, where she'd always retired to her bed in the nude. She could never be so vulnerable here.

But her trousers and vest were gone.

There was no point in searching further because she already knew what had happened. Mariana's girls had snuck into her room once more and taken what was not theirs. What bothered her more was that she'd not seen this possibility and been ready for it.

Yesenia had, however—she recalled now, sighing in powerful relief—slid her daggers under the mattress before retiring to bed.

What would her father think about her past two days? Would he admire her rare restraint or encourage her fire tongue? Would he tell her to hold her ground or wear the hideous dresses they'd prepared for her?

She wished more than anything that she could ask him, to hear his voice guiding her against her impetuous nature into calmer waters. She'd given him intense resistance since she was old enough to run, but she'd always been his lass. It was to him she'd always gone for comfort.

The only comfort he could offer her here was the same tough love, but without the balm of his presence.

Yesenia returned to the sitting room, and the rack she'd tried to ignore. At least ten gowns had been hung for her, all so bloated with fabric that they were stuffed in and overflowing like a pen of overfed pigs. Mariana had taken care to assign Yesenia the colors of the Easterlands, reds and golds and even purple, the favored color of the Rhiagains, of royalty. None of the warmer tones reminding Yesenia of home.

She filtered through them, wearing her disgust like a badge of pride. Not one was tenable, but *none* was not among her available choices, unless she intended to roam Arboriana bare-legged.

Remember who ye are, girl. Being a Warwick 'tis never about comfort. We are above such things. We need only our metal and our mettle.

Yesenia snatched a violet dress—swashed with cloth of gold of course—and forced herself to put it on. It took twelve attempts and some acrobatics she hadn't employed since childhood, but she was at least clothed again.

She walked straight past the mirror intended for self-inspection and went to her bedchamber, where she recovered her daggers and one other thing. She'd nearly forgotten the gift Anatole had given her. Last night, perched at the edge of the too-plush bed, she'd rolled the vial around in her hands, wishing Anatole were still there to guide her. Anatole would know when to use it. When not to.

She slipped the poison vial inside one of the many pockets stitched into the inside of the gown. If nothing else, the Quinlanden women had an appreciation for the practical.

Yesenia couldn't bend to reach her boots, thanks to the untenable restraint of her bodice, so she fastened her dagger belt over the frilled waist of her gown. Upon second thought, she removed it, unclipping the leather extender, and turned it into a thigh holster. Propping one leg up on a velvet chair, she strapped the daggers high enough to hide them under the gown's thick fabric but low enough she could still get to them with a quick enough hitch of the hem.

Tossing a defiant look at Corin's crumpled note, Yesenia left the apartment.

Corin studied his father's intense squint as Chasten peered through his enhancers. Chasten had commissioned the double-lensed device for hunts, but Corin knew his father also liked to take them and climb to the top platform at Arboriana to survey his dominion. When his father was home, he spent a noticeable amount of time up there, often taking Aiden with him. Corin had been up there only once and then was never invited again.

The small tented podium Chasten's men had propped up into the high branches of the Rushwood forest meant Corin was so close to his father, he could smell his veneer of sweat, tinged with the promise of blood lust that he'd ask others to spend on his behalf. Chasten no longer brought his own bows and daggers. He let his men handle the filthy work of hunting and dressing. Later, he'd present whatever kill they'd taken as his own, at the head of a table where no one would challenge his assertion. They'd consume the meat with the expected reverence, offering the Lord of the Easterlands an occasional awe-filled glance, never questioning that to eat meat was against their own code of ethics. As long as it was the lord presenting it, the table could be covered in human flesh and they'd smile, mouths and bellies full, gratitude and admiration overflowing.

Corin would be more focused on not retching.

"Do you see anything?" Corin whispered.

"A doe. Too small." Chasten passed the enhancers to his son. "Would you like to look?"

"Me?"

"Is there someone else here?"

Corin accepted the enhancers, wary of the offer—almost as wary as he'd been of the choice to leave Aiden back in Whitechurch while Corin and his father hunted on Rushwood land. Chasten would be quick to remind him that all land in the Easterlands belonged to the Quinlandens. Corin pretended to not understand it was a reminder to the Sylvaines of Rushwood that he required no permission to take from them.

"I don't see a doe. But I do see…" Corin lowered the enhancers and looked out into the woods without aid. "There."

"What?"

"Elk-kind."

"There's no elk-kind, Corin. That's a *doe*. They're not remotely the same in size." Chasten's disappointment hit Corin in the gut.

But he *had* seen an elk-kind. He returned the enhancers to his eyes, and there it was again, but closer. Without altering his gaze, he handed the enhancers back to his father and pointed. "Right there, just beyond the patch of bluebonnet."

Chasten's skepticism became a form of anger, but he reclaimed the enhancers and looked at where Corin pointed. The sneer playing at the edge of his mouth dissolved. A more serious look passed over him. "I see it." His arm extended to the side, the signal his men had been waiting for. "Easy," he whispered, though only Corin could hear him. "Easy, boys."

Corin glanced toward the shuffling in the bushes below. He averted his eyes, dizzy from the height. His father remained intently focused on the elk-kind, waiting for his men to strike.

Sharp whistles sounded in uneven tandem. Corin's mouth parted as he saw four, five, six arrows sail from all sides, converging on the same spot. He couldn't see the elk-kind without the enhancers, but his father's energetic twitch, followed by an elated groan, confirmed the kill.

"Good eye," Chasten said, and that was that. There'd be no mention of Corin's contribution later, certainly not at evening meal. He dropped the enhancers in the basket. "Now, we wait."

"For what?"

"They'll dress the meat, leave the worst parts for the buzzards." Chasten leaned into a more relaxed pose. "You weren't there to send your sister off to university this morning."

Corin balked. "Saoirse's *gone*? Already?"

"I may keep her in Oldcastle longer than the requisite year, until she's of marrying age. Perhaps…" Chasten seemed to speak his words to himself. "Perhaps it's better that way. Keep Aiden away from her. She can come for visits in springtide."

Corin sat back on his heels. He didn't know which stunned him more: that he hadn't gotten to say good-bye to his sister or that his father might actually take steps to protect one of his daughters. "I wish someone had sent word to me. I'd have liked to have seen her before she left."

Chasten shrugged. "We've got another tick of the sun before the men are done, and I didn't bring you here to talk about your little sister. I thought we might speak, the two of us, on the matter of your foreign wife."

"We spoke yesterday." Corin immediately regretted pointing this out.

But his father's reply was composed, not venomous. "So we did, Corin. I worry I was too hard on you, that you are only trying to make the best of a troubling situation with the Warwick girl." He wrapped his arms around his knees, breathing in the warm morning air. "Aiden has it easier. I recognize this. The Blackwoods are not our enemies, even if they are aberrant in the way they let their women lead. But only a few days in and Yesenia is already demanding she keep her own name? I've never heard of such a thing."

"I'm not like Aiden. I won't put my hands on Yesenia."

"As if she'd let you." Chasten snickered. "She's a wild one. She is. I recognize it. I see the challenge ahead of you. No, you're right not to compare, Corin. Laying hands on Yesenia Warwick will gain you nothing."

Instead of easing at his father's friendlier tone, Corin instinctively clenched, readying himself for the inevitable shift to something more familiar. "I'll find my way with Yesenia, Father. You needn't worry."

"Spying on a Warwick, even under our own roof, will not be as easy as I led you to believe. But you will find your way, yes. I'll help you find it."

Corin didn't bother explaining that wasn't what he'd meant, for Chasten either already knew or didn't care.

"Aiden is, as we sit here, making his own attempt with her."

Corin's spine turned to ice. "An attempt? At what?"

Chasten laughed. "Who can say with Aiden?"

Aiden's absence in the hunting trip made sudden, sickening sense. "How much longer until we return?"

"In a hurry?" Chasten lowered his cool gaze on him. "Have somewhere better to be than here, with your father? Haven't you wished I'd do more with you, as I do with Aiden?"

"It was only a question." Corin's imagination took over, presenting cruel images that veered too close to his fear of the truth. Aiden leering over Yesenia. Cornering her. Laying hands where they didn't belong. Oh, she'd put up a fight, but it would be worse for her. Aiden fed off the suffering of others.

Chasten returned his gaze to the forest. "Be still, Corin. Enjoy the silence. For we both know, it never lasts."

Yesenia had one hand upon the bark—the other, the dagger's hilt—when she felt the shift. It started with the air, an almost imperceptible interruption in the wind's direction. Even the careful nature of the steps could not disguise the intrusion, that way of knowing she was no longer alone, defying even her own senses.

Her fist swelled around the dagger, and she spun around fast enough to halt the intruder mid-stride.

"So angry," Aiden goaded, circling her to the side. "Is violence the only language you know?"

Yesenia lowered her dagger but didn't let up on the pressure. "Violence is the language from which you extract your own power. Though it's decidedly less masculine when practiced upon a woman who cannae defend herself, aye?"

Aiden held out his hands with a practiced smile. "Welcome to marriage."

"Real men donnae have to lay hands on their wives, for they already have their respect."

"Why are you so concerned with what I do with my wife?"

"Why are you following me?"

"You're in my forest. I don't have to explain myself to you."

Yesenia thought of her second dagger, still strapped to her thigh. She couldn't retrieve it quicker than he could be on her. But she only needed one.

"There's something that's been bothering me. Something I've wanted to ask you, but we can never quite find time alone together, can we?"

Yesenia tightened her grip. "I have nothing for you."

"Did my brother satisfy you? Did he truly satisfy you? I heard you, from outside the apartments, but what I cannot decide is whether you enjoyed yourself or if you were simply putting on a show."

There was no gain in either response. To say yes was a lie. To say no was a danger. "As I said. I have nothing for you."

"There is one way to confirm." Aiden's arced path brought him closer to the tree—and to her.

Yesenia twitched her dagger. "Not a step closer."

Aiden took another step. Yesenia released her held breath and cocked her elbow but found herself pinned, from the back, as Aiden grinned at her.

"Hold her there," Aiden commanded. He reached behind Yesenia's bound arms and pinched her dagger, then tossed it into the leaves. His breath coated the side of her neck, threats yet to be spoken. She thrashed only long enough to confirm she was bested, unable to see the face of the man strong enough to withstand her trained resistance.

Aiden traced his bottom lip along the line of her jaw. He edged closer so she could feel the hard press between his legs, a power move she would not allow to overtake her fear.

"Is this the only way you can get a woman into your bed?"

"Not the only way. Just my favorite," Aiden said. He tossed a nod at the man behind her, and Yesenia was upended. Her feet caught the forest floor as the man dragged her off. "She has another dagger somewhere, Mads. Don't let her go for it."

Aiden dropped his sword belt near the tree and sauntered after them.

Yesenia plunged back to the earth, landing on her back. She arched at the pain, but she could see the man responsible for subduing her. Some of her fear left her at the sight of him. He was a large man but had enough idiocy in his face to betray that his size only made him strong, not capable.

She tilted her head back and spat in his face. As expected, he recoiled in disgust, dropping one of her arms as he swatted at the spittle. Yesenia pitched forward, ignoring the pain in her other arm as she nearly pulled it out of place to position the other to go for her second dagger.

124

Mads caught on right as she had it free of the holster, right as she kicked her feet up to arc her legs so she could land erect. Mads yanked her back, hard enough to send stars into her eyes but also to pitch her legs back into the air, where she found herself landing her boots on either side of his neck.

He fell back into the leaves, releasing her altogether in the melee, and when they settled, she had both thighs tightened around him in a headlock. He sounded his affronted grunts against her backside.

With a victorious grin, she pulled her head back up in time to see Aiden's sword pointed at her neck.

Yesenia kept her smile, recalculating.

She rotated her dagger in her hand, pressing the tip to Mads's belly. "Come any closer, I'll kill him." She twitched her thighs. "And I donnae require my dagger to do it."

"Kill him then. I don't care."

Mads's muffled wails were buried in the gust of wind that sent leaves swirling upward between them. He clawed at her with flailing swipes, but she tightened her grip, and his hands went dead.

She rolled her head back at the violation of Aiden's sword tip, pressed into the top layer of her skin. "You're unnatural," Aiden hissed, bowing her even farther back until she was bent so far she almost snapped Mads's neck with her thighs. "A heathen. But I'll break you of these flaws, Yesenia. I'll make you fit to walk our lands and feast on our resources."

Yesenia thought of the poison. She might be able to go for it, but then what? Even if she managed to shove it down his throat, her victory would be short-lived. She'd ruminate on the moment for however long it took for them to burn her on a pyre in the middle of Whitechurch.

Aiden wiggled the end of his sword, driving it into her neck— only more of the tip, but it was enough to send a river of blood down into her the neck of her gown. Any deeper and she'd feel the steel when she swallowed.

Aiden, seemingly satisfied at her immobility, pulled his sword free but kept it close. He reached forward and tugged at the tulle of her gown, grunting at the thick resistance of the fabric. He dug his hand under it instead. His berry-strained tongue passing along his cracked lower lip was the moment Yesenia knew she'd die before she let him go any further.

If I let him best me here, it's the death of me either way. He'll never leave me alone, and I'll never forget how he felt.

She rolled her dagger upward, pointing it at a hard angle into her ribcage, under her chest. "I'll do it. They'll all know why."

"You're lying." He withdrew his hand.

Yesenia's nostrils flared. She joined her other fist to the dagger and clenched her teeth. "Let's find out."

"Aiden! That's enough."

Maeryn.

Aiden spun around in a chaotic swirl of fury. He staggered off to the side, his eyes skimming the forest for his wife.

How long had she been there? What had she seen? Heard?

Yesenia exploited the diversion by rolling off of Mads. She dove for her second dagger and held them both close, backing away. She demanded a sense of calm from herself, but she couldn't shake what had transpired, what had almost happened. She'd been prepared to take her own life, like a warrior cornered in battle. Another few moments, and she might have.

"Your mother has been looking for you. There's some trouble in the courtyard, and your father is still hunting."

The crisis behind her, Yesenia shifted her focus to searching for Maeryn as well.

"Where are you?" Aiden demanded. "WHERE ARE YOU?"

Mads swayed to his feet. He shook off the leaves, cutting a wide berth at the sight of Yesenia several paces away. "Let's leave before these cows get any more ideas, Aiden."

Aiden spun around again and again and then suddenly halted, swaying and drawing his attention back to Yesenia. "This is *not* over. You live here now. In *my* home. *My* domain."

Yesenia was too dazed to respond.

When the men were gone, Maeryn stepped out from behind a nearby tree. Her placid look was a poor match for the fraught situation she'd stumbled into.

Or *had* she stumbled into it? Yesenia wasn't so sure.

"Are you all right?" Maeryn asked, her tranquil tone conveying the practiced nature of her words.

Yesenia wiped the sweat from her brow with the velvet arm of her gown. She couldn't wait to be free of the unbearable drapery. She'd burn this dress, bury the memory that came with it. "Another minute and I'd have had his balls in my palm, doing us both a favor."

Maeryn's grin was as quick as a blink. "Your toughness will not serve you here, Yesenia." She pushed her blonde hair back to reveal a bruise that colored the left side of her face. "I know what you think of me. That I'm weak. That I allow it."

"That isnae what I think of you," Yesenia countered, distrustful of the woman's intentions. "You're married to a monster. I ken he'd treat any other woman the same."

"Your toughness will not serve you here," Maeryn said again. "He wants you to fight. They all do. They're practically salivating at the mere thought of it."

"Aye, and I should have let him rape me instead?" Yesenia asked. "That's your plan, is it? Let them all do as they please, with no repayment for their crimes?"

"You wield your sex as a weapon. So next time, wield it."

Yesenia scoffed, tossing her head into a laugh. "I meant what I said to your bootlicking husband. I'll die before I ever let him near me."

"You took his brother into your bed."

"They are not the same."

"Aren't they?"

Maeryn was both right and wrong, but was Yesenia really going to defend Corin? "Aye, well, fortunately for you, your husband lives another day."

"There is no fortune to be found here. Not for women like us."
Maeryn squinted toward the sun that broke through a patch of
trees. "Coming to the forest alone is a bad idea. You'll not do it
again if you possess the wisdom I expect of you."

"Any more advice, Lady Quinlanden?"

Maeryn twitched her mouth. "None that you'd take anyway."
She lifted her skirts and left.

Corin ran straight to his apartments upon his return from the
hunt. He found Yesenia sifting through a small stack of vellums
at the desk and fixed his eyes upon her shaking hands. She buried
them in her lap and continued reading without looking up.

"How was the hunt?"

Corin shut the door and locked it. "Maeryn told me what
happened." He knelt by her. "Yesenia, are you all right?"

"Aye, ye really asking me that? I can handle your brother." She
rolled her eyes, but the bloom in her cheeks and the slight tics
pulling at the edges of her mouth gave away her truth.

Corin placed both hands on her knees. He noticed two things:
she was wearing one of the gowns, and it was covered in the dark
stains of the forest. "I know you can handle him. I know you can.
But…"

"*Maeryn* told you," Yesenia said, nodding and adding a laugh
at the end that lacked humor. "Ye wonder why that is? Catch the
way she cannae stop ogling you when you're stuffing your mouth
with berries?"

"I have noticed. And I don't care."

"You say that as if you caring would worry me."

He shook his head. "Forget Maeryn. I don't *care* about Maeryn!
I care that…" He made a play for her hands, but she withdrew
them so quickly, he fell back. "You're right to be upset. What he
did…It's atrocious. It's untenable. Unforgiveable."

"Deplorable, appalling, indefensible. Are we done?"

"No, Yesenia. We're not done. I won't let this go."

"You think I cannae defend myself?"

Corin sighed. "I know you can. But you shouldn't have to. This is your home now. He had *no* right."

She drew away entirely and rose, moving upward, into the perch. He understood she went there because it was the one place he wouldn't follow.

"When Father hears of this—"

"Your father encouraged it, you fool," she called back, facing away. Her mahogany hair fell in tangles over her tattered dress. "Why do ye ken you were the one he took hunting?"

Corin nodded to himself, but knowing was not the same as seeing the aftermath. Of seeing what it had done to her.

"Let it go," she said. The light tremor in her voice sent his heart to his boots. "I already have."

Now who's the terrible liar? He fought his careless desperation to go to her, to take her into his arms and insist that it was okay to be vulnerable.

She'd send him flying from the balcony, and he'd probably deserve it.

Corin glanced at the desk and saw a letter from her father. It had been read by several eyes before making it to Yesenia, a fact of which she was undoubtedly well aware. *No matter where your boots strike, you will always be a daughter of the Southerlands* was all he caught before forcing his eyes to avert. He would not contribute to the indignity.

"I'll make an excuse for you, for supper," he said, as a new idea took form in his mind. It wouldn't erase what had happened, but it was something. Something real, something he could do, for her. "Would you like me to bring something up when I return?"

Yesenia shook her head but then half turned and said, "Just some bread. None of that..." She waved a hand.

Corin fought a smile at her small concession. "I understand. When I come back—"

"Leave it on the table," Yesenia answered. She slipped down off the perch and made her way to the bedchamber. The door closed behind her. Locked.

Corin pressed a hand to the desk, still watching the closed door she'd disappeared beyond.

He might have enough time before evening meal to put his idea into action.

TWELVE
THE CHALET

For three days, Yesenia didn't leave the apartments.

The expected fuss from Lord and Lady Quinlanden never came, or if it did, Corin fielded it himself, transferring none her direction. She spent the hours with her thoughts turned inward, returning to the plan she'd lost momentum on: returning home.

Her father and brothers might have moved on, but she hadn't and never would.

She'd yet to hear anything at all from Byrne, which hurt more than she cared to admit. But Khallum's two ravens, in the week she'd been at Whitechurch, only made her heart heavier. He couldn't come out and encourage her rebellion of course, but the way he'd worded his missives made it sound almost as if he was *happy* in his new life, with his new bride. Khoulter's single letter reinforced this, describing Gwyn Dereham as *welcome refreshment*, and he'd added that he was proud of Yesenia for embracing her new life with open arms. He'd even signed it *with love*, and if the circumstances were any different, she would have taken it as a sign he was calling them all to arms.

They know my letters will be read. They know, and so they say what they'd want the king to hear.

These reminders hollowed her. They changed nothing. She was alone here. Without allies. Without family.

No ravens came from Erran. While possible the Quinlandens had held these back, feeling letters from an old beau were not appropriate for a woman newly wedded, she didn't think that was so. She'd left the hard conversation for Khallum, and Erran wouldn't forgive her for it. Nor would she, if their roles were reversed.

Corin left her mostly alone. He returned from his family meals with carefully selected assortments of food he presumed she would eat, and he mostly got it right. Though her appetite had abandoned her, she was not so foolish as to refuse that which gave her strength.

On the second day, Mariana had tried to come see her. *To help ease you, darling, not to chastise you. I only want your happiness, Yesenia. You must believe that.*

Corin sent her away.

No one had come since.

When she woke on the fourth day, the light already having passed to the other side of the room, Corin was sitting on the edge of the bed.

"You're late for breakfast," she said, forcing her eyes closed again.

"I'm not going today."

Her surprise caused her eyes to open once more. She noticed a new glint in his irises, and a feverish energy suggesting he'd been up to something. "Aye? You like punishment then?"

"I want to show you something, Yesenia. Not here but out there, in the forest."

She pulled herself erect. "Donnae ken I like the sound of that."

"I know why you might not be eager to find yourself in the forest again, after what happened."

132

"In the forest *with a Quinlanden*," she amended. "Isnae the forest out to get me."

"Do you trust me?"

Yesenia laughed. "No."

Corin's sigh was more amusement than discouragement. "Can we pretend you do?"

"Why?" Her suspicions returned.

"How about this? If after I show you what I'd like to show you, you have reason to believe my intentions were untoward in some way, you have my permission to punish me in whatever way you deem fit."

She crossed her arms, trying not to laugh at all the strange things he'd packed into one sentence. "Not that I need your permission."

"No," Corin said quickly, hiding a smile. "Of course not."

"But let's say I agree. Ye ken what type of punishment I would offer?"

He nodded. "And that I have no defense against your skills."

His offer was tempting. The past days had offered her more misery than the ones prior, but the forest was no longer safe for her. Nowhere was. That admission was among the hardest she'd ever made, for, until now, she'd never met a foe she couldn't best.

But try as she did, she could see nothing in Corin's imploring expression that promised danger.

"If I hear so much as a leaf move out of turn, expect the next words ye hear to be the Grand Minister reading your dead-given rites."

Corin grinned. "Let's go."

It was just as well that Yesenia had needed several days to herself, for it had taken Corin as long to put his plan together.

But now that she was following him, half-trustful, deep into the same forest she feared, his doubts crept in.

"I ken this is far enough," Yesenia said to his left.

Instead of arguing, he kept on, down the path so familiar to him, he could follow it by the light of sun or moon. That he'd not come here since Yesenia's arrival was a mystery even to him, and his choice to take her there now, an even bigger one.

At last the chalet came into view, sitting sentry at the back of a modest clearing. Over the years it had begun to seem smaller, shrinking alongside his youthful imagination. But it was as unchanged as ever. The clouded windows at the back still held, and the timber cobbling the old cottage together showed no signs of rot. It was as if time itself was suspended there, a sensation that always struck him as he made his approach.

"What is that?" Yesenia stopped moving. He felt her distrust and kept moving, knowing she'd eventually follow.

"A relic from the monastery days," Corin called back without stopping. "Before the Rhiagains created the Reliquary and made the Guardians their own."

"Why are we here?"

Corin reached for the key and slipped it in the lock. He turned back toward her. "Are you coming?"

"Tell me why we're here."

"You asked me on your very first day if there was a place you could go, where no one would bother you," Corin replied. "I regret that the answer I gave you wasn't far enough from Arboriana. That Aiden—"

"No." Yesenia shook her head. "We willnae speak of it."

"He won't find you here," Corin finished. "He never found me here, in all the years I've been coming."

Yesenia stepped slowly closer. "Why? Why come here?"

"For the same reason you're going to." When she was near enough, he handed her the key. He almost told her about Venya, but something stayed his words. "It's yours now. Aiden is always preoccupied just after morning breakfast, until noontide, and then again between evening meal and midnight tea. If you slip out during these times, he cannot follow you."

Yesenia lowered her eyes to her hand, to the key.

"Well, come in!" he exclaimed, shaking off old memories, old wounds. He pushed the door open and awaited her reaction to what he'd done.

Passing him a guarded look he'd come to recognize as normal for her, she brushed past him and entered the room. He felt the beginnings of her rough assessment forming and then her breathing stilled. His held in response, until he heard her whisper, "Corin."

Corin closed the door behind them both and locked it. He'd remind her to always lock it before they left, and though she'd pretend to not need it, he'd also walk her through his other precautions because they'd kept the place safely his for over a decade.

"It took some doing, but I found them. When Mother claimed to have had them discarded, I didn't believe her, so I asked around, among some of the staff who are fond of me. They were in the stables, high up in the loft."

Yesenia went to her trunks and knelt, flipping back the latches one by one. "Why?" She rifled through her belongings and held a set of leather armor tight to her chest. "Why would you do this?"

Corin dropped onto a nearby chair. He leaned forward and watched her sort through her old life, making it hers again. An uncomfortable flutter settled in his chest at seeing her so consumed, her guard down, her words curious and subdued. "I do want you to be happy here, Yesenia."

She snorted and dropped the armor. "Ahh."

"Have I ever given you any indication otherwise? Any indication I agree with the way my family behaves, the way they've treated you? Have I been anything but kind to you?"

"Kindness is a sticky web."

Corin groaned. "Yesenia! Not every gift is a trap." He dropped to his knees beside her. "Not every Quinlanden is your enemy."

Yesenia twitched her nose but returned no barb. She settled against the back of her boots, relaxing some. "You must want something in return."

"No." Corin insisted. "That's not what this is."

135

"Even so." Yesenia inhaled a deep breath. "I cannae accept it without reciprocation. So, tell me. What is ye want? And donnae even *ken* of saying—"

"I wouldn't," Corin said with a light laugh. "And I really don't want anything in return."

"I'm not asking, Corin. I'm telling ye. If ye wish me to see this as a gift, you'll tell me, and I'll do it, so there's nothing between us. No owing ye anything. Aye?"

Corin looked past her, at the small table where he and Venya had shared so many meals. Where they'd played the card game she'd taught him, and then he'd taught her to read and write her letters. It had never been more, but not because he'd never desired it.

What he most wanted was not in Yesenia's—or anyone's—power to give.

"All right," Corin said agreeably. "There is something you could do. Not only for me but for yourself as well. It would make both our lives better." It would do more than make their lives better. It might save hers.

She tilted out her hands, waiting.

He took a pause before speaking. It was still possible she might strike him, but she was calmer than he'd ever seen her, and she was listening. "When we're around my family, we should act as if we are truly man and wife. As if we're happy." He winced, bracing for her to bite his head off. But she patiently waited for him to finish. "When we're in our apartments, I'll never bother you. I'd never so much as *dream* of touching you. But around my family, we…"

"Play happy families," she said, finishing for him. "Coo and gush and fawn and all that other disgusting stuff."

"As far as they know, we've grown to enjoy each other's company and are…" He stopped short of saying, *in love.*

"Aye. Fine."

Corin was stunned. "What?"

"I'll do it. No point in suffering at all hours. Just as long as ye donnae take any of it to mean—"

"No, absolutely not," Corin said quickly. "I'll know what it is and what it is not."

"Aye." Yesenia nodded, returning her gaze to the pile. "Aye."

"There is one more thing…" Corin bit his lip, wondering what prompted the thought.

What flashed on her face terrified him.

"Your daggers."

"What about them?" She narrowed her eyes.

"Can you teach me?"

"Teach you?"

"How to, you know…" Corin reared his hand back and pretended to throw.

Yesenia slapped her knees and laughed. "Aye, well *first off*, ye donnae hold yer hand like that unless ye intend on stabbing the floor."

"You don't know what this floor is capable of," Corin muttered with a brow raise that made her laugh harder.

"Come on then." She leaped to her feet and waved her hands at him. "Come *on*."

He followed her to the other side of the large room. She stood just to the side of the door, centering herself in front of a support beam at the other end. "Stand here."

Corin was jerked into place when she yanked on his shoulders. His heartbeat skipped around as she reached from behind and wrapped her hand over his.

"Take it."

Corin tentatively obliged, but no sooner than he did was she clucking her tongue in reprisal. "Nay, not like that. Like *this*." The way she clutched the hilt in her fist made him blush, and he was glad she was behind him and not the other way around. "No bringing it up over yer head again, aye? Feel this. *Feel* what I do."

He could only nod, heart in his throat, as she brought the dagger up, ear level, and released it with a force that sent him forward a step.

Yesenia released him and went to pull the dagger from where she'd landed it, in the perfect center of the pillar. In a flash, she spun and flicked her wrist, sending the dagger whooshing through the air. It landed inches from Corin's head, sticking into the post above him.

"What was that?" Corin demanded, breathless. Sudden spots appeared behind his eyes as his fear caught up to the moment.

She grinned. "Accuracy."

"You nearly killed me!"

Yesenia snorted, rolling her eyes. "You insult me. If I wanted you dead, you'd be dead."

Corin jammed his finger upward, motioning at the dagger still stuck above his head.

"You asked me to teach you. This is me teaching you. Your turn." She returned and yanked the dagger out, then passed it to him hilt first as if she hadn't just come dangerously close to sticking it between his eyes.

"Go on. Take it."

Corin forced back his hesitation and accepted the dagger. Without her support, the full heft of it hit him. The heat from her palm still warmed the patinaed leather. He went to raise his arm as she'd done, but she buried her face in her hands, shaking it.

"Not like you throw a ball. Too much arc and it's over. You've lost. You're dead." She wrapped her hand around his, fastening it tighter to the hilt. "Again."

Corin stuck his tongue to the roof of his mouth. He held his breath and tried to remember how she'd done it but could only recall the way her body had felt pressed against the back of his.

When he cocked his arm, she crossed her arms and watched.

Corin sent the dagger sailing toward the pillar, where it clanged and fell to the floor.

The silence of her disappointment sent a throbbing ache straight to his chest.

But then he heard it. Her cackle started in the back of her throat and had her buckled over as she lost herself to a fit of laughter.

Corin gaped at her, insulted, but then he was joining her, ensnared with delight at seeing her set aside her grudges and her loathing for whatever this was. He bowled over his knees, shaking with laughter as he eyed the dagger lying pitifully on the floor.

He looked up in time to catch her eyes and the playful gleam reflecting back as she laughed with him. She grinned as she retrieved the dagger, still watching him, her smile spreading a soft light over her face and her dark waves of hair covering one eye.

"I cannae decide whether to continue subjecting my dagger to such abuse," she said, rolling her tongue under her teeth as she held back more laughter. "Or if it's worth it just to see how dreadful ye are."

"Hopeless, am I?" Corin squared his stance in an intentionally terrible way.

"Utterly," she proclaimed, handing him the dagger once more.

They were still laughing when they stepped beyond the forest and into the lively courtyard of Arboriana. Workers turned toward the sound, exchanging knowing glances that confirmed they would share what they'd witnessed with the right people. For good measure, Yesenia slipped her hand into Corin's, adding a brief wink. His return grin was conspiratorial. His quick squeeze of her hand was something less obvious.

Happy families, she thought to herself, wondering how she'd not thought of it first. Lord and Lady Quinlanden would be thrilled, and so would the rest of the Arboriana, except Aiden. He'd be blue in the face when he saw it. But if Corin was a successful husband, Chasten would rein in his elder son.

They made their way up the Golden Stair. Yesenia caught sight of Lady Mariana on her way down, flanked by attendants.

This would be too easy.

She cupped her hands around Corin's cheeks and buried her tongue in his mouth, heightening the kiss as she locked her mouth tight against his, allowing it to become like the ones she'd shared with Erran: consuming, chaotic…like the ones Corin had perhaps once shared with someone too.

When Mariana was close enough Yesenia could hear her steps, she pulled back. Corin's soft exhale affirmed what she knew already, that she was an excellent kisser. That, for him, this would be no chore.

"Lady Quinlanden," Yesenia said with a reverent nod, Corin's hands still bound in hers. She feigned a dreamy expression, like she was still recovering from the kiss. "My apologies. We didnae see you."

"None taken," Mariana said with a blossoming smile. "You've been gone all day. Shall I ask?"

"Best not, Mother," Corin teased. He swayed closer to Yesenia.

"Perhaps you two would rather take evening meal in your apartments?" Her question was hopeful. There was only one right answer.

Yesenia bit her lower lip, eyes on Corin. "If that's all right."

"It's more than all right, dear. Lord Quinlanden will understand. He'll be much pleased, in fact."

When Mariana had passed, Corin's mouth parted with the start of a shocked, soundless laugh.

"I assume that will do?" Yesenia asked. "That I was…convincing enough?"

Corin nodded, breathless. "A little too convincing."

THIRTEEN

THE PRIDE OF WHITECHURCH

Corin rolled his tension through his shoulders as the Quinlanden men commenced their farcical monthly ride through Whitechurch.

First they passed the guildhalls. Men were just arriving, Chasten's trip timed perfectly to appear right at the start of their day. They all dropped into bows, waving as they came back up with beaming smiles. These were the men the Quinlandens looked after, took care of. They were the keepers of the professional guilds, the only place in the kingdom where blacksmiths, armorsmiths, clothiers, and others could come to appeal for better licenses or to apply for new trade agreements.

Every Reach should have their own guildhall, Corin thought. But as long as the Quinlandens rode high in their favor with the Rhiagains, the Easterlands would retain this exclusive control, just as they had over the Council of Universities and even Reach-neutral institutions, like the Sepulchre and the Reliquary.

Next would come the unbreakable line of inns. Here was where the middle class stayed and spent their coin—high enough born to be seen along Whitechurch's glory row but not high enough to be invited to stay at Arboriana. These were the ministers and magi, of the Reliquary and Sepulchre, the masters of the universities at Oldcastle, the leaders of the guilds, and heads of the Great Families of other Reaches.

"What a beautiful day," Chasten declared, closing his eyes as the sunlight spread over them. Corin braced himself for what would come next, and he was not disappointed. "To be a Quinlanden."

Aiden snickered. "Always a good day to be a Quinlanden."

Corin filtered the rest of their words out and traced the remaining path in his head. He found turning his thoughts to the predictable passage of this monthly sham kept him from dwelling overlong on the grotesque showing. Chasten would always say their leaders must be seen, but he was the same man who climbed to the highest perch at Arboriana every morning. His father was here to read the moods of these men, who had wound themselves no higher than the middle of the vine of Easterlanders. His presence wasn't the comfort of a leader, paying his respects to the working class. It was a warning, to the same group. *We are always here. We are always watching.*

"Where are the stonesmiths?" Aiden mused aloud as they came to the end of the guildhall row. The arched entrance, crafted from marble easily as rare as the kind found at Arboriana, had a chain looped through the metal handles.

"Pilgrimage to the Seven Sisters of the West," Chasten explained. "For granite and marble."

Aiden snorted. "If they spent half as much time in the Eastern Range, they might find we have the same to offer, or better."

"The Eastern Range is a bereft catastrophe of raised land that only hinders travel," Chasten replied. "There is no shame in taking from the other Reaches what we cannot find in our land, only in the pride that would prevent it."

Aiden returned to riding in silence. Corin hid a smile into the side of his vestments, but Chasten caught it. Returned one.

"You've done well," he added to the end of it, so swift a shift that Aiden whipped his head upward in confusion. "I don't know if you've broken her, but you've won her over."

"I didn't have to break her," Corin said, proud even though the show of affection they put on for Arboriana was only that. "Yesenia and I understand each other. We like each other."

It was beginning to feel like the truth. Although they always dropped the act when they returned to their apartments, retreating to their own interests, tensions between them had calmed. Yesenia no longer answered every question with a bite. Sometimes, he even found the right words to elicit a smile from her. Two weeks had passed since his gift of the chalet, and she'd even invited him to continue his lessons with daggers. She'd given up training him to throw them and focused on how to hold them, how to jab.

"Not too much, I hope," Chasten replied. "A productive marriage aids the Easterlands. A happy marriage aids only you."

"Should have just let me continue with her, Father," Aiden said. "There'd be no misunderstandings between me and her either. She'd understand well enough who her master was."

"Yet she responded best to a softer hand."

"That's only if you care how she responds at all," Aiden retorted.

"Perhaps the king was on to something, assigning her to Corin," Chasten said, thinking aloud. "He knew she wouldn't break on the knee of a man who tried to tame her." He laughed. "Apparently she only needed to be *understood*."

Both men laughed together, hollowing Corin's small victory with his father. It didn't entirely dampen his spirits though. The hint of closeness he shared with his guarded wife had left enough of a mark to produce a spark of excitement at the thought of seeing her again. He wondered if she felt it too, or if her acting was better than he thought.

He pondered how she was faring on her own ride with Mother and Maeryn, down Slattery Row.

"I've been more than patient." Chasten's deep voice cut through Corin's thoughts. They rounded the small bend in the wide road, coming upon the gleaming white row of inns. "As close as you are now, you have something I can give to the king. I know you do. The question is whether you've grown *too* close and have confused your loyalties."

Corin's spine clenched as he sat taller, singed by the gaze of his father and brother as they sought to pick from his silence anything that might reveal the holes in it. He had once shrunk under their scrutiny, but to do so now would cast doubt on his and Yesenia's agreement.

He had to tell them *something*. Something that would satisfy them without harming Yesenia or her family. Something meaningful but innocuous.

But what?

"She's clever, but she's still a woman," Aiden was saying. "Women are incapable of keeping secrets."

Women invented the keeping of secrets, Corin thought. "She's angry about her vellums being read before they're given to her."

"That's not information, Corin. That's a statement of fact," Aiden replied.

"There's more, I hope?" Chasten asked.

Corin wound his hands through the reins, burying his desperation there. "She...as you can imagine, says nothing of worth in her own letters, as a result."

"We know. And?"

This was safe, wasn't it? If what Yesenia had told him was true, it wouldn't matter if Chasten and Aiden knew about it. They'd be powerless to decipher it. "She told me...that the Warwicks have a code. They only teach it to other Warwicks, never to staff or even allies. It's unbreakable. She's going to begin writing her letters in this code, and it will signal her family to reply with the same." Sweat from his palms soaked the bridle. "Unfortunately, we won't be able to read it."

"A code," Chasten mused aloud. "That's brilliant, son. Just brilliant."

"Even if it doesn't help us?"

Aiden cackled. "You think we cannot break a Warwick code? We employ codebreakers who have cracked the codes of all the great houses of the realm. Father's right. This *is* brilliant. She'll hand us everything we need."

"We'll know what she's been collecting on us," Chasten said. "Her next vellum should be very telling."

"Unless you warn her off," Aiden accused. "If you do, we'll know."

"I wouldn't. I won't." Corin's mouth was so dry, his lips stuck to his teeth. He'd walked straight into this one, and there was no backing out. If Yesenia didn't use her code, they'd think he'd tipped her off. If she did, she might say something that would put her in serious danger. She might even say something treasonous.

And if she does, shouldn't that be enough for you to abandon her cause? To realize what your father and brother have been trying to tell you all along, that she's your enemy? Even Yesenia herself never claimed to be anything more or less.

Chasten slowed his mare as they neared the end of the row of inns. Beyond were buildings in need of repair, families in need of food and provisions.

Aiden and Corin turned with him, aimed away from the desperation, and returned down the same path, past the same glittering establishments that represented the pride of Whitechurch.

Mariana rode in the center, with Yesenia and Maeryn flanking her on either side. They made their way through the forest this way until they neared what appeared to be a small village.

As the path narrowed, they all drew closer together.

It wasn't only Yesenia's imagination that everything seemed darker here, from the shade of the buildings to the filth lined along the road's edges. The road itself required careful navigation, as it was broken apart in places, grass and weeds growing in absence of repairs. Pale faces peered from behind clouded windows. Those outside, sweeping, peeling, and churning, slipped inside at the sight of the three women in their ornate gowns riding down the narrow alley.

"This is Slattery Row, the dregs of the Merchant Quarter," Mariana announced with a sweep of her arm, her satin sleeve grazing the horse's head. She affected overdone nods at the few stragglers who hadn't disappeared back into their homes and shops, earning every one of their aghast gawks. "I meant to take you both here sooner, but instead I prioritized getting you acquainted with Arboriana. I attempt to come here monthly, in offering. Saoirse and Gretchen joined me in the past, and now the two of you will step into this tradition."

"Where is Saoirse?" Yesenia asked. She hadn't seen the girl at all since supper the first night.

"She left for university." Mariana's neck tightened, her head pulling back. "Where she belongs."

"So soon?" *Without saying good-bye?* she almost added.

"If anything, nearly too late."

"What, exactly, are we offering?" Maeryn asked, catching up with Mariana's speech. She passed an uneasy look to Yesenia but returned her gaze forward before Mariana noticed.

"Why, our presence, of course." Mariana seemed surprised at the question.

"Are we going to enter any of the shops? Speak with anyone?" Yesenia asked.

The look Mariana gave her was authentic bafflement. "Why would we do that?"

Maeryn pursed her mouth with a pained frown.

"Is there not something we could do? Something we should be doing?" Yesenia kept one eye on Maeryn, wondering if she should follow her lead. "With these gowns alone, we could feed the whole row."

Mariana shook her head and returned to her empty greeting of the few citizens still outside. "You lead with your heart, Yesenia, not your mind. As women, this is in our nature and therefore tempting, but we must think like our men if we are to serve them."

"I donnae ken your meaning."

Maeryn shot her a wide-eyed, muted headshake from her other side. Mariana remained silent.

"Why would we want to think like men who would starve their own people?" Yesenia realized, suddenly, that the Easterlands made no special concessions for their own. If they weren't highborn, they were treated no differently than a Southerlander.

"Starve them?" Mariana's practiced smile cracked. "Is it not their own choices that led them into starvation? Into poverty? To hand to them what should be earned would teach them nothing, Yesenia. *Nothing*. We are here today, always, to show them what is possible, for those willing to do what is necessary."

Yesenia laughed bitterly. "There isnae a thing they could do to be sitting where we are."

"You're here, aren't you?"

"I'm a Warwick of the Southerlands, and I am not beneath you," Yesenia replied. "But neither are the rest of the men and woman of the Southerlands beneath me. Or the Easterlands."

"If you insist," Mariana said with an upturn of her brows. "But your Southerland principles mean nothing here. Your father's people might look upon him and see a man who works for his people, but it is the *people* who must work for *him*. Your father's rift with our own king stems from such tactless values. If his men worked harder, if he paid more in taxes—"

"Taxes for *what*? So the king can send more of his gold to you?"

Mariana snorted. "Instead of lapping at the well of your father's lies, you might learn something from us. It's a choice you can still make, Yesenia." She pointed at an older woman nursing two children, one from each teat. The soft shrill of screaming children inside told of a much larger family. "You see? She's older than I am, but she'll never learn, will she? What has she, eight, nine, ten children inside? She cannot even feed one, but she'll have twelve more, until her body gives out on her."

Yesenia was at a loss for words. It was clear Mariana believed everything she'd said. Maeryn's cautious glare was even harder to read, but the Blackwoods were popular with their people in the Westerlands, which was unlikely to have happened if they shared these cruel values.

Yesenia lowered her head with a soft smile at the nursing woman. The woman recoiled in response, mistaking kindness for cruelty. And why wouldn't she? It was all they'd ever known from their liege lords.

"Your eyes linger overlong, Yesenia. Quickly, like I do. Nod, divert. They mustn't think they are favored, or they'll show up at Arboriana with their list of demands, smelling like cow dung and mold."

Had Mariana always been like this? Corin had said she'd been a Skylark, numbered among the Great Families of the Easterlands but lower in the overall hierarchy. Perhaps she'd simply adapted, in order to be accepted by those considered higher born.

It didn't matter. Yesenia would never end up like her. She'd hopefully be free of this marriage and this wretched family before their behavior began to feel normal.

The road tapered further, forcing them to ride single file ahead. Mariana angled herself into the lead followed by Maeryn, who shook her head at Yesenia when she passed and fell in behind their mother-in-law.

As the women struggled with their horses down a steep hill, Yesenia turned back toward the nursing woman. The dark saucers under her tired eyes were lit by the moonlight, the resigned anger in her face settling into every wrinkle and crack. Yesenia met her eyes as she reached inside the small purse sewn into her dress. She removed all the gold coins inside and placed them upon a hitching post, stacking them carefully so they didn't fall to the broken cobbles and draw Mariana's eyes.

The woman turned away, crowding the infants against the door.

"Yesenia, are you coming?"

Yesenia waited another moment for the woman to return her eyes forward, but her fear and loathing were greater than her hunger. Yesenia left the coins anyway. If not this woman, someone would find them. Someone would eat better.

It wasn't enough. Not nearly enough.

"Aye. I'm coming," she called ahead, knowing the precise shape her nightmares would take later.

Yesenia had been unusually quiet throughout the evening. At supper, she'd smiled at all the right words and moments, fooling everyone but Corin, who could sense her tension in the air between them.

When he laced his fingers through hers afterward, their final performance of the evening, she seemed to forget herself for a moment. With a stunted grin and a squeeze of his hand, she fell into place so they could continue up to the apartments.

She'd gone right to the desk, and there she sat, eyeing a stack of unused vellum without drawing one from the pile. Her hand tapped an uneven beat on the soft wood, hushed but hard sighs interspersed in the spaces between.

"Are you going to tell me?" Corin leaned against the doorway leading into the bath. He thought of calling for hot water for her, but he wanted to know what was troubling her so he could address it, not distract her from it.

"What?" Yesenia looked up, her face splotched and the same red in her eyes, though there was no evidence of tears, new or old. "Ahh. I was off tonight, aye? I'll be more mindful."

"I'm not worried about what others think right now," he said. He took a step in but didn't crowd her. That sort of intrusion of space was never welcome from her, a thought he'd catalogued with her other likes and dislikes that he'd picked up over the past weeks. "I'm worried about you."

Her laugh was muffled. "Are ye now?"

"I am."

"Save that worry, bottle it, and use it for those who have *real* need of it." Bitterness dripped off the end of every word, but it didn't seem to be directed at him.

"Slattery Row," he whispered, understanding all of it then. What she'd seen. How she'd felt. The resulting change in her.

Was this another secret he could safely share with Yesenia Warwick?

Would she want it?

Corin dipped through another door, the one leading to the bedchamber. Behind the bureau was a rack built into the wall, and from this he pulled two cloaks from the row of them.

He returned to the sitting room and tossed one to Yesenia. She sputtered under the velvet and drew it off of herself with an incredulous look.

"Put this on, and come with me."

She groaned. "Another one of your little surprises? Not in the mood."

Corin pulled the cloak over his shoulders. He'd draw the hood when they were clear of Arboriana. "You will be for this one."

FOURTEEN

LAOCH

Yesenia held fast to Corin's hand until they reached the stables. No one stopped them nor even looked their way. These days, it was accepted by the residents of Arboriana that Corin and his foreign bride were in love. She wondered what being in love might feel like if it ever really happened to her.

"Once we clear Arboriana—"

"I know," she said. "Hoods up."

Corin nodded and secured his saddle, while she did the same. He was quick about it, and she was still fastening her buckles when he swung up to mount.

That Yesenia had been able to keep her horse when the Quinlandens had taken everything else was a blessing she'd not, in her anger, spent enough time counting. She ran her hands down Kheerai's silver mane, whispering her the words of their homeland, and then leaped up.

Corin tore off before she was even settled in the saddle. She angled forward, urging Kheerai to match his mare's pace. When she caught up, he glanced over in acknowledgment and then aimed his eyes forward until they cleared the back gates.

It was the second time she'd exited Arboriana this way today.

He slowed when the path shifted from solid stone to the packed dirt of the crooked forest path. Tossing a quick nod her way, he let his hood fall back.

"Are ye gonna tell me where we're going?"

"You haven't figured it out?"

Yesenia scowled at him in the darkness. Too bad he couldn't see it. The moon was their only light until they cleared the uneven path that wound downward and around, at last leading into the Merchant Quarter and Slattery Row.

"Your mother tell you what I said to her today?" She didn't want to think he'd bring her here to chastise her, after the scrap of trust they'd forged between themselves, but why else was he being so evasive?

"No," Corin answered. Only his mouth was visible from the side, the rest of him hidden behind the emerald scoop of his hood pooling at his neck. "But I'm sure it's nothing she hasn't heard from me before about this place."

They reduced their speed further when the hooves hit the broken cobblestones. The rancid odors that had ripened in the sun of the day were gone, replaced by welcome aromas that reminded her of home: rich, meaty stews, salted tubers, and yeasty loaves, scents topped with the spill of ale, fresh and old. She missed the Southerlands so much that thinking about it had become a weakness she could no longer indulge.

"Which is?" she asked after a soft pause.

"That the people here starve for one reason and only one reason. Us. *We've* done this. We've caused this. Don't you believe for a second, Yesenia, that it wasn't intentional either. Starving men cannot raise arms. Starving men cannot fight back against what's been done to them."

A swell of heat rose within her at the passion in his words. She wouldn't have guessed him to feel so strongly about anything. "It took me aback, to see your father treats his men as he treats ours. I shouldnae have thought he took from us to give to his own."

"They're all the same to him." His lips curled in resentment. "He doesn't even see them as men. They're no different than the beasts he hunts."

Yesenia stared forward. "It affected me so because…" She drew a breath. "It reminded me, I ken, of home. Of what much of my homeland has been reduced to because of men like the king and your father. My own father, he…gave as much as he could of what we had. Sold our tapestries, our nicer furnishings. Warwick heirlooms even. Sold them right back to the same men who'd stolen from us, so our men could eat."

"I'm sorry."

"Why? Isnae your doing."

"I'll confess, I'm glad you can see the difference now, between men like my father and me."

"Donnae ken if I'd go that far." She grinned but kept her eyes on the coming approach to Slattery Row. "Why use your hood at all if you've already removed it?"

"Catch."

Yesenia fumbled the heavy pouch he'd tossed her way, recovering just before the gold coins could spill over the path. There were so many of them! A whole bag, enough for many people, not just one. She glanced at him, her eyes wide with wonder.

"My father can't know," he explained. "Or he'll put a stop to this."

"How often do you do this?"

"As often as I can get away." He maneuvered his horse off the road, the cobbles fading again to dirt at the edges of the unkempt lane, and dismounted near a rickety gate. "We'll tether them here and walk the rest of the way."

Corin reached for her hood and pushed it back from her face. He looked at her.

"I thought…"

"Only for the ride. They know me here." He chuckled. "I don't suppose they'll ever tell."

When they'd secured their horses, Corin reached for her hand, a reaction born of new instincts, but seemed to remember himself with a wince.

She pulled away, but not without a short smile to show him he'd committed no trespass. Her two realities had become blurred for her as well, never more so than now when she observed him walk through the Row, handing out gold to everyone he saw. Men, women, children, he had something for all of them. She broke free of her awe and joined him, gathering energy as they swept down the rickety road, delivering hope to every place lit up in welcome of the man they lovingly called *Laoch*.

"Laoch? Why do they call you that?"

"I don't know," he said, smiling at a young girl he addressed as Elsa.

"You do know," Yesenia challenged. She accepted a sweet roll from Elsa's basket and offered a gentle moan once she inhaled it. "Aye, I ken that's the best sweet roll I've had in my life, lass."

Elsa's cherubic cheeks flushed. "I helped Mama make them. Want more?" She thrust the basket at Yesenia, who beamed at the sweet gesture but couldn't ever take so much food from Elsa or her family.

"Save them for yourself, lass. I'll enjoy another, next time I come."

"You'll come with Laoch again?"

Yesenia's gaze fell on Corin. "Aye, if ye tell me what that name means."

Corin shook his head and turned his attention on a young boy who wanted to show him a drawing he'd made. With a deftness bordering on political skill, he managed to admire the boy's art while also responding to the half dozen others vying for his attention.

"It's one of the Old Languages, Lady Yesenia. Most don't speak them anymore though. Lord Quinlanden has forbidden it."

"You can say anything ye like to me, Elsa."

"Mother says it means 'hero.'"

She felt Corin's shame without looking at him. Unlike his mother and father, who channeled their usefulness into the point-less endeavor of being seen, Corin didn't want to be seen. He wanted to *help* but on his terms, quietly and without the pomp other Quinlandens would have demanded in exchange. These men, women, and children of the merchant class were more kin to him than his own blood. He knew their names, their stories, their hopes, and their fears. He shared them.

"Aye, well that secret is safe with me," Yesenia told the girl, though her words were as much for Corin. She'd misjudged him, but how and to what extent, she'd yet to decide.

A whole crowd had gathered around them, painting a stun-ning contrast to the barren ride she'd taken earlier with Corin's mother. They ushered in close, clamoring not just for the gold Corin offered but because they'd missed him and had so much to share. He asked a man, Fergus, about whether he still thought the midwinter would be easy on crops, and he shared a tender embrace with an older woman named Claire, whom Yesenia rec-ognized from her ride with Mariana. The images of this woman breastfeeding earlier were clarified, as Yesenia learned she was raising her grandchildren after the sudden death of her only daughter. She'd spent weeks trying to push her body to remem-ber how to produce milk.

Corin whispered something in Claire's ear just as the small boy from earlier, the one with the drawing, tugged at Yesenia's cloak. She looked down and grinned at him.

"Can I draw you too, miss?"

"That's Lady Quinlanden, Tristan! Ack, boy!" a man cried out in reprimand.

"Miss is fine. Yesenia is even better," Yesenia replied, kneeling to his height. "What's that ye said? Ye want to draw me?"

He nodded and showed her what he'd waved at Corin moments earlier. He'd sketched his charcoal upon the back of blood-stained butcher paper, but she could see clearly enough that the drawing was meant to be Corin. The soft eyes peering from beneath a heavy cloak were enough of a giveaway, but it was the warm smile he'd captured, shockingly well, that snared her.

"Is that all the paper ye have? What they wrap the meat in?"

"The widower comes around with it once a fortnight. He gives me what's left, after he passes round the meat."

"Would you like me to bring you more? Without the blood? Vellum, perhaps?"

Tristan's cheeks burned bright red. "I don't mind the blood, miss. Vellum is far too valuable."

She'd bring him her own stack of vellum next time, she decided. "You can draw whatever ye please, Tristan. As long as ye promise to show me next time, aye?"

Tristan curled his lower lip inward as he grinned. "I promise."

"Laoch! Eh! You're late!"

Corin was already making his way toward the woman who'd called out to him. Yesenia clapped Tristan's shoulders and then squeezed through the crowd, trying not to lose sight of where Corin had gone. She found him locked in a tight, warm embrace with a woman his mother's age.

"Mara, this is my wife, Yesenia. Yesenia, Mara."

Yesenia had never been presented in such casual introduction before. Her conditioning caused her to bristle, but she liked the simplicity of it, the absence of airs and formalities removing all the expectations from the moment.

"Pleasure to meet you, Yesenia. Any love of Laoch's is a love of ours." Mara said the words genuinely enough, but a hint of sadness played in her glossy eyes. "It's been too long. Months. You promised you'd never let it get that long."

Corin hung his head. "I know. But I…"

"No need to say it. We all live it. We all know it," Mara answered, gathering him in her arms again. When they ended the hug, she left one arm draped about his waist. "Come, come. The littles are with my mother this week, and Lorne is two pitchers ahead."

"He's passed out, you mean?"

"Might be halfway to the Guardians by now."

Corin laughed with the woman, the two sharing something intimate that Yesenia didn't belong to.

But then Corin turned back with a beckoning smile and opened his free arm. Surprising herself, she fell into it, letting him shepherd her inside.

The subtle, ocher-hued illumination from hanging candelabras was a welcome change from the darkness of the row. She looked around at what was clearly a tavern, absent of patrons. Upstairs was presumably an inn.

"Sit, sit." Mara ushered them both toward a table in the corner. Before Yesenia had her cloak off, the woman slapped a pitcher of ale sloshing onto the table, and two mugs beside it. "I think we still have enough stew for two bowls. Now, don't drink that too fast, Laoch. That's from Lorne's experimental batch. I saw two men lose their bellies over it today, forgetting themselves, and as for Lorne...I can only hope he'll rise early enough for the morning patrons."

"You're no fun," he replied, teasing her, and she swatted the air in response, running off to grab the stew.

Yesenia could still hear the joyful din of the crowd gathered outside.

Corin poured them both a mug. He washed his back in one mighty gulp and filled himself another.

"Ye heard her!" Yesenia exclaimed, laughing. "Easy!"

"You're too used to seeing me do as I'm told," he countered. The light caught his blue eyes, making them gleam in the auburn glow. "Or cowing in fear."

"This the real you then, aye? A tavern lush?"

"That's what you take from tonight?"

Yesenia smirked. "No, that isnae what I've taken from tonight."

Corin brought the mug back to his mouth, let it linger there as he said, "I've been showing you who I am this whole time. You just didn't believe me."

"Can ye blame me?"

He shrugged, licking his lips. "No. But I can *outdrink* you."

Yesenia met his gaze, issuing a silent challenge. She downed her mug and, with a belch, slammed it down. "Well, fill it up then!"

Corin's mischievous twinkle sent another laugh rippling through her, which heightened again when she studied how well he handled his drink. Like a Southerland man.

"Why didnae ye want them to tell me? About the whole Laoch business?"

Corin wiped his mouth on his sleeve. "Because I'm not a hero, Yesenia. Them thinking that only underscores how terrible my family has treated them. Feeding them? Getting to know them? Those are the essentials all men should expect from their lord. I want to be their friend, not their savior." His eyes flashed with the start of his drunkenness as he shakily refilled again.

Yesenia let his words settle without response. She nourished the comfortable silence that followed, turning to her ale and allowing her mind a reprieve from the darkness of the day.

By the time Mara returned, they were both dizzy from the ale. Yesenia cackled at Corin's crossed eyes when he tried to stand, and she slammed her hands on the table to urge him on.

"Where do you think you're going, drunk as you are?" Mara chided, an overfilled bowl of stew in each hand.

Corin swayed as he held the empty pitcher aloft.

Mara clucked her tongue. "No, you'll sit and eat some first. Then I'll *think* about bringing you some more." She turned her eyes on Yesenia with a playful glance. "This your influence?"

Yesenia rolled her lips inward with a devious shrug.

"Ah, get on with it then, before you both shit yourselves," Mara urged. When she'd stopped laughing, she let her eyes linger on Corin. "It's good to see you smile again, Laoch."

When she was gone, Yesenia asked him what Mara had meant. Corin set his gaze on some fixed point in the distance, his lips moving in his indecision.

"There was someone. Once. Her name was Venya," he said with his voice low, still looking off into the tavern proper. "Mara was first her employer and then her adoptive mother, and this was where I met them both, here at their inn. I loved her, and now she's gone."

Yesenia settled onto the bench. "What happened to her?"

"She died. At Arboriana." His cheeks flexed. "I should never have taken her there. We were happy enough here and at the chalet."

"Our chalet?"

"Is it ours? I seem to recall giving it to you outright," he said. "I thought I was doing you a kindness, but…perhaps it was for me. So I could be rid of it—and her."

"Ye donnae have to tell me," Yesenia said quickly, snaking a hand over and landing it on his arm. "Donnae feel as if ye must."

"I'm telling you because I want to," Corin answered her. "I never touched her. What you and I did, your first night here… That *was* my first time."

Yesenia cracked a grin. "Aye, ye don't say?"

Corin's dour mood lightened at the jab. "I wasn't that bad, was I?"

"Wasnae pleasure that brought us to that point. You know that."

"Nah, of course not." Corin shook his head.

"I had someone too," Yesenia blurted. Was it the drink? Was it the way Corin watched her now, hanging upon the anticipation of her next words? "A boy. Man. Doesnae matter. Ye said to me that night that ye sensed…I had experience. Aye, well I did…but was only with him. With Erran. I made it seem like there were more, but it was only ever him. I…" She stopped before the wrong word could tumble out.

159

"You loved him," Corin said.

Yesenia lifted her shoulders. She fingered the empty mug, wishing for more to appear so she could wash the words away. "I donnae ken what love means. Not that kind of love."

"What kind of love do you know then?"

Yesenia smiled as she remembered the way the seafoam crested into the cove…how the spray of salt and sand lingered upon her cheeks when she stood high on the cliffs. "Home. My father. My brothers. Aye, even my cow of an aunt. Salt and sand, and everything and everyone in between."

"I'd like to see it someday."

Yesenia waved her arm at him. "Will never happen."

"You wouldn't want me there."

"*They* wouldn't want you there," Yesenia countered.

"You still don't trust me, do you?"

Yesenia didn't know how to answer his question.

"Well, I trust *you*, Yesenia. Maybe I shouldn't." He buried a belch into the crook of his elbow. His words slurred more now. "But I do. In spite of you. Because of you. I trust you, and I'm going to prove it by telling you something no one else knows."

Yesenia tossed her head back and forth. The motion made her ill. She tried to tell him not to do it, but she had to stop and fight back the upending sensation washing over her.

She remembered then that she had stew in front of her, untouched. His had grown cold as well.

"Venya's adoptive family are magic practicers. I've helped them keep this secret for years," he said, in what he must have believed was a whisper.

She tapped her hand against the air, motioning for him to lower his voice.

He winced and spoke lower. "They're healers."

"Stop talking," she replied.

"Why? You won't speak a word of this to anyone."

"You *cannae* know that."

"But I do," he said. "I know you. And I know that when I tell you that if anyone finds this out they'd be executed for the illegal use of magic, you'll take the secret to the end of your promise."

"*Corin*," she warned. "You're drunk. I'll pretend you didnae just admit conspiracy to treason."

"They can't afford an education at the Consortium of the Sepulchre in the Skies, Yesenia. They can hardly afford to keep the tavern running and the children fed. They aren't the only ones either. What are people who cannot afford to go supposed to do? There's no other way to obtain permission to practice magic. The Sepulchre makes no concessions for poverty. So tell me, what are they supposed to do?"

"Why are you telling me this?" She looked around to be sure they were still alone, that Corin's admirers hadn't slipped in unnoticed. "Why, if you've kept this secret so long, would ye tell me, a Warwick?"

"My *wife*," he said.

She breathed out. "Corin, donnae be a fool."

"Why am I telling you?" He repeated her earlier question back to her. "Look in my eyes, Sen. See the real me, as I see the real you." He gestured behind him. "These are your people too. It matters not whether they pay taxes to the Southerlands or the Easterlands, their plight is the same. Your love of them is the same, as mine is."

She hadn't missed his slip when he called her Sen, but it was at the bottom of her concerns. "Should I find Mara? Get some more ale?"

"If something happens to me, you have to promise."

"What? Why would something happen to you?"

"*Promise* me, you won't let them starve. You'll find a way to continue this."

Her heart raced in fear of the way he spoke the words, as if he'd seen a future she hadn't. "You're speaking nonsense."

"You know I'm not."

"Of course I'd…Guardians, Corin. Nothing will happen to you! You ken I'd let it?"

He closed his eyes, swaying toward the table. "You might hate my family, Yesenia. But I don't think you hate me anymore."

Yesenia sighed. She pushed his stew closer to him, jiggling the spoon. "Of course I donnae hate ye, you fool."

He opened his eyes with a slow blink. "You'll come with me here again? Next time?"

Yesenia nodded with a light shrug. "I did promise the boy, anyway. Tristan."

"Good." He closed his eyes again with a drunken smile. "And yes to more ale."

FIFTEEN

A CHALLENGE OF HONOR

Chasten and Aiden waited on the lower veranda at Arboriana, sitting atop plush divans, sheltered from the light rain by the bowing fingers of an old willow.

Corin spotted them before Yesenia did.

It was habit to play up the expected affection between them, but her laughter, this time, was real. The way she fell upon his arm as she recounted the night's events might have been born from the pitchers of ale they'd shared, but it had become something more, something he feared would disappear with the clarity of morning.

Corin shelved the worry for later. His father and brother weren't merely socializing, not at this hour.

"Where have the two of you been off to?" Aiden asked, rising. Chasten remained in his seat, his face impassive.

Yesenia was quick—quicker than he could ever be. She pressed her lips to Corin's neck with a soft, girlish moan. "Your brother took me to the forest, plied me with ale." She tilted her head forward to kiss his chin. "Plied me with something else too."

163

Aiden puffed up in response. Chasten betrayed nothing of what he was thinking.

"Only whores act in such a way." Aiden seethed, pushing the words through his teeth.

Yesenia's playful smile faded. "Ahh, and what does that make you, slinking about in the woods, using your strongman to hold me down and *still* not getting any?"

Corin's protective arm at her back wasn't an act. "He knows what he is. Let's go on to bed."

"Yesenia can go on to bed," Chasten said evenly. "I'd like you to stay."

Yesenia passed Corin a worried look. He nodded to reassure her that it was fine, knowing she'd see right through him.

Her eyes were on the other men as she kissed Corin, lingering to whisper, close to his ear, "If you're not up in fifteen minutes, I'm coming back."

She feigned a smile at Chasten and Aiden and sauntered past them, toward the Golden Stair.

"She's written nothing. Said nothing." Chasten at last stood. "You warned her."

"I didn't," Corin insisted. His relief mingled with confusion. Why *hadn't* she used it? "I don't know why she hasn't used the code."

"Yes, you do." Chasten stepped down from the veranda. The edges of his robe brushed the marble, creating a trail of red satin. "And before you waste breath lying to me, let us understand, son, that you'll never convince me you didn't warn her, directly or otherwise. So we'll move on from that, and you'll give me something else, because our king, our ally? He is no doubt by now wondering if we've been influenced by traitors and turned coat ourselves."

"Something else…but there…there *isn't* anything else." Corin's desperation rose in time with the menacing look growing on his father's shadowed face. "She'd never tell any Quinlanden anything that could harm her family. Not even me."

"The two of you spend your days with your tongues rammed down each other's throats," Aiden said. "You expect us to believe you can win her over like that and she tells you nothing? Nothing at all?"

"I don't expect anything from you, Aiden, ever," Corin retorted. Fury flashed in his eyes as the ale wore off. His anger spread over the pleasant drunkenness that had laid a soft hand over the evening.

Aiden groaned, rolling his eyes toward his father. "I told you, he'll never be strong enough for this. He's too soft. She only tolerates him because he's pretty, like a woman."

"Or because he's kind," Chasten stated, but there was no compliment in his words. Tension choked the air.

Aiden snorted. "Women like *that*—"

"You know *nothing* about a woman like Yesenia Warwick," Corin hissed, a touch of his earlier courage still lingering. "And you never will."

Aiden exchanged a knowing look with Chasten. "You see? Now can we try it my way?"

"And by your way, Aiden, do you mean having Mads do what you cannot on your own?" Corin asked.

"Perhaps," Chasten said. It was unclear which brother he'd responded to. "From where I sit, neither a rough hand nor a soft one has broken her. Will this really become my burden? Have *both* my sons failed me?"

Aiden glowered from the top step. "To be fair, Father, we don't *know* if a rough hand will break her, because I never got to see it through."

"You mean she bested you," Corin said to remind him.

"I mean—"

"Enough," Chasten said, his tone gradually firming. "Corin, I will give you one chance, and one only, to tell me something that would be of interest to the king. Anything. If you cannot, then I am forced to assume that either your loyalties have shifted to favor our enemy or you are simply inept in your duties. Neither outcome will be favorable for you, or her." He took another step closer, blocking Aiden from Corin's view. "It's no crime to care for your wife. I love your mother. I married for love, a Skylark as you know, which was not the marriage my father would have made for me. Even his threat of disowning me was not enough to sway me from her."

"That's not true," Aiden replied. "Why are you trying to make him feel better with lies?"

Chasten swelled, inhaling. He ignored Aiden. "But my father didn't disown me, and do you know why?"

Corin shook his head.

"Because he saw that love had not changed me. That I was still the son of a lord, and I knew my duties. Your mother loved me no less when I was forced to share with my father how her father's bookkeeping failed to include rents from over a hundred farms. She loved me all the more when I used what she told me about her brother, guilty of a similar crime. Are you understanding this?"

Corin sighed, crossing his arms. He tried to nod, but he thought only of Yesenia counting the minutes. If she returned here, with her blades…

"Your love for your wife exists separately of your love for your Reach. A good wife understands this. If you love her—"

Aiden gagged.

"If you love her," Chasten continued, "then you can protect her. But you cannot protect her *and* her family, Corin. I swear to you that I'll never let any harm come to Yesenia if she becomes an informant for us, just as I never let the Skylarks come near your mother. I won't let Aiden touch her. I'll leave you alone to live as you choose. I might even gift the two of you with your own land." He reached forward and brushed a blond hair from Corin's eye.

Corin nearly screamed.

"*Do* you love her?"

Corin's voice broke. "Yes."

"Then give me something I can use, and I will spare her otherwise inevitable agony. Give me something, and I will keep Aiden from going to your apartments, right now, and taking what we need."

Corin's knees turned to jelly. He couldn't count on Yesenia being able to fend Aiden off forever. Eventually, he would find his way through her barriers. Eventually, he might even break her.

The problem was Corin had nothing *to* give his father. He'd never asked her anything. He didn't want Yesenia to tell him something that might put him in a situation like this one. It was Corin who had overshared. Who had—

He looked up. He did have something, something that would bring no harm to Yesenia or her father but might satisfy Chasten. It might even earn Yesenia the annulment she still seemed to want so desperately…even if his own desire for it had waned in potency.

"There is one thing," he said, swallowing and standing taller. He kept one eye on the Golden Stair beyond Aiden, in case he saw her come down. "She came to this marriage already…" Even if Yesenia wouldn't care, he refused to use words his brother would. "She was not a virgin bride."

Aiden cackled. "Are any of the Southerland girls?"

Chasten held a hand to his side, silencing his oldest son. "Are you certain?"

"She told me herself."

Chasten's slow exhale was worrying. He turned his head to the side in thought, a slow smile spreading across his face. "This is more important than you know."

Corin pressed his tongue to the roof of his mouth to suppress his panic. "Oh?"

"Your brother might be right about Southerland women, but daughters of lords are held to higher standards, even there. The king asked all the lords that day in the tent if their daughters were intact."

Corin cringed at the word intact.

"Khoulter Warwick said yes. It won't be enough to annul the marriage, nor would I dare suggest that to our king, but it may be enough for something else."

167

"For what?" Corin asked, trying in desperation to not sound how he felt.

"How Khoulter is dealt with will be up to King Khain, won't it?"

Aiden jumped down both steps with a sly look. "*Now* can we call her a whore, Father?"

It happened so fast. Corin didn't recall rolling his arm back, only his fist landing squarely on the side of his brother's jaw. He got a second punch in before Aiden recovered himself, but Chasten was quicker.

"*Corin*! What's gotten into you?" Chasten pushed him back, off the path. "Remember yourself!"

Aiden opened his mouth, flexing his jaw. The blood pooling on his tongue glistened in the moonlight as he spat out, "He knows exactly who he is, Father. Why can't you see it?"

"There's no competition you wouldn't win. Let that be enough," Chasten warned him. "Corin—"

Corin recoiled, stumbling back into the edge of the garden as he shook his already-swelling hand.

"Competition," Aiden said. He licked the blood from his lips. "You're right. That's what we'll do."

Chasten and Corin both whipped their head at him.

"Tomorrow," Aiden said. He lifted the hem of his vestments and backed up the stairs. "Under Easterland law, I am challenging Corin to combat."

"No," Chasten said. "Absolutely not."

"Oh, yes," Aiden pressed. "I am *entitled* to this, as the aggrieved. And you are forbidden from stopping me, under the same law." He looked past his father, at Corin. "Who will be your second?"

"Me," Chasten said through clenched teeth.

Aiden was aghast. "Father?"

"If you would bring shame to this family by challenging your own brother to exchange blows, like field hands, then yes. I will stand with Corin."

Aiden shook his head in disbelief. "*He* attacked *me*!"

168

"And are you a man, who lets that go, or a child, who wants more?"

Aiden backed closer to the entrance. "You'll both find out what I am tomorrow."

"You don't have to do this, Father," Corin said when Aiden was gone. He was only half present now, his thoughts still reeling from how suddenly everything had shifted. "I can find my own second."

"He's acting like a bloodlusted fool. If he blunders into the challenge like this, he'll kill you, and his regret will come far too late," Chasten said blandly. "But you'll cry mercy before he does. You understand?"

"You'd let him win?"

"No. *You'll* let him win. He's not wrong, after all. You *did* hit him." He clapped a quick hand on Corin's shoulder. "He shouldn't have called her a whore, because she's your wife now, and we don't speak of our kin like that. But he wasn't wrong, son. Her behavior before coming here was untenable for an unwed girl. And while I have promised not to harm her, and you can count on me being a man of my word, I cannot speak for what the king will do when he discovers she came to this marriage under deception."

Yesenia slammed her hand against the bureau before he could finish speaking. "*No*, Corin. You cannae do it."

"I have to," Corin answered with a helpless sigh.

"He wants a lawful excuse to kill you, and you've just given it to him."

"He doesn't want me dead, Yesenia. He just wants to humiliate me."

Yesenia thrust a bucket of cold water at him, left by one of the attendants. "That'll be twice the size tomorrow, if you donnae tend to it."

Corin regarded his fist in surprise. "I've never hit a man before."

"Chose the wrong one to start with." She paced the far end of the bedchamber. She wanted him to think she was angry at him, but he'd learned to read her better, and what he saw in her tense shoulders and the occasional twitch of her jaw was fear.

"I don't have a choice here. He challenged me. The law prevents me from refusing." Corin sank his hand into the cool water. It sent a stabbing ache straight to his head but slowly numbed.

Whatever happened to him tomorrow would not be so easily soothed.

"Fine," she said. She held her arms out. "Then I'll be your second."

"You can't."

"I can, and I will."

He shook his head. "I don't make the rules, Yesenia."

"Aye, ye just break them?" She turned toward the perch. "Tell me what he said…what he said that caused ye to be so foolish."

"It doesn't matter." Corin swished his hand in the water, which was already warming. He felt the pulse in his finger joints. No weapons were allowed during a Challenge of Honor, only whatever skills and limbs the Guardians had given a man. If his dominant hand didn't heal overnight…

"Of course it matters!" She swatted at the gauzy curtain. "You never used to so much as look at either of them wrong, and now you've gone and hit yer brother, for something he said? Aye, well I wanna know, and you're going to tell me."

Corin sometimes wondered if Yesenia Warwick was harboring some magic of her own, for she always saw through to the truth of a matter. But would she want this truth? Even as vulnerable as she'd been earlier that night, she relied on her own strength to guide her.

"Tell me," she commanded. "Or I'll go ask Aiden myself."

"Don't," Corin said quickly. "Don't go anywhere near him."

"Why?" She narrowed her eyes, as if sensing she'd pinned him closer to confession.

"It's not…" Corin pointed at his head. "I was drunk. I reacted to something stupid he said. He always says stupid stuff. I let him bait and hook me, like a fish."

"No," Yesenia replied, drawing the word out. "No, Corin. You donnae want me to know is the truth of it. The question is why."

"Maybe if you weren't so damned pigheaded about letting others stand at your side!" He didn't know where the accusation had come from, only that he meant it, wouldn't take it back. "We *know* you're strong, Yesenia. Everyone knows! But it doesn't mean you can't ever accept help from someone who cares about you."

"You mean you?" Her eyes were steel, but her mouth twitched.

"*Yes*, I mean me."

"You want to stand at my side? Then tell me what was said."

Corin shoved the bucket to the floor and stood. "You already know. He said it before you went upstairs."

"Aye, called me a whore again, did he?" Yesenia laughed.

"It's not funny," Corin replied. "And it was less funny the second time he said it. *How* he said it."

"I donnae care what Aiden Quinlanden thinks of me. Nor should you."

"He can *think* as he pleases." Corin's hand throbbed, but he didn't return it to the water. If not for what he would face tomorrow, he'd prefer it this way, swollen and bruised, reminding him he didn't have to always cow to his brother and father. That he could be more than their whipping boy. "But he cannot speak about you that way."

Her grin froze. "Donnae want another man speaking of your possessions so?"

"Stop ascribing things to me that you *know* are not true!" Corin boomed, kicking the tin of water by accident. "Guardians' sake, Yesenia, you know better. You know that's not how I am. Not *who* I am."

Yesenia crossed her arms and spun away.

"Is it so hard for you, to accept kindness from another?"

"Kindness is punching a man in the face?"

"You twist my words," Corin answered. "And in doing so, you wound me."

"You are far too easily wounded, Corin. It's your greatest weakness." Her earlier fire had died. She moved her head to the side, one eye regarding him over her shoulder. "I would mourn you if you died tomorrow. So you cannae, ye ken?"

Corin nearly laughed. It was the closest she might ever come to saying she cared too. "Father is my second. He won't let that happen."

"Or," Yesenia said, again facing him. "He assumed this role so he could be certain it does."

"He's still my father, you know. He's not a good man, and he has little use for me, but he doesn't want me *dead*."

"Aye, and how certain of that are you? Enough to go down there tomorrow without a plan?"

Corin threw out his hands. "What, then, do you recommend?"

Yesenia's gaze scorched him, but for once, it didn't compel him to turn away. He bathed in it, inviting more of the same, and when she saw he wasn't afraid of her, she softened.

"We could run away," she said.

Corin choked on his laughter. "And go where? Where in this kingdom would they not find us?" he asked. "Who would ever go against Lord Quinlanden of the Easterlands and his best mate, the king?"

"You introduced me tonight to dozens who would."

"I'd never put them in such a position. My father would raze Slattery Row without another thought."

"My point was only that such men do exist."

Corin brought his swollen fist to his chest, nursing it there. "But I could never face them again if I ran from my duty. My honor."

Yesenia sighed. "There's no honor in this, Corin. 'Tis only heartache."

172

"Maybe," he said in agreement. He lowered his eyes toward where he knew, beyond the heavy fabric of her dress, her daggers were strapped. "If he does kill me—"

"No."

"If he does," Corin said, more insistent, "you take Kheerai, and you run. Don't wait for the final blow either, Yesenia."

"This is madness! Are you listening to yourself?"

"Don't wait for him to fell me, or it will be too late. Be ahead of it, so you'll already be long gone before they send the men after you."

Yesenia listened halfheartedly as Mariana explained to her the sordid history of challenges in Whitechurch and the rules of the present challenge. She forced herself to pay mind to the rules and filtered out the rest.

The rules were simple.

No weapons.

No magic.

No poisons or underhanded methods.

The fight ended when someone cried mercy or someone died.

Any last hope she still harbored that they'd call it off disappeared when she watched half of Whitechurch stream through the courtyard of Arboriana at the base of the hill.

Yesenia allowed her mind to wander when Mariana's words did. She feigned greater interest in the view at the top of the hill, from which she could almost see the cresting waves of the White Sea. That same water lapped upon Southerland shores. It was enough to make her sick for home all over again, if she wasn't already sick about something else.

This was real.

This was happening.

This was not some drunken bloodsport in the town square. It was the only two sons of the Lord of the Easterlands fighting to what would likely mean the death of one. She already knew which side Chasten was on, but did Mariana know what was at stake? Was that the explanation for her hasty rambling, leaving no space for response?

Yesenia was awake when they had come for Corin, before the sun had even risen. She watched from the bedchamber door as they escorted him out, and their eyes met; anticipation lived in his, like he expected a confession from her, something fit for the finality of the day.

She had given him nothing but a nod. Anything else would be surrendering to what others believed inevitable.

"Look at them all. Like ants, swarming over discarded food," Maeryn remarked. She looked lovely in her emerald gown. Despite the disgust in her words, she wore the unaffected look that Yesenia had come to know her by.

"There hasn't been a Quinlanden on this hill for over a hundred years," Mariana mused, a whimsical note to her voice. "You might say most residents have waited their entire lifetime for this."

"Waited for it? Like it's an entitlement?" Yesenia shifted from one foot to the other as her anxiousness swelled. Where was Corin? And Aiden? Mariana said they'd fight upon this very hill, under the ancient sycamore that shaded half the courtyard. And where was Chasten?

"Well. It's not an average day when two Quinlandens meet in challenge. Even the last time, it was only one, challenging a Sylvaine."

"Who won?" Maeryn asked dryly.

"The Quinlanden, of course."

"What's your prediction for today, Lady Quinlanden?"

Mariana, flustered, adjusted her shawl. "I wouldn't deign to put words to it."

Yesenia squinted at the shift of the clouds when it released the glare of the sun upon the crowd. She scanned the faces, but there was no sign of the Quinlanden men until a hush fell over the onlookers.

Everyone shifted their eyes to the west, where Chasten and that wastrel Mads Waters carved their way down the path and up the hill. When they began their upward crest, Yesenia at last caught sight of Aiden and Corin, behind the men chosen as their seconds. They both wore their ceremonial vestments, not remotely fit for fighting. From their faces, Aiden was proud, beaming; Corin's eyes were low, defeated. The end had already been decided. A din of speculation passed through the crowd.

"It will be fine," Mariana assured them.

"Aiden will kill him," Maeryn said. "But I suppose that solves one problem for the Easterlands, doesn't it?"

"Not for you though, aye?" Yesenia replied. "Not that it would make a lick of difference. He's never so much as glanced your way, has he?"

"I don't know what you mean, Yesenia. I have my own husband to be concerned with."

"Sorry, dear, what was that?" Mariana's face froze as it followed the small train of men.

Maeryn's eyes flitted toward Yesenia.

Yesenia refused to meet them. She didn't need to know Maeryn's intentions to know there was trouble behind them.

"It's really too bad they don't allow weapons, isn't it? I understand you've turned Corin into a proper man out there in the woods."

"You understand far less than you think ye do." Yesenia's hands turned to loose fists. The men were almost there.

"Hush," Mariana chided. "Chasten will speak now."

"Great people of Whitechurch!" Chasten called to the gathered, his arms wide in a messianic gesticulation. "Our challenge today is unlike any the Reach has ever seen. Both my sons, my only sons, will raise their fists in an effort to right what has been wronged between them. But the law is the law." Chasten's arms returned to his sides. "And let it not ever be said that Chasten's sons were above it."

175

Yesenia stepped away from the women to see better. Maeryn made a derisive, slighted scoff.

Corin and Aiden tossed their outer vestments to the tall grass. What they wore beneath wasn't any more practical, only slightly less trussed than the women. Mads took his place behind Aiden, and Chasten behind Corin.

"You know the rules. Death or surrender. Only the Guardians know the outcome," Chasten said, for those standing at the hilltop.

Yesenia inhaled through her nose. Her fists squeezed tighter.

"On my count, you may begin. Three."

Aiden squared his stance. Corin stood straighter, his strategy less clear.

"Two."

Yesenia lowered her head to her arm to dab at the sweat already taking over her cheeks and forehead.

"One. And begin!"

Yesenia gasped, along with everyone else, when Corin struck the first blow. Aiden's head flew back as Corin's fist landed just to the left of his nose, but he recovered quickly, too quickly for Corin, who was sent flying into Chasten's arms by Aiden's side kick.

"Come on, Corin," Yesenia whispered. She put more distance between herself and the women. She ticked her nerves off down her fingers, tapping the rhythm of her fears into her triceps.

Corin bounced back in time to field a double blow from Aiden. He dodged the third, but the blood pooling at his hairline, falling into his eyes, allowed Aiden to come in for an uppercut that flipped Corin onto his back.

"Oh, Corin," Mariana said and repeated his name over and over. Maeryn glared at her mother-in-law, but the woman's practiced indifference had a crack in it, worry creeping in at the corners of her eyes and mouth.

Aiden closed in and fell upon Corin, but the crowd gasped once more when Corin recoiled his feet and launched them into

Aiden. It was Aiden's turn to regain himself, but Corin didn't move from the ground.

Yesenia leaned in and saw blood not just at the edges of his mouth, but inside.

No, no, no, no, no.

Aiden's cocked head suggested he saw it too; he observed the opportunity to finish the fight. This time when he came down on Corin, all that could be seen were his elbows flying left and right as he pummeled Corin.

"Call it!" Chasten cried out. "Corin, for the love of the Guardians, call it!"

But Corin couldn't call it. Corin was no longer conscious, and Aiden wasn't stopping.

Yesenia's chest seized with her sense of time, everything falling to a crashing halt at once. Her eyes took inventory of what her mind was still assimilating. The bloodied frenzy upon Aiden's face confirmed what she'd known from the start. Chasten's expression, dazed but confident, was a poor match for the words he'd be remembered for when they hoisted Corin's body upon the pyre in remembrance.

Yesenia was not fully aware of herself as she dropped to her knees. As first one hand, then the other slid up her left thigh, only to retreat again.

No weapons. You donnae know the consequence if you draw them.

She became more aware of herself when she noted her choice of gown for the day. Soft and loose, no unwieldy ribbons or stays. She shrugged it down off her shoulders and tugged it over her waist. It fell to the ground, and she stepped out of it. Her tunic was light—and freeing.

Yesenia felt Maeryn turn right as she was again rising, moving, *flying* toward the two men.

Chasten caught her in his peripheral moments before she rolled her chest downward, bounced her palms off the hard earth, and spun her legs upward. Aiden cried out, whipped back by the force of her boots on either side of his neck. She snapped away, landing right as he fell back into the grass.

He struggled to sit, to catch up to the sudden violent shift in the fight, which gave Yesenia the time needed to drop her boot down onto his neck.

Aiden sputtered, flailing. She ground her heel deeper, aware of the others closing in on them.

Yesenia held both of her hands out, turning her head between Chasten and the guards, and even blubbering Mads.

"Anyone comes closer and I relieve his body of a head!"

Chasten stuttered to a halt. He shot urgent nods at the others to do the same.

"Yesenia, this is not the way." Chasten spoke slowly, like she were a child. "The fight will end soon."

"It's already ended," she stated, seething. With a glower, she added "*mercy.*"

"Only one of the fighters can declare mercy," Chasten answered.

"Aye? Well, how ye ken he's gonna do that when he's not even *breathing?*" The urge to cry was sudden, powerful. Inexplicable. She raised her head, her voice with it, and called, "As lord and father, you can stop this! If you donnae…if you let this go on, then you confess before all gathered that you allowed one son to be murdered by another! That you *endorsed* it."

The dark pall that fell over the crowd, who had only moments ago been caught in the fever pitch of the fraternal feuding, shifted Chasten's confident gaze to a panicked one. Someone from the back yelled it out first—"Mercy!"—and then others joined in. It became a chant, and Yesenia joined in, crying the word louder than anyone as she pumped her fists toward the sky. Her breath briefly caught at the sound of both Mariana and Maeryn joining in.

Aiden stopped wriggling under her boot. Yesenia met Chasten's eyes, and the look he returned chilled her. *You won, girl. But at what cost?*

Chasten nodded. He raised his hand, drawing the crowd to silence.

"As Corin's second, I declare mercy on his behalf!"

Thundering applause greeted the announcement. Yesenia dared not look at Corin, who had yet to move.

"Step off my son," Chasten commanded.

Yesenia only half heard him. Her pulse pounded in her ears, her eyes. Her mouth was so hot, she was afraid to swallow, for fear of ingesting fire. She could only think in the moment, the second.

"Step. Off. My. Son."

Yesenia removed her leg. She hobbled backward, returning to the moment, to herself. She finally allowed her eyes to shift toward Corin. He lay as if dead. He might be dead. She dared not think it. She dared not chase the sorrow that followed such a promise.

The ground threatened to rise. She swayed at the surge of blood to her head. She was vaguely aware of Chasten kneeling to tend to Aiden, and she wondered, fleetingly, if she'd gone too far, but she didn't care. Aiden was a monster, and if she'd vanquished him, well, there could be worse legacies.

Yesenia dropped to the ground beside Corin. She was afraid to reach down, to confirm, one way or another, a truth that would decide her next move.

Before she could, Corin's chest lifted, shuddering, and fell. He sputtered a mouthful of blood and groaned.

She coiled back to attack when a shadow fell over them, but it was only Maeryn. Yesenia had only the first of the two words out—*leave us*—when she noted the tears rolling down Maeryn's cheeks.

"Help me, then," Yesenia barked. "We need to get him to the apartments."

Maeryn's eyes widened. She nodded. Yesenia all but read her thoughts. *We'll never get him so far on our own*, but Maeryn was wrong. Yesenia would drag him to the Southerlands before she stopped for breath. Alone if she had to.

No one joined them. No one stopped them. She and Maeryn each took a side, slipping their arms behind him and draping his limp ones over their shoulders. His feet dragged the tall grass until he regained a glimpse of consciousness, but it didn't last.

While everyone else was drawn to Chasten and Aiden, Yesenia and Maeryn dragged Corin down the hill.

Corin blinked the bedchamber in and out of focus over the space of several hours. With every shutter of his eyes, something in the background shifted.

Yesenia, at his bedside, muttering to herself while she dressed his wounds.

Yesenia, arms crossed, pacing between the curtains of the perch.

Chambermaids, refreshing basins of water with fearful peeks in Yesenia's direction.

He attempted, with each flutter of wakefulness, to speak. Nothing emerged, not from his chest, nor his throat, which felt wedged with wool. His lips bore the memory of Yesenia's failed attempts to feed him cool stream water but none of the relief.

Corin pushed himself into longer spells of consciousness. Trying to sit was a mistake he regretted immensely, but it drew Yesenia's attention—who was, once more, pacing the perch entrance—and she was at his side before he could settle back into a less painful repose.

"You're alive," she accused.

The iciness of her delivery startled him into a laugh, which turned into a regretful groan.

"You surprised or disappointed? Or both. Can't tell."

"I told ye what would happen."

"Never said you were wrong." Corin rolled to his back, scrunching his face as he searched for a way to rest that wasn't excruciating.

"Ye wanted him to kill you? That it?"

"That a serious question?"

Yesenia dropped onto the opposite edge of the bed. "I've been thinking, about your girl. Venya, was it?"

Corin was too taken aback at hearing her name to nod or respond.

"Aye, well, ye didnae say how she died, but I have a guess. Will ye humor it?"

Corin blinked in place of a nod.

"It happened here, you said. I expect ye got careless. But it wasnae *your* hands that saw it done. I know who did it, same as you do. I willnae say his name here. Will only give him more power he doesnae deserve. But you going to join your lass?" Yesenia shook her head. "Isnae gonna happen. Neither is you feeling all sore about yourself, or about the last seventeen years of your life, living among snakes."

Her words gave him pause. Had that been his intention? That he couldn't answer quickly was answer enough. "Careless, yes," he said, the pain keeping him from complete sentences. "Never with you."

Yesenia fidgeted with her hands. "I willnae say again that I donnae *need* you to defend me, Corin. Nor do I want it." She lowered her head with a sideways look at him. "But I ken the sacrifice ye made to do it."

"And I…" Corin struggled with the words, but he needed to say them. "Don't need your permission to defend my own wife."

Yesenia's scowl erupted into a grin. "I do like ye better not so agreeable."

"I'm worried," he said. "No one has ever…" Corin groaned. "Challenged Aiden like you did. Certainly no woman."

Yesenia lifted one shoulder. "He'll try to kill me next, no doubt. Doesnae mean he'll succeed."

"Even trying—"

"It's fine," she said. "I'm fine." Her eyes lowered with her last two words. He noted it.

"I don't think you should leave this room alone anymore."

Yesenia laughed. "What, for all time? Or just until I ken a way out of this marriage?"

That hit him harder than he was ready for. "That's still what you want?"

"'Tis not what you want?"

"Yeah. Of course. Of course it is."

She turned away again. He wished she hadn't, so he could read the effect of their exchange in her eyes, discern the truth. It might even help him unlock his own, which was more confusing than it had ever been.

"If you can just help me stand," Corin said. "I can make my way to the settee."

"You'll stay in that bed," Yesenia snapped. "With the door locked."

"You're going to take the settee?"

"I'll be right here," she said, then whipped her eyes toward the open doors of the perch. "Cannae trust your own kin not to sneak in an assassin to finish what your brother started."

"He won't. Not after the way it ended."

"He may not want his name on it," she said, sighing. "But that isnae the same as not wanting it done. Now rest, Corin."

"You need rest too, Yesenia."

"Aye," she said. "Eventually."

SIXTEEN

THE PRINCE WHO HAD PROSPERED

Yesenia unrolled the squashed letter that had been read by an untold number of eyes before finally being delivered to their apartments. She expected another weak-minded gushing from Khallum about his newly wedded bliss, or a to-the-point hello from her father.

Instead, she finally got what she'd wanted all along.

A letter from Byrne.

> *Dearest Sister,*
>
> *I know you are cross with me for my failure to write. It's not for any lack of thinking about you, which I do often and with great fondness. There are many things I miss about the Southerlands, but none so much as you.*
>
> *Do not let my delay speak in place of my words. Though, I cannot help but point out that you have not written to me either, Sen.*
>
> *It has taken me this long to find the words that you will not wish to hear, no matter how I choose to say them. But here they are, just the same. I am happy in the Westerlands. It's very*

different from what we know, but Asherley is kind, and the people of Longwood Rush, and the Reach, are loyal and passionate. They love lord and land equally and have welcomed me beyond what I could have ever imagined.

All you have ever wanted for me is to be well. While this may not be the way you saw this happening, that I am happy should be enough. I hope that it is. There has never been anyone whose opinion ever held more weight for me than yours. Fear of it has been the cause of my delay.

Despite all of that, I have not forgotten our last conversation before we both left for our new lives.

I have not forgotten all your sacrifices, for me.

I have not forgotten that I might not even be here, if not for you.

If you say the word, you know where my loyalty lies.

My greatest hope for you is that you've reached a place of contentment of your own. That the urge to reach for your daggers has eased. That maybe, even, you have discovered happiness of your own.

If not, I am ever your most loyal brother, in all things, until the very end.

In salt and sand,
Byrne

Yesenia swung her head away from the letter, now stained with the tears she'd not been quick enough to stay. *Of course* she wanted him to be happy! How could he even suggest…

She rocked to her feet. Byrne, content with a life in the Westerlands? It wasn't the Easterlands, true, and the alliance between the Southerlands and the Blackwoods of Longwood Rush was stronger than any other in the kingdom. Their greens and legumes kept disease away from the miners of the Southerland Peninsula. There was no enmity there.

But Byrne was a *Southerlander*—salt and sand through and through, even if he had been a late bloomer. Lovely that he had a wife he could stomach, but how could that ever compare to the life he *should* have had, with a bride of the Southern Reach? With a Rutland, or a Law, or, Guardians, even a *Garrick* would have been a better choice for a man born to a Warwick lord!

How was it that both of her brothers had fallen so easily into foreign marriages, and she, the only daughter, was the one still trying to preserve the sanctity of their Reach? The only one who hadn't forgotten who she was…and that the man who had ordered these unions was the same one stealing from them and giving to their enemy. An enemy Yesenia was living with.

But that word…enemy. It no longer felt so potent when she thought of Corin. The Guardians were said to not make mistakes, but they had, in placing him with this family. He would have been more at home in the Westerlands, among the Blackwoods. He trusted too easily. Bowed even easier. In her experience, he was someone to watch, to be wary of, but he simply didn't have the cunning his brother and father were born with. Who he showed himself to be was who he was.

In the beginning, this had made her cautious. Now, it only angered her. His flippant disregard for himself, for his *life*, had almost got him killed, and one day would. Yesenia wouldn't always be there to save him from himself. And did she want to be? *I want to go home. I want to be with my own people,* she told herself, constantly, hourly, daily, but then she'd find herself thinking of the future here and her role in it.

She didn't want to be married to Corin Quinlanden. She *knew* this was true. It must be.

But she didn't want him to die either.

Yesenia tried to set her brother's words aside as she waited in tense impatience for Corin to be escorted back to the apartments, safe.

They'd allowed Corin to choose his own guards. It was an empty gesture, as Yesenia had been quick to point out, for though they had *some* loyalty to him, it would never be as great as their loyalty to their lord.

Yesenia hadn't wanted him to go to the meeting at all. Said he'd be walking into a trap. Corin couldn't disagree. But since the day of the fight, Whitechurch had been buzzing about nothing else. Their prior desire to see the blood between brothers erupt had turned to concern for the one who'd almost died. They deified the benevolent, loving lord who had cried mercy on his son's behalf, showing that fatherhood could be both a strength and a weakness.

The people didn't know *what* to think of Yesenia. The reception was mixed. She was either a wildling saltlicker requiring a firm hand or a loyal wife who had risked everything for the man she loved.

The Easterlanders, above all, loved a good story.

All these things conspired to help Corin, which was such an unusual phenomenon for him that he didn't know how to use it to his advantage. He was the Prince Who Had Prospered, the son half of them had forgotten existed at all until standing witness to his near death at the hands of the more important one.

All this bought his safety. For now.

"Thank you for coming," Chasten said. They sat outside in the courtyard, where they could be seen. Even a private call for peace was theater for a Quinlanden.

Aiden wore a wrap around his neck to hide the purplish-black bruise left by Yesenia's boot. The healer sent to both brothers' chambers had perhaps forgotten to tend to it, but Corin thought it more likely that Aiden wanted it left alone, so everyone would remember Yesenia's crimes against the Easterland heir.

Aiden seemed to have something to say but held his silence.

"Did I have a choice?" Corin asked. "It didn't seem so." Despite Yesenia's care of him, and the healer's fastidious work, the trek down the Golden Stair had still been arduous.

"We are at an impasse, after what happened that day."

186

"That day." Corin coughed, following it with a short laugh. "As if it were years ago."

"Much has happened since. Time has passed differently," Chasten replied. "Tomorrow will be a week. Neither one of you has spoken to each other. Broken bread together. You have not left your apartments at the same times, nor have your wives. I had to cancel the Autumnwhile Jubilee for the first time in…I do not even know if it's ever been canceled before. This cannot go on."

"I agree, Father," Aiden said. "Corin's beast of a wife should be banished, so Arboriana can return to as it was."

"That is not an option available to us," Chasten said evenly. "The way forward is bricked with peace, and I would like both of your help to pave it."

A scornful sound from Aiden carried across the table. "There can be no peace as long as that trollop lives in our trees."

Corin cocked his head. "I didn't realize we had any trollops living in our trees."

"You have always been rather *slow*."

"Perhaps," Chasten stated, interjecting, "that may be a problem that will solve itself, once the king reads my raven. But for now—"

"What raven?" Corin demanded.

"I did tell you the king would be interested in hearing that Lord Warwick lied about his daughter's history."

"Why…" Corin scoffed. "Why does that even matter? Who cares if she was not a virgin? Aiden was not."

"You were," Aiden replied.

"I was," Corin said, unashamed. "And I was proud to give that gift to Yesenia."

"Do you listen to yourself? Do you ever think before you say stupid things?"

"The king had a goal. An intent. He would have married Yesenia into one of the houses no matter her past deeds or experiences."

"That is rather beside the point though," Chasten said. "Lord Warwick chose to lie about it. The king needs to know when his subjects are practicing deception."

"Deception!" Corin exclaimed. "Maybe Lord Warwick didn't know. I'd like to think he didn't, for a man so invested in his own daughter's sexual habits is unnatural."

"I was well aware of every last thing Gretchen did, under this roof or no, and there was *nothing* unnatural about that interest."

"Everything?" Corin countered with a hard glare at Aiden.

Aiden shifted his eyes away.

"Remember the fine line we discussed," Chasten said after an uncomfortable silence, "between caring for your wife and serving your Reach. Be grateful you can do both with this revelation you've given me. It isn't Yesenia who will be punished for lying to the king, after all."

"Her father deserves no punishment," Corin said. "He's done nothing wrong."

"That will be for King Khain to decide, won't it?"

Corin threw out his arms. "You said you wanted to meet about peace. What peace can be found at this table?"

"Indeed," Chasten said, nodding at both of his sons. "My idealism was misplaced, but I'll not brook another outcome here, boys." He pushed back from the table, sweeping his gaze over the people in the courtyard pretending to not listen. "I'm declaring this feud over. No calling challenges. No retaliation. Over."

Chasten made a dramatic exit, slipping behind the platform and back toward the Golden Stair.

"Just remember, Corin," Aiden said when their father was gone. "You were the one who wanted this. Who invited it."

"I didn't invite you to try to *kill* me. That you even tried—"

"I wasn't trying to *kill* you, Corin." Aiden's jaw flexed as it clenched. "Father was supposed to step in. He was *supposed* to be the one to let me know when it had gone too far, so he could call it and be the hero, while you learned a valuable lesson. Ask yourself, why didn't he?"

Corin glared at him. "Instead, my wife had to do it."

"Ah, now *her*? I absolutely want *her* dead, as much for your sake as ours. No matter what Father says about it, I will *never* forget what she did. The wedge she's put between all of us." He flopped back with a heavy, drained sigh. "Guardians, brother. Is she *really* worth all this trouble?"

"How would you like me to answer that, Aiden?" Corin asked. "No matter what I say, you'll find ways to sink your teeth in and tear me and my words apart."

Aiden closed his eyes, rolling his head against the chaise. "We didn't always fight like this, Corin."

"Didn't we?"

"Not like this." Aiden rolled forward again. He plopped his elbows onto his knees. "I can...I can *almost* see what you like about her. She's feisty. Smart, for a woman. But she uses neither of these traits to move our house forward."

Corin laughed. "And why should she?"

Aiden blew out a breath and reached to clasp a hand on Corin's knee. "Let's...for once, for a spell...talk about other things. Like Father would want."

Corin snorted, turning his head to the side. "Other things?"

"Actually, I had an idea...on how we might make up for the cancelation of Father's Autumnwhile Jubilee. While we're at it, maybe come up with a truce we can both live with?"

"You want to talk about *celebrations*?"

Aiden sheepishly grinned. "I have an idea, as I said. Wouldn't it be nice for us to work together, for a change?"

190

SEVENTEEN
THE WHISPER AND SIGH OF DUSK

When Corin didn't return after an hour, Yesenia made a decision.

She could sit, wallowing in helplessness, or she could remember who she was and take back some control.

She slipped out, dodging the young attendants charged with spying on her, and made her way down the Golden Stair. Corin's meeting was in the courtyard, so she exited the back, into the first violet whisper of dusk falling over the forest.

There *was* beauty there. It was impossible to think of the woods of the Easterlands without remembering who controlled them, but she finally saw its promise—its ancient call of thick-barked trees, which she couldn't wrap her arms around, and the undergrowth older than anyone alive in the kingdom.

But the treachery of Quinlanden against Warwick was just as old, and it would linger just as long.

Yesenia knew the way by heart. She'd practiced the importance of timing, coming and going only when Aiden was preoccupied. Over time, she realized her adherence to it was more for Corin than herself. Long after she'd figured out how to extricate herself from this cursed Reach, the chalet would continue to serve a purpose for him. She might not want a life with Corin Quinlanden, but she was no longer so indifferent to his suffering.

As always, she unlocked the door and slipped inside the chalet. She was kneeling to unstrap her daggers when she remembered she hadn't locked the door behind her. The key wasn't in her vest, which meant she'd left it in the lock.

She almost backtracked to retrieve it, but there was no point. No one knew she was there, and she wouldn't stay long because she needed to hear everything that had been said to Corin by his father and brother.

From that, they'd decide what would happen next.

But first.

Yesenia released both daggers, setting one upon the table. She backed up until she hit the post, feeling around the floor for the raised floorboard that would help indicate direction later. She closed her eyes. She hadn't done it this way in a long time, and she feared she'd lost the skill.

Not this too. Too much has been taken. My home. My father. Byrne. Erran. Not this too.

She raised her arm into position. Cocked her elbow. Then, she flipped around, facing opposite of her target.

You know what to do. You need only do it.

Yesenia spun in four circles and faced the right direction. She'd lost her sense of bearing, but that was the point of the drill. To use her other senses.

I know you. I know where you are. What you are.

Eyes squeezed shut, Yesenia released the dagger. It sailed from her hands, traversing the space of her held breath, which she released only when she heard the satisfying thud of the tip landing in wood.

A beaming grin spread across her face. There it was, in the post on the other end of the room, off-center but there.

She pulled the dagger from the splintered wood but froze midair, alert to something new.

Yesenia lowered the dagger. Almost as an afterthought, she sidestepped to the table to retrieve the other one and made her way toward what sounded like, but could not be, the key turning in the lock.

She shifted, so both daggers were gathered in one fist, and tried the door.

Locked.

Locked from the outside.

Locked by whoever had followed her, taken the key, and left her without a way out.

Her thoughts whirred out of order.

Windows, I could try the windows. They're tiny, but I can contort.

Aiden is with Corin. This isnae him.

But that means they've done something to Corin. Harmed him? Locked him away?

I need to know who it is. I need to know, so I can decide what to do next.

Whatever happens, do not lose even a single dagger.

Yesenia braced herself and called, "I know you're there!"

She stumbled sideways at the sudden force against the outer wall of the chalet. It sounded like water but thicker, enough that she heard it as it slid down the exterior wood.

"Show yourself! Unless yer a coward, aye?" More of the same viscous substance sloshed against the outside. "Have to lock me in to best me?"

"Locking you in," Mads said in response, "isn't even the fun part, you freebooting strumpet. Hearing your cries, your begs for mercy, are all the payment I require. Told Aiden I don't even need a return favor for this one. He'd be doing me a great honor."

Yesenia pressed one hand to the wall, listening. He'd stopped his splattering and was silent, save for the faint sound of shuffling.

"Do you even hear yourself?" she called through the thin walls. "Doing your master's bidding? Cannae even think on your own?

193

Do on your own?" She stopped speaking to pick up any hints of what he might be doing, but she could hear nothing distinct. "Will ye always lick his boots so hungrily?"

"Aiden is my friend," Mads said. "We are united in thought, in deed. Had he not asked this of me, I'd have done it anyway. For the Easterlands."

It sounded like he was sanding something, and Yesenia at last understood.

She backed away from the wall and returned both daggers to her thigh holster. Immediately, her mind turned to the windows. There were two, both up high, built for light but tucked away for privacy. She'd almost decided which one to go for when a ball of flaming cloth, wedged in a jar of glass, smashed through one and sent everything around it into immediate flames.

"Shite," she whispered, just as a similar crude fire starter burst through the second window.

"All right," she said with a controlled exhale. "Nothing I cannae handle."

Yesenia knelt, ripping a wad of cloth from her skirt. She wrapped it around her face, tied it at the back, and went to recover the remaining chairs before the fire consumed them. Already, one had lit up in response to the fast-spreading flame, and she was too late to save the table.

Or the trunks Corin had gone to such trouble to recover for her.

She coughed into the cloth, which did little to protect her from the black swirling smoke that moved even faster than the flames. Outside, she heard the maniacal cackling of Mads Waters. She'd kill *him* first. Aiden second. Let the king send her to the Wastelands, to the prison camps he'd built upon stolen Southerland soil. It was still home in a way the Easterlands could never be.

Pained tears streamed down her cheeks. The cloth wasn't enough. She could tear off more, but there wasn't time. The chalet was entirely ablaze now, leaving her a disjointed, hazardous path to either window.

Instead, she pressed one hand over her nose and mouth and lifted the chair above her head with the other. The heavy wood exhausted her in only a few steps, and she knew what that meant: she'd already taken in too much of the deadly smoke.

Yesenia hurled the chair at the wall underneath the window. As she made her way to it, she artfully dodged the falling timber and flaming sinkholes crashing all around her. She tried to right it but had to sit, to pause, to find anything clean to inhale. She pulled aside the cloth and pulled her dress up over her face, but it did no good. Her eyes were seared from the smoke, rolling tears down her sooty cheeks. She swayed as all the good air left her lungs, replaced by what would kill her if she could not dig deep and find *something* to draw from.

Pulsing shallow breaths against the inadequate fabric, Yesenia hoisted herself upon the chair and stretched for the sill, using her hands as her only guide in the thick, dark clouds that removed vision from her senses. She felt around, slicing herself upon the shards of broken glass, dismayed to realize the chair only brought her high enough to grab the ledge. She didn't have the strength or the purchase for what she had to do.

Find it. Find it or die.

Yesenia reached again until both of her bloody palms gripped the frame. She pulled, kicking her legs for support, but her hands slipped, and she fell back to the chair.

She swayed into the wall. Her breaths became gulps, a new desperation creeping in as she accepted this was the moment that would decide her life or her death, and every second bled her chances of the former.

Yesenia hopped the chair twice, turning it so its back was against the wall. On a good day, her balance would need to be perfect to get this right, but in her haze of exhaustion, of the slow hand of death reaching out to greet her, there was even less room for error.

She had to hoist herself high enough to reach to the outside of the frame if she had any shot of climbing out.

Yesenia swallowed the acrid fear gathering in the back of her throat. It singed going down. Her flesh burned too, she'd only just realized, but there was nothing more to do than acknowledge it and *go.*

With a stuttering, wounded breath, Yesenia leaped against the wall, tipping her boot against the chair's back, and launched herself as high as she could. Her underarms landed with an excruciating thud against the shattered glass spiking the frame, but she *held,* fast, tight, aware of the thicker streams of blood coursing down her arms and into her dress. With the last of her vigor, Yesenia shrieked into the night as she kick-climbed the wall, pushing herself outward into the cool air, into the last sigh of dusk. Death awaited her on either side of the window, but if Aiden and Mads wanted to finish her off, they'd have to work harder for it.

Her body rushed to greet the earth, and she accepted, welcoming the darkness that followed.

Yesenia wasn't in their apartments when Corin returned. His suspicion flashed immediately to Aiden, but Aiden had been with him.

Corin did this more frequently now, cataloguing every open question into a nefarious purpose. She was probably at the chalet and would be back shortly. She'd said she wanted to be here when he returned, but he'd taken longer than expected, so she'd left. In boredom. Defiance.

Corin searched for something to busy himself, but his dread didn't leave him. Was it the way Aiden had lingered, catching him in questionably casual conversation after their father had left, like he was purposely stealing time? Corin had seen right through the light, cheery words, but his wounded heart, that'd always wished for a brother he could be friends with, overruled the warnings sounding in his head.

I have an idea, as I said. Wouldn't it be nice for us to work together, for a change?

Aiden had rambled on about some half-cocked idea for a new festival, but then he'd brought the conversation to a jarring, abrupt end. The switch in his brother, as he turned from feigning fraternity to his disgust of it, was so abrupt that Corin thought there must have been something to signal it.

Corin's worries returned. Yesenia was *probably* at the chalet, but what if she wasn't?

There was only one way to know, and he'd have to risk Yesenia's ire to confirm it.

He pulled his cloak from the rack and shrugged it on. The unsaid rule between them was that the chalet was hers unless she invited him. She'd been generous with these invites in the almost four months since, more than he'd expected, but in return, he respected the agreement. She'd left no note indicating where she'd gone, or that he should follow.

But he could handle her fury, if it meant confirming his dark suspicions were only that.

Corin saw smoke before he'd even cleared the rear gates of Arboriana. It billowed in dark blooming puffs from some distant point in the forest.

He reminded himself that accidental fires happened all the time, usually an untended campfire or a worker careless with their pipe. Forest fires were a way of life, especially now, in the dry season.

Exhaustion coated him like a thick, cloying blanket he couldn't shrug off. Returning up the Golden Stair and back down had taken what little energy he'd possessed, and this ride threatened to do him in altogether.

For once, he let his fear take the reins, pushing everything else aside so he could just *ride*.

He gathered his robe around his face as he drew closer. His vision started to blur. The air around him was an impenetrable blanket of grey, the occasional peek of color from the trees and sky causing more confusion, not less. The loss of his vision threw his exhausted confidence into doubt.

A harried crunch of leaves tore his attention to the left, where he just made out the form of a man racing away from the fire's direction. Corin called out, but the man stumbled only once before continuing on.

Corin's mare bucked in resistance. He couldn't take her farther without risking her too, but he had a sense he'd need her. He dismounted, reaching around for a tree to tether her to. When she was secured, he pushed on.

He lost his hearing when he neared the clearing in the forest. The screaming hiss of fire, interspersed with violent crackles, was all-consuming. He coughed into his cloak, knowing it would not protect him for long.

Flames rose off the chalet, licking nearby branches. Jagged, ever-changing peaks of orange and deep red were eaten away by the blackening spreading all over everything in its wake.

Corin's heart plunged to the forest floor.

"YESENIA!" he screamed. The end of her name dissolved into another fit of choking coughs that nearly sent him to his knees. The urge to curl up against a tree was so utterly powerful, but if he gave in, he would regret it for the rest of his life. "YESENIAAAAAAA!"

He pulled his face into a grimace when a hard pillow of smoke whooshed at him. It burned, everywhere. His eyes. His flesh. The inside of his mouth, now coated in ash. He was too late. Anyone trapped inside would already be gone.

He realized, suddenly, who the fleeing man was.

Mads.

Aiden *had* been stealing time, for the one who'd always do whatever he needed or asked. When questioned, he could say truthfully that he hadn't lit the fire that had killed Yesenia Warwick.

Corin removed his cloak and fastened it around his head so only his eyes showed. With a glance at the smoke-dark sky, he said a silent prayer to the Guardians.

He jogged to the rear of the chalet, to the windows. Before he could contrive a way to climb through them, he spotted her.

Yesenia lay on her side, curled into the dewy grass. Inching closer, he saw blood. Soot. He called her name again, but she didn't move. Didn't so much as twitch.

He swallowed his fears born of terrible revelations and rolled her onto her back. Her bloody arm flopped back against the grass, her head lolling to the side. Blood was everywhere, though the cause was not immediately evident. Layers of dark soot, cut with tears and sweat, told a more poignant tale of her struggle.

Corin leaned in. His fist closed over blades of tall grass, his breath held as he listened for hers, praying for even a hint of an exhale. He laid his hand over her too-still chest. Time stopped. Even the smoke hung in midair, awaiting its next command.

His hand rose with her chest. She still drew breath. Shallow. Infrequent. But there. Corin cried out in relief. He tasted the first of his own tears.

He yanked at her cloak, but it didn't budge. He had to get her into fresh air, *fast*, or what little life lingered in Yesenia would be snuffed out forever.

I'll kill him. With my own hands. And I won't send someone else to do it. I'll kill him, even if it kills me too.

She wouldn't survive the night without aid, but he couldn't take her back to Arboriana. There were too many unknowns there. Too many adversaries. Was his father in on it? His mother? Any physician in the castle would report right back to their lord. He could find another one in another town, but she didn't have that kind of time left to her.

Corin dug his heels in and hoisted Yesenia into his arms. Her arms draped to the sides, lifeless. Her long dark hair, singed at the ends, brushed against his shirt, promoting a painfully juxtaposed memory of it brushing across his bare chest their first night together.

Once confident he wouldn't drop her, Corin lowered his head and ran, past the blazing chalet and dodging the flame-covered needles and branches falling from the sky. He didn't know where this burst of strength had come from, only that he wouldn't question a gift that might mean the difference between failing Yesenia and saving her.

Corin didn't stop until he spotted his mare, still tethered.

He laid Yesenia carefully over the back of his saddle, mounted, turned down a different path than the one he'd entered, and rode for her life.

EIGHTEEN

THE THING WITH THE BIRDS

It took several attempts before Yesenia's eyes accepted her command. With each blink, something new materialized, crafting fresh confusion that clung to her nausea, then deepening it. A plain bureau. A cracked window, caked in filth. The light, at first bright, had faded to the dim ochers of candlelight and evening.

There were sounds too. Footsteps traversing uneven boards. The soft settling of mugs and bowls. The *slosh* water made when wrung from rags. Whispers too, though these only started near her. They always traveled beyond her hearing, which of course meant whatever was being said was being said about her.

In the midst of the murkiness lingered a sense of safety. Her last memories were violent, terrifying, but she had nothing to bridge all of that to all of this. It was this sense, she supposed, that quelled the fight in her, letting it rest a while longer.

"Yesenia?"

She knew this voice. This man.

No sooner than these thoughts left her did she appreciate their absurdity. Of course she knew this voice, this man.

There was more recognition beckoning, still beyond her reach.

She rolled her head toward the sound and opened her eyes, this time without the struggles of past attempts. Corin's expression shifted from wonder to worry and back again. He rocked in his seat, chewing at the bottom inner corner of his lip in anticipation.

"Where am I?" she grumbled.

"The Misty Merchant."

"Where?"

"The inn, on Slattery Row. Remember, that night…"

"Aye." Yesenia tried to pull herself forward, but the expulsion of energy only drained what little she'd had. "How did I get here?"

"Well, I…I brought you. When I saw the smoke, and I followed it to the chalet, I thought…" Corin lowered his eyes toward his sooty palms. "And then I found you."

"You?" Yesenia struggled to piece together the order of things. She recalled wiggling out of the window, collecting more gashes than she could count, and landing, and then…

Then nothing. It ended there. It should have ended there, if Aiden had had his way.

Corin nodded. "I'm so sorry I didn't know. That I didn't come sooner." He again looked up, and the details in his face stitched the moment together. Uneven lines cut through the soot on his cheeks, the aftermath of tears. His brilliant-blue eyes sparkled brighter than ever behind the mask of his efforts.

"It was Aiden," she said. She turned her head to the other side, searching for something to wet her throat, which still burned with the same intensity as earlier. Corin picked up on her need quickly, handing her a mug of cider that she promptly emptied. The relief was delicious, but the taste of ash in her mouth made her gag.

"I know," Corin said when she was done. He returned to his chair. "I should have known sooner."

"What I was trying to say," Yesenia answered, finally able to push more than a few words out at a time, "was that it wasnae your doing, Corin. Ye cannae keep living in his shadows, for you'll only catch his foul leavings. You're better than that."

Corin's attention shifted at the arrival of Mara. She blocked the glow from the tavern as she leaned against the doorframe.

"You poor thing. How are you feeling? Would it be too much to feed you?"

"I'm not hungry," Yesenia said, trying to smile, to show the gratitude she was only beginning to comprehend. "Thank you, Mara."

Mara tapped the rag in her hand against the door, nodding. "You'll regain your appetite soon enough. Are you all right otherwise? I haven't practiced my healing on anything so dire in years. Most come to me with scrapes, bruises, illness. If Corin had come any later…" Mara shook her head at the unsaid words.

"I ken…" Yesenia winced, shifting. "I know the sacrifice you made to help me. I willnae forget it. I will repay it."

Mara batted her hand at the air. "I don't want repayment, Lady Yesenia."

"Just Yesenia. Please."

"I did it for Corin. Not for all the gold he brings to our poor quarter, but for his heart, his companionship. He doesn't leave his coins on posts to be collected. He drops them into our hands, sups with us, celebrates our joys, and mourns our losses. He is one of us."

Yesenia absorbed the light sting about the post and the coin, but the warmth in Mara's rosy cheeks softened the reproach. "What an honor that must be."

"The honor is ours," Mara said. "And he was in poor form himself when he arrived, damn near hanging off his horse, holding tight to you. I tended to you both, and now I'm in need of my own rest." She met Yesenia's eyes. "It's clear to me the love and fondness he bears you. You are welcome here, Yesenia. You need not wait for your mother-in-law's dutiful but meaningless rides. Nor even Corin's visits. Come on your own. I'd like to know the young woman who has snared our Laoch."

Yesenia nodded as the woman left. The door closed behind her, and it was then Yesenia noted the din of patrons filling the tavern beyond.

"I *will* repay this," Yesenia told Corin. "No matter what she says."

He shrugged with a light twitch of a smile. "She won't accept. If you really want to show your gratitude, then you'll take her invitation. Come to her on your own."

"She was only being polite."

"No," Corin replied, insistent. "Mara has no use for politeness that doesn't serve her."

Corin rocked to his feet and moved to the corner, near the window. He breathed in, a stilted, shuddering breath full of the day's events. When he spoke, he dropped his voice so low, Yesenia strained to hear. "It was Mads, at Aiden's request. I had a feeling… It was strong, but I ignored it, like a damn fool. A feeling that Aiden was up to something. I ignored it because it was so nice, for once, to hear him speak to me like a person and not some dog he enjoys kicking to the corner."

"Nay," Yesenia said, cutting in. "I willnae listen to this from you anymore, Corin."

"No?" He thrust his hand toward the door. "I can go."

"Stop being a bairn. I'm not insulting you." Yesenia pressed her palms to the straw mattress and pushed up so she was sitting. "Come here."

"Why?"

"Will ye just do it?"

Corin approached the bed. She groaned and whipped back the thin cover, nodding at it.

"You want me in the bed?"

"Not if you cannae get your mind straight."

With a wary stare, Corin slid in next to her, leaving one foot on the floor.

Yesenia strained to see him clearly in the dim flicker of candlelight. "You were very brave back there, Corin. I'd be dead if ye hadnae come. Do ye ken? I'd be dead, if not for you. You are not who they think you are."

Corin's head hung. He avoided looking at her directly. "I've decided I'll go to my father. I'll tell him what Aiden has done—"

"Absolutely not," Yesenia retorted. She stretched her hand toward his and laid it over the top, wincing at the tug of flesh so recently healed. This, combined with the shock of his warmth melding with her own, gave her words the briefest pause. "No. You say nothing."

"Why?" Corin snapped his incredulous gaze back to her. "So their crimes can again go unanswered? So they can try again and again, until they're at last successful? Until they finally kill you?"

"They'll know they've bested you." She worked to calm her words, conscious of how they might incite him. This Corin sitting beside her was changed, but a man transforming was a man dangerous to himself. He would sacrifice himself if she let him follow his whims. "And you can never, never allow that. Never give them more than they've already taken."

Corin swung his body toward her. "How are you so strong, Yesenia? How?" The corners of his mouth drew back as his expression crumbled. He bit down on his lower lip at the start of fresh tears. "You're like a wall that I cannot climb."

Yesenia rolled forward and kissed him. He released a sob against her mouth, and she grabbed for his face, drawing the kiss deeper until at last he relaxed.

"There's no one here," he said. "You didn't have to do that."

"I never do anything I donnae want to do," she replied. She leaned back against the wall and inhaled her first breath that didn't taste of soot. "And walls keep you safe, Corin, but they're not the whole of you."

He passed the back of his hand across his eyes to dry his tears. "How I wish I had that gift. To shut out everyone and everything, and be hardened."

Before she even said the words, she was astounded at her intention. Was she going to tell *this* man *this* story? A story she'd never even told Erran? The consequence of this falling into the wrong hands was catastrophic. Byrne would be at best ridiculed, at worst...

Even as she recited all the reasons telling Corin Quinlanden about Byrne and the birds was a terrible idea, she knew the words would come all the same.

"I do have weaknesses too, Corin." Her voice quavered. She didn't recognize it. "My little brother, Byrne, is one."

"Love isn't a weakness, Yesenia."

"Isn't it?" She dropped her hands back into her lap. "Byrne, he's always been special. Different, I suppose ye could say. Definitely not what most men think of as salt and sand. Khallum thought we should harden him, and aye, I tried that, but some men...Well, they just are who they are. There's no changing it."

"Maybe it's not about changing him."

"Aye, but it is, if it means keeping him safe. Safe from himself."

"And you've had to do that, I take it?"

"I have, aye, but..." There was still time to rescind her words. She didn't have to say them. She sighed. "One day, we came upon Byrne in a small thatch of woodland off the coast, Khallum and I. He was alone, cowered over a semicircle of what I first thought were rocks. We didnae know..." She inhaled. "We didnae know, and would we have gone up to him at all, had we?" She lifted her shoulders. "I donnae know. But we did. It was Khallum who saw it first, who realized what we were dealing with. He called back something incoherent, but it was in his eyes, ye ken, that I saw we had a big problem."

"They weren't rocks," Corin guessed aloud.

"Nay," Yesenia said. "They were not rocks. They were birds. All dead. Hundreds of them. More, perhaps? I didnae count. I was scared to. I could hardly breathe. I hated myself for it, but I couldnae help but wonder, did Byrne *do* this? Did he kill them? I *knew* it wasnae possible. But was it?"

Yesenia rolled her lips inward, wetting them as she searched for her next words. There were none existing to pull from. She'd discussed it with Khallum exactly once and then they'd let it die.

"Khallum, he was tugging on Byrne's collar, screaming at him, not in anger but fear. Just screaming, and Byrne, I didnae ken he had such strength in him, but he didnae *budge*, not an inch. He was so fixated on the dead birds. It was like…like he'd joined them, as little sense as that makes. But it's how I felt, watching him, his lips moving without words, his eyes flitting around from bird to bird to bird."

"What happened to the birds?"

"How did they die, you mean?"

Corin nodded.

"Dinnae know," Yesenia said with a shrug. "Predator. Illness. Poisonous flora. But it's what happened after that matters."

She cleared her throat, fixing her eyes on a small picture hanging on the far wall. It looked to have been drawn by the boy, Tristan. "He wouldnae leave them, no matter how we fought. And ah, we fought. Khallum especially. He couldnae handle things he couldnae explain, and aye, he went wild. I dragged him away, had no choice. We left Byrne with the birds and returned home. When he didnae make it for supper, we told my father and the Widow he was practicing his swordcraft in the armory, and I've never felt so sick about a lie. Not for the lie itself, ye ken, but what we were protecting. For all we didnae know. For all we might never know. No one else had seen him, but…" She remembered Lem and Garrick bullying Byrne, and wondered, for the first time, if she and Khallum *had* been the first.

"We went out after supper to try to convince him once more, but then there he was, walking along the path with an armful of these dead birds. He towed a wheelbarrow behind him, full of the same. When he reached the keep, he collapsed. All these dead birds just rolled to the ground, and he rolled with them. He curled into a ball, in the middle of them, and sobbed."

Yesenia's eyes stung, but this time it wasn't from the lingering smoke. She dabbed at them with the back of her hand, blinking to keep the rest where they belonged. "By this point, we were more afraid of what our father would do if he came upon this strange scene. We tried to clean up the birds, but Byrne wasnae himself at all. He wouldnae let us *near* them. That night, Khallum and I took shifts inside the door of the keep, staying awake to be sure no one happened upon Byrne and his birds. But then in the morning..." Yesenia swallowed. "In the morning, when we went outside, we found him out there, still with the birds. But the birds...the birds...the birds were *alive*."

"*What?* How?"

"All of them, swirling around Byrne like he was their master, like he commanded them. All I could do was gape like a dumbstruck bairn, my eyes on the birds, on him. I kept thinking of all the eyes of the courtyard. Not real people, mind, but the shrubs and the cobblestones and the sand, all of it witnessing this, knowing more about what it was than I ever would..." She trapped a sob as her voice broke. "How? How did he do it? I donnae know, Corin, and I never will. Byrne never explained it. He never spoke of it. And so, neither did we, not after that day. But it could only be magic, aye? And if it could only be magic, then Byrne practicing it without approval from the Sepulchre was as good as a death warrant."

"That's...I honestly don't know what to say," Corin whispered. "Did anything like that ever happen again?"

"No. Never again. Not before, not since."

"Why would you tell me?" Corin asked, clearly still making sense of her confession. "To use your own words, why share anything with me that could be perceived as a weakness?"

Yesenia bristled. "Should I not have? Ye gonna go tell your father?"

"Yesenia, no, that's not what I meant." He slid his hand over hers. "I shouldn't have said it. It's only...It feels like trust, from you, and you've never trusted me like this before."

She glanced down at their joined hands. A strange thought hit her, that she didn't even mind it. That his touch had become a comfort. "I told ye because...I wanted you to understand no one is born strong, Corin. I learned to be strong. For others. For those who donnae have their own strength."

"Like me?"

Yesenia shook her head. "Have ye not heard me? You are *not* who they think you are. You are *not* weak. Weakness is what men like Aiden, men like Chasten, wedge behind their shields and spin to hatred. Ye donnae bully someone because they are less than you. Ye bully because they aren't."

Corin, too, stared at their hands, still pressed together. He wiped more tears on the back of his sleeve. "What now?"

"We go back. We pretend nothing is amiss."

Corin scoffed, his head shaking. "I don't have that skill, Yesenia. I can't pretend that my brother didn't try to kill my wife. That my father might have had a hand in it."

"You can," she urged. "And you will." She twined their fingers together and brought the knot to her mouth for a brief kiss. After, she released him and swung her legs over the opposite side of the bed. She squeezed her eyes to fend the wave of dizziness that snuck up to remind her that only hours separated her from the terror at the chalet.

"You still want out of this marriage?"

The vulnerability in his soft, searching tone gave her pause. She turned to look at him over her shoulder. "Aye…I do. But not because of you, Corin."

"Is there not…another place, another world…"

"If there is, I donnae know it. Do you?"

Corin appeared on the other side of the bed with clothing that was not hers. Her dress had been destroyed in the fire, of course, but these were garments more suited to her. Trousers, a blouse. No doubt he'd had some hand in picking them.

"If going home is what you most want," he said, turning to let her dress in private. "I'll find a way to help you do it."

Yesenia's eyes went to her arms, tracing the dozens of light, white scars lingering from her escape from the chalet. Healing only took things so far. Would they always be there, reminding her?

"You heard what I said?"

"Aye, I heard it," she said, shimmying into the trousers that were slightly too big.

"And?"

She spun back around, her shirt half-buttoned. "I don't need your help with this. I'd prefer you didnae get involved. Will only cause you more trouble, with the others."

Corin's eyes traveled to the swell of her bosom as she finished buttoning the shirt. Was it desire? Remorse?

Did it matter?

He cleared his head and looked up. "I don't need you to save me from them. I'll help you because it's what I want. I don't know what we are, Yesenia, or what we're doing. Pretending, not pretending. Enemies, not enemies. Half in love or not at all. What I do know though…" He stepped toward her and reached to guide her hair to the back. "Is that if nothing else, you're my friend. I failed the only other one I ever had. I won't fail you, if I can help it."

"Friend," she mused to herself. She'd had friendships back in the Southerlands, though none had been remotely like this one. "Aye, that'll do, I ken. Friends."

"Friends, who kiss when other people are looking," he said, grinning. "And sometimes when they're not."

"Donnae get ahead of yourself there, *Laoch*." She pressed her tongue to the back of her teeth as she exaggerated the name.

He narrowed his eyes with a playful twinkle. "I *ken* I was a hero today, *aye?*"

Yesenia's jaw curled in horror. "Donnae ever do that again."

"Donnae ever what?"

"Keep that up, you'll wish you'd left me at the chalet."

He laughed to himself. "You're well enough to ride? One of the children found Kheerai roaming the woods and brought her here. But you can ride with me on mine if it's easier."

Yesenia cocked an eyebrow. "With you? On the same horse together, you panting in my ear? You'll need to set fire to another building I'm in for me to agree to *that*."

The moon was high when they passed through the gates of Arboriana. They made their way to the stables, where Corin helped Yesenia down, ignoring her prideful swat.

He indulged himself a good look at her. Mara had done well in healing her, but some wounds were beyond the touch of magic. He saw it in Yesenia's eyes, in the slight draw of their corners. When she laughed or smiled, they took a moment to catch up. The hollows of her cheeks were more apparent now. Her loose dark hair waved around her jaw like waves framing the gentle arch of her mouth.

He scolded himself for noting her beauty amidst the horrors of the day.

"Why ye gaping at me like that?"

"Just making sure you're all right. Before we go in."

He braced for some wisecrack, but she instead nodded.

"I'm fine," she said to assure him. "Will be quite the challenge not taking my hands to his neck when I first see him, but I'll manage."

"I'll be fighting the same battle."

"Lady Yesenia."

They both turned at the sound of a guard, but it was not one man centering the space between the barn doors, but a dozen. Beside the one who had spoken stood Chasten. They all glowed in the pale light of the moon lighting the path behind them.

"We were—"

Corin's father raised his palm and the guards swarmed in, filling the barn.

"Lady Yesenia." Chasten said it this time. "I regret to inform you that your father, Lord Khoulter, has fallen. He is dead."

"He...*what?*" Yesenia pushed the words out, caught in her choked breath.

"Some illness," Chasten said, adding a flippant tilt of his chin. "He went swiftly, I'm told, and your brother has already assumed the mantle of Lord of the Southerlands."

"My father?" Yesenia whispered. She swayed, and Corin caught her in his arms before she could go down.

"Yes," Chasten said evenly. "Where your father has no stomach for war, I've yet to learn the ways of your brother. Thus, I'll be denying any requests for leave, for you to return for the dead-given rites. You can mourn him from here."

Corin glared at his father as he held her. "Are there no limits to your cruelty? How can you deliver such a message, in such a way? How can you deny her the right to return and lay her own father to rest?"

"What's more..." Chasten went on in the same light tone. "After the unfortunate events of the day, there are now secrets that can never leave the Easterlands."

"You cannae keep me from my own home!" Yesenia howled.

Corin held tight to her.

"You cannae stop me!"

"I assumed as much," Chasten said, "and have arranged a cell for you in the dungeon. It's the nicest one, as these things go, reserved for just such an occasion. You won't starve."

"You did *what?*" Corin demanded.

"I cannot trust that Yesenia will obey my wishes. If she tells her brother what happened in the woods today, he might raise arms, and while I'd not deny myself such a pleasure as cutting down every last man boasting salt and sand, the king would not approve. Nor can I trust that in your mawkish coddling of each other, you haven't spilled your own treasonous truths."

Corin unraveled Yesenia and thrust himself in front of her. "You will not *touch* her. You would not dare."

The guards shuffled in tense anticipation.

"Would you like to join her?"

"Father! This is *madness*. Even for you!"

"Guards." Chasten clapped his hands once.

Corin turned and buried himself against Yesenia until they were ripped apart, half the guard on Yesenia, the other half keeping him from her.

"You cannot do this!" Corin screamed, stretching against his restraints. He watched Yesenia surrender without fight, and it was wrong, all wrong. Chasten couldn't mean this, and Yesenia...

"YESENIA!"

She disappeared beyond the corner of the barn.

"Yesenia! I won't let him do this!" He wrenched one arm free, but another guard was on him in an instant.

"You make one move. One step," Chasten warned. "And you join her."

"You think I'm scared of you?" Corin rasped as incredulous tears cut down his face. What a fool he'd been, thinking that *anything* he did had escaped his father's notice. To believe *anything* was safe from Chasten's machinations.

"I know you're scared of me. But I don't like the look in your eyes right now, Corin. I don't like it one bit. If the threat of imprisonment doesn't stir you, then here's one that might."

Corin spat at his father's feet.

Chasten regarded it with casual amusement. "Are you done? Because you need to hear this, and you need to hear it clearly, as I never say anything I don't mean." Chasten's head fell to the side. "You go after Yesenia? I kill her. I send her head back to her brother to be burned on the same pyre as her father. And when the king asks why?" He measured his words, speaking each one with a meaningful pause between. "I will make sure he, and all the kingdom, remember Yesenia Warwick as a traitor to the realm."

Chasten spun and marched out of the barn.

The last thing Corin saw, before the hilt of a sword sent him to the darkness, was the red snap of his father's cloak catching the wind.

213

SALT AND SAND

NINETEEN
SPIDERS AND RATS

Yesenia lay prone on the rough straw cot, watching the biggest spider she'd ever seen weave an impressive web in the corner of the sparse cell. In the insufficient light provided by dying sconces, she couldn't make out details, but it was evident her orb-like body was swollen, poised to erupt.

Soon there would not be just one large spider, but dozens.

Yesenia rolled to the side, spiders forgotten. A small pile of dishes was chaotically stacked by the cell door, untouched for days. When she wasn't watching the pregnant mother build her empire, Yesenia mused over the plump rats jumping from dish to dish, their weight hitting the clay, beating an unintentional song on the bars as they filled their bellies with the food she refused to eat. None of them had died, as far as she could tell, but these were Quinlanden rats, so perhaps they were immune to poison.

The wineskin she'd given into on the second day. The agonizing burn as it went down, as it settled, was enough to fight off the worst of the hunger pangs, but that wouldn't be true for much longer. Starvation was no way to die. She'd seen it all her life, in men who worked themselves into their grave, bellies so empty they were naught but bones.

But she'd rather die by her own choice than that of another.

The dark humidity of the place was suffocating. She'd removed her pants days ago, and not long after, other layers had followed. She now donned only the shirt Mara had left for her at The Misty Merchant in what seemed years ago, not days.

Occasionally, she thought of the poison vial still rolled in her garments. She'd been dedicated about removing it each night, to avoid crushing it in her sleep, and replacing it in the morning when she re-dressed. They'd taken her daggers but had somehow missed the small ampoule.

She'd held fast to her gift from Anatole, believing he'd meant it to be used for a singular purpose when he'd given it to her. She understood now what that purpose was—and what it wasn't. What it had never been.

A few drops would end this misery.

Was there another way out? If there was, it better present itself soon, because she *would* starve if she was stuck in the cell much longer. Bribing the guards, with gold and even sex, had fallen flat. Their fear of their lord surpassed even their strongest base desires.

There'd been no visitors otherwise, not even Aiden or Chasten. Her strength was no match for the girth of the metal, nor the complexity of the lock. It was the most robust prison she'd ever seen, built into layers of stone and sediment underneath Arboriana. A prison like this hadn't been constructed for incidental troubles. The rest of the cells might be empty, but they had a purpose to serve.

A few drops. It will be fast. They might defile my body, but a Southerlander has no such sentimentality for the flesh.

Her belly howled for food. This was new in the past two days. Her anger had silenced all else competing for her attention, but her anger was sleeping in the shadows, awaiting address, which she could offer at any time.

She had nothing to tell her poor belly, nothing to give except the lingering, undecided promise to end their shared misery.

Wasn't it always going to end this way? Had there ever been an outcome where she could've come to Whitechurch and led a peaceful life? Would not Corin's life have been the same in Warwicktown?

No, she answered herself swiftly. *His life wouldnae have been easy, but he'd have had nothing to fear from me or mine.*

From time to time, she wondered what they'd done to Corin after dragging her off. Even clear of the barn, guards sliding her away like trash, she'd heard Chasten's threats. It didn't make her less hurt that Corin hadn't come. It didn't ease her hurt because he'd shown her he was so much more than his father's footstool, and to have been wrong about that...That *did* hurt.

Beyond the cell, the stone walls wept with water stains. The construct of the prison was impressive, built close enough to the sea as to be almost impossible. Would the stone hold forever? Would the sea eventually reclaim this place?

Maybe three drops. Or even four. Why parcel them at all, like I'm saving the rest for someone else? Take the whole fecking vial. Aye, leave nothing to chance.

Yesenia pressed her hand to the roll at her waist. She trailed her fingers downward, exposing the ampoule. It fell into her palm.

Anatole never told her what it was. She'd only assumed it would be a swift death. What if he'd handed her something that would invite great pain?

The unmistakable ring of metal hitting stone shot her straight upward on the cot. Sometimes the rats knocked things about, but it was the trod of boots that piqued her alertness even higher. The guards rarely ventured down there at all, unless delivering food, and it was long past her final meal of the night.

She reached behind her back to bury the vial under a patch of straw and then went to the bars, listening.

"*Yesenia?*" A shouting whisper.

219

Corin.

He'd come.

Alone?

She wrapped her hands around the bars and waited.

"Yesenia!"

His approach was broken by the rattle of bars as he checked the other cells along the way to hers, at the very end of the row.

"Here," she called, ridding her voice of any emotion that might be read and used against her. There was too much she didn't know. Why he was here. Who had sent him. A reasonable explanation for the absence of the shuffle of guards behind him as he inspected each space.

Corin jogged the rest of the way. She met his eyes as he stopped just beyond her cell. For several strange moments, neither said a word. She had nothing *to* say, but ahh, Corin looked like he did, yet he held back.

He held up a ring of keys with one hand, and with the other, he reached into his pocket and withdrew a loaf of bread, then passed it through the bars. She hesitated before accepting, still wary of so much in the column of unknowns, but she was *starving*.

Yesenia nodded her gratitude, turning away in shame as she shoved the loaf into her mouth.

"I am so sorry for what's been done to you. This is *abhorrent*," he whispered, furiously fumbling through the ring, trying every key. "My father will pay for this, Yesenia." He tried more keys, all the wrong ones. Sweat poured down his temples. "I know you don't think much of my abilities in that regard, but every man has his limits. My father has found mine and stormed well across that line."

Her mouth was too full to argue.

"I desperately wanted to come sooner. I *would* have come sooner if it had been possible. Finding a way to you is all I've thought about, day and night, since the barn." His words were rushed now, as if afraid he'd never get them all out. "There are two guards per shift. They're no ordinary men. My father plucks them from smaller villages, the best fighters. I couldn't match them for strength, so I had to find another way."

His mouth tilted in frustration when, key after key, he came up short. "I used the entirety of my gold, what I've stored away all these years to take down to Slattery Row. It wasn't nearly enough, so I stole as much as I could carry from my father's treasury, and *that* was enough to send both the guards anywhere in the kingdom, to live as handsomely as stewards. It had to be bigger than their fear of my father, and it was."

"I'll replace the money you had for the Row," Yesenia whispered, stunned. "Every last coin."

"I don't need you to replace it. I just need you to be all right."

"We're alone then?"

"I dismissed them in the middle of their shift. No one else comes down here, not if they don't have to." Corin's face lit up in delighted surprise when the lock sprung. He laughed, glancing between Yesenia and the open cell door.

Yesenia threw the rest of the bread on the cot and leaped into his arms as the door swung wide.

"Oh!" he exclaimed, adjusting quickly and cupping her bottom in his palms when her legs tightened around his waist, locking together. He seemed to have more to say, looking up into her eyes with a wild, excited flush, but there was nothing here now that needed words.

Yesenia wound her fist in his hair and kissed him so deeply he fell back, spinning around and slamming her against the inner cell door. She squeezed her thighs around him and reached down to tug her shirt up.

Corin thrust her harder against the bars, stretching his hands over her head to grip the thick steel as he deepened their kiss, grinding his leather-bound bulge against her bare flesh. Yesenia bit down on her lip as she reached to free him from his pants. She guided him in, but her hand was forced away when Corin drove in so hard, it knocked the air from her lungs.

She slid her hands up the bars, twining some of her fingers through his as he crashed into her. His passion transformed him, became him. He nibbled at her neck, sliding his tongue up her sweaty flesh until it was again on her mouth, into which she released her pleasured groans as he slammed her against the metal with such power, the bars trembled in their housing.

A sharp wave of pleasure swelled between her legs. Yesenia bit down into his shoulder to bury her scream, but it only drove Corin wilder, faster, harder, until her vision flooded with stars.

"Ah, Guardians," she moaned as it overtook her. The responsive throb of her release made Corin scream, and he sent the muted sound into an open-mouthed kiss just as he pulsed, shuddering against her.

He held her like that for several moments, surrendering to the occasional rogue jerk. She felt him go soft, then harden once more, and ah, she wanted it, in spite of herself—in spite of everything, she wanted more—but it wasn't safe here.

Yesenia wrapped her arms around his neck and slid down the bars. She gave him one last lingering kiss and then went to gather her clothes. "Now what?"

Corin leaned into the bars, breathless. "We aren't going to talk about what just happened?"

"Did you want to?"

"Not now, of course not." He recovered himself with a shake of his head. "Now what? Well…Um, I have both our horses waiting just beyond Arboriana. I've packed provisions, and a change of clothes for you. We should send a raven ahead to Warwicktown, so they know we're coming, but not until—"

"Warwicktown?" Yesenia asked. She dropped her belt. "We?"

"Yes," Corin said swiftly, still gathering his breath. "We leave right away. We'll send a raven announcing ourselves, as I said, once we've cleared my father's lands. I don't want your brother accidentally mistaking us for enemies."

"You're coming?" Yesenia finished dressing, moving through the motions slower as she replayed his words, accepting their meaning. "To Warwicktown?"

Corin's expression shifted. "Do you not want me to come?"

"It's not that," Yesenia said. As she fastened her belt, she remembered the poison. She couldn't leave it here. "Your father will kill you, when he finds out what you've done."

"My *wife* is my only concern now. What my father will think, or what he will do, is far from my mind, Yesenia."

Her own father…Yesenia buried the thought, as she had these past four, five, six, however many days she'd been there. Thinking of Khoulter, of what this loss meant to her, had no place amidst a bid for survival.

It was Khallum now. Khallum was lord, and his icy Northerland wife meant the Southerlands once again had a lady. Khallum would accept Corin, if it was what Yesenia wanted, but what of the rest of the Southerlands? The only thing worse than a Rhiagain was a Quinlanden. There was no room for exception or nuance when people were starving.

Yesenia only realized she'd been holding her breath when she started again. "The Southerlands are very different, Corin."

"I know. But you came to another world and survived. It seems only fair that I can do so now, for you."

"Donnae do it for me. Donnae throw your life away, for me." She glanced around. "*This* was enough. More than enough."

Corin reached for her hands. She looked down at them in confusion. "You are my wife," he said again. "And though I don't expect you'll ever admit it, you'd have done the same for me. Now, let's get the bloody hell out of here before someone wakes up."

"Warwicktown?" She let the effect of saying its name settle over her. *Home. Khallum. The sea. Feck, even the Widow. But not… not my…*

Not now.

"Warwicktown," he stated, dropping her hands and heading for the exit. He looked back and caught her digging through the straw. "What are you doing?"

"Nothing," she lied, closing the vial tight in her palm. "Thought I'd lost something."

Corin's lightly cocked head betrayed his suspicion, clouding his smile. "It's midnight. We have another three ticks of the moon before the new guards come to switch shifts. That should give us enough of a lead." His grin deepened, eyes brightening. "Oh! I almost forgot."

She watched him sprint back down the corridor and kneel to lift something. As he returned, she saw what he had.

Her daggers.

Corin handed them over. "Can't leave without these, can we?"

"Corin…" Yesenia's voice dropped to a whisper. She rolled the leather over in her hands. With a flick of her wrists, she turned it and fastened the belt to her waist. "Thank you."

Corin lifted one shoulder in a shrug, but pride gleamed in his eyes. "There's no more reason to wait. We should go."

Yesenia joined him, slipping her open hand into his as he guided her toward safety—and home.

TWENTY

WARWICKTOWN

Khallum had ordered a sizable retinue to welcome Yesenia home. They would meet her at the border to escort her to Warwicktown in a manner worthy of a lady of the Southerlands. This alone wouldn't surprise her, even if she'd scold him later for the unnecessary pageantry.

What would surprise her—and, he hoped, lift her spirits—was who he'd sent to greet her.

He'd hear about it soon, along with the other stories she brought with her. Stories he was certain would bring him to fresh rage all over again. Yesenia had known her life in Whitechurch would be dangerous for her, and Khallum had dismissed her fears.

He leaned into the broad open window overlooking the sea from the Hall of Warring as he awaited her arrival. How this view had changed for him, since the death of his father. He'd sat at this table for years with Khoulter's men, pretending to be one of them. He thought he'd have so much more time before he had to be.

Yesenia had come too late to attend Khoulter's dead-given rites, but the raven Corin had sent ahead of their arrival explained why. Khallum would kill Aiden Quinlanden one day. The man would suffer. He'd scatter the bootlicker's parts across the kingdom so he'd never find peace.

But Yesenia needed a lord more than a brother. The comfort she required—the stalwart salt and sand strength of their land and people—was what awaited her. To speak of Khallum's vengeance would be to spark her own.

He turned at the shuffling of feet and saw Gwyn hovering in the doorway. She wrapped one arm lovingly around her belly, the other propped against the frame. Her red hair flamed wild around her rosy cheeks, flush with the throes of pregnancy.

Khallum wasn't supposed to enjoy this. Yesenia had all but called him a traitor for taking so easily to his beautiful Northerland wife. But what of it? He'd done well. He already had an heir on the way, and Gwyn was as eager to give him more as he was to help her do it. The Southerlands would not want for stability, least not where he was concerned.

If he'd done nothing else right, he'd done this.

Was it a crime to enjoy it? To enjoy her?

"Aye?" he asked. "They're here then?"

Gwyn nodded. She wrapped her shawl tighter at the chill drafting off the sea. "They've just entered Warwicktown."

"Is he with her?"

"Is who with her?"

"The Quinlanden lad."

Gwyn eyed him strangely. "I should think so, Khallum, seeing as it was his signature on the raven. He *is* the one who rescued her from that terrible prison."

"And another thing…" Khallum tapped his fist against the window's natural plaster, an amalgamation of bird shit and barnacles as old as the keep itself. "Why would she let him send the raven? That's not Yesenia's way. Does he have her under some kind of charm? Some spell?"

Gwyn shrugged. She didn't know Yesenia. He didn't know why he'd said it at all, to her.

"Will you tell her? The truth about Lord Khoulter?"

Khallum paled. He turned his eyes back toward the crested waves rolling in on the tide. "I donnae ken I will, no."

"You don't think she deserves to know?"

"Deserves to know? That the king probably killed our father for lying about what she was doing in the cove, with Rutland?"

Gwyn sighed into a slow nod. "I suppose you're right."

"You suppose?"

"If what Corin said in his vellum was true, Yesenia's honor must be defended."

Khallum bristled. He inhaled a lungful of briny air through his nose, welcoming the burn. "You'd have me start a war, when I've only just become lord?"

"Is that what you'll tell her?" Gwyn asked, pressing gently. "When she arrives, seeking the succor of her brother, her lord, her protector?"

"The Quinlanden lad kens himself her protector now." Khallum gruffed. "I cannae decide what grinds me worse, her trying to rebel, or her falling in line."

"Will you turn her away?"

Khallum scoffed. He passed his fist over his nose and again looked at the sea. "Nay. Of course not." He flexed the hand he'd cut a little too deep into. He could only now turn it to a fist, all these months later. "I made a vow. Even if I hadnae…" He coughed and spat. "She's my sister. She's our Yesenia. And she's come home to us."

Gwyn shifted in place. Her judgment lived in the air between them. Desire surged through him, along with the full weight of her disapproval. Even when she was cross with him, he wanted to fuck her. *Especially* when she was cross with him.

"Aunt Korah has gone to greet them. We should be there as well."

"Has she?" Khallum shook his head. "Aye. All right." He rolled his neck back and forth, transferring the stress of the past months into the open air. "Let's go."

Yesenia dropped onto the sandy path with a satisfying thud. She ground the heels of her boots into the land—her land. Home.

She wrapped Kheerai's reins around her hand and led her the rest of the way. The soft impact Corin created when he followed her lead was the only foreign thing left in her sphere. If he had something to say as he took in a world opposite his, he kept it to himself.

Yesenia paused to absorb the roar of the sea, letting it roll over her like a tide in transition. She pressed her hand to her chest, trapping her grief. She'd missed the dead-given rites and the pyre. Chasten had taken these sacred moments from her. Byrne told her they'd called a celebration tomorrow, to remember Khoulter properly and welcome her home, but it was hardly consolation for what had been lost.

Byrne wrapped an arm around her waist and winked at her from the side. Who was this young man guiding her with such confident airs? The command in his step as he led her toward the keep caused her to question if this *was* her brother, and not some changeling sent by the Westerland witches.

He hadn't brought his wife though. He'd been back in Warwicktown over a week and planned to stay a few days longer now that Yesenia had returned. All this and more he'd revealed on their somber approach to Warwicktown, as the sand drifted from the black of Iron Hill to the tan of Goldthorpe and then the golden shore of home.

Yesenia had listened to her brother speak—so freely, so charmingly—about his life in Longwood Rush, but she'd heard little and would remember even less. Her father was dead. What else could matter? Not even Byrne's strange transformation could distract her heart from such acute pain.

If it ever becomes unsafe for you in Whitechurch…unsafe, ye ken, for you, tough as ye are, hard as ye are…I willnae let even a king stand between me and my lass.

Yesenia turned her shudder of sorrow into shivers when a briny gust swept off the cliffs. Autumnwhile was their longest season in the Southerlands, and their most volatile. More ships would sink in these few months than in all the others combined. These were the storms that necessitated the rebuilding of keeps and the close tending of bairns and barns. Terrible as they were, there was a comfort in knowing what was. In knowing none of it was centered in grudges or politics. The sea and sky took indiscriminately.

The Widow's gauzy black veils snapping on the wind pulled Yesenia into the moment. Her whole face was covered, as was the rest of her, as her reverent steps carried the respectful, funereal strides of mourning. Yesenia supposed Korah *was* mourning. She and Khoulter had no other siblings and had been close once. Khoulter hadn't just been solving for his children's needs when he'd invited his sister to live with them. He'd gained back his oldest friend.

"Yesenia. Darling." The Widow clasped Yesenia's cheeks in her palms. "I can see in your eyes what you've endured. You poor dear."

"Aunt Korah."

Kheerai snuffed at Yesenia's side.

Korah's inspection lingered a few more moments and then she shifted it to Corin. "And you, lad. Seeing ye up close like this, you're not what I expected."

Corin tried to smile. "What were you expecting?"

Korah knit her brows in study of him. Her answer never came. "Such crimes against a Warwick will not go unanswered, Yesenia. You can be sure of it."

"Aye, Korah, Father might've let you speak for him, but I have my own words," Khallum said, appearing in a break through the Widow's retinue. His words were playful though, as was the soft squeeze he laid upon his aunt's shoulder when he brushed by her.

Yesenia gulped a shuddering breath. Khallum. He'd changed too, though in less obvious ways. Lines around his eyes, and between them, betrayed the work Father had left for him. His youthful dress had been replaced by the heavier armor their father had enjoyed, but that was not all that was weighting him down.

His light way with the Widow revealed a happiness there too, between the spaces of the rest.

Beside him stood his wife, Gwyn, fiery and radiant, a child already on the way.

Yesenia went to address her brother as her lord, but Khallum had her in his arms, in a bear of a hug, before she could. Her face hidden in his massive shoulder, Yesenia buried a hard sob and let him hold her.

"You're home," he said low, a soft gleam in his eyes. "You're home, Sen."

Yesenia bit the inside of her mouth, nodding. It was her turn to say something—to, at the very least, introduce Corin. But speaking was impossible.

"Corin." Khallum nodded at the man. The brief twist in his lips was the only sign of his discomfort of standing with a Quinlanden. "Thank you for escorting my sister home. You didnae have to do it, and I ken your father will make you pay for it. If there's anything I can offer in gratitude, say the word."

"I...I don't require anything in return, Lord Warwick." Corin's confusion became Yesenia's understanding.

Khallum was dismissing him.

"Quinlandens do nothing for free," the Widow replied, her more familiar air of wisdom returned to her. "I ken not even this pretty one comes without a cost."

"He's staying," Yesenia asserted. "Corin will be staying *here*, in Warwicktown. With me."

Khallum cocked his head at the same time the Widow gasped. "Aye? With you?"

"Aye. With me."

"*With* you, with you?"

Yesenia nodded.

Khallum passed a wide-eyed look to Byrne. "Ye certain? Dinnae need to put on airs here, sister. This isnae the Easterlands. You're free to do as ye please."

Yesenia detected Corin's stiff panic at the thought of being banished to a guest's chambers, left to fend for himself in a foreign land hostile toward anyone bearing his name. But he'd done this for her. He'd done more for her than he should have. She could do this for him.

"*With* me," she affirmed. Her eyes caught Corin's from the side, and she read his relief. "He's to be welcomed into our keep and Warwicktown with the honor due a guest of the Warwicks. No one will trouble him for his name, nor any other cause."

"As ye wish, then," Khallum said with another brow raise. "Shall we?"

Several grooms rushed forward to take their horses. Yesenia gave Kheerai one last loving pat and sent her off.

Corin fell in next to her as they followed the procession. An urgency of unsaid words draped over him, spreading to her. If he thanked her.,.if he even *dared* suggest, however unintentional, that she was being soft, especially after the way Khallum had looked at her...

"It will be all right," he said instead. "You're home now."

Yesenia retired to the corner of the room with her ale. She kicked the chair back against the wall and propped her feet up on the old card table no one used anymore. Her brothers sat at the larger table, nursing their own mugs and each, in their own ways, appraising her choice to sit away from them. That they didn't understand was a sign, as much as any, of how much had changed in the tumultuous months since the Epoch of the Accordant.

"It was a proper send-off," Khallum was saying through disjointed nods. "Not a single Great House of the Southerlands wasnae represented. They flowed up into the hills, so many of them. They all loved him. Wasnae like our grandfather, was he?"

"I donnae ken it, Khallum. An illness? Father?" Yesenia said, shaking her head. "What did the physician say?"

"There wasnae a physician, Sen," Byrne answered. "It was that quick."

Assured though he spoke, he wasn't so much changed that Yesenia didn't catch the lie in his words. But what was the lie? What did he, and apparently Khallum, wish to keep from her?

"Nothing is that quick. Warwicks are tougher than that."

"Aye, but it *was* that quick," Khallum replied. "Sen, I know ye feel like ye missed out on the rites, but the celebration tomorrow? Aye, that's how we honor Father. We take the piss with each other, we drink until all we can see is the sky and stars, and we remember who *we* are."

"We have our share of anger," Byrne said, "more than we know what to do with. But we're together now. Father would have wanted this."

"Father would have wanted this?" Yesenia asked. "Tell me, what about 'this' would've whet the happiness of Khoulter Warwick?" She polished off her ale, and Byrne gingerly approached to refill it. She blinked her thanks.

"Now what?" Byrne asked, looking between them both.

Yesenia trained her gaze on Khallum, as the only one with the power to answer.

"I mean, now what do we do about the situation in the Easterlands?"

"Aye, eh…" Khallum sighed. "I've sent my own raven to Lord Quinlanden. Advised him t'would be unwise to bring men down here, looking to retrieve ye. Told him I ken what his son did, and what he did. That unless he wants the whole of the kingdom to know it, and the ratsbane besides, he'll stand down."

Yesenia dropped one foot to the floor. "You sent that to Chasten Quinlanden?"

"Aye." Khallum held his palms in a shrug.

"When?" Panic settled in. Chasten knew she and Corin were in Warwicktown.

"Same night Corin's raven reached me. So, eh, what was that, Byrne? Two nights ago?"

"Aye. Two nights ago."

"And?" Dread burned in her chest. "Any response?"

"Nay." Khallum quaffed his ale. It foamed around his beard, also new, and Byrne mimed the need to clean it. Khallum grunted, passing his forearm over his face.

"Nay? *Nay?*"

"It means *no*, Sen—"

"I ken what it means. It's the silence from the Easterlands I cannae interpret!"

"Ask your husband," he said, then chortled. "Aye, didnae even flinch when I called him that? Still making a bid to get yourself out of the marriage?"

"Apparently I'm the only one," she replied, her tone flat.

"Isnae an answer. Why is he here? Why not send him back?"

Yesenia stiffened. "Ye said it yourself. He'd be punished. I saw with my own eyes how far Lord Quinlanden will go against his own blood. Willnae have Corin's on my conscience."

Khallum grinned. "Plenty of apartments here. Could've had his own. Aye, could've sent him to the gatehouse. To one of the inns in town…"

Yesenia dropped her gaze into her mug. "He didnae leave me to suffer in Whitechurch. I'll nay leave him to suffer here."

"Charitable," Khallum said. "He'll brook no trouble from us, but I ken taking him beyond the keep would be a mistake."

"Are you staying forever?" Byrne once more sounded as she remembered him.

"She just got home, Byrne. Let her get her feet under her, a night of rest first."

"But if you do stay forever," Byrne said. "What will Corin do?"

"I donnae…" Yesenia shrugged. "We've not discussed it."

"Would you like him to stay?"

"Byrne! Guardian's cock, can ye take a hint? Does she look like she kens the future right now? Cannae even hold her ale properly, look at her."

Yesenia slammed her chair down on all fours to refute the low slight, but the ground rushed up; an unsteady wave passed behind her glossy eyes.

"See?" Khallum looked at Byrne, pointed his arm at Yesenia.

"It is late," Byrne replied. "Sen, I'll walk ye to your room."

She waved him away. "Nay. I'll go alone."

Hurt sank into Byrne's expression. "You're angry with me. For what I said in my raven."

"Angry with you? For being happy?" Yesenia snorted. "Well that wouldnae be very *charitable* of me, would it?"

"Drunk." Khallum emphasized with a rap of his knuckles on the table.

"I can take your anger," Byrne said softly. "I want to see my sister happy. I want to see her accept that she can be and that she deserves to be. That love can be so much more than protection."

Khallum made a retching sound in his mug. "We done?"

Yesenia's eyes swelled with abhorrent tears. "Aye. We'll talk more…tomorrow."

"Oh, the celebration," Khallum stated, interjecting before she could leave. "Ye should know, Sen. The Rutlands will be there. Erran, I ken, will keep his distance, but his father, his sister…"

Yesenia froze. Of course they'd be there. The Rutlands were favorites. Friends. "Aye…and?"

"Does your husband know?" Khallum failed to hide his mischievous grin.

"He knows there's nothing *to* know," Yesenia retorted. "And unlike my brothers, he listens when I say it."

Khallum burst into laughter. "So he's a fool is what you're saying?"

Yesenia directed scathing gazes on them both and slid her mug onto the larger table. "Good night then."

Yesenia yawned into her elbow, weaving down the hall of her childhood. She passed Khallum's chambers, which were cold and dark, only to realize he'd probably moved into Khoulter's. She wasn't ready to see her brother coming in and out of that room. He already looked too much like their father.

She neared her own, where Corin would probably be asleep, but her attention was snared by a warm yellow light coming from the cracked door to the Widow's apartments. Just beyond was the soft, unmistakable sound of sobbing.

Yesenia sagged with her guilt. She should go to her aunt, offer comfort. It was the right thing to do. It was what her father would want. But where would she find comfort to give when she had none for herself?

It was the addition of Corin's voice that made her turn away from her chambers and keep moving toward Korah's.

She pressed her face near the gap in the door. Corin sat next to Korah on her lounger, one hand over hers, the other bracing across her shoulders.

"They don't exclude you out of ill intention," Corin assured her. His hand moved in soft strokes along the thin black fabric. "They're all in pain, and they're fortunate to share a closeness that brings comfort to each other."

"They've never wanted my comfort."

"I don't know your nephews, but I do know Yesenia. She's not likely to ask for it."

"Aye. Just the same."

"I'm sorry I never had the privilege of knowing your brother, Stewardess Holton, but he must have been some man to have left such an impact on so many."

The Widow wheezed into her handkerchief. "You're kind, to comfort an old woman in her grief, even if ye are wrong."

"You are not old," he said lightly. "And you have lost someone irreplaceable."

"Aye." Her warbled voice returned. "I know how Khoulter's children see me. How they always have. I'm not their mother. I never said I was, but I did my best, aye? I did my best for them."

"A mother is duty bound to her children," Corin said. "An aunt gives because she has chosen to. They know that."

"Do they?" The Widow laughed. "No, I donnae ken they do. But you're a sweet lad for saying so. For sitting with me."

"I'll stay as long as you like," Corin said, smiling at her. "And tomorrow, you'll be at the celebration? Yesenia asked me to go, and I could use a friend."

"Nooo…" She patted his knee. "I ken that's for the young ones. Not for knotty widows like me."

"Come with me," he said, insisting. "I'll easily overshadow you on the list of the unwanted. They'll pay no mind to a knotty widow when a bootlicking Quinlanden walks in."

The Widow laughed. "You're brave, coming here. I'll give you that."

Yesenia rolled away from the gap in the door. Her pulse quickened and she pressed a hand to her chest, to quell it. What was happening to her? She could hardly breathe, her words tonight had not been her own, and now this? How would she manage at a celebration if she couldn't even assert control over her own emotions?

She stretched to the tips of her toes and quietly returned the way she'd come.

TWENTY-ONE
BREAKING THE PATTERN

The trill of music reached them before they'd even left the keep. Corin tilted his head to listen, to try to patch it together with the world he knew back home. Fiddles and bagpipes, Yesenia explained, before he found the words to ask. Khoulter's best mate, Rylahn Rutland, had brought the traveling musicians in from Leecaster Bay, she said. They'd been a favorite of both men when they had still been running around as boys.

A rich, gamy scent permeated the soft breeze, mingling with the unmistakable brine of the shore. Roast boar, Yesenia said, because it was Khoulter's favorite. The aroma drifted, smoke coating the burnt-umber-colored tent tops, creating a blanket of color that stretched for miles. Dozens of banners, all boasting the crested wave, were spread around the party and down into the sand. This entire night was an homage to a man they'd all loved.

There were far more in attendance than he'd expected. Though everyone of political importance was already there, inside the several dozen tents erected at the top of the jutting sea cliffs, the shoreline below was streaked with the bobbing torches of thousands of celebrants: men, women, and children from all societal classes. Everyone from merchants to beggars had closed shop and hitched rides to Warwicktown to celebrate the too-short life of the lord who had sold his own belongings to see them fed. From the white cliffs of the eastern shore to the miners of Warwicktown and the Golden Coast, everyone was represented.

"You donnae have to eat the boar," Yesenia whispered, with a spirited shoulder nudge. She had him by the arm, earning them their share of curious glances. Some, more than curious. Some, bordering on threatening. It had only been a day, and the whispers about their Southerland lass and her bootlicking husband had swelled as high as the tide lapping at the driftwood deep along the shoreline.

"That's generous, thank you," he retorted, grinning at her. "But won't that give me away as an Easterlander?"

"There isnae enough boar in the world to disguise a tree-dweller," she teased.

She'd been like that all day. Playful. Bordering so close to affectionate that it sent his emotions on a hilly path. Corin absorbed everything she offered him, and he turned it into the courage he'd need for the evening. He wasn't afraid of the Southerlanders' ire, but he didn't want to steal focus from why they'd gathered—to be the cause of her pain, if that happened. If she hadn't insisted he come, he would have stayed behind, out of respect for the Reach and the Warwicks.

He almost had anyway, until he'd realized her impish way with him was a pretense to mask her grief. She'd not spoken of her father once, neither on their tense flight from Whitechurch nor since arriving in Warwicktown.

Nor had they spoken of, or repeated, what had happened that night in the cell.

"We're late," she mused aloud as they both took in the massive crowd of celebrants teeming from the tents. "Just the way I like it. Donnae need anyone cooing or cawing over me. I'm home. That's that. Nothing to talk about."

"Nothing at all?" He laughed, gesturing toward himself.

"Ye flatter yourself. There's enough ale here for men to forget their own name."

"Let us hope."

She pulled on his arm, stopping them. The light in her eyes faded to something more serious. "Aye, Corin, there isnae a thing to it. Talk to them. Be one of them. Donnae lord over them or act above it. 'Tis no different than Slattery Row, not really. Be *one of them*, and they'll warm to you, once they see you're not what they expect. Maybe not right away, but they will. Ye ken?"

Corin nodded. "I promise to try."

They entered the tents, and the din of sound mounted to sensory assault. The rise of a thousand conversations competing was disorienting as he searched for the few faces familiar to him but found none. Instead he was met with diverted gazes and paused conversations as men and women of the Southerlands tried to make sense of how the daughter of their beloved lord tolerated Corin's presence.

Yesenia aimed them toward a center display housing a long line of kegs.

"Best ale in the kingdom," she said, slushing a mug as she thrust it at him. "Drink."

Corin, squinting one eye at her, took a sip. He had to press his hand to his mouth to keep from spitting it out. He held the cup away from himself and pointed at it with his free hand. "What's *in* this?"

"More kick, for one. Go on. You'll get used to it. Will turn those blond locks brown quick enough." She snaked a hand up and tousled his hair.

The less Yesenia was her usual self, the more he worried. He wanted to enjoy this side of her, but he knew her better than that.

For her, Corin forced himself to ingest more of the rancid swill she'd erroneously called ale. He *did* want to fit in, almost as much as he wanted her to be happy with his performance. It would help if she'd offered some hint of her expectations. She couldn't really want everyone to think she was happy with her Easterland husband, could she? What role had she assigned him, in her mind and for them?

"Sen!" Byrne cried out, from somewhere. His hand poked through the top of the crowd, waving as he made his way over. The siblings embraced and then Byrne turned toward Corin.

"You came. That's brave."

Corin laughed. "Your sister brings it out in me."

"Mm." Byrne passed his gaze over Corin. "Aye, that she does."

"Where's Khallum?" Yesenia asked. She adjusted her dress, shifting from one foot to the other.

"With Hamish and Sam." Byrne glanced behind himself and then at Corin, before looking back at her. "Erran isnae here."

Yesenia's neck pulsed, the first indication of how thin a line she was walking. "For the best, that. Have you seen Anatole?"

"Aye, he was looking for ye earlier," Byrne said. His eyes narrowed, and Yesenia turned to follow his gaze.

Corin, perplexed, did the same and spotted the source of their ire: two young men, passing fearful glances between them as they cut a wide berth to avoid Yesenia.

"They better not..." Yesenia muttered through a clenched jaw. "Not here."

"Let it go, Sen," Byrne urged. "Look, they're plenty scared of you."

"What's going on?" Corin asked, raising his brows with his confusion.

"Just the Garrick boys. Fecking rats." She grunted, shaking her head.

"Sen!" A wispy redhead in a crimson gown flew in behind Yesenia, nearly bowling her over. Yesenia spun, laughing, and they embraced.

"Sessaly," Byrne explained to Corin. "Erran's sister."

Did Byrne assume Yesenia had told Corin about Erran? How much did Byrne think Corin knew, to speak so casually of the young man his sister had been in love with before the king assigned her in marriage to her enemy?

They watched the girls whisper to themselves. Throwing Corin an apologetic glance, Yesenia mouthed the words *be right back* and scurried off with Sessaly in the direction of a gathering of other girls their age.

"Old friends?" Corin asked. He picked up on a few rogue words from nearby conversations. *Bootlicker. Tree-dweller. Outlander.* One of them included an old man, who caught Corin's eye. Corin awkwardly raised his mug in cheers. The man dragged his gaze up and down the Easterlander and then shook his head in disgust.

"Aye. Though…" Byrne scratched the back of his neck. "She's acting more keen on them now than she ever did before. Sessaly Rutland is a chinwagger. Yesenia never had the time for it."

Corin had spent more time with Venya's family after losing her, to feel closer to her.

He emptied his ale.

"Might slow that down," Byrne chided with a grin. "Need to last the evening, aye?"

Corin grunted and refilled his drink, forcing himself to *not* follow Yesenia's movements. He took in the enormity of the fete as his eyes swept the crazed energy flowing between the tents. The air was ripe with food and drink and smoke. Laughter was the language of choice. This was no somber, funereal remembrance. They'd called it a celebration, and they meant it.

Byrne read his silence. "Donnae fuss yourself over Yesenia and Erran. Past is past. Erran has a wife of his own now."

Corin turned back toward him. "Does he?"

"Khallum and Father saw to it when Yesenia left. They were afraid he'd go after her and start a war. They decided to settle the matter for good."

Corin pretended to not be relieved. "And he's not here tonight anyway."

"Aye, well he will be. His father, Steward Rutland, planned most of the celebration." Byrne took a swig of his ale and dragged his gaze over the sea of celebrants. "If Sessaly is here, Erran is here, somewhere."

Fortune had favored Khallum with his friendships, but that had never been more true than tonight, when they all instinctively fathomed the needs he couldn't articulate.

Round, lovable Hamish kept tight to Gwyn, sending her through a whirlwind of introductions she'd never remember in the morning. Hamish's joviality disarmed her and turned what would have been a chore into something resembling entertainment. Most of the locals were taking to her pleasantly enough. They'd saved their distrust for the Easterlander.

Sam, when he wasn't mouthing to himself about the cost of every little thing at the celebration, had an eye on the Widow, striking the perfect balance between engaging her in light talk and complimenting everything, from the way she handled her grief to the lace she'd chosen for her cuffs.

Erran was missing, but his absence was what Khallum most needed. What Yesenia needed, and she'd thank him if she knew.

I know you loved my father too, Erran. But he'd want Sen to forget her troubles tonight, aye? And we both know, the two of you together, t'would be a world of trouble for ye both.

Is she happy? Does she love her husband?

Those are nay longer your questions to ask. Remember your own wife. Remember Mariel.

"You look lost for purpose," Gwyn said, sidling in beside him. He lightened at the arrival of her distinctive warmth. Such a surprise she was to him, every day. The locals hadn't entirely thawed toward her yet, but they would, just as he had.

Some were born of salt and sand. Others were remade.

"Aye." Khallum laced his hands atop his head. "I donnae ken where to begin."

"Steward Rutland took care of that for you. You're not here to fuss over details, my love. You're here to draw strength from your people."

Should he tell her he'd almost not come at all? Would she think him weak if she knew he'd spent the better part of the early morning sobbing by the shore, like a bairn?

Of course she would. She wouldn't say it, but she'd think it.

"How'd ye manage to shed Hamish?"

"His wife stole him away," Gwyn said pleasantly. "She's an interesting woman, Yanna. Hard to know though." She wrinkled her nose. "A bit like Yesenia."

"Eh?" Khallum spotted his sister flocked by a gaggle of young women, daughters of stewards, all girls she'd had little time for in her old life. "What about Yesenia?"

"I said she's hard to know."

Khallum curled the corner of his mouth in a grin as he took notice, for the first time that night, what a stunning gown Gwyn had chosen. The emerald set her hair aflame. "Have I told ye how beautiful ye look tonight?"

"No, nor do I require you to ply with me flattery. You know that," Gwyn replied, scolding him, sharpening her tone at the end. "I'd like to befriend her, Khallum. But I don't suppose she likes me very much."

Khallum pursed his lips. Someone passed him an ale, which he tossed back, then handed the empty mug to someone else. "She doesnae *know* ye, Gwyn. She only returned yesterday, and on the end of an ordeal that would leave anyone sideways. Last time she saw you, the king was fecking all our lives about." He kissed the top of her bare shoulder. "She'll need a sister. Her place is in the Southerlands; I see it now. She'll need you."

"Yesenia strikes me as a woman who never leaves you confused on her feelings. She doesn't trust me." Gwyn rolled her shoulders and plastered a smile. "What do you make of Corin?"

Khallum flared his nostrils. "I'd prefer not to make anything of him at all."

"You think he's dirty, like his father?"

"How can he not be?"

"But Yesenia believes—"

"Yesenia cannae decide *what* she wants. Trust me. Lass could outwit and outfight most men in this Reach, but when it comes to how she *feels* about 'em?" He snickered.

"You didn't answer my question," she stated. "Are we safe with him here?"

Khallum shrugged his hands out, pinching his shoulders together. "You tell me, Gwyn. The Derehams never stopped trading with the Quinlandens. You know them better than I."

Gwyn recoiled at the accusation. "I don't know them any better than you. But we have one here, now, in our home—"

"I cannae say one thing out of one corner of my mouth and something else out of another," he snapped. The words were more for himself. "I told her to make the best of her marriage, even after she *begged* me to let her stay. Aye, well she's making the best of it, and I willnae kick her down the other end of the coast when she's sacrificed more than any of us."

"As you say," Gwyn said pleasantly. She took a deep breath and looked around, searching for an escape. "Aunt Korah is all by herself. I'll go to her."

"Aye. Do that."

Gwyn lifted her skirts and sauntered off without another word.

"Something wrong with Lady Warwick?" Sam asked, from behind.

Khallum spun around. "There ye are. Aren't ye supposed to be tending the Widow?"

"She gave me the slip." Sam tsk-tsked himself. "I see Gwyn has taken up the charge."

"You seen the tree-dweller?"

Sam nodded. "Byrne has him."

"And no sign of Erran. Right?"

"So far."

Khallum held his mug aloft. Sam met him for the toast but set it aside, untouched, when Khallum drained his ale.

"She looks happy, Yesenia," Sam said. "Not nearly so…"

"Stabby?"

Sam chuckled. "Aye. Why do you suppose that is?"

"Not what I ken you're implying. Yesenia is all salt, all sand. She understands duty and honor. We do what we must. That's all."

"Of course," Sam said quickly. "Couldnae ever be more."

"Keep an eye out for Erran, would ye?"

"I will, but he did promise, Khallum. We should take him at his word."

"Fools who lead with their heart are easily parted from their promises." Khallum clapped him on the back. "I need a word with Steward Nye. You have my back? In case you're wrong?"

"Always."

A large man with the thickest hands Corin had ever seen reared up behind him, sending Corin's heart into his chest and his ale into a nearby woman. She shrieked and chucked the remainder of her drink at him in retaliation.

"Corin Quinlanden, aye?" the man said, nodding exuberantly as Corin swiped his hands over his ale-stained jerkin. "Feck-all. Ain't kidding, they were, what they said about tree-dwellers."

"I'm sorry," Corin said. He shook his hand to expel the sticky beer. "We haven't met. You are?"

"Hamish Strong," the young man said with a proud tilt of his chin. "Son'a Steward Strong, and mate of your wife's brother."

"A pleasure to meet you," Corin said when he regained his breath. Someone handed him another ale, which was the second time a drink had appeared so fortuitously. If that had happened in the Easterlands, he'd suspect poison. But something as surreptitious as poison would be an insult to these men. "What is it they say about…tree-dwellers?"

Hamish rolled his head back. Licked his lips. "It's in the skin, they say." He gobbled Corin's cheeks in his meaty fists and laughed. "Like the rear of a bairn. Too soft!"

Corin half chuckled with him. He couldn't discern whether the man was making nice with him or insulting him. He suspected a little of both.

"Cannae keep your palms off anything, ye old louse?" another man said, laughing with Hamish but in a more reserved manner. "Samuel Law. Son of Steward Law and confidante of Khallum."

"A pleas—"

"Not necessary," Samuel said with a swipe of his hands. "We're all kin tonight. Lord Khoulter wasnae a formal man, nor will we be as we celebrate him. Did you meet him, Lord Quinlanden?"

"Corin, please," Corin replied in a rush. Byrne had been gone a while now, and he'd been the only thing standing between Corin and outright aggression from some of the Southerlanders. "And yes but only briefly, at Termonglen."

"I heard they made ye all rut like pigs in heat, front of all," Hamish said, his eyes wide.

"No, thankfully," Corin said, shaking off the uncomfortable imagery this produced. "It all happened very fast and then we were all sent home."

"Very fast is how most wives 'scribe their marriage night." Hamish roared, slapping Sam on the arm. "Get it, aye, Corin?"

"I get it," Corin said. He searched for Yesenia and found her speaking with a tall, thin man he almost recognized.

Samuel followed his gaze. "That's her personal guard, Anatole. The one your father sent back."

Ah. "My father did a lot of things that don't sit well with me."

"Still your father though, in'e?" Hamish countered.

"The Guardians don't give us a choice in these matters," Corin muttered. He stretched to set his ale on a nearby stump, but someone again exchanged it for a fresh one.

246

"Aye," Samuel replied. "Sometimes they get it right though. Khoulter was a good man *and* a good father. His love for his lads and lass was as true as the sea."

Hamish raised his mug in a toast but didn't wait for the others to join in before gulping it back. Foam painted his red beard. "I like me ale the way I like me women. Biting all the way down."

Corin spotted Yesenia break free of Anatole, moving through the crowd. "Hamish. Samuel. If you'll excuse—"

"Hamish, *for the love* of the Guardians," Sam said, chastising his friend with a wearying look. "This must be very overwhelming for you, Lo…Corin."

Corin tightened his face into a forced smile, one eye still on Yesenia. He didn't like the look he'd seen on her face, only a flash of it, a crack in the careful veneer she wanted no one to untangle. "Aside from being keenly aware of how others view me, it's been fine, actually, so far. I think I'll like it here. But I really do need—"

"Ye came at the right time!" Hamish boomed and whistled. The odd, urgent look he passed to Samuel was brief but not so quick that Corin didn't catch it. "Aye, the storms will blow a man to Beyond." He braced his jaw. "Ever, eh, seen storms like that, Corin?"

"Not like that. No."

"We'll need to teach you how to handle yourself on a ship, of course," Samuel added with a nervous shift sideways, transfixed by something else.

Yesenia had almost disappeared, but Corin's eyes snapped to a man running after her. It wasn't Anatole. She seemed unaware she was being followed, never changing her pace, but the man's quickened, narrowing the distance between them.

"I really need to go find—"

His third attempt was thwarted by both men moving to block him.

"Let's see what the other end of the tents has to offer, right, Hamish?"

Hamish's easy smile turned to a gnarled frown. "Aye, Sam. I ken that's exactly what we should do."

Khallum's friends nudged Corin forward. He tossed one last helpless glance over his shoulder, but Yesenia was already gone.

Yesenia pitched forward into the balmy dusk, gulping her first breath of fresh air of the evening. When she hit the grassy sand, she kept moving, downward along the side of the cliff until she found a gap between the rocky crag that she recognized as a place she'd played as a lass.

She slipped inside. The opening was narrow, with little room to move around, but she didn't need to move. She needed to be free.

With an exhausted grunt, she backed into a pile of rocks and rolled her face into her hands, kneading her fingers through the hair she'd allowed the Widow to make into ringlets for her earlier. Her natural curls were too loose, Korah had said, like it were a personal failing.

Add it to the list, Yesenia thought as she pulled hard, salty breaths in through her nose and exhaled them open-mouthed, her eyes closed and pressed into the heels of her palms.

Warwicktown was the one place in the kingdom she shouldn't have to pretend, and yet it was all she'd done tonight. Tomorrow, they'd run their mouths about how happy she looked, how *lovely,* never knowing the darkness rotting her from the inside out.

Except Anatole. Her master of subtleties. He'd seen through the careful act, which shouldn't have surprised her, but why did he have to say anything? Why couldn't he have let it go, just for tonight?

"Sen?"

She looked up and straight into the eyes of Erran Rutland. He hung along the side of the rock, one foot into the small enclave, the other hovering behind.

"Erran?" Her voice croaked. "I didnae see you inside. I thought—"

Erran rushed in and gathered her in his arms before she could finish. The insistent crush of his mouth ushered her back to simpler times, when her heart had been fuller than she'd ever realized.

But these were not simpler times.

Yesenia dropped her head, breaking the kiss. She backed away to create space between them.

"Forgive me, Sen." He reached for her, but she didn't budge. "I know the timing…tonight being…but I just didnae want you to be alone."

"Erran…" Yesenia sighed. The ache in her chest spread to her shoulders. "I'm not alone. I'm surrounded by my people."

"But I knew you wouldnae let anyone in. Ye never do."

"So I'm broken, you mean?"

"That isnae…oh, Sen." Erran sagged against the rock wall, moaning with his exhale. "I never thought I'd see you again. When Khallum told me—"

"No. Leave it."

"When he told me—"

"LEAVE IT!" Yesenia ripped off the oatin shrug the Widow had made her wear over her dress, complaining of her bosom being *too ample*. All these concessions she'd made, for others. The dress. The hair. The shrug. The giggles and smiles. "I donnae have it in me, Erran! I didnae then and now…" Now, what? Where did the end of her thought fall?

"It's all right. I'm not angry," he said, hands held out as if she were a danger and not someone he'd once claimed to love.

"Aye? Well, that's good." Her words ran together. "For I'm not apologizing."

His face crumbled. "I donnae want to fight with you, Sen. I've missed you so. I was in such a dark place when you left. I didnae know how to climb my way out of it, and I almost…was your brother and your father who fixed it. I had no choice."

Yesenia scrunched her face. "No choice in what?"

"Three months, it's been, since Mariel and I wed. Was your father and brother who arranged it." Erran lowered his eyes. "But seeing ye here now, like this, I'd throw it all away for you, Yesenia Warwick. I'd throw everything away for you."

"You're married…" Yesenia's words caught with her gasp. Her heart was impaled upon the sudden stab of pain. "I was coming *back*, Erran. I told Khallum. He *knew*…"

Erran's strained voice wrenched the invisible blade stuck in her chest. "And how could I have known that, Sen? How?"

"Because you know me!"

"And the Yesenia I knew wouldnae ever have let me suffer without telling me herself! She wouldnae have left her *brother* to say the words!"

Yesenia drew back, panting. She met his eyes, as sad and wild as hers.

"I wrote to you. If you'd have just responded to *even one*…"

Yesenia threw out her arms and raised her chin. "I never got a single letter from you."

"I sent ye over a dozen. Poured my heart out, which wasnae easy, I ken, knowing that those tree-dwellers would read them."

They both braced when a chilled wind roared through the enclave. Yesenia ran her hands over her bare shoulders with a shiver. She thrust a hand out in refusal when Erran tried to come help.

"I loved ye then, Yesenia. I love ye now. Nothing has changed for me."

"*Everything* has changed!" Yesenia cried. "*Everything*, Erran. You have a wife now, and do ye ken me for the kind of woman who would wreck a hearth like that? And me…"

Erran moved closer. "And you," he replied with an echo. "I saw your husband in there."

"Ye have eyes then. Good for you," she spat. She had to get control of her heart before it beat so hard and so fast it sent her unconscious.

"You brought a Quinlanden, *here*. To the Southerlands," he accused.

"That *Quinlanden* saved my life. *Twice*." She emphasized the last word, glaring. "I donnae need to explain myself to you. I never did."

Erran laughed. "Aye, because explaining yourself might have saved us all this heartache. I might've known ye loved me sooner, so we could have already been wed when the king called upon you."

Yesenia narrowed her eyes to thin slits. "Who said I loved ye, Erran? Not me."

He recoiled, as wounded as she'd expected he'd be. "That was cruel."

"Life is cruel."

"Why has it always been so hard for ye to say how ye feel, Sen? Would it hurt you so much, to be real?" He held a hand out toward her. She tried not to look at it. Better if she could ride her wave of anger, rolling forward on a sea of resentment. Better for him. For her. For all.

She never should have looked at his face. Her resolve, for whatever it had been, crumbled.

Erran crushed her into his arms. "I'm so sorry about your father, Sen. I'm just so sorry. He was such a good man."

Yesenia grimaced as she sobbed, loathing every tear, every beat of weakness pouring from her and into the chest of a man she *had* loved, but did she still? Was she even capable of it?

Erran peeled back and cupped her face in his palm. "My love. My heart."

"Please…" *Don't,* she tried to add, but her grief had taken over. What a fool she'd been, thinking she could bury it.

Erran kissed her again, and her resistance melted into the damp rocks of the enclave. His hands wound through her hair as he moaned into her mouth, a sound still so familiar she could almost forget any time had passed at all.

But when he went to peel her dress away, she froze. She shook her head, stepping to the side.

"What's wrong? What is it?"

"I just…I cannae!" she stammered, bolting past him and stumbling back out into the open air.

"Yesenia!" Corin quickened his pace to catch up to her, but she was moving fast. She raced ahead, her dress hitched, her hair catching the wind. "Wait!"

The terrain shifted when she hit the small stretch of sand connecting the cliffs to the keep. It gave Corin the opportunity to narrow the distance. "Yesenia!"

She dropped her skirts when she reached the courtyard, but her stride remained purposefully single-minded.

It wasn't until his feet slammed into the stone of the main hall that he stopped to catch his breath.

He knew where she was going.

Corin found her in their chambers, tearing away the layers of her dress. Fabrics, much thicker than the tulles and satins of the Easterlands, were draped over chairs, unlit candelabras, and the floor. He could only watch, incredulous, as she stripped herself down to nothing and wandered between the netting separating their room from the open air, then on to the private balcony facing the sea.

He pressed his palm to the netting. "Yesenia?"

"Aye? What is it?"

Looking at her as she was felt almost like an intrusion. Her flesh was soft, tanned, over a muscled back that flared into hips he'd touched but twice and still felt in his dreams. Her hair fell half over the front of her shoulders, the rest trailing uneven curls down her spine. He noted the soft white lashes in her skin, the whisper-thin scars of that terrible day at the chalet.

When he was lost for response, she angled her head to the side and called, "You just gonna stand there and gape at me or come out here?"

He caught the quaver she tried to hide. "I'll find you a robe."

"No." She returned her eyes to the sea. "You wanted to come to Warwicktown. To know my home. To know me. Well, ye saw it tonight. And now you're seeing me, as I am."

"If that's what you want," Corin said, pressing against the netting. "For me to see you."

"No man in my life has ever asked me what I want." She laughed to herself, tossing more of her curls behind her.

"I have." Corin slid in beside her. He tried to not divert his eyes from the white crests of high tide. "I asked you that when you came to Whitechurch. More than once."

Yesenia smirked. She angled her head away and brought a hand to her eyes before turning back. "So ye did."

"Was it him? Was it Erran?" Corin stripped the jealousy from his voice. "I saw the two of you."

"If it was?"

"It's nothing to me," he lied, "if you want to be with the one you love."

Yesenia sniffled. She folded her arms under her bare breasts. They looked so soft and inviting under the moon's light.

Get ahold of yourself. "I'm not upset if it was. But—"

"Upset? Have ye any right to be?"

"No," Corin said carefully. "And I'm not, Yesenia. But I *am* worried about you."

"Last time ye did that, nearly got yourself killed."

"Do you want to talk about it? What happened tonight?"

"Talk about it?!" Yesenia's mouth gaped in horror.

"I know you don't believe this," Corin said. His heart lived now in his throat, along with the startling, burgeoning realization of what—*who*—had caused this. "But your happiness is important to me. You being okay is important to me. You said to me that you've been the pawn of men, and all I can think about—day and night, whenever I see you, whenever I talk to you, look at you—is how to break the pattern, to be the one who *breaks* the pattern.

Not *for* you, Yesenia, but *with* you. To be so unlike those other men as to be unrecognizable."

Yesenia's head fell forward. She wrapped her arms tighter around herself as her sobs shook her.

Corin's instincts replaced his fears as he slid behind her, gathering her in his arms. Her flesh was so warm it choked his breath. The underside of her breasts brushed his hand, and he had to remember what he was doing there.

Kissing the back of her head, he whispered, "Tell me what you need."

Yesenia rolled around in his arms and lifted her face. She aimed her red-rimmed eyes on his. They glistened, from tears fresh, tears old. "You are a most unusual man, Corin. I donnae ken what to do with ye."

Corin pressed his forehead to hers. Welcomed the hard throb of her heart through her flesh. He said again, softer, slower, "Tell me what you *need*, Yesenia."

Yesenia's lips moved, soundless, as she studied him. What he wouldn't give to know her thoughts, to have the gift of interpreting them so he could give her what she would never ask for.

Then she stretched up on her toes and whispered in his ear.

His sigh melted to a groan.

What he'd been fighting since he'd entered their chambers became a battle lost.

Corin cupped his palms under her ass and hoisted her atop the balcony ledge. Yesenia wrapped her legs around his waist and tightened them, reaching to free him from his trousers when he wasn't fast enough for the urgency of her needs.

She dug her fingers into his ass to drive him in. They cried out together. Yesenia's feral scream was loud enough to wake everyone in the keep, but their pleasure blended into the roar of the sea.

Corin dragged her tongue through his teeth as he drove faster, harder, trying to kiss her when all he wanted was to press his mouth to every inch of her. Even that wasn't enough for her, and she let him know with her iron grip, tightening, urging him to rise to a pace that would send him over the edge far too quickly.

"I can't…I'm going to…"

"Come for me." She purred, throwing her head back. "And then come for me again."

Corin gripped her hair in one hand and crushed his lips to hers as he came so hard, he had to hold her from flying off the balcony.

His knees buckled, but Yesenia still had a firm grip on his ass, and she guided him back into place, squeezing herself against his soft organ to bring him back to life. He didn't tell her it wasn't needed, that the desire in her eyes, the sweat beading atop her breasts, the words she'd whispered—which he'd never get out of his head—would bring him back to life a thousand times over.

Corin lifted her into his arms, backing away from the balcony. She wrapped one arm around his head, reaching down with the other to keep him inside her, to leave not a second to chance.

"Don't stop," she whispered. Her pulse throbbed in her neck. "Not even if I ask ye to."

He passed them both through the netting and then laid her on the bed, falling over her, still joined. He moved in slow rhythm to start, learning the shape of her desire. Her hips bucked to urge him on as she rolled her head back against the pillow, mouth parted, eyes glazed in yearning.

Before he lost himself entirely, he planted kisses atop both of her eyelids. Her brief, soft smile of gratitude placed his heart firmly in her palm.

But that was for later.

There was something else he wanted first.

Something else she needed.

Corin plunged into her, sending her eyes fluttering with her scream. He arced her hips in his palms and gave her everything she'd asked for.

TWENTY-TWO
AN ORE-SIZED PROBLEM

Corin was mesmerized by the waterwheel. He knew he shouldn't stop to watch, when Yesenia was already half-way up the hill, almost to the mine's entrance, but he'd never seen anything like the behemoth power-creator. In the midst of his awe, it occurred to him Yesenia might have felt the same way when she'd first beheld their kingdom in the trees.

The waterwheel was taller than any home or business in nearby Sandycove, a marvel of craftsmanship and innovation that even his father would have admired. It sluiced through the sea, powering the drainage that kept miners safe from the devastating floods that would end a mine, and the men with it. The mines in Warwicktown were dug too close to the land to benefit from these, but they, too, had enraptured him. There, the cavernous belch of the colossal bellows moaned into the open air twice an hour, providing another kind of life-saving relief from the stifling heat within.

"Ye coming, tree-dweller?"

He tore his attention away from the sea, returning it to her. A slow smile appeared on his face at the sight of her, hair everywhere but where it should be, hands splayed on her leather-swaddled hips. She no longer startled him in her anger, and, with several months behind them in their life in Warwicktown, he'd even begun to see these telltale peculiarities as adorable.

That though, he'd never confess.

"Yes, coming," he called back and launched into a jog to catch up.

When he reached her, she rewarded him with a deep kiss and a cupped hand between his legs, both wonderful and utterly torturous. They'd come to spend the day at the Strongsea mine, and there were many hours—too many—before they'd welcome the privacy of their rented bedchamber. "That's so unfair." He groaned. "So, so unfair."

"Ye ken I willnae make it up to you later?"

Corin flicked his eyes downward. "Meanwhile, how am I supposed to hide *this*?"

Yesenia passed her tongue across her bottom lip. "Well, perhaps ye can think of it as a game then?"

"What will be my prize, if I make it the whole day without pulling you into some corner and having my way?"

Yesenia tugged his arms and locked them behind her back. "I could tell ye, but we both know I'm the more imaginative of the two of us when it comes to matters of pleasure."

"Mm," he said, kissing her again and then again. "You'll surprise me then?"

"Do I not always?"

"You do," he said in agreement, drawing his arms up her back and into her knot of waves. "You always, always do."

"We get it. Ye can tolerate each other." Korah huffed up the path, at last caught up to them. Corin had tried to escort her, but her stubborn insistence that she was more than capable of escorting herself had given him this ardent interlude with his wife. "You're not newlyweds anymore though. Going on a year now, aye? Six months in Warwicktown, anyway."

Yesenia peeled away. "There ye are. We thought Steward Strong might've sidelined ye."

"Not all widowers are out stalking for a new wife, lass." Korah dropped her bunched skirts and basket, and she wheezed to the side.

"You're not taking inventory yourself, for a second husband?"

"One good marriage in a lifetime is all anyone should need." She knitted her brows. "Or *want*, for that matter."

Corin grinned at Yesenia. She grinned back.

"Shall we?" Corin held out his arm, and Korah accepted with a coquettish smile. He transferred her abandoned basket to his free hand.

"You tell your brother I said this, and I'll claim you were telling tales," she purred. "But the men of the Southerlands could learn a thing or two about chivalry from your husband, Yesenia."

"This is our most profitable mine in the Southerlands," Yesenia explained as she yanked on the rope to indicate they were ready for the pulley. "Mostly ore and copper but also silver, which is rare on the central coast. Rare anywhere, really. Without that waterwheel, we'd have nothing though. We lose half our coastal mines to flooding, still full of ore and promise. We cannae build these waterwheels fast enough."

"Why?" Corin gripped the small, wobbly basket. He'd imagined something far more sturdy and practical to take them down into the mine, but it was too late to turn back now. These past months, Yesenia had let him into her world, one experience at a time. Once a week, she ventured to a different mine, to bring reports back to Khallum. Sometimes, she was gone for days, even traveling as far as Whitecliffe—where Erran Rutland lived, Corin thought, before burying the fear.

Never had she invited Corin along on one of those ventures. She'd always taken Anatole as her escort. Until now.

"Donnae have the gold," Korah said. "All we mine goes to your kin."

Corin swallowed. "I know. I wish that wasn't so."

"Most of the gold comes from the Wastelands," Yesenia said, correcting her aunt. "The Wastelands used to be ours. The Rhiagains stole the peninsula from under us."

"Is there not gold anywhere else in the Southerlands?"

"Aye, there is. In flooded mines we cannae any longer excavate. There's been ore lines spotted in Blackpool too, promising ones, but as soon we heat that earth, your father will come sniffing, and that, too, will be gone."

Corin seldom thought of his father these days. Though a long way off from being a Southerlander himself, he felt less and less like an Easterlander with each day that passed. His life in Whitechurch seemed like a history belonging to another lifetime. Only occasionally did he still wonder why his father had so easily let them stay, not even so much as responding to Khallum's return message. Why he'd said nothing at all.

The air thickened as they descended. A ripe, rotten scent had him wrinkling his nose, but it did nothing to either of the women, who were used to it. Yesenia caught sight of his manic efforts to stay centered in the basket and chucked him under his chin.

"You'll be all right," she promised with a wink. "It's not our finest cart, but we spent all our gold on the wheel. There's more room at the base, so ye willnae feel like the walls are gonna eat ye."

"I know the walls aren't going to eat me," he mumbled in defense, but she'd leaned over the edge, peering down into the mine.

"Never liked this one," Korah said with a shiver. She smoothed her skirts and lifted her basket from the floor of the cart. "Like an oven."

"We'll add the bellows when we can," Yesenia said. She startled Corin by leaping out of the side of the basket.

260

She urged her mare on, toward town. They'd stay in Sandycove and arrive back in Warwicktown midday the following day. The Strongs had invited them to stay at their keep, but Yesenia had politely declined. "Iron is the crux of our trade. Iron is what we offer the Westerlands, in exchange for food that will keep the scurvy from our men. Food we cannae grow here."

Corin absorbed her point. Korah, riding on the other side of him, said nothing.

"Surely Byrne can negotiate something?"

"Byrne has no power in the west," Yesenia stated. "His wife holds it all."

"Sounds familiar," Korah quipped.

Corin exhaled. "What do we do?"

"We?" Yesenia shook her head. She rolled the tension from her shoulders. "'Tis Khallum's problem to fix now. We were just there to flash our smiles and find the truths they ken we're too pretty to understand."

"If only there was a Reach just to the north of us that we could trust to trade with," Korah mused aloud.

"What can *I* do?" Corin said, this time loud enough only for Yesenia to catch.

She tried to grin. "'Tis I who owes you something tonight."

After a light supper of stew and ale, Yesenia told Corin to head up to their room and she'd meet him there. She was too tired to give him a decent excuse, though he waited for one, and he only did as she asked upon realizing there was none to be had.

She watched him ascend the stairs and wave from the door before she started speaking.

"Aunt Korah—"

"So ye are keeping secrets from him," Korah said. She leaned back in her chair with crossed arms. "I thought it was odd, mind, the way ye paraded him before all the men, but I suspected ye had your purpose."

"My purpose…" Yesenia's sigh was as heavy as her heart. "There's nothing to be read there. It was the right move. If he's to live here, he needs to be safe."

"Mm." Korah fingered her empty mug of ale. "What is it ye donnae want him to hear?"

"I need something from you." Yesenia splayed her fingers on the table, her eyes cast down at them. "When I was a lass—"

"You're still a lass, married or no, but go on."

"Ye tried to give me this foul, green drink in a vial. I said no because at the time I didnae need it."

Korah lowered her chin. "You want to prevent a bairn from growing?"

Yesenia swallowed. Nodded.

"Why did ye not ask me when ye arrived here?"

"I—"

"It's been *months*, Yesenia, and all this time, you've been sharing your bed with him. Why now?"

"I was a fool not to ask sooner. I know it. Nothing ye can say I have not said to myself."

"Aye. So *why now?*"

Yesenia pursed her lips and shrugged out her hands. "I dinnae ken."

"You do," Korah replied, pushing. "And I ken I do too."

Yesenia groaned and sagged forward. "Can we just agree that I need it and let that be it?"

Korah shook her head in disbelief. "You're not playing pretend here, lass. That man is your husband. Not just in name either. Not anymore."

Yesenia kept her eyes on the table.

"Would ye deny it?"

Yesenia shook her head.

"You've gone about it all backward." Korah tapped her nails against the wood and leaned in. "The time to ask would've been when you first came home. But now?" She fell back again. "If you willnae say it, I will."

"Say what?"

"You're scared."

Yesenia whipped her head up in offense. "When have I ever been scared of anything?"

"You were scared of how ye felt about that Rutland boy, and you're scared now."

Yesenia passed her tongue back and forth in her mouth. "Is this the price for the vial? I have to listen to this?"

"You have a duty to give that man a child."

"I have done more than my share of duty!" Yesenia lowered her head at the attention she'd collected. "You know that," she said, quieter.

"Perhaps 'tis my fault, for telling ye there was no joy to be found in marriage." Korah sighed. "Duty aside, I can see, plain as the day, how ye feel about Corin. Guardians know why they paired my poor niece with a tree-dweller, but who are we to question? It doesnae change your truth."

"Aye?" Yesenia's nostrils flared. "And what truth is that?"

"Your fear will split your heart in two, and it will destroy his."

"I donnae need this…this…*assessment* of yours. Will ye help me or not?"

Korah pushed back from the table. "I'll think on it. But I ask that you do the same. Some decisions cannae be unmade, Yesenia. Not everything has to be a fight in order to be enjoyed."

Corin gripped the slivered edges of the old table in the inn. The walls were thin. He jammed his tongue against the roof of his mouth to keep from screaming.

Yesenia stood and wiped her mouth. "Was that a surprise worth waiting for?"

He swiftly nodded and stumbled a step as his knees regained power. "That was incredible." He reached for her face, still panting. "*You* are incredible."

She half rolled her eyes but turned her head to kiss his palm before peeling it away from her face. "Everything is a novelty in the beginning."

"I'm not worried about that."

Yesenia unhooked her belt and draped it over the chair. She'd prepared her assault for him the moment she joined him in the room. Neither of them had even undressed.

Corin buttoned his trousers. "Are *you*?"

"Worried about sex when there's now another mine that cannae produce enough to feed us?"

Corin exhaled. "You're right. I'm sorry."

"Why are you apologizing?" She leveled her words like an accusation. Her clothes came off in violent heaps, reminding him of the night of her father's celebration.

Corin started to rebut, but the truth of his answer changed his words, shaping them into a confession. "I've apologized for everything, as long as I can remember. I do it when I feel cornered but also when I feel helpless. I think I've gotten better at reading your needs, Yesenia, but I still have a ways to go. Forgive me if I don't always know the words you need."

Wearing only a filthy blouse, Yesenia propped herself against the ledge of the paned glass. "You're not responsible for your father's crimes. I donnae hold ye as such. I did once, aye, but I donnae now. You could've spied on me, reported on me, but ye didnae. So can we put it in the past? Your apologizing for things ye didnae do?"

Guilt flushed the warmth from him. He *had* reported on her, even if he'd chosen seemingly safe things to share, and he'd done it for *her*, not for his father. If she ever discovered this, she'd never see it that way.

The reality that he could lose her to such a misunderstanding hit him like a stone wall.

But they weren't under his father's thumb anymore. They were in the Southerlands, where they were meant to be. With whom they were meant to be.

Corin nodded. "I'll try. The guilt will always be there, but I'll try, for you."

"For yourself," she countered.

"For us," he amended. "For whatever future we have ahead of us, Yesenia. I *can* be more than a release in the bedchamber." He approached her, his heart escalating with every step. "You can talk to me."

The immediate suspicion that appeared behind her eyes broke his heart. It lasted only a moment, but it was why he still apologized to her, the reason he spent every moment they were together working his mind around how to be the man she needed, not just the one she wanted when she needed to forget.

"It's Khallum's mess," she said and turned her head to the pane, pressing her cheek to the cool glass. "Nothing to talk about."

"I can see it's weighing on you." She smelled of mine dust and sweat—her commitment to her people and her kin. "You didn't have to take me today, but you did."

Yesenia twitched her head. "Had to parade you out there someday. Might as well have been today."

Corin looped his arms around her waist, easing her feet from the ledge. She wouldn't look at him. He followed her face when she jerked it away, determined, this time, to not give in so easily. "Can it not be more than that?"

Yesenia locked eyes with him, the first sign of a smirk appearing around the edges of her mouth, but then she looked away again. "Does it have to be?"

"Is it not?"

"Corin, I donnae ken—"

"I *love* you, Yesenia Warwick." His pulse leaped so high, his eyes throbbed. He'd done it. He'd said the words, and now that they were out, there was no taking them back. "I *love* you."

A sharp gasp caught in her throat. "Why would you say that to me?"

"Because it's true. I do love you."

"Nay." She shook her head, swallowing. "You're just…You only know kindness. You were kind to me at Termonglen when I had shite on my boots, you were kind when I arrived at your tree castle, and you're being kind now."

"No." Corin pressed his forehead to hers.

She fought it, shaking her head away, but didn't leave his arms.

"No, Yesenia. Kindness is only a part of me. Kindness kept our lives from being worse when we were both in a hopeless place, but *love* can make both of our lives better."

"Stop it," she whispered.

Corin kissed the corner of her eye. "I can keep the words to myself if you don't want them, but I won't stop feeling as I do. I won't pretend anymore that we're just having fun, making the best of it. It's more than just play to me."

Yesenia's voice cracked. "Love isnae real."

Corin's head shook. "I know you don't believe that."

"It's a cage for a woman to climb into."

"It will never be a cage with me."

"It's balancing on a blade's edge and expecting not to get cut."

"You fear I'll hurt you."

Yesenia's eyes swam with tears un-spilled. "I *know* you'll hurt me."

Corin released her. He stepped back. "You're right."

Yesenia sniffled, tilting her chin. "So we agree. You cannae promise that's not what would happen."

"I won't promise you something I can't," Corin answered carefully. His hands trembled at his sides. Why did it feel as if his heart was both so full and so drained? "It's in our nature to be imperfect, and the imperfection inescapably causes pain to others. I would never hurt you intentionally, Yesenia, but I will hurt you. It's inevitable. And when I do, I'll spend whatever time, words, or actions are needed to make it right again."

Yesenia hopped off the ledge. She brushed past him, knocking him off balance, and slid into the bed.

He spun around, incredulous at how she could still so easily shut him out, push him away. "Is this how you want to leave it?"

Yesenia coiled the blanket around her without response.

"I thought we'd moved beyond this. I thought—" He clipped his words when he felt rage tinge the edges of his thoughts. It scared him, not because of what he might do but of what she had already done to him. How far gone he already was and how hard it would be to ever come back from the loss of her.

"Fine." Corin searched for his cloak and went to a chair in the corner. He sank onto it and tossed the cloak over his head. "Good night."

TWENTY-THREE
BLESSINGS AND FELICITATIONS

"Nmy one? None at all?" Khallum spread his palms against the dining table, gripping the soft wood with the pads of his fingers.

They *should* be having this conversation in the Hall of Warring, but he didn't allow women in there.

Yesenia bristled at his reproving glower. "I cannae find new ways of telling ye; Corin is *not* his father. Doesnae *like* his father. *Speak* to his father. So, no, he has no influence in the Easterlands. You'll keep him out of this."

Khallum turned his head to the side as he shook it. "Ye need to learn, now that you're married, that men protect their women, not the other way around."

"You think I'm protecting him?" She pointed all her fingers at her chest. "Or do ye just not like when you're told the way of things?"

"I'll send Hamish to the Strongsea mine, make some sense—"

Yesenia slammed her hands onto the table. "Ye have your sense! The Widow gave it to ye. *I* gave it to ye. There isnae more

273

to be had, unless ye plan to confess, at last, that ye have *no faith in me at all!*"

Khallum repositioned himself in his chair, stuttering through a sigh. "That isnae it. Ye know that."

"What else can it be? Hamish is a blubbering fool. If I thought ye meant well, Khallum, you'd have at least sent Sam, who knows his way around a ledger!"

"I just have to be sure, Sen. That's all."

"By sending a man to confirm what the women already told ye?"

"By sending a man," he said, in a placating tone that stirred violence in her heart. "To put his name on the report."

"What good are the reports when it's our own king responsible?"

"We have to keep a record. Ye know that. If it's in writing—"

"It does us feck-all good, in writing or no!" Yesenia jumped to her feet. "And no, Corin cannae go back to his father and ask him to stop stealing from us. If he did, that codswallop would only steal more, for the joy of seeing us squirm and starve."

Khallum closed his eyes to steel himself. "What, then, do you suggest?"

"Me?" Yesenia pulled her chin in with an incredulous widening of eyes. "Why, I'm just a woman, a stupid little fool with no use to a man beyond the price I can fetch."

"Too late for that. Ye spent all your dowry, and I cannae very well wed ye off when you're already married."

Yesenia set her jaw. How things had changed since Khallum had stepped into the lordship of the Southerlands. She'd counted their friendship among her dearest treasures, but the feeling was no longer reciprocal. He'd shed it in favor of authority.

"Then I want Mother's land."

"Eh?"

"Mother's land. For Corin and me." It was strange, thinking of Corin in these terms when they hadn't spoken in two days. It was her fault, like all their arguments, but her stubborn anger hadn't subsided enough for an apology.

It was more than that though. To apologize, she'd first have to confront her feelings, whatever they were.

"Why?" Khallum shrugged.

"Why do ye ken? This isnae my home anymore."

"Sen—"

"Donnae *Sen* me! I'm either your sister, your friend, and your partner, *or* I'm the woman ye cannae trust to do business on your behalf, but I cannae be all those things!"

Khallum rubbed his temples. "Fine. Ye two wanna live in Iron Hill, so far from the sea—and us? Donnae let me stop ye."

"I'll make the arrangements myself. You willnae have to lift a single finger," she stated.

Khallum shuddered into an exasperated sigh. "Fine!"

She turned to go, but he called her back.

"There's one more thing, Yesenia."

"I've had quite enough of ye today, thank you."

"The Rutlands will be joining us for supper and will be staying overnight before returning to Whitecliffe. They'll be arriving within the hour."

Yesenia gripped the door and spun. "*What?*"

"I know," he said, exhaling. "I know. I tried to put Steward Rutland off, but after everything he did, for Father, for us…There wasnae a thing I could do."

"Couldnae even do this one thing for me?"

"This one thing?" he parroted and leaped to his feet. "I forbade my best mate from attending our father's celebration, a celebration you left early, for *you!*"

Yesenia's chest heaved out of sync with her breaths. "Oh, aye? Lotta good that did, Khallum. He came anyway—"

"What? When?"

"Cornered me outside, wanting to talk about how we left things, and *that's* why I never returned to the party."

"Sen. I didnae know."

275

"Aye, well ye do now." Yesenia slammed the door and left.

Corin had at last come face-to-face with his wife's first love.

Erran Rutland was a comely man. His dark hair and eyes were reminiscent of the Southerlands, but the softness behind his gaze and his temperate mannerisms betrayed his upbringing in the wealthiest town of the Reach, Whitecliffe. Where Khallum ran roughshod over a conversation with his artless, boisterous proclamations, Erran's thoughtful pause before speaking, the genteel folding of his hands in his lap, not splayed across the table like the others, felt more like home for Corin than he liked.

He'd pictured Yesenia's love as another version of Khallum, not Byrne. Not a harder version of himself.

Yesenia's intentional avoidance of Erran when they sat for supper did nothing to put Corin's wounded heart at ease. Khallum seemed to note it too, frowning each time he caught it.

And then there was Sessaly, the dazzling younger sister with a mischievous twinkle in her eye, which intensified Corin's already-frayed nerves.

"We apologize for the short notice, Khallum," Rylahn Rutland said as he accepted a mug of ale from Korah. Circumstances had become so dire that the Warwicks had only two cooks, and the family had taken to serving themselves. The only place Khallum wouldn't trim expenses was in their guard, which seemed to grow by the day.

"Nonsense," Khallum replied, his voice gruff. "Drink up. Eat up."

"Yesenia, you're looking lovely these days," the steward said with a smile. "That flush in your cheeks isnae the wind's doing, I expect."

"I donnae ken," Yesenia muttered as she dug her fork through her mashed tubers.

Korah's skirts rustled as she slid into her spot opposite Khallum. "Much has changed, Rylahn. Our children have all been forced to grow, have they not?"

"All too true," Rylahn said in agreement. "Sessaly here is soon to be married to Law's second son, Aliksander. Sam, it seems, was already contracted, but a Law is a Law."

"How lovely!" Gwyn exclaimed. She clasped her hands together, then let them fall to rest over her swollen belly. "Where will you have the wedding?"

Corin, following Korah's eyes, saw how Gwyn had missed the point. Sessaly, he deduced, had once been promised to Khallum, same as Yesenia had been to Erran. A son or daughter of Whitecliffe could marry only a Warwick if they had intentions of elevating their already-lofty station. Both their children had and would marry laterally—not only that, a second son for Sessaly, who must have been one of the greatest prizes in the Reach— when the Warwicks were chosen for other purposes.

But there was no enmity in the steward's voice. It seemed to Corin his choice of words were intended to call only brief attention to the obvious before putting it to ground for good.

"Congratulations, Sessaly," Corin said, managing a magnanimous smile that masked his racing heart and thoughts. Yesenia hadn't looked at Erran, but she hadn't looked at Corin either.

"Thank you," Sessaly said with a brief nod. "Lady Gwyn, I must say, I'm delightfully surprised to see you've joined us, so far along."

Gwyn chuckled with a longing glance at her belly. "Our physician insists confinement will come any day now, but I feel perfectly fine. No need to hide away, until I must."

"Women hiding away in their confinement is for the men anyway," Yesenia groused. "So they donnae have to ken anything so unpleasant as childbirth, or see their women as anything less than objects of their desire. Never mind that the whole thing is their fault."

Erran snickered, as if he were in on her little dressing down.

Corin's belly clenched.

"If you're waiting for a denial, Yesenia, you'll be waiting a long while, I expect!" Korah exclaimed, drawing laughter from the table. "Bringing a child is a woman's business. Making a child, that's a man business."

A deep flush shot down the center of Yesenia's cheeks. Corin tried to catch her eye but couldn't.

"And why shouldn't it be a man's business?" Erran said. "Perhaps a man belongs in a birthing chamber, with his wife. Sen is right. He did put her there, after all."

"I know I didnae hear that correctly!" Khallum boomed, laughing with the steward.

"If you believe this so heartily, brother, you'll get that chance soon enough," Sessaly said in a delighted tone.

"Oh?" Gwyn asked.

Erran looked ready to climb into his plate and become one with the tubers.

"My brother is being shy, so I'll share the joyous news on his behalf. Mariel is with child!" Sessaly patted her brother's shoulder with a devious grin. "A new generation of Rutland heirs."

Yesenia screwed her lips and trained her eyes on her plate. "Aye? Congratulations."

"I...eh, Sess," Erran said, his focus on Yesenia, "a touch too early to be sharing such news."

"Well, it's been shared!" Sessaly exclaimed. "I hope to offer my own husband such a swift success."

"Mariel has done well," the steward agreed. "As I know you will too, lass. Has Byrne any news of a son?"

"Not yet," Khallum answered. His gaze, falling briefly on Yesenia once more, had turned to worry. He directed it back to the others. "I ken what we're really here for—"

"And you?" Sessaly leaned past her brother to get a better look at Yesenia. "All I hear about these days is Yesenia and her foreign husband. How they cannae keep their hands from each other, not for all the decency in the kingdom."

"Sessaly," the steward warned. "Such news is offered, not demanded."

"I wanted to thank you, Steward." Khallum pressed on. "For all you've done. You were a true mate to my father, and your son is a true mate to me. The Rutlands will always have a place at this table."

Corin kept trying to snare his wife's attention, but she had it buried in her food.

"Aye, and in your cove, no less," Sessaly quipped.

It happened fast. Yesenia launched herself across the table and had Sessaly by the throat in the same move. The erratic song of wood on stone filled the air as everyone at the table pushed back to deal with the situation.

"Sen," Erran said, in the gentle lilt of a cautioning lover. He wrapped his hands around the ones she had at his sister's throat.

Corin angled himself in, wedging Erran out. "It's okay," he whispered. He reached toward the table, where she was on all fours, and scooped his arm under her thighs. "This isn't worth it. Never let them see what they can take from you."

Yesenia released Sessaly. The girl fell back in dramatic repose, clutching at her neck between gasps.

Yesenia turned her eyes on Corin for the first time that night. The flecks of gold in her dark irises were brighter, torched by her agony and anger. The rest of the room faded into another night, another memory.

She broke away as everyone slowly returned to their seats.

"Felicitations on *all* the new blessings heaped upon the Rutlands," Yesenia hissed through clenched teeth. Her eyes flicked toward Corin so fast, it felt like an attack, but as her next words settled on him, he forgot all the ones before. "Corin and I will be welcoming our own heir in the springtide, blessed be the Guardians in their bountiful favor. And with that, you'll excuse me, for food and I no longer agree with one another."

Yesenia's boots echoed as she stormed from the room.

Corin clutched the back of a chair before his knees gave out. Erran's questioning eyes burned through him, but he had no answers.

Was it true? Had she said it to hurt Erran? Had she known that, in doing it this way, who she'd really hurt was Corin?

"Sorry, Khallum, I'm going to—"

"No," Korah said, decisive, as she pushed her chair in. "I'll go. This is women's business."

Korah found Yesenia in the cove. She'd been watching her niece seek solace there since she had been a young girl. Lost, motherless. It was only in the past years Erran had been added to the reprieve.

And now Corin.

Korah was all too aware Yesenia would not want her here. She knew what her niece thought. That Korah was old, out of touch, and too mired in duty to understand matters of the heart.

But Korah had once had her own Erran. Her heart, too, had broken when she'd had to give him up.

Unlike Yesenia, Korah had never grown to love her husband.

"I want to be alone," Yesenia said.

"I sense the lie in those words, even if you do not."

"I'm fine. 'Tis nothing more to say than what was said."

"You may have nothing to say, Yesenia, but I do." Korah propped herself on a nearby rock ledge and sighed. "When ye came to me, for the brew…"

Yesenia looked away.

"Did ye know?"

Yesenia shrugged. "How could I know anything for certain? I have no one to guide me in such ways. I wasnae well, but it could have been anything."

Korah winced at the slight. She had always guided her niece as best she could. "Are you certain now?"

Yesenia didn't answer.

Korah sighed once more. "I suspected as well, Yesenia, which is why I wasnae keen to offer ye the brew. It prevents a bairn well enough, but if one is already coming along, it would mean death, for the bairn. Death, often, for the mother."

"If ye knew, why say nothing? Why not tell me?" The desperation in Yesenia's voice was heartbreaking. Did she not see what a joy this could be? A husband she could love, and a child born of that?

"Your anger is a frightening thing to behold," Korah answered.

After a beat, Yesenia laughed. "You aren't really afraid of me, are you?"

"Not afraid of you," Korah said slowly, "but afraid of pushing ye so far away, you're beyond my help. Aye, *that* I'm afraid of."

"You want to help me? Really? Aye, I remember your wisdom well. *Lie back and remember the Southerlands.*" Yesenia snorted.

"Practical advice is in itself a form of love," Korah said. "And I do love you, Yesenia. Ye may not see it, or want it, but I have watched you grow from lass to woman, and my heart has captured every step of it. If my advice is archaic to you, it is because this world, too, is archaic, and I would spare you the pain of discovering that the hard way. But you're quite fortunate, for you have loved not once, but twice."

Yesenia looked upward. "Everyone says that word. Do they really know what it means?"

"You do," Korah said, insistent. "Erran is a good man. Corin is a good man. But only one of them is your husband."

"Corin. He's…" Yesenia trailed off, sighing into her hands.

"He's what, lass?"

"He doesnae know me! He has this…this *idea* of me, and it's all wrong. He says he loves me, but he doesnae ken the darkness in my heart, the salt and sand in my blood that keeps me from being who you and father and everyone else wanted me to be."

"I donnae know what that means, Yesenia. Perhaps neither do you."

"I donnae deserve him!" Yesenia howled the words. They echoed off the stone, leading into the silence that followed.

Korah nodded into her understanding. She'd read Yesenia's pain incorrectly, seeing it as pride, and knew it was something far worse.

Fear.

"Is it so hard to think he might love you because he *does* see these things?" Korah asked.

Yesenia whipped her head back and forth. Her hair stuck to her tear-stained cheeks. "No. No, he said he sees the real me, and I ken he's only seeing what he wants to see. And when he realizes… ahh, when he at last *sees*, he'll know this for what it has always been, doomed from the start."

Korah crossed her legs. She listened to the distant roar of the sea as the tide began its interminable shift. "Well. Now there's a child."

"Aye." Yesenia's tears dripped from her jaw, falling to the sand. "I should've left him in Whitechurch."

"For his sake, or yours?"

Yesenia nestled her face against the rock wall. "That was a horrible thing I did. Telling him like that, in front of everyone. I wanted to hurt…"

"You were going to say Erran. I ken you meant yourself."

Yesenia hung her head.

"What's left, Yesenia? What's really keeping your heart in a vise? It cannae be the worries of your homeland. The people are warming to your husband, lass. Anatole's reports are more promising every day, and ye know he gets to the truth of a matter, reading whispers as he does. I ken I've developed a soft spot for your man myself. He has a good heart."

"I know. Too good. Too good for *me*."

Korah bristled. "Now, listen here—"

"Yesenia?"

Korah stood and turned toward the intrusion.

"Guardians," Yesenia groaned. "Erran, ye need to go back inside. Now."

"Listen to her, lad," Korah insisted. Ahh, what a mess the boy was. She'd been the one to find Mariel, brokering the deal between her brother and Steward Rutland in midnight vellums. The boy would throw it away and, with it, his reputation. "You donnae belong here. You are not welcome here."

Erran thrust his hands outward and looked past her. "Can we talk? Please? For five minutes? It's all I ask."

"Absolutely not!" Korah exclaimed. "Yesenia, ye tell this boy—"

"Fine. Fine!" Yesenia screamed. She stood and backed into the lap of foam at the edge of the cove. "What's five minutes to me anyway?"

"This isnae a good—"

"I'm fine, Aunt Korah. He has something to say, he'll say it, then he'll go. Right, Erran?"

"Aye. I promise."

Korah flashed Yesenia a wary look. But she'd done what she could. Then. Now. Unlike the boys, who'd clutched her skirts in their desperation for a replacement mother, Yesenia had always done her own thing. Always would.

She'd said all she could say. Yesenia's happiness would not be decided by Korah's words.

They'd be decided by Yesenia's choice.

"Is it true?"

Yesenia crossed her arms and turned away. She focused instead on the sunset tickling the sky with orange and red to the west.

"Is it?"

"Why would I say it if it wasnae?"

"I thought…" Erran scratched at his beard. It was new, like so much else was about him. "I ken ye just wanted others to think you were happy, but when doors were closed—"

"What?" She whipped around. "That I'd pine after ye, rest of my days, while ye dropped your seed in your new wife?"

"What choice do I have? I *have* to bring an heir…I'm the only son…but you…"

"But me?" Yesenia asked. "I'm just supposed to swaddle myself and live a monk's life?"

Erran's scrutiny of her was so piercing, it stopped her breath.

"I'm a fool," he whispered. "'Tis not about warming your bed, is it? You *love* him."

Yesenia groaned.

"You've fallen for him. You've done it, haven't ye? Bad enough, were it any other man, but a *tree-dweller*, Sen—"

Yesenia jumped forward and clapped her hand across his mouth. "I have had more than my share of others calling my husband that!"

Erran peeled her fingers away. "Just tell me, so I can move on."

"And have ye not already?"

"Or…" Erran's words were rushed. "Is it that ye donnae want me to *move on*, but ye donnae *want* me either? That what it is? Ye willnae outright reject me because ye want me to keep showing up in your cove, whispering my love, begging ye to run away with me?"

"No," she said, her voice strained. "I really…" Yesenia swallowed to rid herself of the dryness stuck in her throat. "I want to move on. And I want you to move on. I want us to do that… apart."

The sound of boots hitting the rocks outside the entrance turned their eyes.

Corin.

Erran laughed. "Ye take *him* here now?"

Corin pushed past Erran, but he didn't come to her right away. He stood between the two of them, passing a glance back and forth.

"If I'm interrupting…"

"You're *not*," Yesenia insisted. It was important Corin knew it. That no matter what hurts she'd laid upon him, this was not one of them.

"Good." Corin stood tall, wearing confidence in his eyes. "Erran, it was an honor to meet the man who once loved my wife, before I did."

Erran's jaw went slack.

"But as I do love my wife, I'll have to ask you, with all respect, to leave her be. Stop following her into cracks and coves. Stop confusing her."

Erran turned toward Yesenia, but her eyes were fixed on Corin.

"She can speak for herself," Erran replied.

"I think she has," Corin said. "It's time for you to listen."

"Yesenia?"

Corin turned his back on Erran. "Come back with me, Sen. There's nothing either of us has said that cannot be mended."

"*Yesenia*," Erran howled. "This cannae be what you want."

Yesenia's legs moved before her mind bid them to. The searching commands of her once love blended into the background, mingling with the sea. Corin gathered her into his arms and held her there, one hand at the back of her head, the other wound around her back.

She tilted her chin back, and for the first time in two days, Yesenia looked willingly into the eyes of her husband. She read the hurt there, the confusion. It was a reflection of her own, though she was the cause of both. "I donnae ken what I feel, but I know where I belong." She hardly recognized her voice. It was as surprising and foreign as her words. "And where you belong. Here. Both of us. Right now. Together."

Erran made a pained sound and retreated from the cave.

Yesenia went on. "I dare not think so far ahead, or in such absolutes, as you can. I want to but—"

Corin kissed her. "You don't have to. Your words are your own. I only ask that you not shut me out."

Yesenia nodded against his mouth. "I'll try. For you. For us."

"For our child," he said. "It's true then?"

"Aye. It's true."

Corin crushed her into his arms. He laid his head against hers as he sobbed. "A real marriage. A real life. Yesenia, Yesenia, Yesenia…"

Yesenia closed her eyes and rode the rise and fall of his chest.

TWENTY-FOUR

BETRAYAL

Yesenia jolted awake.

Her first reaction was a pointed glance toward her daggers. They were still on the nightstand. Close enough to draw. Her clothes were where she'd discarded them in the night's passion, in various heaps upon the floor of their bedchamber.

Corin remained sound asleep, his head tucked into the crook of her arm. She kissed the top of his head and peeled him off without waking him.

The beat of hooves was closer now. She dressed quickly and secured her daggers. If this was what she suspected it was, then they'd have to work to take her down.

Her eyes fell on sleeping Corin.

The blanket bunched just below his waist, leaving the rest of him exposed.

His soft, untroubled breathing turned to snores every few beats.

The desire to pause here, live in *this* moment, was palpable.

But the horses were almost there. She had to tell him. Had to wake him.

Yesenia knelt on the bed and leaned in, pressing her lips to his ear. He roused with a start, hearing her words, his eyes responding to the severity of them before the rest of him did.

"Are you sure?" He kept his voice low. "Are you *sure,* Sen?"

"Aye," she said, matching his tone. "It was always going to happen one day, Corin."

"No." He shot up in the bed. His hands tangled through his hair. "No, it wasn't. He let it go. He let *us* go."

"Where's your sword?"

"My sword?"

"Aye, the one ye never wear."

"I never wear it because I don't need it."

"You'll need it now."

Yesenia went to the window and pulled the curtain. Dust flew in whirls around the arriving men sweeping down the hillside and into Warwicktown. Soon, she'd see the violent crimson and obscene cloth of gold, topped by that ludicrous plumage that belonged on birds, not men.

Corin shimmied into his clothes behind her. "How long?"

"Not long. They—" Her words ended abruptly. Her brother's banners appeared on the other side of the dust. His men were geared for war.

But not with the Easterlands.

"What is it? What do you see out there?"

"Betrayal."

Yesenia and Corin waited in the courtyard for Khallum and his men to arrive. Corin watched her from the side, trying to gauge where her mind was at. That she intended to fight was apparent, but fight what?

He should have seen it sooner. The crimson robes, swashed with cloth of gold and feathers, flying high. He'd missed those details because there were only two of them in the whole company, in a throng of otherwise Southerland men.

Yesenia hadn't missed it though.

Khallum, at the front of the pack, dismounted, and so did a man Corin recognized but had never been friendly with: Drystan Sylvaine, Steward of Rushwood and father of Gretchen's jilted Ash. *I guess Father made peace with them after all.*

"How dare you," Yesenia challenged as the two men approached. Corin was surprised to not see her hands on her daggers, but though she was gutsy, she was also clever. There was no battle. It was an ambush.

Khallum looked as if he hadn't slept in days. He regarded his sister through bleary eyes, a scratch in his voice. "Let's go inside, Sen."

"Aye, just us? Or all the other men ye brought to subdue me?"

"They aren't for you," Khallum said, with a hard eye toward Steward Sylvaine. "We'll speak of it inside."

Corin took another glance at the gathered men. The other Easterlander was a steward as well, of Oak Hill, which had once been Southerland territory. His father had chosen neither of these men by chance, but his reasons were yet unclear.

"You used to ken what these men were to us." Yesenia tensed, her nose and eyes flaring. "Father's been with the Guardians for mere *months*, and you'd already betray him."

"*Inside*," Khallum said, this time a warning. "Unless you want everything said here to be carried to their beds and turned to fishwife gossip."

Yesenia stepped toward her brother with a finger raised. "Whatever it is, I'll never agree."

"Let's go inside."

Drystan Sylvaine nodded at Corin. "Always good to see you, Lord Quinlanden."

"I'm not him anymore," Corin replied. "But you must already know this."

Yesenia grasped for Corin's hand. "Aye, he's a man of the Southerlands now. Isnae enough gold or men in the world to bring us back to Whitechurch."

"We'll see," Sylvaine said, dropping his pretentious smile. "Lord Warwick?"

Khallum grunted and turned to go inside.

Corin squeezed Yesenia's hand. "We'll figure it out."

"Your optimism is misplaced," she answered as she turned and pulled him along with her. "As for mine, it's officially dead."

"An *agreement*?" Yesenia asked. "You signed an *agreement*, with the *Quinlandens*, on behalf of...*who*? Not me. Not Corin."

"I wouldnae have let a single bootlicker on our land without one," Khallum replied with a defensive recoil. "We donnae just invite them in, Sen. Not like you."

"I brought my *husband* home." She flopped back in her chair. "Ye know, the one you and father bade me make the best of? How many sides of your mouth are ye capable of speaking from, Khallum?"

"I can see this is troubling for you both," Steward Sylvaine said, folding his hands in a pleasant, patient pose. "Will you not let us at least discuss the terms of the agreement? They're more favorable than you're anticipating."

"Any terms that force us to return to your Reach cannae possibly be favorable," Yesenia snapped.

"My Father knows we're making our life here," Corin said. "We're moving to our own keep soon, and Yesenia—"

Yesenia pressed a hand to his knee before he could tell the man about their child.

"Yes," Steward Sylvaine agreed. "And your father has been more than fair in indulging this dalliance—"

"Dalliance?" Yesenia echoed, stone-faced. "I ken your lord must have also told you, then, what led to us fleeing your lands in the dead of night? Not exactly a dalliance."

"Lord Aiden had nothing to do with what happened in the chalet, and Lord Chasten regrets that he wasn't aware of it when he chose to imprison you. A misunderstanding he hopes you'll come to look past. When Lord Quinlanden finds the man responsible, he'll see him justly punished."

Yesenia threw her hands out. "He already knows the man responsible. Choosing to do nothing isnae any form of justice I'm aware of. Aye, I bet he didnae even punish the ugly one either? Mads?"

"Yesenia," Khallum said with a short sigh. "Can we get through this?"

Yesenia crossed her arms and passed her gaze from one man to the other. "So eager to be rid of me? Aye, tell us then."

Steward Sylvaine unrolled the scroll. Yesenia withheld her gasp at seeing her brother's signature beside Lord Quinlanden's. This was...There wasn't a word for this. Khallum could call it whatever he wanted—an agreement, an armistice—but that, *that* was an alliance between men of warring Reaches. A war that would never end.

She flashed her gaze between the two men and the words on the vellum. Corin had already finished reading and fell back in his chair, both hands over his eyes.

"I see." Yesenia rolled the vellum and chucked it at the air beyond her brother's head. "So these tree-dwellers threaten war, and instead of raising yer own arms, as ye wanted, as Father would've wanted, you'd sell your own sister back to your enemy?"

"Did ye even read it?" Khallum asked, booming in exasperation. "Did ye? I didnae sell anything, Sen! You want this marriage to your tree-dweller, then your home is *there*, in the Easterlands, for that's *his* home, and he's the husband!"

"That's never been my home," Corin replied. "I've never felt more at home anywhere than I have here, where half the men tolerate me and the other half loathe me. And that, *that*, is still better than living in my father's realm."

"Your father and brother would be aggrieved to know it," Steward Sylvaine said.

"My father has long been the architect of my misery, and my brother, the all-too-eager builder."

Yesenia pulsed her hand on his knee.

"Ye didnae read it, did you?" Khallum asked again. "You're off-limits to anyone there, ever again. Lord Quinlanden, he cannae touch ye. His son, his allies, this man sitting at our table… none of them. No trickery. Not steel, not poison, not prison, not anything. And not only you, Sen, but your husband. It was *I* who made them include Corin in their promise of safety. By returning, you prevent a needless war between our Reaches, and you'll be safe. Your husband will be safe."

"No one in the Easterlands is safe. Not even this minion he sent to assure us," Yesenia said. "That ye believe a word of it…that ye ken a signature on a page means *anything* to a man who would wish his own son dead—"

"Lady Yesenia, I was there," Sylvaine stated, interjecting. "Lord Quinlanden was heartsick at what he saw between his sons. He is grateful to you for your timely intervention."

Yesenia snorted. "Ye enjoy dining on his spleen, yer head so far up his arse?"

"It's done. We signed the agreement in Blackpool," Khallum said. "This will always be your home, Sen, but Corin is your husband. You've made this clear to all of us. You belong where he belongs. Even you must know this, in your rage for me."

Yesenia shot to her feet. The sudden shift of blood sent stars into her eyes, and she had to grip the table to steady herself. "Has it really come to this, Khallum? That ye would turn your back on your own sister, rather than fight for her?" She gaped down at her healed palm. "You swore a *blood oath*. An unbreakable bond."

Khallum hung his head. "Ye donnae ken what it is to be a lord, Yesenia. What Father has left for me."

"I *do* ken it. I've been here these months, helping ye sort it."

"Ye donnae," he said, looking up. She hated how the sight of his fatigue tore at her heart. As a boy, he'd tired so easily of politics, and she wondered, even then, how he'd manage to run the entire Reach one day. There should have been decades more before he had to do it. He would have learned so much from Father in that time.

Yesenia knew one thing. Her father might have agreed to the king's demands, but if he were sitting where Khallum was, he'd have raised the whole of the Southerlands against the Easterlands before letting such a travesty come to pass.

Yesenia drew a dagger, and all three men jumped. She pressed it into the underside of her chin. "I would rather die than go back."

"Aye, drop the dagger. Guardians," Khallum said, sighing again. "Always a fight with you, Sen. Why?"

"I'll put an end to the fighting right here, Khallum."

Corin jumped to her side and grabbed her upper arms with a careful shake. "Yesenia, forget your brother, forget Sylvaine. Forget them, and look at me."

"Move away, Corin."

"You'll have to kill me."

The shock of those words from his mouth broke her focus. "Do you want to go back?"

"I want to be wherever you are." He flicked his eyes, ever briefly, toward her belly. "I'll ask my father for some land. I'll get us out of Whitechurch. We'll figure this out together, I promise you. I promise, Yesenia. Just please, put the dagger away."

"Did you know?"

"You know the answer to that." Corin sucked in a deep breath and snaked his hand toward her other dagger. He drew it quicker than she could stop him, and he pushed the tip to his neck. "I go wherever you go. If that means to the Guardians, so be it."

Corin pressed the tip into his flesh hard enough to send a trickle of blood running down his neck.

"Put it away, you fool," she hissed.

"No."

"This is really what ye want? To again live in a prison?"

"I'm looking at the only thing I've ever wanted badly enough to die for."

As Yesenia slowly lowered her dagger, the shock of Khallum's embrace enveloping her from behind knocked her from her feet. It was both an act of restraint and love, and she despised him for mingling these two things, for making her feel so helpless and confused.

"I *haven't* forgotten my blood oath. I will raise the whole of the Southerlands if he comes near you, or that bairn," Khallum promised in her ear, low enough just for the two of them. "But right now, we have no choice. Ye ken? No choice, Yesenia. There were thousands of men in Blackpool when I rode up. There are thousands more ready to come. If ye donnae go, it willnae be a war. It will be a *massacre*."

Yesenia asked the carriage to stop twice before they even reached the border. Corin held her hair as she vomited into ditches. He rubbed her back while she sobbed between expulsions. Held tight to her as they climbed back in, moving farther toward her misery.

And his.

But what she needed was his strength, not commiseration.

"Just rest," he whispered and pulled her head down onto his lap. "We'll handle this one moment at a time. We have each other, Yesenia. That's all that matters."

Long after he thought she'd fallen asleep, she said so softly he had to lean down to hear it, "Donnae ye get it, Corin? We could be whatever we wanted in the Southerlands. Whoever we wanted. When we return, none of that is true, nor will it ever be again."

She said no more, leaving Corin to ponder the true meaning of her words as he smoothed her hair back off her face, directing his hollow stare to the plush velvet of the seat across from him.

TWENTY-FIVE
A LORD'S METTLE
BUT A MONSTER'S HEART

I won't spy on her. I won't let you or Aiden speak to her as you have in the past. And if Aiden goes *anywhere* near her, I'm well within my right to kill him."

Chasten curled back on the divan. He ran his middle finger down the outer edge of his mouth, deep in thought.

Corin had never been proficient at reading his father, but it had somehow become worse. Before he'd known this happiness, toughening his skin had been enough to survive the day. He'd only thought he'd known pain, until he'd seen Yesenia endure it.

"None of that sounds unreasonable," Chasten said at last. "She is with child, after all."

"How could you know that?" Corin immediately wished he hadn't asked it. Questions like that had always been his father's font of power.

"It didn't require spying, if that's what you're inferring. I can see it, and so could you if you weren't blind to her." Chasten laughed to himself. "The truth is, I knew before you did."

"What?"

"Three of our seers foresaw it. You're fortunate the child is yours, or we'd be helping her rid herself of it."

"Who else's child could it be?" Corin snapped. But was it not a relief to hear this? That his fears about Erran were unfounded? She'd told him nothing had happened, but fear wasn't rational. Fear played by its own rules. He was a fool for ever doubting her, but a relieved fool nonetheless.

"Who knows? But it's yours. Maeryn was evidently never with child to begin with, so Aiden is working to fix that. I *was* tempted to have your child sent into exile, as it would not do to have Aiden come in second to you, but Lord Warwick was very insistent in his wording. Neither you nor her, nor any child she carries or births, are to be harmed or punished. Even *I* cannot spin the idea of exile into a positive outcome."

"No one cares about who comes in first, other than you."

"You'd be surprised, Corin. You'd be surprised."

Corin folded his arms and leaned back. The air outside his father's perch rustled with the first stir of a midwinter storm. "Why did you even sign that? I thought you welcomed a war against the Southerlands."

"I do, yes," Chasten said, his mouth playing at a grin, "but the king? He's made it clear that is the *opposite* of what he wants. The Warwick way would scorch the earth. They'd drown and burn their mines until there was nothing left. We'd arrive to collect a barren land and the ire of a king who enjoys, more than he'll say, watching us simply hate one another."

Corin was taken aback by his father's openness. His words bordered on sedition, so why share them with the unworthy son? The unpredictable one who had chosen his enemy wife over his flesh and blood? "Why…Why make us come back at all?"

Chasten poised to answer with a deep intake of breath, but Corin kept talking.

"I know how you feel about me. How you've always felt." Corin leaned in, his words pouring forth with courage he didn't recognize and that might soon leave him. "I know I disappoint you. I see how the disappointment vexes you. It was relief I saw in your eyes when Aiden nearly killed me."

"Yes. To some of that," Chasten replied. A darkness soon followed, spreading over his careful expression. "But had Aiden… had he killed you…he'd have taken two sons from me that day. Your disbelief in that doesn't make it less true."

Corin burst with laughter. "You've never punished Aiden for a single one of his sins! You encourage them! You're glad he's the way he is, so he can do what you will not."

"He has a lord's mettle," Chasten said with a soft sigh. "But a monster's heart."

"Wonder where he inherited that from."

"I taught Aiden to be cold," Chasten admitted. "But not cruel."

Corin shook his head. "Ah, if what you think you offer is merely coldness, I would hate to see your cruelty."

"You are my son," Chasten said more firmly. "I know I have not always made you feel that way."

"Not always?" Corin gaped at him, slack-jawed.

"Gretchen is more like me and could have done more for this family had she been born a man. You are more your mother. As the head of this house, I shouldn't have punished you for this, but instead found you a role suited to your unique strengths."

"I don't want or need a role in this family." Corin slowed his racing pulse. He lowered his head into his palm. "I just wanted, then and now, to live in peace."

"You are a Quinlanden," Chasten replied. "There is no peace to be found in that. Your son or daughter will be the heir to the Easterlands until Maeryn produces her own."

"No." Corin shook his head. "Maeryn will bear him a dozen children, if that's what he wants. Yesenia and I are to be left alone. That was the agreement—"

"You aren't listening to me, as usual. We are saying the same things, Corin. No one will touch your wife or your child, not because of this agreement, which means little to me, but because of who your child may be, one day, if Aiden fails."

"Aiden won't fail." Bitterness dripped from Corin's tongue, running down his throat and into his heart. "He never does in your eyes."

"You and Yesenia, vexing as this is to me, are popular here. Your *love*, or whatever it is, is something the common people admire. Her unnatural but theatrical rescue of you has kept all their tongues wagging, and your return will be celebrated."

"Ahh." Corin smirked. He shook his head. "I knew there was more to it. "

"I want you to be my ambassador for the merchant class," Chasten said abruptly. "This goes beyond the beggar girl who fell from one of our perches. Yes, I knew about that. I'm not angry. Someone has to deal with them, and few are capable in the way you are."

"You never cared before about the merchant class."

Chasten set his mouth in a tight line. "There have been some… skirmishes, in some of the towns."

"Skirmishes." Corin snorted.

"We must subdue them, before they gather more moss and swell into something bigger."

"What does that mean?" Corin swallowed the tremble in his voice.

"You don't have to *pretend* to care for their well-being, as we do. They know this. It's why they adore you."

Though his father's words were an invitation, everything about the conversation screamed warnings from within. "Is that all?"

Chasten looked surprised by the question. "Are you so ready to be rid of me, when you've only just returned after almost half a year away?"

"Yes."

Chasten laughed. "You've changed."

"Also yes."

"Very well. I've arranged for separate apartments for you, until Yesenia is safely delivered."

"Not necessary."

"But happening, just the same."

"No. She needs me right now, and I'm staying with her, in *our* apartments."

"Maeryn will be with her during the day, and your mother will tend to her in the evenings. What she needs now is to debride herself of the past months so she can bring a healthy Easterland child along. Your emotions will only confuse her."

Corin jumped to his feet. "You can't keep me from my wife. I won't allow it this time. I won't allow the same mistreatment, of her or of me."

Chasten sighed open-mouthed, his exhalation becoming a light smile. "Then consider that these will be her wishes by the time you make it back to her."

"Yesenia *wants* me at her side."

"But will she when she learns of how you fed us information about her? When she learns you agreed to spy on her?"

"*What?*"

Chasten joined him on his feet. "As I said. Neither of you will come to harm. The child will be the safest in the realm. But that child belongs to the Easterlands until Aiden can fulfill his own duty. Aiden is with Yesenia now and has explained things as they are. She now knows that you spied on her, for us. So, it is not I who will impose this separation. I expect she will choose this all on her own."

"No, no." Corin shook his head. Once more, his father had led him down a path he hadn't predicted, and he'd followed, easily, willingly, *foolishly*. "She'll understand why I did it. She'll know nothing I told you was damaging."

"Will she care? I don't think she will. I've never met a bigger firebrand. Not even your brother wears that crown." Chasten fixed his collar and smoothed out his dressing gown. "If what passes between you is truly love, she'll see fit to forgive you when the time is right. For now, this will keep her focused on what's important until she's safely delivered."

"Why would you do this?" Corin hated himself for asking, for giving his father yet one more thing to hold over him, but he had to know. No matter the answer, he needed to hear it in his father's words.

"Everything I do, always, is with the Easterlands in mind."

"But I'm your *son*."

"I gave you what you want. You are now free to associate with the merchants without hiding it from me. Is that not a gift, Corin? Is that not a father attempting to understand his son?"

"You've taken more than you've given, though I've come to expect that as your personal standard," Corin spat. He narrowed his eyes. "But you're wrong about Yesenia. She knows me. She knows I would never betray her."

Chasten cast his eyes upward. "Then go find out who's right. The apartments are prepared for you, just the same."

TWENTY-SIX
FOOL THAT I WAS

Yesenia hurled the remainder of her stomach into the basin. It seemed impossible there'd been anything left to offer after the past hours of violent disruption. She wanted to ask Mariana, Maeryn, *anyone* if it was normal, but she had no women in her life with whom she shared such a level of intimate trust.

The Widow would know. She'd tell me everything I needed.

The thought hit her like a punch to the gut.

"That's it. Let it out." Maeryn rubbed her palm over Yesenia's sweat-drenched tunic.

"Let what out? Cannae be anything left." Yesenia dropped back onto the cold stone and accepted a clean cloth from Maeryn with a brief, grateful smile.

"It was like this for me, in the early days," Maeryn said. She rose and went to collect the pitcher of wine. "It goes away."

Yesenia realized the implication of Maeryn's words. "I'm sorry, Maeryn. Truly."

"There was no child, Yesenia. I thought he'd leave me alone if I was expecting, and I suppose wishing for it was enough to

301

convince my body to behave accordingly. It worked, for a while."
Maeryn stopped mid-pour. "They'll take an interest in your child,
Yesenia, and you must know it for what it is. Corin cannot be seen
to deliver the first grandchild."

Yesenia scoffed. "Isnae Corin delivering anything."

"Your time away has softened you." Maeryn handed her the
mug, and Yesenia shakily drew a sip.

Yesenia swished the wine in her mouth and spat it into the
basin. "Say what you mean, Maeryn."

"They may claim the child is Aiden's."

Yesenia laughed, fighting another powerful wave of nausea.
"None would believe it."

"They believe everything their lord tells them. What they
don't believe, they have no choice but to swallow anyway."

"Well, I wouldnae allow it," Yesenia replied. "Nor would
Corin. Ye ken I've changed? Wait 'til you see my husband."

Maeryn turned away. "I expect I'll be seeing more of him than
you will, for a while."

Yesenia snickered. "Right."

"They made up separate apartments for him, Yesenia. You
don't have to believe anything I tell you. Watch. Listen. Their
actions speak their intentions louder than any words."

"But that's...nay. They signed the agreement. There are con-
sequences for breaking it."

"Where in the agreement does it state husband and wife must
share an apartment? Where does it state that Aiden cannot claim
what is not his? There are not words enough that could stop them
from their designs."

"Aye?" Yesenia pressed the cloth to her mouth. "And what have
they planned for me? To give my child to you? Dispose of me?"

They both turned toward the thuds of many footsteps. Maeryn
whipped her head back and whispered, "You should not have
come back. Either of you. It was a mistake."

"I didnae have a *choice*."

"You couldn't remain in the Southerlands. That is not the same as having no choices." Maeryn said her words so quickly, Yesenia had to replay them in her mind to grasp them.

"Where are you going?" Yesenia's eyes followed Maeryn's harried movements, and she shuffled out of her privy chamber. Yesenia tried to push herself to her feet but stopped when the light from the other room became obstructed.

Aiden's frame swelled to fill the doorway. "Let's have a chat, you and I."

Yesenia's hands scrambled across the stone, in search of anything she could use to defend herself. Her daggers were…Where were they? At one time they'd been in the other room, but the past day had been a haze of sickness and confusion. Were they still there?

"I'm not here to harm you, Yesenia." Aiden stepped inside and closed the door. Bolted it. The echo of his boots colored her first true fear of him; the first time she'd had no protection, not even her own strength.

"Liar."

"Not physically anyway." He settled on the edge of the steel bathing basin. "I see you enjoyed your time away with my brother."

Yesenia dragged herself across the stone and fell back against the wall, panting and glowering.

"I'm not going to touch you. Your brother saw to that. Pity." He gripped the edges of the tub and watched her. "Corin is not who he seems."

Yesenia snatched the bile-covered cloth nearby and draped it over herself. It was a meager attempt. There weren't enough linens in the world to keep his eyes away.

"Jealousy becomes no man," she charged. "Least of all the one who cannae see fit to hide it."

"I am jealous of Corin," Aiden agreed. "He got the better wife in the deal."

"Maeryn might be a better wife if she wasnae in constant fear for her life."

Aiden shrugged. "Or perhaps she'd be a worse one. We'll never know. But I didn't come here to speak of Maeryn—or even you, my dear. There are things you need to know about your husband, things we've kept to ourselves for now, but no longer see a reason to."

"Whatever words ye have, they're wasted on me."

"I must know. All these months…Could you see it? Even a hint of it? When he lay on top of you, making you scream for him, did it even once jump into your head that he might not be what he seems?"

"I know who Corin is," Yesenia said, swallowing. Her belly turned. "And I know who you are."

"He's a Quinlanden, same as me."

"Your name is the only thing you two share, and he'd be rid of that too, if he could." Yesenia's eyes narrowed. "Say what you mean and leave me."

Aiden shrugged as if to say *no need to be unreasonable.* "He's been spying on you since the day you arrived."

Yesenia laughed, burying another surge of sickness against her sweaty arm before it could emerge. "Leave."

"He has." Aiden went on. "To be fair, Father gave him no choice, but does that matter to you? Only weak men fall in line. Corin put up a fuss well enough, but he did it just the same. Do you know why?"

"I donnae believe you." Yesenia pressed the words through clenched teeth. She pushed a strand of matted hair from her eyes. "And you'll leave me now, or I'll puke on your pretty little jeweled boots."

"He told us about the Southerland code."

Yesenia cackled, falling back again, exhausted. Her eyes swam with sweat and tears. He'd say anything, anything at all, to break her. "Everyone has a code, bootlicker."

Aiden tapped his boot against the basin. "That's true. We said as much at the time. So then, he told us something else. Something *far* more interesting."

304

"Nothing you've ever said is the least bit interesting."

"He told us," Aiden said with an exhale, "that you came to your wedding night no longer intact."

Yesenia's arrogance crashed.

"Ahh. Now do you see, Yesenia?"

It *was* a betrayal, but for reasons Aiden couldn't possibly understand. She'd shared that truth amidst others more personal. She'd trusted him not with her facts but with her heart. "Ye called me a whore yourself," she said. She tried to smile. "Should be no surprise."

"Oh." Aiden laughed. "Definitely no surprise, Yesenia. Not to me nor my father, nor any man with eyes. But the king? Well, it was a surprise to him."

"Why do I care what the ratsbane thinks of me?"

"It isn't about you," Aiden said. "It's about the lie your father told in that tent in Termonglen. He said yes when the king asked if you were intact."

"And? My father wouldnae have known any of it."

"He *lied* to the king, Yesenia."

"It wasnae a lie if he didnae know!"

"That isn't how the king saw it." Aiden rose, throwing his shadow over her like a damp blanket. "And so, a very sudden illness befell an otherwise healthy man. All because—"

"No." Yesenia rolled to her knees, wobbling as she tried, and failed, to stand. "You repulse me. Your lies sicken me." She retched, dry-heaving on the ground by his feet. "You have underestimated me, turn and turn again."

Aiden reached into his pocket and pulled out a scroll. He dropped it on the floor.

"Don't have to believe me, saltlicker. You can read it in the king's own words."

Yesenia slid forward on the floor just as he spun and marched out.

She laid her face against the stone, one eye on the discarded vellum. Breathed in. Out.

Yesenia reached for it.

Corin would hear her words every moment of every second of every hour of his life.

They would become part of him, weaving through blood and bone and flesh.

Nothing before they were said, nor anything after, would remain.

I trusted you.

You told me I could trust you.

You made me believe it.

Fool that I was, I did.

And not only…not only that…but I…but I…

I loved *you.*

I loved the man responsible for the death of my father.

Corin tiptoed into the bedchamber, set to the alternating sounds of Yesenia retching and Maeryn's inelegant comfort.

He opened the drawer and removed her daggers, then fastened them around his waist, under his dressing gown.

She'd never believe he was taking them to help her.

She'd never believe another word he said, ever again.

ABSENT A DAM,
THE RIVER FLOODS

TWENTY-SEVEN
FOUR RAVENS

A hooded Yesenia darted down the Golden Stair without lift-ing her glance. Few paid her notice at all, but those who did returned to their own business quick to assure her she hadn't been recognized.

Once on the ground, she adjusted her pace to fit in with oth-ers gathered in the courtyard, for work or play. She clutched the empty basket close, knowing anyone nearby would take it as a sign she was committed to her assigned task as just one of the many servants of the sylvan princes in the trees. No one would question her focus. They were all dreadfully aware of what happened when one of them failed.

Her garment belonged to one of the chambermaids. Some of them were fond of Yesenia, but none would have had the courage to give it to her. *Maeryn* had stolen it. Yesenia had accepted the suspicious gift with one hand, and with the other, prepared to defend herself for the inevitable betrayal that would follow it.

And my daggers?

Maeryn could only shake her head. Whether she didn't know the answer or had declined to provide it, Yesenia couldn't know.

Yesenia hadn't found the poison either, though she'd searched for it herself. She'd never even told Corin about the vial.

A younger version of herself wouldn't have agonized over the loss of such things. Her present unease didn't come from doubt of her ability to defend herself without weapons, but having them made matters decidedly simpler.

It wasn't only herself she was defending now.

Free of the courtyard, Yesenia tucked the basket behind a tree and ran for the stables. She flung the door wide with a celebratory sigh. She'd made it so far without getting ill, but being locked away for several weeks had rendered most of her senses unreliable.

Yesenia clucked her tongue at Kheerai and planted a kiss on her nose. "Not tonight, lass," she whispered and moved on to another mare, one she'd never seen any of the main family use. The saddle on the rack behind her was cruder than Yesenia was used to, but it would do.

"Let's be kind to each other. I'm carrying precious cargo," she said before urging the mare onward, out of the stables and into the start of a fresh rainstorm.

"Yesenia!" Mara clapped both hands to her mouth, hesitating only a beat before rushing to free her of the drenched cloak. She exhaled into a gentle smile when she noticed the swell under Yesenia's gown. "Then it's true. What a blessing for you both."

"Word travels swiftly," Yesenia muttered, trying to return the smile in spite of her mounting dread. "Thank you for allowing me in."

"Nonsense." Mara glanced behind her, into the warm light of the teeming tavern. "If you were hoping for subtlety, this is a bad night for it. The whole Row is here when it rains, and some visitors from across the Reach just arrived."

Yesenia cast a frown back toward the door. "I cannae be seen, Mara. Is there somewhere else?"

"I won't hear of sending you somewhere else. I'll get you a fresh cloak so you're not recognized, though these men would die before they ever sang to a Quinlanden."

Yesenia accepted the garment, warm from its placement near the wood stove, and covered her shivers with it. "Thank you for this."

"You're so pale. So peaked." Mara's calloused hand pressed against Yesenia's cheek. "Has anyone been looking after you?"

"In a way."

"When have you last eaten, girl? Weeks?"

"Everything I eat…" Yesenia made an arcing gesture from her mouth.

Mara nodded. "That will pass. From the looks of you, soon. If you can trust me, there's broth I make that will restore some of your strength without you having to give it right back. The smell will have you holding your nose, but the result is worth it."

"I trust you, Mara," Yesenia said as she leaned against the stove. The warm metal heated her straight to her chilled bones. "It's why I'm here."

Mara tilted her head. She again glanced into the tavern behind her. "Oh?"

"Are your ravens monitored by the Quinlanden Guard?"

Mara met her eyes with a bitter chuckle. "They have no fear of us. They know we could invite every corner of the realm to insurrection, and still they fear nothing."

"Good," Yesenia said with a quick glance past Mara, into the tavern, at the roar of raucous laughter. "For that's roughly what I intend to do."

Mara's smile faded. "What's that?"

"I need to get word to my brother, and I need to do it without Quinlanden eyes on my words."

"Your brother? Lord Warwick?"

"Aye."

"How strange." Mara leaned in. "Is there a reason you two didn't just come together?"

"Sorry?"

Mara shook her head and held out an arm. "Come with me."

Corin returned his quill to the inkwell and lifted the vellum to blow on it. He pulled it back, re-read, then blew some more as he watched the ink shift from glistening black to a more muted charcoal.

Only a light tremor had passed from his hand to the paper, despite the violent wave of fear traveling through his blood like a company of enemy forces.

He jolted when the door opened. Relaxed again when he saw it was only Mara. He smiled, rising to greet her, but his tension ignited again when he saw she wasn't alone. A hooded figure entered behind her.

Mara nodded without a word and closed the door as she exited, leaving him alone with the newcomer.

The hood fell back. Yesenia's wan face peered back at him.

"Sen." Corin stumbled into the desk. A hundred thousand words rolled forward, the ones he'd thought and prayed for and wished he could say, ones she would understand.

But he could only exhale, leaving them unspoken.

"What are you doing here?" She nodded at the desk behind him.

He hesitated. He'd always been open with her with his intentions, but she was no longer open to receiving them. "Writing your brother. You can hate me for however long it suits you, but Khallum needs to know my father has broken the agreement. He needs to decide where his loyalties lie, for you and for our child."

Yesenia passed her glance around the room with a slow nod. "Aye...I ken you and I had the same intention there."

"What?"

"I need to get a raven to Khallum, and I suspected this would be the only safe place to do it."

"How…How did you get out?" Closer to the light, he saw her better now. The crescent shadows under her eyes, extending down toward her hollowed cheekbones, left him anguished in his powerlessness. In his mind's eye, he watched himself trail kisses across each mark of evidence of her suffering, leaving her whole in his wake. He ached for a time when she would have welcomed it.

"Maeryn helped me. I expect she'll reveal the cost soon enough." Yesenia walked toward him. He edged aside to allow her space. She grabbed the letter but didn't read it. "I have something to say, and once it's said, I willnae ever revisit it. The pain is too sharp."

"We don't have to—"

"I know you didnae kill my father, Corin. I know ye did what ye had to, to keep me safe here. You had no choice. His blood isnae on your hands."

Corin gripped the back of the chair. "Yesenia, I…"

She let the letter fall to the desk and turned. "I know I'm not a reasonable woman."

Corin held his arms out, and she walked into them. He buried a laugh into her wet hair, kissing her scalp. "I decline to respond."

Yesenia craned her neck upward and let some distance fall between them. Corin's hands brushed her arms and then fell back to his sides.

"I had too much time with my thoughts. Way too much." Yesenia's cheek twitched. "Usually, this is a road to disaster, ye ken? Spending that much time in my head has never served me."

Corin nodded to show he was listening.

"Erran accused me of being in denial. I ken I *have* been in denial, about many things, but I didnae learn that lesson from Erran Rutland." Yesenia reached for one of Corin's hands. She placed the tips of her fingers on the inside of his and let them hang there. "I fought so hard, Corin, to loathe you. To see ye as

I've always seen Quinlandens. It was easier to hate ye than to accept you might be different."

He pushed his tongue to the top of his mouth when his pulse quickened. He didn't know where this was going, but there'd be no coming back from wherever it led.

"So when Aiden comes to me and tells me ye spied on me and had my father killed, well, that's like serving a hearty stew to a starving man, innit?" Yesenia looked away. "I ate it right up because hate, in the end, is easier than love. It's certainly safer, aye?"

"It's not safer," Corin replied. He wrapped their fingers tighter together. "I've never been more scared or vulnerable than when I let hate guide me. Loving you…" He bit his tongue to keep the rest of his words down. This wasn't what she wanted. It would be unfair to say it.

Yesenia's eyes widened as she nodded. "Aye, you're right. It's not safer, but it is *easier* to live thinking you already know how a story will end. Leaves no room for being wrong, for being *hurt*."

"I never meant to hurt you." Corin's chest shuddered as his first tears spilled.

"Cannae love someone who's incapable of hurting ye. 'Tis not love if there's nothing to lose." Yesenia lowered her eyes and then raised them again. "I do love ye, Corin. Against all my resistances, which you've addressed and removed, one by one."

Corin was undone at her words. He tangled his hands in her matted hair and crushed her into a kiss that skimmed only the surface of his agony these past weeks of separation. She wound one arm around his back, tugging them closer to the desk with the other, until he'd lifted her up on it.

Piece by piece, he removed every piece of cloth separating their flesh. He could only gaze in awe at his wife, glowing even in her sickness. The soft arc of her belly made him harder, as he remembered the acts of love that had created life.

"I donnae know the old me," Yesenia said, watching him. "I donnae want to even recognize her, Corin. She's not welcome here. Help me forget her."

She reached for his head, and with a flutter in his belly, he realized what she was finally inviting him to do.

All those months he'd tried to give her pleasure, but she'd always steered her own hand there instead, afraid to be so exposed, keeping her guard gathered closest around this part of herself.

As Corin tasted his wife for the first time, he felt his old self slip away, joining the remaining ghosts of his past.

"You didn't know I was here? When you rode out alone?" Corin asked when their residual moans faded to sighs.

She watched him pause in the middle of shimmying into his trousers as if a soft, delightful wave of euphoria had hit him. He sagged against the wall to steady himself and tried again.

They'd lost the better part of the past hour to their reunion. After he'd delivered her the most delightful pleasures, she'd returned the favor, but neither of them were satisfied—neither wholly healed from the rift. She'd begged him to take her from behind as she'd gripped the desk and muffled her screams into his forearm.

Even that hadn't been enough, but it had to be, for now.

Yesenia tousled her mussed hair and re-dressed, recovering her clothes from the desktop with a matching sway in her movements. "No. I didnae."

"So all these things you said…"

"I would've said, next time I saw you." She grinned, her cheeks flushed. "Probably. Took some courage."

"Then you came here to—"

"Aye. We had the same intention. I guess it shouldnae surprise me anymore, but I like that it does." She hopped off the desk and leaned in to kiss him before turning back toward the letter on the desk. "Let's finish this before dawn, before we're missed."

"There's…something else." Corin fixed her cloak at the neck. His mouth pulled in at the corners.

"I ken there always is, aye?"

317

Corin stepped past her and pulled the middle desk drawer open. Inside were her daggers.

Yesenia's heart swelled in relief. "Thank the *Guardians* it was you. I thought..."

"I'm sorry I couldn't tell you, but there wasn't any way to. And..."

"I know." Yesenia reached inside for her dagger belt. The familiar heft pulled a soft sigh from her. "Thank you, Corin."

"Yeah. Of course." Corin shuffled. "So, the letter. Read it, tell me if it's what you'd say. If we should change anything."

Yesenia was still fixed on the daggers, and a new thought, one that surprised her as much as it would Corin, took over.

She unlatched the belt and held it out to him.

"What are you doing?"

"My belt-wearing days are behind me until this bairn is here," Yesenia said. She snaked it around his waist and adjusted the buckle to the last hole. It barely fit. "I could wear them on my thigh, but whenever I do, I seem to invite the kind of trouble I'd like to avoid right now."

Corin gaped down, shaking his head in disbelief. "Are you sure about this?"

She laughed. "I *was*, until I saw that scared look on your face."

"It's an honor that you'd trust me with your most prized treasure." Corin was nearly breathless.

Yesenia kissed the corner of his mouth. "*Was* my most prized treasure. Now I have you—and this bairn that I ken we're both gonna have to fight like mad to protect. Aye?"

Corin nodded. His eyes brimmed with fresh tears. "Aye."

"Right. Where's the poison then?"

"Where's the *what*?"

Yesenia paled. "I had a vial of poison, wound into the gown I wore when we were forced back here. Where is it?"

"You...since *when*?"

"Since before I came to Arboriana."

"And you didn't *tell* me?"

Yesenia balked. "I'm telling ye now."

Corin dragged his hands against his face. "Ahh, well, then *no*, Yesenia, I do not know where your sacred vial of poison has run off to."

"Isnae funny, Corin."

"Am I laughing?"

Yesenia glanced back at the desk, one hand on her belly. *My son,* she thought, despite it being too early to know such a thing.

"Let's send our raven and then I'll help you find it," Corin said.

"It's not lost," she said, still eyeing the flickering candle and the vellum. "Someone has it."

Corin paced by the door. "Then you're staying here. They'll think you brought it to kill my father or brother. There's no way you can return there now."

"I stay here, they'll find me. They'll raze the whole Row. You know this."

"If they know you have poison—"

"*Had* poison."

His face darkened with his fear. "Yesenia!"

She went to him and cradled his head in her hands. "This isnae a game anymore, Corin. That poison could appear anywhere. In anything. Anatole chose it especially for me, so I could make a quick escape."

"Were you going to use it…against me?"

She shook her head. "No, that never…never occurred to me. And though it was given to me for defense, if I'm to be honest with you, I only ever truly considered using it on myself."

Corin's shock hung over them both. "On yourself? Yesenia…"

The pain in his eyes caused her to lower hers. "A woman knows when she's been bested. When it happens, she goes out on her own terms."

"Then it's good you told me, for I'd never, ever, *ever* let you do it." Corin kissed her. He pressed a second kiss to his palm and laid it against her belly. "I won't lose either of you."

Yesenia looked away, toward the small window. Beyond, the rain had turned to snow. Her gasp was quick, sharp. How beautiful the sight was. How rare it was, for a girl raised on the hard promises of salt and sand to behold such a thing.

"Aye, well," she said. "I willnae so easily surrender what came so hard earned." She turned back toward him. "We send four ravens. Each on a different path. One to Khallum, one to Byrne, one to Erran, and one to Hamish. We can trust that if any one of them gets the message, it's as good as Khallum getting it."

Corin nodded. "How long will it take him, to raise his men to arms?"

"Longer than is safe for us," Yesenia answered, locking her fear away. "Are you ready to be Lord of the Easterlands?"

From the shock on Corin's face, it was apparent he'd never considered it. "I…I don't know…No. No, I'm not."

"Our safety and the safety of our people is the priority. Neither can be safe as long as your father and brother are leading."

"Our people." Corin smiled. His bleary eyes blinked closed. "I've never heard you speak of the Easterlands as your own."

"It's your family that stains the Reach with treachery. The people of the Easterlands are the lifeblood of the land. *Their* land. They are no different than the miners or freebooters of the Southerlands. It's time they have what is rightfully theirs. We can give that to them, Corin. If we donnae muck this up."

"We just have to survive until Khallum gets here."

She threw her head back and laughed. "Aye, that all?"

"If we can't…if this gets worse, if this…"

"Then we make our stand." She gripped his hands tight in hers. "Together."

Corin followed his shaky breath with a slow smile. "Together."

TWENTY-EIGHT

THE MISTY MERCHANT

Mara finished emptying the tavern. She shooed out all but a handful of patrons, carefully selected: her husband—Lorne—a woman, and two men.

She bolted the door and craned her neck up at the stairs, calling out for someone to come down. Yesenia met Mara's eyes as the woman ran her hands over her arms, as though chilled. Snow had once more turned to rain, pelting the uneven stones of the Row beyond.

Yesenia glanced at Corin. His nearness was enough to steel her frayed nerves, but she was never far away from the understanding that every second here was a second stolen—a second that could bring the Quinlanden Guard in swarms.

His tight smile betrayed his shared worries. In his eyes, he wore the love she needed to see, before they heard what Mara and the others had to say.

Yesenia leaped up, nearly knocking her chair over, at the sight of the man Mara had called down the stairs.

"Anatole!" Yesenia yelled his name in a violent, rushed whisper and dashed to greet him. "What? You *devil*. How?"

"It was in the agreement that you could have your own men and women, Yesenia. Ye know, the one you didnae read," he said, accepting the squash of her hands atop his. "But your brother feared they'd have me dispatched before we arrived at Arboriana, claim it was brigands or some such. He bade me wait—and hide. I remember ye telling me about this place, what it meant to you. I've been here for going on a week, waiting for you."

"Waiting for me?" She dropped his hands. "How could ye have known I'd come here?"

"I didnae," he said with a fractured laugh. "But I hoped ye might, or I'd be finding myself a wife and settling down."

"Why come at all, if ye thought they'd dispose of you?"

"Khallum asked me to. He said you'd need me but that I wouldnae be able to serve ye properly from where the tree-dwellers live." He shot a half-apologetic glance to Corin. "That I should wait in safety for ye, until the need arose."

"The need has arisen," Mara declared, drawing her arms in swooping motions to encourage everyone to gather around the large table at the center of the tavern.

As they shuffled into place, Mara nodded at Lorne. He was behind the bar, balancing four pitchers of ale that sloshed with his uneven gait. Tristan, the young boy who'd drawn the picture of Corin, appeared behind Lorne with the mugs.

"Thank you, son," the other woman said with a soft nuzzle of the boy's cheeks. "Pass them around, there you go."

Thank you, Yesenia mouthed to Tristan as she accepted her mug.

"I forgot to bring your picture tonight, Lady Yesenia. 'Tis a poor thanks for all the vellum you brought me." His smile deflated.

"Just Yesenia," she said gently to remind him. "But there will be other nights, Tristan. I ken it will be well worth the wait."

He beamed in response and went to deliver the rest of the mugs.

"Right. Everyone have their ale?" Mara asked. She slid in at the end of the bench. "Laoch, Yesenia, you can trust every man, woman, and child in this room. Yesenia, Riona is my sister. Callan is her husband, and Tristan is their son. Laoch and my family are already well acquainted. And Antioch…" She nodded at the final man. "Would you like to introduce yourself?"

The man fiddled with his dark hood. "I come from Streamstowne, near the western border of the Easterlands. I'm only the first emissary to arrive. Others are coming."

"Coming, why?" Corin asked.

"While the two of you enjoyed yourselves in the Southerlands, your father again raised the rents across the Reach by another ten percent."

"Antioch." Mara clucked her tongue. "Save your ire for the deserved ones."

"But they're already double what they should be," Corin stated. He swallowed a mouthful of his ale, letting it sit in his mouth before swallowing. "Guardians. There's no low my father won't fall to."

"You really haven't heard of all the smaller uprisings, in the lesser cities?" Callan asked, his face wrinkled in surprise.

"My father mentioned some skirmishes, but he seemed to think they were nothing."

Mara laughed, looking at the others. "Why does that not surprise me, eh?"

"So we've come," Antioch continued, "to do something about it."

"We?" Yesenia looked around. "How many men are ye expecting? Whatever it is, triple it, and it still wouldnae be enough to challenge Chasten Quinlanden."

"We're on your side, always, but Yesenia is right. If you're planning some kind of uprising, I hope your plan is more solid than this," Corin said with wide eyes.

"No. But it will be." Antioch turned his heavy gaze on Mara. "You didn't tell them then, did you?"

"There wasn't time," she said. Her shoulders rolled back in a touch of defense. "First Laoch showed up, in distress, and then hours later, Yesenia. But their plans are a match for ours, Antioch. You might say the timing is the most fortune we've seen in many years."

"What's going on here?" Corin asked, looking from one to the other.

Riona spoke. "Laoch, you have been a friend to the Row, a friend to all of the Easterlands, since you were a boy. We have oft wondered how our lives could be…if *you* were our lord."

"You're serious?" Yesenia whispered. She fell back in her chair. Timing and their own distress had caused them to overlook the changes in Mara—and the men and women of the Row. They'd been planning something for months, and that it was coming together now, when she and Corin were back, was only wind for their flame. "This is happening?"

Corin's laugh turned into the high pitch of a cornered animal. "Riona, Mara. You both know…no." He shook his head. "It cannot be me."

"Why not you? You have the constitution to be a fair lord, a loving one. No one knows that better than we do," Mara replied. To Yesenia, she said, "The details came together while the two of you were away…and still coming together, piece by piece. But now we see that timing is as important as intention. The two of you are in very real danger. You yourself said they might take your *child*. Laoch has spent his life trying to improve ours. We would do the same for you and save the whole Reach in the same breath."

"I'll take your ravens beyond Whitechurch and send them from somewhere safer," Antioch said. "Lorne, you'll ride south and send the hundreds we prepared tonight, to go out to every corner of the Easterlands."

"No," Anatole said, speaking for the first time since they'd settled around the table. "Let me take Yesenia and Corin's ravens. If I'm caught, they'll just send my head back to my mother. If you're caught, they'll know what you're up to, and your plans will be over before you get the chance to see them through."

"They'll raze the Row. They'll cut ye all down, like dogs." Yesenia's panic traveled to her hands. She set down her mug before she dropped it. "What you're suggesting…It takes *years* of planning. Not months."

"With respect, Yesenia, this *has* been years in the planning," Mara replied. "But it was Laoch's happiness, seeing him with a wife, building a family, that spurred us to make it happen now. It showed us we could yet have a leader who led for the people, not for themselves. But you can't do that if you aren't even safe yourselves, can you?" She softened and reached a hand over, covering Yesenia's. "The Row is only wood and straw and stone. It can be rebuilt. Our people are stronger."

"I know," Yesenia whispered, lowering her eyes. "But…"

"No buts. This is our choice. That we can also protect the two of you in making it happen is how I know it's right. That the timing is right."

"We respect this choice," Corin said, glancing sideways at Yesenia. "We do. As we love and respect all of you. But wait until you're ready. I beg of you. Yesenia is right; they will cut you down without losing a moment of sleep over it. Wait until you're really ready. We'll stand by you. You know we will."

"*You* don't have that kind of time, Laoch."

"We'll make it," Corin said. "We have to. My father and brother will answer for what they've done to the two of us. Lord Warwick will come."

"It will be weeks before he can get here," Lorne said. "Is that a chance you're willing to take?"

"It's our chance to take," Yesenia answered, flattening her palms against the table with more restraint than she felt. "We willnae watch our friends die to protect us. You have already suffered too much. That isnae…no. Corin, we should go. We've been gone too long already."

"What precisely has you so upset?" Mara asked. "You think you don't deserve friendship because you're higher born than us?"

Yesenia squeezed her jaw tight to keep from crying. "I *know* I don't deserve your friendship, Mara. And I willnae have your blood on my heart too."

"Yesenia, wait!"

Corin raced behind her down the slick cobbles of the Row. When he caught up, he spun to in front of her, choking a sob in his throat at the sight of her face curled in grief, her tears mingling with the rain.

"We cannae let them do it, Corin. It's hard enough you and I have to fight to save our child, but to know we could lose them too? And that they could lose everything?"

"They heard you. They heard us," he said to reassure her, pressing her face to his chest. "Khallum will come. He'll come, and we'll fix this, and then we'll join them."

"They'll make you lord."

"That's not going to happen. Do we even need a lord? Maybe it's time the Reach is given back to the people."

Yesenia sniffled and pulled back. "As if the king would ever allow such a thing."

Corin nodded. "We could give it to a Sylvaine then, or—"

"Not tonight." Yesenia pulled her hood up, shuddering into the last of her sobs. "Tonight we just have to survive, Corin… tonight and for the next few weeks, until Khallum can raise arms. That's all."

"We will."

"You donnae sound convinced."

"I have to be, because even trying to envision a world without you in it, without you and me together, is worse than any nightmare my mind could conjure."

Yesenia leaned up to kiss him. She left her mouth resting against his. "We cannae return together."

Corin sighed. "You're right. I know."

"I'll go first. Come to me later, when you can. I know they want us apart, but I'd like…I'd prefer we combine our strength for the days ahead."

Corin softly laughed. "Can't even say you need me? Even now?"

"I need nothing," Yesenia whispered and kissed him once more, her lips still lingering upon his as they spread into a smile. "Except you. I will always need you. Our son will need you." She cocked her head. "I'll need you, Corin, for the days ahead. That better?"

"Better." He straightened her hood. "Ride safely."

"If they donnae let you come to me, I…" Yesenia's voice caught. She sucked in her lip.

"I know." Corin pressed his mouth to her forehead. "Go, my love."

TWENTY-NINE
THE MATTER OF THE POISON VIAL

Yesenia paced between the gauzy curtains billowing out onto the perch. She had one eye on the door, the other on her privy chamber. She'd hardly touched the hunk of bread on the table, or the broth Mara had sent her home with, but her stomach churned as if she'd consumed a great feast. She couldn't discern the line between her pregnancy sickness and her fear of the unknown. Both kept her from full fighting form.

Hours had passed since parting with Corin in the cobbled alley. He should have been there by now, with her, and his absence sent her mind down dark spirals. He'd never make her wait, not if he hadn't encountered trouble. Something had to have happened.

And Anatole, where was he? Had he safely sent the ravens and returned to The Misty Merchant?

When would she even know?

It would take a day for the ravens to reach their marks, but a week—two, more reasonably—for any help to arrive. Four, if she were being honest with herself.

Yesenia pressed her palm to the wall and panted through harried, desperate breaths. He should be here. Corin should *be* here. His absence was—

The lock clicked in the chamber door. Her attention darted toward the sound, but it was Maeryn who stepped through and closed the door behind her.

"Yesenia? Are you all right? I heard Mariana couldn't find you when she came to look in on you, and…What happened to the cloak I borrowed for you?"

"I left it behind a tree, with the basket."

"I see."

"Where's Corin?"

Maeryn's eyes passed over the room, as if it contained the answers Yesenia was less willing to offer. "I haven't seen him in hours." She looked at Yesenia. "When did *you* last see him?"

Yesenia dodged the question. "I feel fine. I donnae need your aid tonight." Yesenia's throat constricted in response to the lie. "Thank you for the cloak. I was able to ride in peace and get some needed air, untroubled."

"Mm." Maeryn indulged in another inspection of Yesenia. "You don't have to tell me your truths, Yesenia. But I could be a friend to you here."

"There's nothing to tell. Apparently to be with child in Arboriana is to be a prisoner. That doesnae sit well with me."

"We both know you didn't go for a simple ride."

"If we both know there's no aim in talking about it then, aye?"

"I'm worried for you."

Yesenia looked away. *Corin, where are you?* "Most of the sickness has passed now. I thank you for helping me through it, but it willnae be necessary any longer."

"That's not the source of my worry, Yesenia." Maeryn folded her hands in front of her. "I realize there is no trust between us. I realize…perhaps…that how I approached your arrival may have played a part in this…"

"If there's no trust between us, it isnae only your doing," Yesenia replied, harsher than she'd intended. "But there's only one person in Arboriana who has my trust. My *husband*. He's the only one I need at my side right now. So if you ken ye wanna help me, Maeryn? Find him. Bring him to me."

Yesenia kept no mind to the passage of time, so when the first touch of orange beyond the forest's horizon appeared, fresh panic came with it.

It was morning, and Corin still hadn't returned.

She rushed to the perch and strained over the edge, but there was nothing to see but the rustling canopy of trees. The rear court-yard was empty at the early hour.

Had he stayed at the Row? It seemed unlikely. He'd promised to be right behind her. They both feared drawing Chasten's wrath upon their friends. He *must* have returned, and if he'd returned, then he'd either gone to separate chambers, or, or..,

Yesenia ground her jaw and rolled her head.

No.

She'd never been one to let her thoughts run, and it wasn't the time to start.

If Corin was in danger—no, not *if*, it was time to face the situation for what it was—then remaining here, waiting, helped no one. Maeryn presumably had had no luck, if she'd even tried. Yesenia was wrong to have asked her, to have assumed anyone would be as loyal to Corin as she would...

She searched the apartments for a clean cloak and whipped one of Corin's from a gnarled hanger on his side of the bedcham-ber. She'd just thrown it on when the outer door swung open, and the echo of boots filling the room became the only thing that mattered.

Yesenia's eyes darted across the room in feverish assessment. Her daggers were with Corin. The poison was lost. There was

331

a lantern, and she might hit two of them if she swung it hard enough, but—

She looked up and straight into the eyes of her father-in-law.

"Going somewhere, Lady Warwick?"

Yesenia's belly clenched. She jerked her mouth into a smirk. "Aye, I see ye know my name now."

"I've always known who you are," Chasten said smoothly. He reached into his vestment and pulled out a wad of vellum. He slammed it onto the bedside table. "Did you really think that *anything* could be sent in my Reach that I didn't know about?"

She swallowed the urge to share exactly how much he didn't know, what his people were plotting right under his nose. "I sent a hundred," she lied, grinding her toes into her boots and reminding herself to *breathe*. "What do you have there? Two?"

"Three," Chasten answered. "But you knew there were three. Because you didn't send a hundred, did you? You sent three. And here they all are."

We sent four, you treasonous eel. She dug her heels in, hoping the look she wore was the one he was expecting.

"Perfectly good messenger ravens, shot from the sky. I'll send your brother the bill of remit."

Yesenia didn't ask about Anatole. If they'd caught the ravens in flight, it was still possible the messenger had been spared.

"Nothing to say for yourself?"

"My ravens spoke for me clearly enough, I ken."

"Not only for you, but for Corin. How did you turn my own son against me? Against his home?"

"Me?" Yesenia laughed.

"Your brother can't save you this time. Even if you'd gotten one of these traitorous missives through, your fate will have already been decided. Today. Here. Yours and Corin's both."

Yesenia's eyes narrowed. "What have ye done with him?"

"Oh, you might say he's waiting for you—waiting for all the others, who get to see you both for who you are and decide the nature of the punishment dealt to traitors to their land. To the Easterlands."

"Funny word, that," Yesenia spat. She held out her hands, her wrists joined. "Would be wise to bind me, Chasten. I ken ye know I'd best ye, even in my delicate condition."

Chasten shook his head with a chortle. "I'll be happy to bind you, Yesenia. With *gladness.*"

"Like father, like son."

Chasten raised a hand, and four guards rushed in. He nodded for them to restrain her, and she laughed through her terror, arcing her head back to meet his eyes.

"Cannae even do it yourself? You really are afraid of me. Puts so much of my time here into perspective. Aye. *So* much."

"Your *perspective* will be the death of you, your husband, and your child." Chasten snapped his gaze to the door, and the men dragged her off.

"Oh, by the way. I found something of yours." Chasten's steps thundered from behind. He stepped in front of Yesenia and the guards and dug something out of his gold pouch.

The vial.

Yesenia licked her lips. Deep down, she'd known he had it. How could he not? She'd been too careful to misplace it.

Would Chasten make her drink it?

Worse, would he give it to Corin?

"At last, I've discovered the means to silence Yesenia Warwick," Chasten taunted, closing the vial in his fist. "We'll see what the Easterlanders have to say about the foreign whore come to assassinate the lord of the East."

Yesenia was upended when the guards flung her out the door and towed her down the Golden Stair.

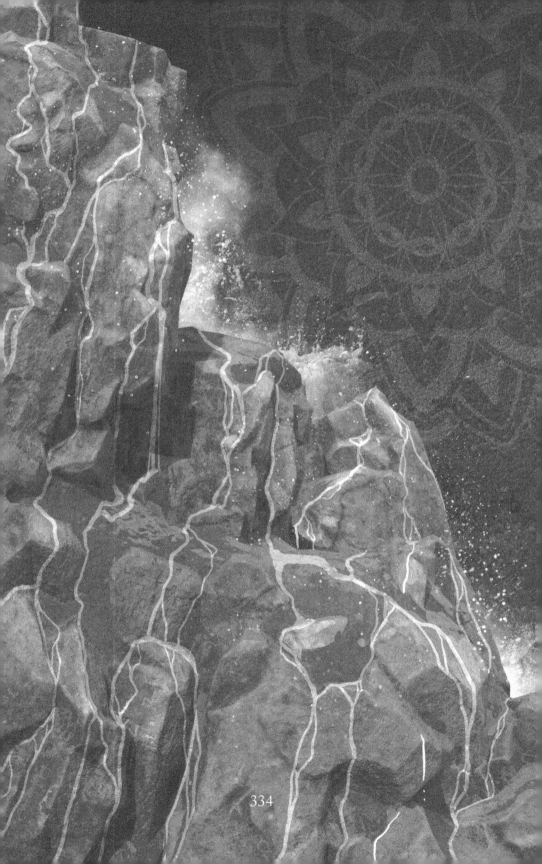

334

THIRTY
THE WILL OF THE PEOPLE

"What he's done to me, he could do to you," Corin said to Aiden. His brother was the last person he wanted to speak to, but words quelled the unending wave of chills that were rocking him from within.

The hard center of midwinter had come, and the air smelled of snow, but his shudders were amplified by something far deeper. The guards had taken his cloak, so he was experiencing every icy stab as the coastal wind met the storm rolling off the Eastern Range.

Briefly, he wondered if they would sentence him to exposure for his perceived crimes. In his fear, he let his imagination take him there, but he refused to see Yesenia with him in these visions. No matter what happened to him, she had to survive this. He'd take the punishment for them both, in whatever form spared her life.

There were more Easterlanders present than there'd been to greet Yesenia, or even Maeryn. They bowed inward as the court-yard first met and then far exceeded capacity. If he climbed the

335

hill—which he could not do, bound as he was—how far would he see the men and women of the Reach, stretched into streets and alleys? And what were they all thinking, coming here to observe what might be the execution of their lord's son and daughter-in-law?

And child, he tried not to think.

Who had brought them there? His father? Mara and her cohorts?

"That you truly believe this, Corin, is why we're standing here." Aiden carved a jagged smile onto his face and waved at the interminable crowd.

Was it his imagination, or did Aiden sound almost afraid?

"We're standing here because you tried to kill my wife, and I wouldn't allow it."

"Your wife is an unnatural abomination who never should have been allowed inside our borders," Aiden hissed. He sighed, softening. "But that is not your fault. The king doesn't always get it right, does he? But you didn't have to *follow* her! Could you not have just let her escape, and then let the king deal with it?"

"No," Corin said, staring ahead and away from him. "I could not."

"Because you love her?" Aiden whistled in through his teeth, still offering curt waves to the gathered. "Father regrets his early feelings for Mother. They weakened him when strength would have guided him toward a steadier path. An *easier* one. Is it that she paid you mind when no one else would?"

"To answer would be to offer you a truth you don't deserve."

"You don't deserve *this*," Aiden barked. He looked away but then straight at him. "Does it surprise you that I think so?"

"No," Corin said. Even without looking, he felt the swell of the growing crowd as more arrived, as those already there passed their questions among themselves. "For you know what I said before is true. This could as easily be you. It might be, one day."

"He has no other sons." Aiden lifted his head, twitching his mouth into a series of stilted grins aimed at the people arriving.

"Do you think he wants to do this, Corin? You've left him no choice. The people will expect strength from him now, not weakness. And over a *foreigner*. You stupid fool."

Corin almost laughed. "The people?"

"I tried to help you," Aiden grumbled quietly. "With her. You'll never see it that way, but it's exactly what I was doing, and you—"

Sharp gasps ripped through the crowd, bringing an uneasy silence. It passed through like a wave, reaching as far back as Corin could see.

Chasten burst through the arched entrance, followed by four guards restraining Yesenia. The bold smirk she wore might have fooled everyone else, but Corin saw through it, straight to the terror taking hold of her. Her practiced grin froze when their eyes met; the light tremble of her mouth almost gave her away, but she kept her gaze moving, leaving him behind.

"Are the criers stationed throughout the crowd?" Chasten asked Aiden. He didn't look at Corin. It was as if he weren't there at all. "They'll hear everything and pass it along?"

"All across Whitechurch, and I've sent more to the borderlands. I'm told they're bursting through the town gates."

Chasten frowned. "So many?"

"And still coming. How far did you spread this message?"

"Only through Whitechurch. The capital citizens must have sent their own ravens into the other towns." He frowned, passing a hand over his face. "They have stronger feelings about this than I realized. The Reach will not abide a foreigner come to kill their leader."

"Father…Can we not just set an example of the trollop? We could say she bewitched Corin, that she—"

"If anything, I bewitched her," Corin said. He shivered in the wind, watching Yesenia, who had her back toward him as she surveyed the throngs, her head high. "And you'll never get me to say anything otherwise."

"It's beyond that now, son," Chasten said, looking at neither of them. His expression bordered between disturbed and charged as he stepped upon the platform to address the crowd. "We're beyond that."

Mariana and Maeryn spilled out of the entrance wearing matching looks of terror. They were ushered behind Corin, out of his sight.

Aiden nibbled at the corner of his mouth and glowered at Corin's side.

"Great people of the Easterlands! Of Whitechurch! Of the Eastern Reach!" Chasten called. He waited for the first crier to sound his words into the crowd before continuing. "It is with unspeakable sorrow and immutable dismay that you are called here today, to my home and our capital. As your lord, I cannot lie to you. I cannot deceive you, as my own son and his foreign bride have deceived me!"

"Just say it was her idea, Corin," Aiden said through clenched teeth. "Father will forgive you. The *people* will forgive you."

"No." Corin tried to catch Yesenia's eyes but sensed her purposeful avoidance of his.

Chasten pumped a handful of crushed vellums toward the sky. "An incitement of insurrection! Written by the hands of both my son and his wife, calling for the vile filth of salt and sand to storm our borders and bring war to our land!"

Corin couldn't read the shock that fell like a veil over the crowds. He heard the criers bounce the words down the line, and the silence that followed trapped his breath in his throat. Would his father let him speak? To defend himself?

No. To defend her. To save her.

"I hear what you do not say in your silence!" Chasten called. "For nothing, in all my years, has given me such pause as treason committed by my own son. My own flesh, my own blood."

Mariana sounded a clipped wail.

"Fortunately for us all, I stopped these ravens from reaching their intended audience. You may all rest easy in the knowledge that there will be no war within our borders. But our problems are not ended with this crushed rebellion. For we now know what Lord Warwick sent his sister back to us to do."

Chasten raised a vial in the air.

Corin knew what it was before his father said it.

"Poison! Intended for me and my heir. So that my second son and his indecent wife could take our places, infusing our land with their filth and lies!"

Chasten turned back toward his sons. Corin braced for the evil he'd find in his father's eyes, but all he saw was sadness. Had Chasten convinced himself that his lies were true?

His father returned his impassioned gaze to the masses.

"But though I am your leader, I am also a man, and I am weak in the face of my own son's betrayal. My heart would lead me to go easy on him, even now, when I know he would have stood over my body and laughed as his wife fed me her poison."

Corin's breath quickened. If Yesenia would just *look* at him, just once...

"And so," Chasten said. "I have called upon the people to decide their fate."

Corin tensed at the pitch of his mother's fresh sobs...the rustling of skirts as Maeryn attempted to comfort her. But Mariana was no better than her husband, Corin realized—now, at the end of his life. She'd surrendered her kindness for power, and this was the price. He didn't want her to suffer, but she would.

"You have seconds to save yourself," Aiden urged, leaning close. "What is *wrong* with you? Even if you love her, so what? There are others, Corin! Other women...other *loves*, if that's what you fancy."

Corin swallowed and pointed his gaze at the crowd that would decide his fate.

"You stubborn fool!"

"So I will present to the people of the Easterlands three choices," Chasten cried. He waited for the message to spread. "*Three* choices. I will recite them to you now, and I ask for silence until I finish. Once I've shared with you these choices, I will again

339

speak them, one by one. As I come to the one you believe to be the right course, the right choice in answer of these crimes, you will cheer your support of it. The choice with the loudest cheers, the voice of the will of the people, will be the one I honor, no matter how my heart will fight it."

Chasten stepped down and accepted a mug of wine. He swallowed it and rolled his head and neck before stepping back up. "Criers, are we ready?"

Several minutes passed before the message traveled from Chasten to the end of the line and back to him. The closest crier lifted his thumb in confirmation.

Yesenia, please. Look at me.

She stared boldly ahead, her tangled hair catching the breeze like a flag.

"Choice one!" Chasten waited for the words to pass. "Permanent imprisonment in the cells of Arboriana! Choice two, execution upon the hill, by way of the Quinlanden tradition, hanging!" His voice choked. He waved away the page, who offered him more wine, and continued. "And choice three, so it can be said that I have truly given you a fair assortment of options, we free them and allow their sickness to spread across the Reach, inviting the very war I seek to prevent!"

"Guardians, Corin." Aiden's exhale was long, drawn out. "Pray for the gallows. Your agony will come to a swift end at least."

"You expect me to believe you aren't enjoying this?" Corin bit down on the quaver threatening to lace his words. "That this isn't what you wanted?"

"Disgusting of you to even suggest it."

"Your conscience, or whatever remains of it, will find no solace from me."

"Corin—"

"You have all been presented with your choices. Now, it is time for you to make one," Chasten called.

Yesenia wriggled in the hold of the guards, but she didn't turn.

Corin, until this point, had elected to see the crowd as a unified being. As one person, magnified into thousands. But when his eye fell upon Mara, standing near a tree with Lorne, his knees buckled. Suddenly he knew them all, every last face. Whether he recognized them or not, knew their names or not, they were his people. His *friends*.

At the thought of them witnessing his fate, his first true panic settled into his blood and bones. *Go, go!* He wanted to scream, but between the wind and his father's words, there was no sound he could make that would prevail.

"Choice one. Imprisonment."

They all waited, restless, as the criers passed the message down the line. Seconds passed. Finally, a few rogue cheers sounded from outside the courtyard. Chasten turned back toward Aiden with a frown and a shrug, as if to ask *did they not understand?* Aiden tossed his head back and forth, sharing the same confusion.

"Tell them again," Chasten called to the nearby crier, who nodded and sounded the choice through the crowd once more.

But only a few more cheers joined the weak chorus.

"Again?" the crier asked, but Chasten shook his head.

He stepped to the side, in a fleeting daze, but recovered quickly and called, "Choice two, people of the Easterlands! Execution."

"They really want you dead, I suppose," Aiden murmured.

But silence greeted that option as well.

Yesenia bowed her head. She shook with laughter.

Corin glanced again at Mara. Her face was stoic, but her eyes reflected her love. She offered a nod.

"Execution!" Chasten yelled, his voice straining despite the absence of sound. The crier again passed his message, but there was no reply, not from the courtyard nor the streets of Whitechurch or beyond.

"They don't understand," Aiden said, still providing unwelcome narration. "They're confused."

"We'll see," Corin replied, his eyes still on Mara. His sense of dread deepened, but it was no longer fear for himself or Yesenia,

341

but something else. Something darker and infinitely bigger than them both.

"All right then. Your final choice is that I free them both—"

Chasten's words died in the thunder of cheers. It shook the ground, rippling outward from the courtyard and into the streets as the criers passed the message.

Aiden gasped. He whipped his confused glance to Corin and then to Chasten. He tried to say something, but Corin couldn't hear them over the will of the people.

Chasten turned back. "We'll do it again. They're confused."

"They're not confused!" Mariana cried out, brushing past Aiden to confront her husband. Her voice carried through the melee. "You gave them a choice, and they have decided, Chasten. You must honor it."

"They cannot mean it." Chasten ran his palm across his mouth. "Do they not understand that there would have been *war*, on our lands? That there *will* be war if we allow this to go unpunished? They cannot possibly."

"The people aren't the fools you take them for," Corin spat. "If you wanted us dead, you should have seen to it yourself instead of leaving it in the hands of citizens who have suffered needlessly in the shadows of your reign."

Chasten's attention flew wildly over the still-booming cheers. He stumbled in his confusion, trying to speak to the people once more, but even the criers could not quiet the masses.

He leaned in to whisper to Aiden. Corin strained to hear.

"There are more of them than us," Aiden answered. "Tenfold, at last count, but they keep coming. From all over the Reach, it seems. I could send for more forces—"

"No," Chasten snapped. "They'd never make it on time." He wagged a finger at one of the guards. "Go to the crier and demand silence. I have…I have something more to say."

"If you go against their wishes, they'll swarm—"

"Trust me, Aiden."

"What's he up to?" Corin asked, but Aiden, wide-eyed, only shrugged. In the place where relief should be, terror took hold. If his father denied the will of the people, Aiden was right; they'd storm through Arboriana and mow down everything in their wake. He wouldn't get to Yesenia in time to usher her to safety.

"The people have spoken, and I shall respect the will of the Easterlands!" Chasten called when he had a break in the noise. He waited for his words to carry before moving on. "But as it was *my* life that was threatened, I now call upon another tradition, as is my right, as the offended one."

Chasten pivoted and extended his arm toward Corin. "In recompense for the attempted assault on my person, I challenge my son, Corin Quinlanden, to a Trial of Mastery."

Aiden gasped. "He's not serious."

Corin's breath caught.

A Trial of Mastery.

Of *skill*.

"The rules are simple. A series of spars of swordcraft. The fighter who claims the upper hand claims the round and takes his right to deliver a single wound to the other before the next round begins. But…" Chasten paused as the message spread.

"But with one adjustment to the rules, to allow for the unique circumstances that brought us here. As it was poison that nearly took my life, it is poison that inflicts the wound upon the defeated at the end of the round." He raised the vial. "We will add this to a carafe of wine, diluting it. The defeated will draw a sip upon their loss, and on the rounds will go until the battle is decided by the death of the one who at last succumbs to the poison."

"When's the last time you even held a sword?" Aiden asked. He'd gone pale.

Chasten turned to face Corin. "Do you accept this challenge?"

Corin fumbled his words. Fear settled into his fingers and his toes, choked his tongue. "I…you will honor the will of the people, where Yesenia is concerned?"

"I will send her back to Warwicktown. Your child will be declared a bastard."

"Alive. Untouched. Unbothered."

"Yes."

"You're already conceding," Aiden said. "Are you not even going to fight?"

Corin glared at his father. "Say it, so all can hear it. Say it so that you cannot go back on it!"

Chasten repeated the words to the guard, who carried them to the crier.

Corin lifted his chin. In his mind, he saw Yesenia laughing with him as they moved down the coastline of her homeland… her eyes falling back as she surrendered to him in pleasure. How natural it had felt to hear her declare her love for him in The Misty Merchant, and how complete he felt to have received it.

"I accept," he called. His voice croaked.

"He doesnae!" Yesenia bellowed, straining against the guards as they reluctantly turned her to face him. "For he cannae!"

"Yesenia, what are you *doing*—"

"For my husband didnae even know about the poison!" She screamed the words at the crowd. "I never told him. It was *my* justice to exact. So, ye see, Corin cannae accept this challenge because he wasnae the assailant." She licked her lips and directed her glare at Chasten. "But aye, Chasten Quinlanden, *I* accept."

"No. *No!*" Corin wailed the words. "You…Yesenia, no, *no,* you take yourself and our child back to the Southerlands, you *go*—"

"You cannae beat your father at swords," she said evenly. "But I can."

"Daggers are not swords!"

"Do ye trust me, Corin?"

"With my *life*, but—"

"Aye, that's what I'm asking for now. To save your life. Because for me? There isnae one awaiting me in the Southerlands now. Not without you."

Corin dropped to his knees. "I'm begging you, Yesenia. I am *begging* you not to do this."

"Guardians, Corin, stop groveling and let her do it," Aiden said.

Yesenia stepped closer, still restrained. "It's done. Your father has issued a challenge. One only I can accept."

Corin lowered his head and sounded a defeated sob into the icy air.

"If I win," Yesenia said to Chasten. "Then no Quinlanden will come near me or my husband ever again."

"If you lose?" Chasten asked.

"If I lose, you're well rid of me, but you must still respect the will of the people. You send Corin to my brother. Alive. Untouched. Unbothered."

"How can you trust I will?"

Yesenia whipped her head around, nodding at the crowd. "I donnae trust ye, Chasten. But I trust them."

Chasten cast his eyes away, nodding. "Let her go. Prepare the chalice."

The guards released her, and she dropped before Corin.

"Do you believe in me?" she whispered, this time just for him. She gathered his face in both her hands. "Trust me?"

Preparations were already underway behind them. The crowd rippled with nervous, uneasy energy. All of it seemed so far away, belonging to another world, another life.

"Why did you do it?" Corin bowed forward again with the weight of a fresh moan. "Why, why could you not have let me do it? I'd have gone to my death happily, knowing you and our child were out there somewhere, living, thriving."

"Ye think I could go on without you?"

"Guardians," he whispered, breathless, throwing his head back. "Yesenia."

Yesenia brought Corin's lips to hers. She pressed her forehead against his as they stuttered through their terrified breaths.

This couldn't be it.

They had not come this far for...

Corin trapped a howl in his chest.

"It's my turn, Corin. Simple as that. Khallum will look after ye if the worst comes to pass."

"What if it does? What if my father kills you?"

She kissed him again without answering and rose to her feet.

THIRTY-ONE
A TRIAL OF MASTERY

Yesenia paid no attention to the setup of the event. She was aware, of course, of the thousands of eyes watching her, Easterlanders whispering and wondering at the woman who would risk not only her own life but that of her unborn. Aiden's blustery pacing also hadn't escaped her notice, nor had Chasten's careful inspection of the precise measurement of poison to be added to the carafe of wine he was confident he'd never sip from.

What she did expel from her sight, her mind, was Corin. Once they'd freed him, she was only vaguely aware of him as he shrugged away his mother's attempt at desperate comfort and went to join Mara and Lorne. He only maintained distance because Yesenia had, perhaps cruelly, told him that if he wanted to ensure her death, he'd keep pulling at her nerves with his fears.

Yesenia drew from a skill as known to her as her name and forced her own reservations into a shadowed corner of her mind. Fear had never served her for good. It subdued her natural talent, replacing it with distracting desolation. Corin was right. She had no skill with a sword. She'd only held her father's and Khallum's,

347

which was enough to know the long steel weapons were not intimate enough for the combat she desired. Dwelling on it would hand Chasten a victory, however.

She remembered Anatole's words from that night in The Misty Merchant, meant for her alone. Was he there, in the crowd? Had he fled to the Southerlands, or had he returned in a box?

Maeryn stepped to her side with an unusually heavy gait. Yesenia turned and saw Maeryn's arm drooping with the weight of a sword she could barely carry.

"Where did you get that?" Yesenia asked with a baffling flash of amusement. Maeryn's free hand clutched her shoulder as she flinched from the heft. "Weren't hiding it under your dress."

"I went to my chambers to retrieve it after you decided today was a good day to be a hero."

"Aye, I kenned that much, but why do ye have it?"

"Asherley has our ancestral sword, The Betrayer. This one belonged to my grandfather. I had no use for it, but I hadn't the heart to leave it behind. He bequeathed it to me upon his death. Seemed a sacrilege." She lifted the corner of her mouth. "Or perhaps I just saw a glimpse of a future where someone else might need it."

Yesenia eyed the sword, thinking. "They'll bring me one from the armory."

"They'll bring you a rusted piece of tin that won't cut a pie, Yesenia."

"Why?" Yesenia caught sight of Chasten backing away from the carafe and pulling his sword, flexing it to and fro in his hand with a light spin. "Why would you give this to me? We're not friends, are we? You've had your eye on my husband since before I arrived. With me out of the way, he could be a comfort to you."

Maeryn blinked with a slow look at the sword, still resting against the stair. "If you die here, he'll die with you. Maybe not today, and maybe not here. But Corin won't survive the loss of you *and* your child. You're a fool for taking his place, but I understand why you did it."

Yesenia tightened the leather binding her hair in the back. "No one else does."

"He'd never be a comfort to me," Maeryn said. "But without him, there's no one to temper the madness of the Quinlandens. Corin only thinks he's powerless, Yesenia. He's done more for the people than he knows. Absent the force of a dam, a river floods unabated."

Yesenia reached for the hilt, then shifted the sword to her dominant hand. The heft didn't sway her as it had Maeryn, but her muscles were trained for sharp, quick thrusts. Chasten would know this. He'd attempt to tire her and then close in for the finish.

She nodded. "Thank you, Maeryn."

Maeryn squinted at the midday sun falling over the hushed crowd. "None of them wanted you punished. They made it exceptionally clear. Together, they are a force capable of defeating the Quinlandens and all who back them. Why don't they now, when you are most likely stepping up to face death anyway?"

"Tradition," Yesenia said, spinning the hilt in her hand. "Without our rituals, our customs, we're just beasts, aye?" She winked. "But have *some* faith in me, Maeryn. Greater men than Chasten Quinlanden have underestimated me and come to regret it."

The rules were as simple as the last time a challenge had played out in Arboriana.

Swords only.

A tournament of skill.

No blood drawn.

When an opponent was dealt what would otherwise be a fatal blow, the bout would be called, and the loser would drink. This would continue until one opponent had consumed enough of the poison to perish.

No outside intervention or aid.

Any disregard for the rules would end the match, and the offender's fate would be decided by their opponent.

No exceptions.

Yesenia swung the sword in impressive arcs in the final moments before Aiden declared the match was starting. Corin couldn't forget that his father had used his sword before. On beasts. On men.

"We're clear on the rules?" Aiden asked. His chest rose and fell in wild beats. Corin had never seen him so shaken. "No questions?"

Yesenia held her sword out to the side, squaring her stance. "Not from me, bootlicker. Aye, Chasten, we good?"

Corin held his breath and beseeched the Guardian of the Unpromised Future, a fickle guardian from whom he'd never asked anything, to spare his wife and child, at whatever cost to himself.

"We're good."

Corin braced at the clang of connecting steel. Mara held tight to his shoulders, while Lorne stepped to his side.

Chasten forced Yesenia's sword down and back to the side, but she hopped away before he could use it to his advantage.

They began again.

This time Chasten swung his sword downward in a sideways trail from his shoulders, aiming for her legs. She jumped, but the steel caught her heel and flipped her onto her back. The crowd drew its breath in tandem, but before Yesenia could make it to her feet, Chasten had his sword tip to her neck.

"Regretting taking his place yet?" Chasten asked. He reached down to offer her a hand, but she rejected it. She bounced to her feet and went to the table.

"Breathe," Mara whispered to Corin. "There's nothing you can do for her now, except make it harder."

Yesenia gripped the edges of the stand, eyeing the carafe.

She hesitated only a moment. She pulled the wide cork and took a hard swig.

"That's more than a sip!" someone from the crowd yelled, but Yesenia just wiped her mouth and raised her sword for the next round.

"Lord Quinlanden should take one, even it up!" another called.

"Willnae be necessary," Yesenia cried. "No one will say I didnae accept my losses like a warrior."

Cannae love someone who's incapable of hurting ye. 'Tis not love, if there's nothing to lose.

I do love ye, Corin.

Lorne caught Corin before he could go down. He braced him without a word.

Aiden gaped at Yesenia for several moments. With a shake of his head, he asked, "Ready?"

"Aye," Yesenia called and went to charge, but Chasten had her, once more, at the end of his sword.

With a shrug, Yesenia shoved his sword away from herself and returned to the table.

"I can't." Corin choked through his breath. "I can't watch this. I can't let him kill her. I—"

"She asked you to trust her, and it's what you're going to do." Mara's reply was firm.

"Two sips, Mara! What if that's enough to kill her?"

Mara nodded at Yesenia, rolling her shoulders and bracing for the third round. "Does she look dead to you, Laoch?"

"Again!" Yesenia cried, and this time when Aiden called the round, Yesenia spun and swung her sword upward, catching Chasten's steel in time to keep his from her neck. She spun again, hurling it downward, and they clashed, back and forth, for a full minute before backing away and resetting their stances.

She pulled her sword out to the side again, but when they connected, she coiled her elbow back and thrust the sword at his belly, her hand coming to a shaking stop before she pierced his flesh.

Chasten's look downward was equal parts shock and horror. "That was clever, Yesenia, but next time I'll be expecting it."

Yesenia pulled herself erect and nodded behind her. "Drink."

The crowd was restless now. Guards lined the bottom of the steps in a meaningless show of protection. The people had stopped talking among themselves and were poised, alert, as if awaiting another command.

Chasten ripped the carafe from the table. He uncorked it and took a small sip. When the onlookers called him out for his cowardice, he took another and shoved it into the guard's arms.

He lifted his sword, but a bout of unsteadiness took him. He stepped sideways, blinking through the unwelcome change. His sword swayed to the side.

"Again," Chasten called, and Aiden announced the fourth round.

Corin's pulse pounded in his ears. He could no longer hear their grunts or the connection of steel, over the sound of it. Time slowed around him. Voices blurred. His own thoughts joined the words of others, and all he could see, all he could feel, was Yesenia.

I do love ye, Corin.

Against all my resistances, which you've addressed and removed, one by one.

Yesenia screamed as her sword dodged his block and came down against the side of his neck. She bowled forward and clutched her belly as Chasten slammed past her to go drink once more.

"She's fine," Mara chided when Corin's instincts pushed him to go to her. "Be still, Laoch. It's almost over."

"She's dying," he moaned. His fingers and toes went numb. Memories from the past year streamed through his vision, out of order. They should have run when they had the chance. They should have taken a ship and sailed to Beyond. Anywhere. Anywhere but here.

Chasten swaggered back toward the fight, but an abrupt shift in his gait sent him flailing to his knees. He pitched forward as a stream of blood spewed from his mouth, a crimson spray painting the alabaster marble, while hundreds of gasps ripped through the air.

Yesenia walked over and knelt at his side. "Call it off, Chasten. You donnae have to do this. No one has to die here."

Chasten's mouth fell wide as he laughed, blood staining his teeth and tongue and dribbling down his chin. "You hide it well, but another sip, Yesenia, and it's over for you."

"Another sip, and it's over for *you*," she replied. "But it doesnae have to be."

"I don't understand," Corin whispered to Mara, time and sound at last catching up, evening out. "Why is he so much sicker than she is?"

"She's not sick at all, Laoch," Mara whispered, straining to reach his ear. "For the poison cannot harm her."

"It's *poison*, Mara!"

"Her man, Anatole, suspected she'd use it on herself one day if she felt she had no other choice. So he crafted it from the same elements and minerals the Southerlanders have eaten, breathed, and drunk for centuries. It cannot harm her." Mara nodded toward the fight. "And now, at last, she knows the purpose of this gift."

Aiden called the fifth round, and before Chasten could even lift his sword, Yesenia had him at the tip of hers.

"Call it *off*," she cried. "You take that sip, you die, you old fool."

Chasten stumbled—half crawling, half walking—and used his hands to pull him along and up, onto the table. He balanced on his forearm and tried to grip the carafe, but it fell from his hands just as a stream of the tainted, garnet liquid coated his mouth and tongue. He collapsed to the stone, his hand falling to the side.

"Father!" Aiden howled.

Mariana's following scream tore through the fractured silence that had taken hold.

"What's happening?" Corin asked—as the might of the Easterlands shed the remainder of their restraint and stormed the stairs.

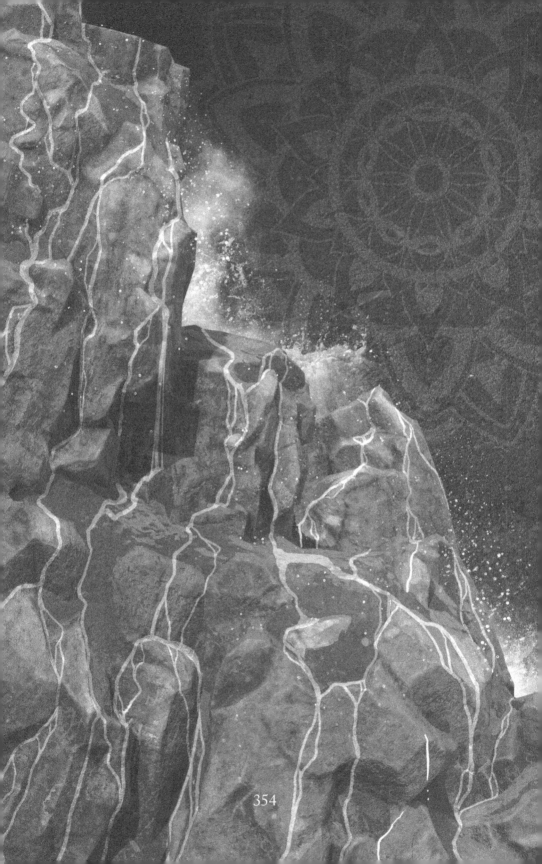

354

THIRTY-TWO

THE SUN
THAT BANISHED THE DARKNESS

Corin slumped in his father's seat in the great dining hall. He hadn't intended to sit there. Someone—or several someones—had aimed him there, and in his daze, he'd lost the last of his fight. Hands from all around clasped his shoulders as they passed, milling in until the hall was filled with men and women of the Reach. Not one of them would have been extended an invitation to dine with their lord before today, but, at least for the moment, the Easterlands was lord-less, and it was time for the people to have their say.

Aiden was tied to the chair to Corin's right. Gagged. *It's not necessary,* Corin wanted to say to them. *He's been bested, and he knows it. By the time the king gets wind of it, it will be too late, and the king doesn't want war anyway.*

But it wasn't his place to decide what they did with Aiden.

Yesenia, to his left, wore a look that mirrored his own. Her eyes blinked, and her mouth was parted, her expression laden with the weight of a death that had not been her fault but would attach to her conscience just the same.

Without breaking her gaze, she passed one hand to Corin under the table, and he took it. She shuddered into her exhale.

It sounded of relief, darkened by detachment. They both felt it, each for their own reasons and caused by their own battles, but it brought them together, perched on the edge of a great transformation.

Yesenia released his hand and wrapped both of hers around her belly. Her eyes closed.

Corin's mother was there as well, and so was Maeryn, but they'd been relegated to the corner, held in place by the same guards they'd once commanded.

It had begun to snow.

Antioch, sitting at the far end of the table in the seat opposite Corin, rose to his feet. The others flipped their gazes his way and waited for him to speak.

"What happened today," he stated, then cleared his throat before continuing. "Will be spoken of in every corner of the Easterlands for generations to come."

Nods were passed around the table in response. Corin looked at Yesenia, but her focus was on Antioch.

"Lady Yesenia, we all see the burden you carry in your heart, the guilt, and would free you of it. Chasten Quinlanden starved our children, burned us out of our homes when we could not pay his exorbitant rents, and sold our men to the Wastelands, to *prison camps,* to remind us what we were to him—what we would always be. *You* have freed us from his campaign of terror, and we will carry this burden from here."

Yesenia bowed her head, eyes on her open palms. "You cannae take this burden from me, Antioch. I have taken a life. No matter how reprehensible his actions, that man was my husband's father. I appreciate the sentiment, all the same."

Corin whipped his eyes toward her, shocked. "No, Sen. *No.* If your guilt is for me, turn it away. He called this down upon himself. You even...You offered him *a way out.* He *chose* this. If it had been you, lying dead on those stairs…" Corin bit down on his tongue, unable to finish.

"The new life you carry is our purpose now," Antioch said. "For in you grows the heir to the Easterlands."

His words caused her to look up. "Why would you say that?" She pointed her palm around the table. "The Easterlands belong to all of you now. Not Corin. Not me. Not our child. Why, after all this, would you find purpose in *that*?"

"May I?" Mara asked Antioch. He nodded and sat, while she stood. "Yesenia. Laoch. It may be hard for you to understand this, for you've only seen our world through your own eyes. We never wanted to sit in your father's seat. We never wanted to dine at his table or spin our garments with cloth of gold. We only wanted a lord who would not take from our tables to build his own higher."

"This is the chance to pick one of your own!" Corin cried. He jumped to his feet. "Mara, Lorne, even as you say this, you *must* know it's madness to not take this opportunity to invite real change."

"We are inviting real change," Mara said, remaining calm. "*You*, Laoch."

Aiden squirmed in his bindings. Whatever he tried to say was buried with his gag.

"No," Corin whispered. He backed up a step. "I don't accept it. We don't accept it."

"All Corin and I want now," Yesenia said, "is to live quietly, in peace. To raise our son in peace. You'll brook no fight from us. Aiden is no threat to you now. Mariana and Maeryn can return to their families. Arboriana is yours."

"Dear, you are not listening," Mara said. "One day, it will no longer be a Quinlanden lording over us from their perches. And it will be a good day. But we are *years* from such a future. The choice alone would take us into civil war—or worse, for the king knows if a lowborn takes this seat, it will encourage similar rebellions all over the kingdom." She looked around the table. "Am I wrong?"

357

No one disagreed. A few vocalized their support of her words. Antioch nodded.

Corin slipped behind Yesenia. He dropped both hands on her shoulders and was heartened when hers slid over the top of his. Even the touch of her flesh was strength. There was nothing he couldn't do with Yesenia Warwick at his side.

Except this.

But as their words washed over him, a new idea formed. One that might bridge the gap between now and a time when the Easterlands could be returned to the people, as it had been centuries ago, before the Rhiagains had arrived on their shores and decided things.

"Mara, Antioch. Everyone," Corin said. Yesenia squeezed his hands as he took a deep breath. "Tell me, what would be your asks of the ideal lord?"

"Halve the rents, making them reasonable again," Mara said quickly, with a nod at Antioch. "And the taxes..."

"They're criminal," Antioch said. "You pay the crown eight percent. You charge us forty. Where does the rest go?"

"The right to keep the crops we grow, and profit from anything sold from our land," said someone Corin didn't know.

"And a majority consensus if any of these things should require change. Change that *must* benefit the people, and not only the lord," said another.

Words and ideas flew across the table, passed around like a hearty meal among family. Yesenia aimed her eyes upward at Corin with a soft, knowing smile. She approved. Would they?

Corin waited for the exchange to die to a din before speaking again. "We put it in writing," he said. "All of it. It becomes law." He forced himself to look at his brother. "And Aiden, as the Lord of the Easterlands, is bound to follow it. His council will be comprised of men and women that *you* pick, Mara, Antioch. Men and women who will see the Reach is governed as the Reach wishes to be governed."

"Laoch!" Lorne cried. "Your brother is more of the same. He's your father, reincarnated into a younger body with greater cruelty."

"Aiden's cruelty is known to me *and* my wife. All too well," Corin replied. He bowed down to kiss the crown of Yesenia's head and then began his circle of the long table. "What he feels, what he desires, those are his troubles to deal with. If your needs become law, then he has no choice but to follow them. If he fails to, the Easterlands returns to the people, and he suffers whatever consequence you deem appropriate."

"Corin!" His mother hissed. He'd almost forgotten she was there. It was better for them both if he did. Whatever warmth she'd possessed had been offered as sacrifice in her worship of her husband.

"If a Quinlanden in this seat is what you most desire, then this proposal is more than fair. It will satisfy the king, so that he does not wage his own war on the Easterlands and decide things his own way," Corin said. "I would see that every last thing you desire is part of this agreement, and it is signed in Aiden's blood—in *my* blood, as a promise that should the time come, should he fail, I will stand at your side, as I have in the past, and will lead the transition of power away from the Quinlandens to the leader of your choosing."

Antioch shrugged his hands. "Do we care, my friends, who it is sitting high upon their perches, if they cannot take from us? Most of us had never even seen the face of Chasten or Aiden before today. We'd never have to see it again."

"Do you really not want this, Laoch?" Mara's voice caved. She tilted her head to the side and offered him the most motherly look he'd ever received. "All this time…I was wrong to assume, but can you blame me? You have so much to give."

"And I'll give as much as I can, for the rest of my life," Corin answered her. "My life would be meaningless without service, and I know I can speak for Yesenia when I say she feels the same."

Yesenia nodded, watching him.

359

"But my days at Arboriana are behind me. My family, my *life,* is out there, with you." He stopped behind Mara's chair. "I was born in the wrong place. I would see that my son is born in the right one."

The stirring around the table was hard to read, but the looks exchanged between Mara and Antioch were clear enough.

The name of the man running their Reach had never mattered to them.

It was everything else that came with it.

"We'll prepare the declaration," Antioch said. "But will he sign it?"

Corin met Aiden's panicked, bloodshot eyes. "A nod will do, Aiden."

Aiden's throat bobbed. His eyes closed as he jerked his head into a wild nod.

"There is not a guard that exists, Aiden, large enough to withstand the will of the Easterlands. Not yours, not the Knights of Duncarrow," Corin said. "And if you find that hard to believe, they'll be happy to prove it to you." He looked at Yesenia and then Mara. "*We* will be happy to prove it to you."

"We have work to do," Antioch said. He signaled for someone to fetch food and drink, and for others to return with vellum. "You're welcome to stay and help us."

"It would be my honor," Corin replied. The crack in his voice allowed some of the relief to set in, finally. "But first, I need a word with Mara and my wife."

Corin said what he needed to say as Mara listened. She nodded throughout and then fell silent.

Mara shifted in her chair. "You are, of course, welcome at the Row, Laoch. You and Yesenia, and all the children you'll one day bear."

Corin held fast to Yesenia's hand, resting it on his lap. "But?"

"Oh, there's no but." She chuckled. "If what you two most desire is life in the Row, we'll make it happen."

Yesenia leaned in. "We wouldnae want to displace *anyone*—"

"Yesenia, my dear, a quarter of those homes are abandoned now. Families who fled for smaller villages when their money and luck ran out. You'd be taking from no one."

"I see it in your eyes," Corin said playfully. "There is a but."

"Not a *but*," Mara said with a slow drawl. "More of an *or*." She rose to her feet, dusting herself off from the habit of running a tavern always in need of a rag. "Give me time to sort it."

"Sort what?"

"A gift," Mara answered. She approached them both, laying a palm against each of their cheeks. "For the mother and father of the Easterlands."

"More like the elusive aunt and uncle who wish to remain nameless," Corin bantered.

"Perhaps one day your names *will* fade, with the hard memories of this day," Mara said. "But none living today will ever forget."

When the door to their apartments clicked shut, Corin voiced the question that had been burning in his chest across the arduous hours since the tournament.

"Why did you not tell me about the poison? About your immunity?"

Yesenia burrowed against his shoulder. "They had to believe I could die. You never could have convinced them that *you* believed it." She peered up at him. "Donnae even try to deny it. I know ye best, but they know ye well enough to ken your heart wears itself most easily in your eyes."

"I thought you were…" Corin pressed his lips tight. "I thought I was losing you."

"I *am* sorry, Corin, about your father. I tried—"

"I know."

"If he'd have only left us alone…"

"He couldn't," Corin insisted. "His pride wouldn't have ever allowed it. And I…I suppose I will mourn him, Sen, in my own way, but I will *never* look at you and see *anything* but the absolute gratitude I feel right now."

"I ken I'll let it slide, ye calling me Sen now. Aye, aye, I noted it. Been noting it for months now."

"Sen." Corin tilted her chin with his fingers and kissed her. "Yesenia. My heart. The veins pumping blood through my body. The sun that banished the darkness from my world."

"Sen will be fine," she said, teasing, and took his bottom lip between her lips. "I suppose I cannae call ye tree-dweller now, can I?"

"It never bothered me." He pressed his forehead to hers. "You never scared me half as much as you wanted to."

"I wasnae convincing enough?"

"I'm sure to everyone else, you were," Corin answered. He wrapped his arm around the edges of hers, letting his fingers trace the arc of her belly. "But I saw through you the moment I laid eyes on you, in Termonglen. I saw *you*. I couldn't have predicted *anything* that happened after." He laughed, and she joined in. "But I wasn't very surprised when I first realized I loved you. Seemed as inevitable to me as the moon rising at night, or the tides rolling in just when we expect them to."

"And when I loved you back? That surprise ye?"

Corin turned and gathered her in his arms. "No," he whispered, kissing the outer corners of her damp eyes. "No surprise. Just profound gratitude."

Yesenia pressed her cheek to his. "Do you still have my daggers?"

Corin recoiled a bit, defensive. "Of course I do. Why?"

She slid her legs over his, straddling him. "Better take them off, before one of us gets hurt."

EPILOGUE

Byrne checked every last one of the chairs. They had to be perfect. Yesenia wouldn't notice if half were on their side and the other half upended, but he would, and others would, and on the day his sister stepped willingly into her happiness, there could be nothing amiss.

"Arboriana could accommodate so much more," Asherley said, but she approached the task with the same meticulous care as her husband did. He was surprised she'd joined him on the trip, but his marriage had been full of surprises, most of them welcome. There were no signs yet of a child, but she was more ardent to the task these days, and so was he. It would happen when it was meant to.

"Aye, but it wouldnae be true to them, would it?"

"You know your sister best," she replied. She splayed her hands on her hips and surveyed the sea of chairs covering the entire clearing, skirting the forest line. "There's a charm to this though, isn't there?"

Byrne squinted into the soft breeze rustling the trees overhead. It felt nothing like home, any more than Longwood Rush did, but as he watched his wife dust pine needles off of chairs, it occurred to him that home could be anywhere. For him, it was with her.

He noted Gwyn and Mara near the altar, each holding a child. Ransom was nearly old enough to go running into the forest on his own, a fact Gwyn seemed all too aware of as she fought her son's wriggling attempts to squirm away.

Torquil, Yesenia and Corin's newborn son, dozed peacefully against Mara's shoulder.

Asherley followed his gaze. "They're both beautiful children."

"Aye."

"Does it bother you we've not had our own joy to welcome?"

Byrne quickly shook his head. "No, it's…isnae for lack of trying." He flushed, adding, "And though I shouldnae say it aloud, I hope our first is a daughter."

Asherley eyed him. "You do? Really?"

"Gwyn is already with child again. The future of the Southerlands is safe with Khallum, with Gwyn." Byrne gripped the back of a chair, still watching the women with the little ones. Asherley's sister, Maeryn, had joined the group, as had the Dowager Lady Quinlanden. The Widow soon appeared as well, fussing over Ransom. "Is that not what you'd want, Ash? A daughter to take your place one day?"

"Women haven't always ruled the Westerlands."

"Was a woman who changed that, as I recall."

"Rhosyn was a Ravenwood. A sorceress. She left her life behind for love when she came to the Westerlands. It's how the Blackrooks became the Blackwoods. Thedyn Blackrook loved her that much."

"I know the story," Byrne said. "The whole kingdom does. 'Tis the reason they call ye the Westerland witches."

Asherley grinned, a twinkle in her eye. "I thought that had to do with the poison we grow in our gardens?"

"You do work hard to keep the rumors alive," he agreed, and they laughed together.

Asherley passed behind him, sliding a hand across his lower back as she went to join the women.

"Father should be here."

Byrne's eyes broke away from his wife at the sudden interruption of Khallum beside him.

"Aye," Byrne whispered. "He should."

"He deserved to see his lass happy. He…" Khallum's thoughts trailed off.

"I think about him a lot, Khallum."

"Aye." Khallum crossed his arms over the ceremonial sash the Widow had packed him for the occasion. "One day…" He tapped a fist against his thigh. "We'll see him avenged, Byrne, aye? Father was right; we have work to do, before we'll be ready. But in our lifetimes? It will be done."

"You mean that?" Byrne's voice caught.

Khallum nodded. "The work has already begun to train our men to arms. I *will* take down this king, brother. One day, I'll turn my eyes to all the other Reaches to join us. And we will *all* take back what is ours." Khallum's gaze fell on the women. They narrowed. "What are the bootlickers doing here?"

"Yesenia invited Maeryn, and Asherley hasnae seen her sister in so long…" Byrne said. "As for the Dowager Lady Quinlanden, her invite was Corin's doing. Says he's learning to forgive, that he feels bad for his mother. Says she wasnae always like this."

"Bigger than what I could offer, were I him."

"Aye," Byrne replied. "But isnae that the purpose of this day, Khallum? To let the past be past?"

Khallum's answer was a short exhale as he scanned the generous but humble arrangements. At the center of them sat a freshly built chalet, a gift from their friends on Slattery Row. The modest cabin was where Yesenia, Corin, and Torquil would begin their life anew.

Byrne shared a moment with his brother, enjoying the silence of the unsaid.

A few celebrants came to take their seats, followed by more, until slowly the rows filled. Byrne recognized only a handful in the crowd, but Yesenia and Corin knew them all. Loved them all.

Khallum coughed into his fist. "Aye, well, I ken she's been doing for the two of us, all of our lives. Time for us to do for her."

Byrne clapped his older brother on the back as they went to take their places.

Corin melted at the sight of his wife, flanked by her brothers, as they led her to him. She'd chosen her practical leathers from her Southerland life, but one of the women had added floral arrangements to her hair, which she wore down, free, and brushed into soft, bouncy curls.

He couldn't take his eyes off her as Khallum and Byrne wound the thick wedding rope around his and Yesenia's wrists, binding them together for the ceremony ahead. Korah blubbered into a lace handkerchief from her seat nearby.

Corin didn't know what to expect from the traditional wedding rites of the Southerlands, but he suspected all he'd remember was how he'd felt as he witnessed her watching him, the love reflecting in the gold flecks of her dark eyes and the soft parting of her mouth as she held back sighs.

Khallum cleared his throat and fumbled with the vellum, unrolling it. "Salt and sand," he read, then again, louder and stronger. "Salt and sand. So begins all sacred happenings. So ends all promises. In the salt of the sea, we are most free, like a bird upon the wind." Khallum swiped his sleeve along his brow, his eyes wide with nerves, and continued. "Or…or a fish in the deep. But the sand is there to ground us, to remind us of our tethers, our bonds of duty and fealty and love."

Khallum tugged at the sash that should've been worn by a Grand Minister of the Reliquary. But the day wasn't about the traditions of the kingdom. It was a choice Corin and Yesenia had made for themselves, to commit to their life on their own terms. Corin knew, as he watched Khallum's eyes swim with tears—as he observed Byrne behind him, fighting the same—that they could not have chosen better men to seal these vows.

"'Tis the lot of a man or woman of the Southern Reach to be both free and bound, both of the sea and of the land that connects it. There can be no greater manifestation of these truths than the joining of the two who have chosen to temper their salt and cultivate their sand together."

Yesenia grinned. "You're more salt and sand than you know, Corin."

"Aye," he said, laughing, twining their fingers deeper into the tangle bound by the knot. "I'm glad ye see it."

"No jumping ahead," Khallum whispered. "Kissing is for the end."

Yesenia bit her bottom lip. Corin could hardly keep still.

"Eh, Corin Quinlanden, son of Chasten, son of Mariana, do you enter this joining heart open, mind willing?"

"Aye, brother. I come before you, heart open, mind willing."

Khallum dusted the vellum and turned toward Yesenia. "And you, Yesenia Warwick, daughter of Khoulter, daughter of Sancha. Do you enter this joining heart open, mind willing?"

"Aye, heart open, mind willing. I do."

Khallum squeezed his eyes, then opened them wide again. "Then I will ask you both to repeat the Five Sacred Promises. Aye, eh, turn to one another. Corin, fold her hands in yours, as you will for the rest of your..." He grinned. "Aye, ye already have. Good. Good."

Yesenia's eyes sparkled with tears. She didn't avert them, inviting Corin to see her as she was, in her raw vulnerability.

His heart had never been fuller.

"Repeat after me," Khallum said. "I have reached into the sand, and the sand has offered me strength. This I offer you, until my promise is spent."

Yesenia and Corin repeated the words in imperfect unison, grinning.

"I have faced the wind, and the wind has offered me breath. This I offer you, until my promise is spent."

"Until my promise is spent." Corin fought himself to not kiss her now, declaring for all the world his greatest weakness, which was also his greatest strength.

"I have mined the gold from our cliffs, and the gold has offered me prosperity. This I offer you, until my promise is spent."

Corin felt the gazes of his loved ones falling over him like a protective veil. This was not the past, where everything he did was scrutinized, in anticipation of his inevitable failure to rise. None who had made him feel that way was there today, except his mother, and he'd invited her more for himself than for her. To give himself to Yesenia in the way he most wanted—wholly, perfectly—he could have no darkness constricting his heart. Not anymore.

"I have submerged myself in the salt of the sea," Khallum said, "and the sea has offered me courage. This I offer you, until my promise is spent."

Corin willed a calm to fall over himself. These were the vows they'd chosen, not the ones forced upon them. He didn't want to forget a single word—nor a single falling tear, twitch of her hand, or nibble of her lip.

"I have faced the deaths of those who came before me," Corin said, repeating in perfect timing with Yesenia, "and death has offered me life. This I offer you, until my promise is spent."

Khallum squinted at the vellum. "I, uh, wasnae supposed to bind ye until the end, I ken, so we'll skip this part. But eh, aye, here we are. It is these vows that bind you. Let this rope rest eternally upon your heart, as a constant reminder of what you have both surrendered but also gained in this union. Ye are now one, and naught but death can sunder this bond."

The applause that followed buoyed Corin up and then he kissed her, skipping his lips across hers as they both withheld their laughter. They at last connected for a proper kiss, which sent an approving ripple through the crowd.

Khallum backed up and drew Sandspire, their father's sword. He nodded for them to hold out their hands while he carefully, his hands shaking, made the cut.

He passed the severed rope to Corin. "Donnae ye ever give me cause to come retrieve this."

"Never," Corin whispered, accepting the gift with a reverent nod.

Mara joined them then, passing Torquil into Yesenia's arms. She pressed the infant against her chest and turned toward Corin with a contented smile.

"That's it. It's over now."

Corin kissed the top of his son's head, then connected again with his wife, lingering as the celebrants filtered down the path, toward the Row, where the evening was only getting started.

Yesenia handed Torquil to Corin. "I'll meet you there, aye?"

He grinned. He held his son and the rope against his chest. "Aye."

Khallum fiddled with the vellum, failing to squeeze it back into the tube. Yesenia waited for him to finish, but when it was clear he wasn't going to get it on his own, she took it from him and stuffed it herself.

"There," she said, patting the top on.

"I'd have gotten it."

"Aye. Of course." She held out her arm. "Walk with me to the Row?"

Khallum stared at the offer before taking it. "I hear the ale is shite."

"Isnae a Southerland brew, but it will take ye off your feet, you underestimate it."

"Underestimated you and look what happened. Ye fell in love with a tree-dweller."

"Not a tree-dweller anymore," Yesenia said to remind him. They found the path and followed it into the Merchant Quarter. "I said some things, Khallum, when I was angry."

"I grew up with that mouth, Yesenia. I ken you'll have to be more specific."

"What I wanted to say was thank you," she whispered, swaying into him with a light nudge. "For today. For stepping into Father's place. I miss him so much, but…Today, it was like he was here."

Khallum nodded, looking ahead. "Aye. I felt it too."

"He would want this, aye? For the three of us, to be happy. But also…also not to forget."

"I've forgotten nothing, Sen. One day…"

"Aye. One day."

"You'll still be spending your winters in the Southerlands?"

"We want Tor to grow up knowing who he is, Khallum. To know his uncles, his cousins, to understand what salt and sand *means,* not just how the words sound saying them. The physician said…" She lost her voice. "He said Tor might be the only one for me, after the trouble bringing him in. So, aye. We'll be there."

"Then he'll be a fortunate lad, to have ye all to himself."

"You and Gwyn, you're always welcome here too."

"Donnae share your warmth for this damp, *green* land, but thank you."

"It grows on you," she mused aloud, squeezing both arms around her brother's one. "Thank you, as well, for coming when Erran received Anatole's raven. Even if there wasnae a war to fight when you got here, that ye came at all…you honored your blood bond."

Khallum settled his cheek atop her head briefly and then peeled himself away. "I promised ye, Sen. I know I disappointed ye along the way, but I'd never abandon you."

"I know."

They reached the bend in the path that would take them into the Row. Yesenia turned when Khallum stopped.

"Ye coming?"

Khallum's slow nod seemed to take him somewhere else. "Aye…eh…just lost myself a moment."

"Well, find yourself because that shite ale isnae gonna drink itself," Yesenia teased and held out her arm to her brother once more.

After watching Torquil pass through the arms of most of the women in The Misty Merchant—and Anatole, who was more keen to childmind than she'd ever have guessed—Yesenia needed a moment alone with her son.

She bounced him near the hearth in the back room, holding him close to her heart as her memories took over, transporting her. She was once again waking in this bed to the sight of Corin's troubled eyes, listening to the tremor in his voice as he awaited her first words following the fire at the chalet.

Had she not been so stubborn, she'd have known her heart then.

Ahh, but she knew it now.

Yesenia pressed her son's smooth forehead to her mouth, humming a song she'd never learned the words to. Her mother had always sung it like this, a soft vibrato of sound and feeling. The Widow had caught her humming it once, not long after Yesenia's mother had gone to the Guardians, and told her the song was called "Reborn in a Mother's Love."

Her gaze caught Tristan's drawings hanging on the wall. He'd improved since he'd switched to the vellum and charcoals Yesenia had given him. Riona had a proper artist on her hands.

Yesenia smiled to herself and kept humming.

Corin's shadow passed into the doorframe. Yesenia lifted her finger to her lips.

Sleeping? he mouthed.

Yesenia nodded. She leaned over the cradle in the corner and let Torquil come to a gentle rest. His small mouth puckered in response to his dreams.

She tugged Mara's quilt over his waist and kissed him once more before turning.

Corin's eyes were bleary from the drink. His slow blink revealed the exhaustion of the day. When he held out his arms, she tiptoed into them.

"I have faced the deaths of those who came before me, and death has offered me life," he whispered into her hair, his words just slightly slurred. "Yesenia."

"Donnae get too soft on me," she whispered back, her words fading against his vest.

Corin spun her in his arms, his feet lightly stepping in time to a dance without song. He led her across the floor of the room where she'd fallen in love with him, listening to his heart beat out of rhythm, an imperfect match for her own.

"I know better than to believe our peace will last forever, but..." Corin spun her, then snapped her close once more. "I would exchange a lifetime of sorrow for just one year where the three of us can be a family, without the rest of the world closing in to remind us who we are."

"Just one?" Yesenia nibbled his ear, swaying in time with his movements. "When I've offered you a lifetime?"

"You're not afraid?"

"No," Yesenia whispered, wrapping her arms around him and surrendering, letting him bear her weight. "Not anymore. For I have submerged myself in the salt of the sea, and the salt has offered me courage."

"Mm," Corin said. "You *were* listening."

"Every Southerlander knows the vows. They're a part of us, like the blood in our veins."

He swept her off her tired feet and laid her on the bed, then climbed in next to her. "I think..." His voice trailed off.

Yesenia rolled her head on the pillow to look at him. "You think what?"

Corin's eyes fluttered closed. He reached for her hand and wound it through his own. "I think I take it back, what I said before. The Guardians could give me a thousand lifetimes with you, Yesenia, and I'd still beg for more."

Yesenia looped her arm under her husband's head and settled him against her chest. As her eyes closed on the evening, she released her thoughts, allowed them to ride the gentle tide sweeping her imagination toward the everlasting allure of a thousand lifetimes as Yesenia Warwick Quinlanden, mother of Torquil and wife of Corin.

The Book of All Things continues with a new story in *The Altruist and the Assassin.*

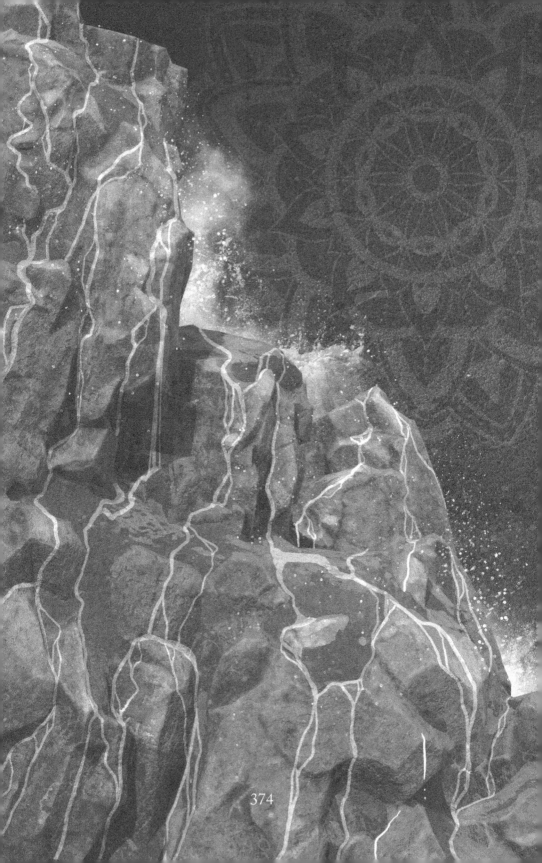

THE FIVE SACRED PROMISES OF THE SOUTHERLANDS

I have reached into the sand, and the sand has offered me strength. This I now offer you, until my promise is spent.

I have faced the wind, and the wind has offered me breath. This I offer you, until my promise is spent.

I have mined the gold from our cliffs, and the gold has offered me prosperity. This I offer you, until my promise is spent.

I have submerged myself in the salt of the sea, and the salt has offered me courage. This I offer you, until my promise is spent.

I have faced the deaths of those who came before me, and death has offered me life. This I offer you, until my promise is spent.

ALSO BY SARAH M. CRADIT

KINGDOM OF THE WHITE SEA
KINGDOM OF THE WHITE SEA TRILOGY
The Kingless Crown
The Broken Realm
The Hidden Kingdom

THE BOOK OF ALL THINGS
The Raven and the Rush
The Sylvan and the Sand
The Altruist and the Assassin
The Melody and the Master
The Claw and the Crowned

THE SAGA OF CRIMSON & CLOVER
THE HOUSE OF CRIMSON AND CLOVER SERIES
The Storm and the Darkness
Shattered
The Illusions of Eventide
Bound
Midnight Dynasty
Asunder
Empire of Shadows
Myths of Midwinter
The Hinterland Veil
The Secrets Amongst the Cypress
Within the Garden of Twilight
House of Dusk, House of Dawn
Midnight Dynasty Series
A Tempest of Discovery

A Storm of Revelations
A Torrent of Deceit

THE SEVEN SERIES
Nineteen Seventy
Nineteen Seventy-Two
Nineteen Seventy-Three
Nineteen Seventy-Four
Nineteen Seventy-Five
Nineteen Seventy-Six
Nineteen Eighty

VAMPIRES OF THE MEROVINGI SERIES
The Island

THE DUSK TRILOGY
St. Charles at Dusk: The Story of Oz and Adrienne
Flourish: The Story of Anne Fontaine
Banshee: The Story of Giselle Deschanel

CRIMSON & CLOVER STORIES
Surrender: The Story of Oz and Ana
Shame: The Story of Jonathan St. Andrews
Fire & Ice: The Story of Remy & Fleur
Dark Blessing: The Landry Triplets
Pandora's Box: The Story of Jasper & Pandora
The Menagerie: Oriana's Den of Iniquities
A Band of Heather: The Story of Colleen and Noah
The Ephemeral: The Story of Autumn & Gabriel
Bayou's Edge: The Landry Triplets

For more information, and exciting bonus material,
visit www.sarahmcradit.com

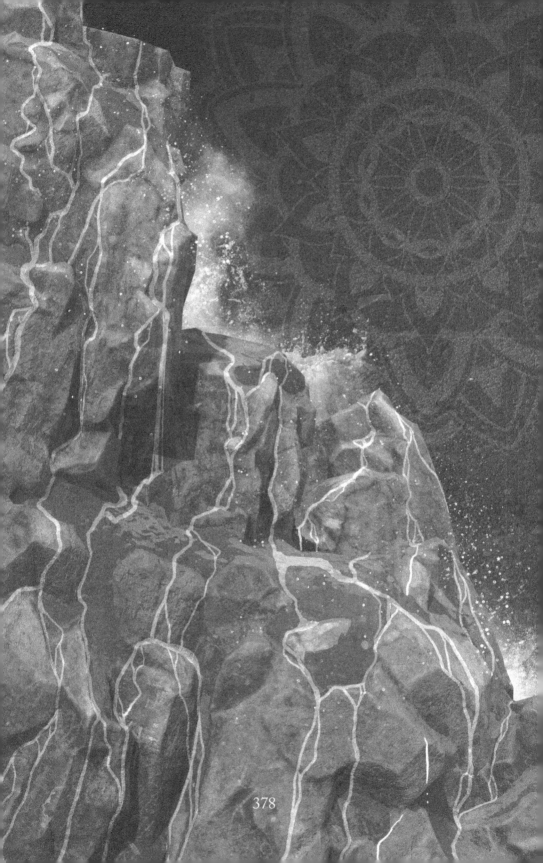

ABOUT SARAH

Sarah is the *USA Today* and International Bestselling Author of over forty contemporary and epic fantasy stories, and the creator of the Kingdom of the White Sea and Saga of Crimson & Clover universes.

Born a geek, Sarah spends her time crafting rich and multilayered worlds, obsessing over history, playing her retribution paladin (and sometimes destruction warlock), and settling provocative Tolkien debates, such as why the Great Eagles are not Gandalf's personal taxi service. Passionate about travel, she's been to over twenty countries collecting sparks of inspiration, and is always planning her next adventure.

Sarah and her husband live in a beautiful corner of SE Pennsylvania with their three tiny benevolent pug dictators..

www.sarahmcradit.com

SARAH M CRADIT

WEAVER *of* WORLDS